GOING LIVE

The President of the United States was dead, victim of a blank-eyed assassin standing in the shadows of a Washington hotel with a gun tucked into his coat ...

There was fear, not only in the places where power dwelt, but among those who huddled around the television sets in their living rooms to watch their President die on screen, while cameras panned in on the puddles of his blood on a dark, wet sidewalk.

For the news organizations – the television networks, radio stations, and newspapers – it was a time of tense, grinding work, when the portentous sound of drums must be intermingled with the hailing of a new chief. It was a time when the best in the business again proved themselves, and it was a time when flaws were cruelly exposed. It was, as James Mellenkoff, president of World Network News, observed bleakly, not a time for an anchor to fall apart, on or off the air.

About the Author

Muriel Dobbin is former West Coast bureau chief for the *Baltimore Sun*, for which she was previously White House correspondent. She was born in Ayrshire, Scotland, and now lives in San Francisco.

Going Live

Muriel Dobbin

NEW ENGLISH LIBRARY
Hodder and Stoughton

The characters and situations in this book are entirely imaginary and bear no relation to any real person or actual happening.

First published in Great Britain in 1987 by Century Hutchinson Ltd.

First New English Library paperback edition 1988

British Library C.I.P.

Dobbin, Muriel
  Going live.
  I. Title
813'.54[F]
  ISBN 0-450-43069-3

Printed and bound in Great Britain for Hodder and Stoughton Paperbacks, a division of Hodder and Stoughton Ltd., Mill Road, Dunton Green, Sevenoaks, Kent, TN13 2YA (Editorial Office: 47 Bedford Square, London WC1B 3DP) by Richard Clay Ltd., Bungay, Suffolk.

With thanks for the professional assistance and advice of Roz Abrams, WABC–NY; Rollin Post and other members of the staff of KRON-TV, San Francisco; and John Chancellor, NBC-NY.

And with special thanks to Elaine Markson for her endless patience.

Prologue

IT BEGAN *at 7:16* P.M. in the newsroom of the World News Network in New York.

What had been a quiet day, winding down, exploded into frenzied excitement with the telephone call from Washington. Frantic questions followed the bulletin from the network's Washington bureau. Was the report confirmed? It had come from Martha Vogel, World News Network's correspondent at the scene, but had she eyewitnessed it? Was it on Associated Press or United Press International yet? Was there anything from the White House press office? From Capitol Hill? Could they confirm? Could they confirm? Confirm? Confirm? The word sped from reporters, correspondents, and editors to producers, directors, the president of the network on the fortieth floor, and the chairman of the board on the forty-first floor.

In the studio, national news anchor Caroline Mitchell, in the midst of a brisk reading of the latest developments in South Africa, heard a warning voice on her Interrupt Feedback (IFB) earpiece telling her to prepare for a bulletin. Her fingers tightened on the sheaf of stories on the desk in front of her, all neatly typed, ready to be read. She heard the terse voice in her ear. Stay calm, she told herself, all I have to do is stay calm and listen. But her heart beat more rapidly, her pulse was quickening, she wished she had a second to close her eyes, look at Caroline in the mirror, and swallow. But there was no time.

She paused after completing the South Africa story and in her usual serene voice told the viewers, "This just in: we have a report that the President has been shot

1

outside a Washington hotel. Please stand by. We will bring you more information as soon as we have it. Please stand by."

In the welcome few seconds of a break that followed, they briefed her: the only thing they had right now was a report from Martha Vogel at the hotel. She had reported that it looked bad. Terry Steiner was setting up at the White House for them now, trying to get to the White House press secretary. But the press secretary was with the President. They didn't know, they told Caroline, if anyone else had been hurt. They didn't know anything else at all in fact. Numbly she thought, What will I say then? I've got to get back in twelve seconds. Her producer said there would be wire-service stuff soon. She could fill with some recent biographical material on the President. But for now that was all. She would have to wing it. "You'll be fine," someone said to her. "Keep calm"—someone else patted her shoulder—"keep talking."

"Ten seconds to air," intoned the producer. The staff was watching her. She felt their eyes on her, but she wanted to close her own, to hide from them, from herself. Everyone was watching, for all she knew, the whole world, and everyone in it, were watching as she took the cue, looked steadily into the camera with those wide, dark eyes, and spoke in the Mitchell voice, with only a hint of a tremor:

"We are getting more information from our correspondent who witnessed the shooting. We repeat, we have a report that the President has been shot, but we do not yet know how badly. . . ."

On the fortieth floor, WNN president and chief executive officer, James Mellenkoff, sat in front of his multiple console of television screens, watching tensely, talking occasionally with staff in the newsroom and in the executive offices. They had to think ahead, prepare now, beyond the moment, beyond the assassination, if that was what had happened. They had to consider the impact of the death of a President, the violent death of another American President. Diplomatic consequences, economic, political. If it was true. But if Martha Vogel had called it in, Mellenkoff and the others knew it was true. In that case WNN had its reputation and its ratings riding on Caroline Mitchell, their solo news anchorwoman, the only national solo news anchorwoman. On this young, beautiful woman who could create such a special rapport with an audience. But. Mellenkoff knew that everyone around was silently thinking their "buts." If Martha Vogel was a veteran who could be counted on, Caroline could only be described as untried in a major news crisis. If WNN was riding on her this moment, Mellenkoff himself and maybe his career were hanging in the balance. But he had never failed before. His judgment about people, personnel, potential stars had been perfect. His people always vindicated his judgment. Tonight would prove he had been right. It would be a coup. For him.

On the forty-first floor, Joel Eliass, chairman of the board of WNN, thought first about the effect on the market as he waited for word on the President. He would unload some stocks, he thought, making a mental note, and settled back to watch Mellenkoff's young anchorwoman. This would test her. Whatever happened tonight —a hitherto healthy President's death, a young star's rise, an unsettled market—the chairman would get some pleasure, as always, in watching events around him and benefiting from them. He would especially enjoy watching this gamble put to the test, seeing whether Mellenkoff's young woman had the professional skill to carry through. On her performance tonight would depend whether she was WNN's star . . . or Mellenkoff's.

In the newsroom and the control booths, there was tension. Writers scurried, telephones shrilled, all movement was rapid. In the studio, sitting before a backdrop of carefully chosen blue, with her fingers clinging damply to scraps of hastily compiled presidential background material, Caroline Mitchell was trying to do what the voice in her ear told her to do, trying to follow its instructions, trying not to register the worry on the faces of the producers beyond camera range. The voice in her ear was alternately soothing and urgent; it advised, it updated, it admonished, it cajoled. This voice, her connection to producers and new information, kept saying, *"keep calm, you're okay. Keep talking. Stretch it, Caroline, stretch it. Stuff's coming in. Fill now. Read some of the stuff on what else the President did today. His schedule. How long he's been in office. Find it. It's in the bio stuff. Repeat the bulletin now. Martha Vogel's doing a live shot at the hospital. We'll throw to her as soon as we can. Okay. Okay, AP stuff's coming in. Something on Carl Olson, the White House press secretary—say something. There's a crew on the way to the hospital. Stay cool. Keep talking."*

She pressed her nail into a paper, tearing it. Could she do it? All those years, all the training, all the practice, all the mikes, all the monitors, all the mirrors: this was it. She was solo, at the top, just as she had wanted. But all it meant was that she was alone. She started to open her mouth. Her throat burned strangely. Could she make it?

The voice kept telling her what to say, what to read, what not to say, reminding her of what you could not say, hissing words like *alleged* and *reported* at her. But as the minutes passed, the voice in her ear grew more desperate, its words more frantic.

At 7:46 P.M. it was all over.

A LIGHT, cold rain was falling, softening the gray November twilight, spattering the shining black limousines lined up outside the hotel. Martha Vogel stood waiting for the President of the United States, preoccupied with thoughts that made her vigil more mechanical than usual. She had waited so often in the rain for politicians. She knew what they would do and what she would do. Often, even what they would say was predictable. She pulled up the collar of her raincoat and noticed that the puddle in which she was inadvertently standing was seeping through the soles of her scuffed brown leather boots.

It had been a long time since she had been a member of a presidential pool, that group drawn by rotation from the White House press corps, assigned to follow as closely at the President's heels as the Secret Service would allow, clocking him in and out of events such as this private reception for political contributors whose past and presumably future generosity to presidential campaign coffers justified their being honored by a private meeting and chat with the candidate. The President frequently extended his stay on such occasions, perhaps in relief that there were neither prying eyes nor cocked ears behind him, because the press were outside in the rain, talking to each other, grumbling automatically, glancing repeatedly at the door beneath the dark red canopy behind which the President had disappeared. That door was guarded now by the blank-faced young men with identical devices in their ears, men who, Martha had once suggested sardonically, were all clones of one superagent.

Depending on the state of world tensions, it was sometimes worth trying to question the President anytime he put his nose outside the White House, but this was not one of those times. There had been an unusual dearth of major crises lately, which, Martha reflected morosely, was probably why she had been asked to take the place in the press pool of one of the regular network White House correspondents, who were all taking advantage of the lull in global drama to keep other appointments. There had been a time when Martha was on the kind of terms with a President that would have made him pause to chat with her, or at least acknowledge her presence. She had been on chatting, interviewing, and even social terms with three Presidents, but not with this one. She was there only because Sullivan, the news director of the Washington bureau of World News Network, had glanced up from the telephone with a faintly impatient expression, scanned the room, and called, "Hey, Marty, how about going over to the Hilton and doing that White House pool? Terry can't make it, and nothing's doing anyway."

People at the White House had seemed pleased and a little surprised to see her when she joined the pool car in the presidential motorcade. "Where've you been?" they'd asked. "On vacation?" "Sort of," she'd said. "Big project, eh?" they'd said, nodding, and perhaps, she thought, being kind, because some of them could remember when Martha Vogel was at the White House every day and on the air every night. That was before Caroline, of course. AC and BC, Martha mused, with a grim little inward chuckle.

Yet she didn't—couldn't—blame Caroline. She had been sure in her own mind that the fault lay with herself. Having reached her thirty-seventh birthday in a business still too much dedicated to the unlined female face, she felt that if she hadn't gotten where she wanted to go by now, she wasn't going to get there at all. Mellenkoff had warned her about that a long time ago. But that was a time when forty was twelve years away and they were both climbing fast. Now he was there and where was she? Standing in the rain outside a hotel waiting for the President and getting wet feet. Which in a way was a symbol of all that had gone wrong. She had never minded being alone, but she had become aware that her solitude had become increasingly empty. When she went home, went out, went to her office, she was conscious of being not only single but solitary. Chatting casually, she had the uneasy feeling that she was somewhere else, standing and looking at herself. Pitying herself. And that was something she had never done before. She had always drawn a clear distinction between pity and compassion; perhaps that was why she was supposed to be so unapproachable, so self-sufficient. And she certainly had been self-sufficient, prided herself on it. That was why she couldn't believe her feeling of groping when it first began to haunt her, a feeling that gradually assumed the dimensions of despair.

She sighed involuntarily, and Tim Kassky, one of her cameramen, glanced over and shook his head understandingly, grimacing at the closed door through which the President should have emerged twenty minutes before. She nodded in return, smiling determinedly, and pushed damp, dark tendrils of hair away from her forehead. She wished she had brought a scarf or an umbrella. But when she left home that morning, she had not expected to be anywhere except her office and her assignment at a hotel where a threatened strike of public-service employees was due to be launched with a press conference. Martha moved a few feet to a half dry patch of sidewalk between two large puddles and glanced around at the little group partly hidden in shadow. Small as it was, she realized she didn't know most of them; that was how long she had been away from what was considered mainstream news.

One young man looked especially miserable—tall and thin, his head down, his hands tucked inside a shabby leather jacket for warmth. Martha felt sympathetic toward him. He was probably another fill-in, and at his age, torn between awe at covering the President, even in such a minor capacity, and the reality of damp gloom and anonymity. His head came up abruptly as he felt her eyes on him, and Martha smiled, but there was no response in his face, which was a streaked white blur before he ducked back into his collar, like a turtle. She sighed again and noticed it was raining harder. She supposed she could call in to the office from a hotel telephone to let them know the President had gone back to the White House, although strictly speaking, she ought to return in the pool car and file the obligatory report to tell the press

that there was nothing to tell. At this hour, most of them
would have gone home, anyway.

Suddenly the door beneath the red canopy opened,
and an agent strode out to the limousine, a signal that the
President was not far behind. The group in the shadows
stirred to life. Martha glanced over at Kassky and checked
her tape recorder and notebook; she still retained faith in
the power of a ballpoint pen. Voices sounded beyond the
door, and the tall, familiar figure of the President was
briefly silhouetted in light, moving quickly into darkness.
She saw his smile, glimpsed the hand raised in greeting as
he walked toward the limousine. And at the same time,
she heard the staccato popping sounds that froze the
moment and the President's smile in her mind.

The dim street became a kaleidoscope of movement
and shifting shadow; the falling body of the President
seemed to fuse with a rising wave of harsh sound, of
shouts and sirens and a scuffling and thudding behind
her. Martha caught a glimpse of Kassky moving into
action with his camera, then swung around to see agents
engulfing the thin young man whose hands had been
buried inside his coat. He did not seem to be resisting
their onslaught; his face was bland, oddly slack. He seemed
to be watching almost with surprise as an agent snatched
from the ground the gun that the young man apparently
had dropped after pressing the trigger. He seemed to
have no further interest in the huddled figure of the
President, now almost hidden by frantic bodies and hands.

The young man looked as though he too were dead,
thought Martha, and she shivered at the phrase as she
edged closer to the group around the President, who was
now being lifted, gently, with great care. For an instant,
past the shoulder of an agent with a machine gun, she
glimpsed the face of the President, the eyes closed, the
fleshy, genial features drawn taut and pallid. Carl Olson,
the White House press secretary, who had been kneeling
beside the President, was getting to his feet, and for a
moment, Martha caught his eye. She had known Olson
for years, since he went to work on Capitol Hill. They
had even dated occasionally. She called to him, desperately, her voice rising in an urgent question.

"Carl?"

He stared at her, and at first she thought he did not

recognize her. Then she saw the tears on his face and saw his head shake, slowly, hopelessly. And she turned and ran, thrusting through crowds, remembering a telephone in the hotel lobby, finding it occupied, rushing down a hallway to a restroom where she remembered there was another wall phone. Remembering where telephones were was something she had learned when she first went to work for a wire service. And suddenly there was the old remembered exhilaration of doing what she knew she did best, of being where history was being made, and being able to tell the world about it. She had not forgotten how, and she had learned to ad lib words as well and as fast as she had once typed them.

The long night wore on, and the drama exploded and spread from the hotel and the wild street scene to a hospital and the White House and the embassies and Capitol Hill, and through it all, Martha went on doing what she did best—performing coolly, efficiently, and eloquently. She did not even lose patience with a shower of semihysterical and incoherent questions from the network anchorwoman, Caroline Mitchell. Her responses and explanations almost made sense out of Caroline's questions. And words of praise came down from the heights of the network, passed from those elevated gray levels. Mellenkoff says terrific job, they told her, and she smiled. Miller says thank God you were there, and she smiled. Eliass told Mellenkoff to give you his compliments, and she smiled. Mitchell's gonna get fired over this, and she shook her head.

It was dawn before they told her to go home and get some rest because it was going to be another long day tomorrow. Mellenkoff had sent another message, they said, to tell her it was the best job of spot reporting he had ever seen. And Mitchell, they reported, was having hysterics in her office because they had pulled her off the air. Martha took a taxi home. She was not tired. She felt light-headed and almost happy. Her apartment was dim and cool, and she turned up the heat and switched on a single lamp. When the telephone rang, she took it off the hook and let it whine into silence, while she wrote a short letter.

Then she ran a hot bath, poured half a bottle of bath oil into it, and lay there in the fragrant warmth for a long time, sipping on a tumbler of Scotch. She felt immensely peaceful, as though nothing remained to think about except the gentle surge of the perfumed water and the smooth sting of the Scotch on her tongue. When she at last climbed out of the tub, she dried herself slowly and wrapped herself in an immense blue velour robe, belting it tightly at her waist. She did not even remember, as she usually did, that Mellenkoff had left the robe at her apartment a long time ago and had been so amused by her fondness for wearing it that he had refused to take it back. She replaced the telephone on its hook and noticed that it did not immediately begin to ring. Looking out the window across the rooftops of Washington, she saw another cold, gray day, with rain sweeping the streets, but not even the memory of the dark and rainy night just past could give her pain. She thought only of how warm and protective the room was, of how soft the robe felt against her body.

Unhurriedly, she went into the bathroom, took a plastic vial from the wall cabinet, and slipped it into the pocket of the robe. Back in the kitchen she poured herself another Scotch and carried the glass into her bedroom, where she placed it on the bedside table, then she crawled under the blue down comforter and arranged pillows behind her head. Swallowing so many little red capsules was easier than she had expected. She lay quietly, sipping the Scotch. When the telephone began to ring, Martha did not hear it.

2

THE PRESIDENT of the United States was dead, victim of a blank-eyed assassin standing in the shadows of a Washington hotel with a gun tucked into his coat. The man who had been Vice-President of the United States was frantically assembling a patchwork administration. Diplomatic alarms were shrilling around the world, as potential policy shifts were measured and weighed in Europe, Asia, and the Middle East. Americans were reacting with that combination of shock, shame, and sick unease that wells up in the wake of political cataclysm. That this was not the first murder of a President made it all the more frightening. Each time, the thunder of a great machine fleetingly out of control seemed closer to those helpless in its path. There was fear, not only in the places where power dwelt, but among those who huddled around the television sets in their living rooms to watch their President die on screen, while cameras panned in on the puddles of his blood on a dark, wet sidewalk.

For the news organizations—the television networks, radio stations, and newpapers—it was a time of tense, grinding work, when the portentous sound of drums must be intermingled with the hailing of a new chief. It was a time when the best in that business again proved themselves, and it was a time when flaws were cruelly exposed. It was, as James Mellenkoff, president of World Network News, observed bleakly, not a time for an anchor to fall apart, on or off the air. Sitting in his carefully designed black-and-white office on the fortieth floor of the network offices in Manhattan, Mellenkoff stared at the New York skyline wreathed in November mist while his mind replayed the soft, icy voice of the chairman of the board of WNN requesting the rationale behind the hiring of Caroline Mitchell as the national news anchor.

"As I recall," Joel Eliass had said in those icicle phrases, "you were most confident of Mitchell's ability, James. Most confident. You defended her to her detractors. Whose doubts appear to have been well-founded. Well-founded."

There had been a pause then, and Mellenkoff, for perhaps the first time in his life, had been uncertain whether to volunteer any comment. It seemed to him that no matter what he said, he would be wrong. Either way, he would have to defend himself, or, unbelievably, defend Caroline Mitchell. Eliass, however, appeared to assume a humble silence as his due.

"There must be personnel changes, James," he resumed. "More than one change."

As the second pause grew longer, Mellenkoff felt his palms dampen, and said, in a voice that was a hoarse echo of its normal commanding cadences, "I understand that."

"You should, James," said Eliass. The click at the other end of the line had left Mellenkoff in no doubt as to the extent of his professional peril.

In another era, Mellenkoff reflected, Eliass would simply have asked for the head of Caroline Mitchell; not that there was much difference between physical and psychological execution when it came to appeasing the wrath of the men who worshiped only the god of ratings. Eliass had made it clear that he placed responsibility for what Mitchell had done on the air the previous disastrous night on Mellenkoff's shoulders. Or rather, what she had not done.

Anchors for the other networks had performed their assassination coverage in a manner that provoked no more than the customary carping of television critics. But Caroline Mitchell had been raw meat flung into the critics' cages. She had achieved the kind of media prominence dreaded by networks fighting against the unisex image of the blown-dry talking head with a vacuum inside. She had carved herself a memorable niche in the hall of television ignominy, and, as Mellenkoff knew from experience, hers would not be the only head that would fall.

He could still taste the combination of fury and fright that had welled in him as he heard his handpicked anchorwoman's voice ascend into hysteria, and listened as she announced not only the death of the President, but rambled on about additional injuries to White House staff and Secret Service agents, which, at the time, were no more than unconfirmed wire-service reports. He had cringed as her composure visibly crumbled, and what she did say became fragmented babble. He knew how much help was being offered her by producers—one of whom was even sitting nearby, just out of camera range, to help her collate fast-moving copy, offer advice, stave off panic. Reports and stories pouring in were underlined at points appropriate for her to read. Reporters dismayed at the on-camera collapse of the network's national anchor had done their best to feed her both questions and answers. Nothing had helped. Mellenkoff thought bitterly she had done everything but foam at the mouth, and he had been afraid that that might be next. He watched the terrified eyes and the quivering mouth, heard her voice waver, and slammed his hand on the marble top of his desk with a force that sent a pile of papers flying to the rug. He was possessed by frustration all the more unbearable because he had no one to blame but himself. She was a flawed model, but she was his model.

"Get her off the air. *Now!*" he had barked. Roger Miller, a vice-president who had opposed the naming of Mitchell as anchor, had urged that they bring in Martha Vogel, a veteran network correspondent who, by chance, had been a member of the press pool covering the presidential attendance at a reception preceding his shooting. Mellenkoff, who had known Martha Vogel for a long time, had watched her performance on the air with as much pride and admiration as he had been horrified by the collapse of Caroline. He had sent her a message of congratulations. But he ordered that White House correspondent Terry Steiner take over from Mitchell. Vogel was too valuable where she was, he said, and he had refused to meet the furious eyes of Miller. He knew Miller was too professional to argue in the midst of the kind of disaster they had on their hands at that moment. He also was aware that, in all the years he had known Miller, he had never seen him so angry.

Mitchell had been removed from the anchor spot, but not before she had broken down, telling millions of viewers, "I'm—I'm s-sorry," while tears welled up in her huge dark eyes.

Mellenkoff had sent up a silent prayer, based on the frail hope that some of the viewers might be gullible enough to believe that the breakdown of the WNN anchorwoman was attributable to her patriotic grief at the passing of a President. But he doubted it. And during the hours that had passed since the President was shot and the marathon aftermath coverage had begun, Mellenkoff had refused to see or speak to Caroline Mitchell, despite her desperate and repeated calls and messages. She had even succeeded in waylaying Roger Miller and persuading him to take with him a scrawled little note for Mellenkoff, who wadded it up without glancing at it. Miller made no comment. He had been more taciturn than usual since their altercation the previous night. Mellenkoff assumed he would get over it. Meantime, he had to deal with what amounted to a salvage operation, with Eliass perched on the floor above like a vulture.

He felt a flicker of nervousness when he called Miller in to tell him to stay with Steiner as anchor for the time being. Miller's face was expressionless. He merely nodded and asked if there were any other reassignments. Mellenkoff glanced at him sharply, but the other man's eyes were blank.

"I'll personally sign off on all assignments today. Funeral, reaction, new administration, this stuff about the killer being a terrorist. All of it. There'll be no more slipups," Mellenkoff said.

He looked up from the papers stacked tidily on his black marble-topped desk to see Miller smile. It was a twisted smile, but it was a smile.

"I say something funny?" asked Mellenkoff, harshly.

"Absolutely not," said Miller, as he turned away. But when he opened the door of the office to leave, a figure burst in, evading his restraining hand. Behind the figure was Betsy Cooley, Mellenkoff's press secretary, uncharacteristically flustered, plucking at the intruder.

"She told me you had called her on the private line—"

Mellenkoff waved a hand dismissively at his secretary. He had not moved in the massive black leather chair, and he had not looked at the newcomer.

"All right, Betsy."

He glanced at his watch and his eyes flickered to Miller, who was standing in the doorway. It still seemed to Mellenkoff that the man still had a faint smile on his face.

"I'll see you at the ten o'clock meeting, Roger. That'll be in fourteen minutes and twenty-two seconds."

He waited until the door closed behind Miller and Betsy Cooley before he glanced up at Caroline Mitchell. His mouth curled in distaste. She looked like a drowned cat, he thought. The wide-set dark eyes were puffy and shadowed in the white oval of her face, and the glossy dark hair hung in elf-locks about the slender neck. Her hands were clasped behind her, he assumed to conceal their trembling. She looked miserable and pitiful and she exasperated Mellenkoff intolerably. He was inescapably reminded of his misjudgment of character.

He had always known Caroline was high-risk material, but Mellenkoff had always taken chances. In policy, in style of coverage, in spending, the Mellenkoff mark was sweeping and distinctive. Like Cain, some of his critics said. But his firm grasp on the network's top job attested to his record of success. He had thrown his influence behind an unlikely concept of a behind-the-scenes news-docu-drama that sat at the top of the ratings for years. He had borrowed the framework of the "McNeil-Lehrer Report" for a network news feature hour that leaned so heavily on emotional titillation spiced with sensation that it swamped all opposition. He had proved he did not bite off more than he could chew. Until now. And he looked with something close to hatred at the cringing little creature who had proved Mellenkoff wrong.

His choice of Caroline Mitchell had never had anything personal about it. He despised executives foolish enough to bestow professional promotion because of personal weakness. He had chosen her because he believed she possessed qualities that he could nurture, polish, and hone. Especially a certain charm that had been compared to a laser beam, producing an inexplicable yet apparently irresistible effect on viewers. Mellenkoff was impervious to all charm, except that of power. In women, he considered charm a frosting that made the cake more palatable. But in Caroline Mitchell, charm took on a new meaning, because it seemed possible that she could transmute it

into the gold of ratings magic. She lacked background
and experience, and the fact that she looked quite a lot
like Jacqueline Kennedy Onassis was, in Mellenkoff's view,
an unpredictable factor. But what Caroline was able to do
was communicate, apparently effortlessly, with her audience. Mellenkoff had seen politicians and actors do it—
sweep audiences up, engulf them, overwhelm them. The
Kennedys had that knack. Franklin D. Roosevelt had had
it. But he had never seen it in a television personality,
with the exception of Walter Cronkite, whose avuncular
reassurance had made him the Santa Claus of the airways.

Mellenkoff had looked at Caroline Mitchell and permitted himself to dream. Now she stood before him, a
slender, sniffling failure, waiting for his forgiveness.

"Well?" he said.

Caroline swallowed. "I had to—talk to you."

"About what? You had your chance to talk last night.
Why didn't you talk then, when the whole world was
listening?"

Her eyes sought the thick black-and-white pile of the
carpeting. "I—I wanted to—I'm sorry."

"I expect you are."

Her eyes came up, wide and pleading. "I—I got upset.
I—it was just that I didn't know what—I couldn't—"

"That was obvious. To the viewers as well as to me."

One hand came from behind her back, reaching out in
a supplicating gesture. "Please. I know you're angry with
me. But I can—I mean I promise I'll—"

Mellenkoff looked at his watch. "I have a meeting."

"What about—I mean—tonight's show?"

His eyebrows rose only a fraction. "You must be
joking."

He flipped open his schedule pad and began to study
it, making occasional notations. When she left, he was
genuinely unaware of her departure, and when he looked
up, Betsy Cooley was standing at the desk.

"The meeting, Mr. Mellenkoff. I just wanted to remind you."

He nodded. "Thank you, Betsy."

He paused on his way past her and there was a hint of
softening in his eyes that had the warmth of a winter sea.
Betsy was a valuable cog in his organization, and he had
no wish to diminish her confidence in her competence.

"By the way. Don't worry about that little—ah—problem, a few minutes ago. I don't expect you to be a bouncer, Betsy."

Her smile was relieved and grateful, and Mellenkoff suspected that that was the only moment of the day when he would be sure he had done something right.

The meetings pyramided, punctuated only by a sandwich at his desk. Stories were assessed for priority and air time. Preparations for the presidential funeral. The new President and his administration. Reports of the killer's ties to a terrorist group. The presidential widow. Congressional reaction. Diplomatic reaction. And gratitude that nothing else of moment was happening in the world, which seemed to be briefly between international crises. Mellenkoff applied all of his substantial expertise to ensure that WNN coverage would be more than adequate. And then Joel Eliass padded into his office to watch the evening news broadcast with him. Mellenkoff felt the familiar knot in his stomach as he saw the crinkled pout of the chairman's little round purse of a mouth in his shiny, pink face.

Eliass's head looked as though it had never caught up with the rest of him. It rested like a tomato atop his massive body. But no one underestimated the power of the computer mind operating inside that tomato. He had been referred to, by a junior executive no longer with the network, as "our friendly neighborhood tarantula." Mellenkoff had never found any reason to quarrel with the comparison, and it came to his mind as he sipped a light Scotch and waited until Eliass finished his Dubonnet and carefully placed the crystal glass on a side table. The chairman gestured toward the triple television console, and Mellenkoff pressed a remote-control button to activate the screen.

They watched in silence. Mellenkoff deliberately did not look at Eliass. (The chairman had once told him he disliked being peered at as though he were expected to sprout something.) On the console was solid coverage; Mellenkoff was not dissatisfied with it, and he began to feel a little better.

"Not bad, James." The voice was dry and cold, but it was not as icy as it had been the previous night.

Mellenkoff nodded. "I thought Steiner did pretty well."

"Any change," said Eliass, "would have been an improvement."

Mellenkoff stiffened.

"By the way," said the chairman, "where is Vogel?"

Mellenkoff frowned. He had wondered about that. After her performance twenty-four hours earlier, he had expected Martha to have some kind of assignment. What she had done was spot reporting. Yet he would have thought some kind of follow-up story might have been assigned to her.

"I don't know," he said.

"She did exceedingly well last night," said Eliass.

"Yes. Yes, she did."

"In fact,"—the chairman's tone was silky—"perhaps she might have been a much better choice than your little Mitchell girl. As anchor, I mean."

Mellenkoff knew exactly what he meant. He also recalled that it was Eliass who had wanted Martha Vogel removed from White House coverage because she didn't smile enough.

"You may be right," he said, and hoped he did not sound too submissive. Eliass liked respect, but not obeisance.

"I think," said the chairman, "we must sit down and talk about some of these things, James. We do not want any repetition of last night, do we?"

"No," said Mellenkoff, "we don't."

"So perhaps a—reassessment? Yes, a reassessment of our resources. Perhaps that is in order?"

The pale-blue button eyes studied Mellenkoff, and the pink mouth snapped together.

Mellenkoff nodded. "I'll set up a meeting."

"Tomorrow," said Eliass. "No. The day after tomorrow. That will give me time to do a little looking around of my own. A little looking around, James, is always a good idea. Don't you agree?"

Mellenkoff's mouth was dry. This, he thought, was what Eliass did best and enjoyed most. The circle and strike routine. He wondered how far the chairman would strike.

"Whatever you think," he said.

Eliass nodded gently, the white-capped tomato bobbing on the thick neck.

"Change is good for all of us, James. All of us," he said.

Mellenkoff waited, but Eliass abruptly rose, with agility surprising in so heavy a man, nodded at the network president, and left. Mellenkoff poured himself another, stronger, Scotch and leaned his head on the back of his chair, closing eyes gritty with fatigue and tension. He did not hear the office door open; he was drifting in a subconscious haze, trying to rein in his speculation on whether Eliass was really on the warpath or simply being his usual reptilian self. He started when he heard a sound nearby and opened his eyes to see Roger Miller standing and looking at him. He stretched, grimacing as he felt the ache in his muscles, and thought how good a hot shower would feel.

"Roger. How about a drink? Imagine you could use one."

It was Mellenkoff's conciliatory gesture toward a man he numbered among the handful he trusted, even if he did find Miller too fastidious in applying his scruples. Not to mention his unnecessary sentimentality. Pouring the drink, Mellenkoff glanced up and noticed that the habitually mournful lines of Miller's rectangular face were as if etched in ink. Roger was beginning to show his age, he thought, then reflected that Roger was only a year older than he. Roger was a worrier: that was probably it. Bit of an old lady, always agonizing about something or somebody. Like that business last night. Sentimental overkill. Mellenkoff dropped in two ice cubes and handed the glass to Miller, who still had not spoken.

"Jesus, Roger. You look like you drowned your grandmother. Listen, I just had Eliass in here, and, for him, he was pretty high on tonight's show. I mean, we all have bad days. And Christ knows yesterday was as bad as you can get. But you can't live in the past. Got to worry about tomorrow now, right?"

Mellenkoff wondered why he was babbling like this to Miller, as if he were trying to ingratiate himself with a man he could fire if he wanted to. He must be more tired than he realized. Mellenkoff shook his head and took a healthy swallow of Scotch and felt a little warmer. Miller was holding his drink, but he had not touched it. In his other hand was a slip of paper. Mellenkoff peered at him irritably.

"What the hell is it, man? Don't tell me we've got another disaster. I don't know that I'm up to it, after yesterday. Roger? For Christ's sake, what's the matter with you?"

Miller held out the piece of paper.

"This came in over the wire. About the same time we got a call from Washington. I thought you'd want to see it, decide what we should do. . . ."

Mellenkoff took the paper and felt the warmth of the liquor seep away. He read the brief wire-service story and walked over to the window so that he would not have to look at Roger Miller's face. He crumpled the scrap of paper so tightly in his hand that when he tried to smooth it out later, the words were illegible. He was grateful for Miller's silence. When he spoke, his voice was hoarse and dry.

"Do we know any more?"

"Sullivan had her building manager check when she didn't answer her phone, Jakes was on his way to the hospital when I talked to Sullivan. She's in a coma."

"She did this this morning." Mellenkoff shook his head in disbelief. "Jesus Christ, why? It was the best work she's ever done. Superb job. She was the only thing that saved us, if anything could have saved us."

"Maybe she didn't think she had anywhere else to go," Miller said softly.

Mellenkoff stiffened. He moved back across the room, his feet soundless on the heavy piled carpeting, and met the other man's stony gaze.

"It's my fault, is that it?"

"Obviously it's more complicated than that. But it's true that what happened with Mitchell last night sure as hell wouldn't have happened with Vogel. Maybe she thought of that."

"Probably not. But she had other problems."

"Obviously."

Mellenkoff gestured at Miller with the white-knuckled hand in which the AP slip was grasped.

"She didn't try to kill herself because Mitchell got the job she wanted. She was too damn much of a professional for that."

"I didn't say it was because of the job. I'm not saying it

was because of you either, James. I'm saying she didn't think there was anything else left."

Mellenkoff stared at him, and there was pain in his face.

"I never thought she—" He stopped.

"Nor did I. But there had to be some clues."

Mellenkoff nodded. "There were."

Miller was silent. When Mellenkoff looked up, his face was expressionless.

"Use a news brief. A collapse. A stroke. Say as little as possible. At least we can spare her that."

"I don't think she'd give a damn," said Miller.

"I give a damn for her," said Mellenkoff, and wanted badly to smash his fist into the twisted flicker of a smile that crossed the other man's long, lined face.

"And the eleven o'clock?"

"Some footage from her coverage last night. Any change in condition. But don't make it sound like . . . like . . ."

"An obituary." Miller completed the sentence for him.

Mellenkoff walked back to the window and stood there until he heard the door close behind Miller. He leaned his head against the coolness of the glass, through which lights and darkness now blurred together.

3

THE CAMERAS and cables were gone and the antiseptic hush of a hospital had supplanted the chaos of the previous day. Yet it seemed to Roger Miller that the emergency area of the hospital, where the President had been pronounced dead, was eerily quiet. Voices of nurses and aides were low. Even arriving patients seemed sunk in silent misery. He had telephoned hospital officials from New York before using the WNN corporate jet to fly to Washington, and he was taken within a few minutes to the office of Dr. Mark Louis, a tall, gray-haired man with weary eyes and a long jaw.

"How is she?" asked Miller without preamble.

"The prognosis is uncertain," said the doctor flatly. "She's still unconscious and so far we haven't been able to rouse her. She's in a coma."

"What did she take?"

"Apparently a combination of sleeping capsules and liquor. Enough that it might kill her, might not."

"You assume it wasn't an accident?"

"We don't assume, Mr. Miller," Dr. Louis said. "We don't know. It's a question of when and how she wakes up."

"If she wakes up."

The doctor was silent.

"Can I see her?"

Dr. Louis hesitated. "She's in Intensive Care. I don't . . ." He paused and looked curiously at Miller. "May I ask whether your connection with—"

"I'm an executive vice president at WNN and I'm her best friend, so far as I know. We want to be sure everything that can be done is being done."

Miller's voice was unemotional, but whatever the doctor saw in the other man's face aroused a flicker of sympathy.

"All we can do now is watch her carefully and wait. I know that isn't easy," he said quietly.

Miller nodded and turned away. The doctor hesitated, then stopped him.

"Just a minute. You're Roger Miller, right? A messenger from your Washington office delivered this a few minutes ago. He said they expected you to be here. Glad I remembered it."

He fished among the papers on his desk and produced a white envelope stamped with the WNN logo.

"Thank you," said Miller and put the envelope in his pocket. Louis watched thoughtfully as Miller strode away, down the long, polished corridor. If that was corporate concern for an employee, it was impressive. The network executive apparently had not traveled by commercial transportation to Washington, given the speed of his arrival after his telephone call, and his tightly controlled manner suggested a far from impersonal interest in the woman who lay unknowing and unmoving in the hospital bed.

Miller walked until he reached a telephone booth in the lobby, went inside, closed the door and opened the envelope. Inside was another envelope addressed to him in Martha's handwriting. Clipped to it was a brief note from Jakes: "I found this when I went to the apartment. I stuck it in my pocket before the paramedics and police arrived, figured that's what she'd want me to do."

Miller's mouth softened as he tucked Jakes's note into his pocket. He held Martha's letter for a moment before opening the envelope, trying to control his dread of what he was about to read.

Roger dear, I'm sorry. I wish things had been different for us. I wish they had worked out for us, and maybe they would have, if I'd been able to think straight sooner. But I couldn't and I didn't, and the only reason I'm getting into what you always called the what-if factor is that I wanted you to know I'm sorry, and maybe I'm most sorry about what-if. I know I did a damned good job tonight and I'm proud of that. But I also know that tomorrow will be another futile day, and I can't think of anything to look forward to. I'm tired of feeling useless

*to myself and everybody else. I missed the chances I
should have taken, personally and professionally. Not
even you could save me from my own capacity for
self-destruction. Now I'm too tired and discouraged to
try to put myself back together. And I'm not going to
ask you to do it for me. God knows you tried often
enough. I know this will make you sad, and, knowing
you, it'll make you mad too. But I did want you to
know that it was always you I wanted to love. Martha.*

Miller read the note twice, noting that the handwriting
was neat and steady. Then he folded it carefully, replaced it in the envelope, and put it in his wallet. He sat
for another moment or two in the booth, staring without
seeing, until he became aware that a woman was peering
curiously at him through the window. He pulled open the
door.

"I'm sorry—" he began.

"Roger?" The tall, dark-haired young woman with
bright, lively brown eyes looked at him questioningly,
and he stared at her, aware that he knew her, yet unable
to fix her face in his mind.

"I'm Jill Starling—Jill Starling Roberts, that is. We've
met a few times at parties. I'm a friend of Martha Vogel
and . . ." She seemed about to add another name and
stopped herself.

Miller nodded. "Yes, of course I remember you, Jill."

She hesitated. "What're you doing here?" she asked,
and her blunt curiosity made him recall her more sharply.

They had talked a lot after Martha had introduced him
to her at the bar at the National Press Club in Washington. Martha liked Jill, who was a reporter for the Public
Broadcasting System, concentrating on investigative journalism without losing her sense of humor and a perspective of the idiocies of Washington bureaucracy. He
suspected that that was why Martha liked Jill, and it was
why he found the younger woman so entertaining. She
had a capacity for cheerful cynicism about her work that
he found increasingly rare in a generation that appeared
to believe it was most important to be earnest. Jill Starling Roberts—he wondered why she had dropped the
Roberts and assumed her marriage had crumbled—had
established herself as a reporter who could be relentlessly

tough-minded without being apocalyptic about the stories she pursued. She had a refreshing eye for the ridiculous and an awareness that what lay under stones might as likely be stupid as sinister. Martha had said Jill was one of the most perceptive reporters she knew. He recalled Martha telling him how she had met Jill when she went to give a speech at a journalism school some years earlier.

There had been another name. Roger shook himself mentally and fitted the handful of jigsaw pieces together. Jill was a close friend of Caroline Mitchell, another of Martha's protégées. His mouth twitched faintly in bitter recollection of Caroline, the WNN national news anchor. Or the ex-WNN national news anchor. Was that the name Jill had bitten back?

He held out his hand. "Jill, you'll have to forgive me. Things have been chaotic."

"I'm sure."

Her expression was sympathetic but her curiosity was clear, and Miller was not about to satisfy it if he could avoid doing so.

"What are you doing—a piece on the hospital?" he asked cautiously, uncertain of what she knew.

She nodded. "Previous dramatic events. It's had quite a few."

"Your people put together a good show last night," he said.

She smiled vividly. "Thanks, I'll tell them WNN said that."

Jill hesitated and Miller reflected wryly that she was probably trying to think of something nice to say about the WNN coverage of the presidential assassination and couldn't.

"Well, I . . . ah . . ." She paused, apparently searching for words, and was overcome with curiosity. "You're visiting someone here, Roger?"

His face and voice betrayed nothing. "Yes. An old friend. A stroke."

"Oh. Those things can be awful. I'm so sorry."

Miller glanced at his watch. "Listen, I have to run, Jill. Get to the airport. Good to see you again."

She nodded, then stopped as she was turning away.

"Hey, I know what I meant to tell you. Martha was absolutely terrific last night. Just marvelous! I haven't

had time to call and tell her so, but if you should talk to
her—"

Something in his face stemmed the flow of her words.
Miller nodded.

"Thank you. If I talk to her, I'll be sure to tell her."

Jill watched his long, lean back disappear down the
hall, out the front door, and into a waiting limousine.
She didn't know Roger Miller especially well, but she
liked him. He had a mixture of the sardonic humor and
baroque courtesy of some Texans, and to Jill, he had
never seemed to quite fit in the emotionally arid world of
ratings and financial returns. Yet he obviously was a
survivor. Whatever his philosophical qualms, they had
been muted enough to allow him to flourish as a network
executive, close to the president of WNN, a man about
whom the usual rumors and speculation swirled. He had
a reputation as a womanizer; his wife was almost never
seen in public; he was said to drink too much; and some
contended his courtesy cloaked ruthlessness. Aware as
she was that gossip was the cottage industry of journalism, Jill had made her own judgment of Miller, basing it
on what she knew to be his devotion to Martha Vogel.
Martha had never been given to discussing details of her
personal life, although she and Jill had become fairly
close over the past few years. Jill suspected that one of
the reasons for Martha's reticence was that her long-
running interest in a different publicly prominent man
received enough attention without her contributing to the
rumors. But Jill had always noticed that when Martha
was with Roger Miller, she seemed to be happy and relaxed. They had laughed together a lot, she remembered,
in the way people laugh when they are entirely comfortable with each other.

Jill walked slowly down the hospital corridor, trying to
determine what it was that troubled her about her encounter with Miller. He had looked gaunt and exhausted,
but that was unsurprising, given the events of the previous day. Sitting in her office later, Jill wondered who the
old friend was, whose illness had brought Miller from his
office in New York, on the morning after his network
had suffered some of the most disastrous major coverage
in its history, to make a visit to a hospital in Washington.
Her line of thought tracked to Caroline Mitchell, whose

name, as Miller had noticed, Jill still could not quite
force to her lips when she spoke of friends. Caroline,
with whom she had grown up in the small town of Glayville, Ohio. Caroline, the little girl down the street who
was so much prettier and more polite than Jill that Jill's
mother repeatedly and sharply made comparison. Caroline of the glossy dark hair, shining dark eyes, and incan-
descent smile. Caroline whom everybody in Glayville
loved. Caroline who was Jill's best friend, partly because
Jill's mother thought Caroline would be a good influence,
and partly because Jill was often sorry for Caroline,
without ever knowing why. She could not remember
when she first became conscious of an odd remoteness
about Caroline, although she did recall being reproved
by her mother for outbursts of frustrated anger and for
failing to "control herself" the way Caroline did. Her
mother had been especially sharp the time Jill had exploded that Caroline didn't have anything to control.
"It's like she's empty," she had asserted. That was a
terrible thing to say, her mother had scolded, just because Caroline was so well brought up.

Jill also remembered that her father, who managed to
restrain his enthusiasm about Caroline, had observed
gently that the kid reminded him of a wind-up doll. Her
father had winked at her, and Jill had felt suddenly that
she didn't ever want to be like Caroline, didn't need to
be like Caroline. She had become a curious, sometimes
puzzled student of Caroline, and the longer she knew
her, the more she came to realize how little there was to
know about Caroline, who was the star of Glayville, the
town's favorite local celebrity, winning beauty contests,
playing the lead in the Glayville Players' productions,
always escorted by her tall, handsome father.

Jill was Helen and Nolan Starling's bright little girl
who was always at the top of her class and usually looked
as if she had been climbing a tree, which was frequently
true. Caroline was Glayville's frosted fairy, an inevitable
success story, and she had made the town's dreams of her
come true. She had become a television star. Jill's mother
wrote to tell her how people turned on their sets every
night to hear the news being read by what the *Glayville
Gazette* called "our own Caroline Mitchell." Jill wondered how they had reacted in Glayville the night before,

when they tuned in to see the local heroine come unglued on the air. She wondered what the reaction had been in the Mitchell house, especially on the part of Caroline's father, Carlton, who doted on his beautiful daughter, constantly caressing her and buying her clothes and trinkets and toys. Jill's father had tweaked her nose and taken her fishing and never noticed what she wore unless it wasn't blue jeans.

Jill had always thought Caroline's father was a little odd. She felt uneasy around him and didn't know why. She remembered her mother talking about how Caroline's mother, Amy, had changed after she married Carlton.

Helen Starling had known Amy when she was slender and lively and funny and laughed a lot, in the days when she was dating Carlton, who lived on the other side of town. On the wrong side of town, as a matter of fact. Almost as soon as Amy and Carlton were married, Amy had turned into a shadow with a fixed smile and Carlton had done all the talking, said Helen. It was about then that Amy started to do a lot of eating. The better Carlton's law practice did, the more locally prominent he became, the more he took to being gently disparaging of Amy. There were rumors about other women; Carlton was such a handsome man. And it was about then, Helen told her daughter, that Glory Swimmers, the editor of the *Gazette*, had taken Amy aside and told her to take herself in hand, and Amy had. Jill remembered her mother shaking her head over the sadness of it all. Amy had lost weight and gotten her hair styled, bought new clothes and chattered like her old self and confided that she couldn't wait for Carlton to see what she called her "butterfly day," when she'd come out of her dowdy cocoon and everything would be good again. But "butterfly day" came and went and Amy stopped talking about Carlton or anything else. She began to drink a bit, and the town was shocked by talk of her picking up men in bars. Such a mixed-up pair of people, said Helen, comfortable in her own marriage to a man who worshipped her and whose idea of a night out was watching football on television with his daughter.

When Caroline was born, Helen told Jill, everyone thought things were better with the Mitchells. She was the most beautiful baby in town, and Carlton couldn't stop talking about her, but nothing seemed to matter to Amy. Caroline was Carlton's only comfort in the end, Helen said piously, and frowned at her husband's chuckle.

By the time Jill heard the official story of the tribulations of the Mitchells, she was in her teens and her opinion of Caroline was irreversible. Without rancor, she had long ago decided that her groping childish assessment of emptiness had been painfully accurate. The voltage of Caroline's charm had grown and her smile was more radiant. But as Jill put it years later, to a man who had fallen into and out of love with Caroline, when you looked into her eyes, there was nobody there. Jill didn't pretend to understand Caroline. She was intrigued by her, especially by her capacity for single-minded ambition, and some of the time she liked her. Caroline could be fun when you least expected it, a wistful child, occasionally a frightened child. Those were the characteristics that most interested Jill, because she had never been able to explain them and Caroline denied their existence. They had grown up together and gone to college together, but their friendship had collapsed when Caroline had had an affair with Jill's husband, mostly because she hadn't anything better to do that night, so far as Jill could tell.

Back in her office, Jill sighed and turned in her chair to watch television reruns of the previous day's tragedy. She smiled as she saw Martha Vogel, tousled, vivid, and damp in a raincoat, doing the best work of an impressive career. Martha was so good, Jill thought. Why hadn't she been made anchor instead of Caroline? She suspected the WNN hierarchy was wondering the same thing at that moment. If she had wanted to take revenge on Caroline, she reflected, she probably couldn't have done anything worse to her than Caroline had done to herself last night. Staring at the footage of rivulets of the President's blood on a dark wet sidewalk, Jill wondered why Caroline had collapsed.

A producer wandered by her desk and stopped.

"Too bad about Martha Vogel," he said. "Wasn't she a friend of yours?"

Jill stared at him. She'd forgotten to call Martha.

"What's too bad?"

"She's in the hospital. Wire story says she had some kind of collapse. Maybe a stroke. It's a bit vague. She's in a coma."

"My God. Where—what hospital's she in?"

It was the same hospital to which the President's body had been taken. A coma. The word touched a chord in Jill's mind: Roger Miller's old friend. She read the brief wire-service story, which said as little as possible and had all the earmarks of careful wording. Jill picked up the telephone and called the hospital. She identified herself as a friend of Martha Vogel and then as a PBS reporter. The hospital official reacted to both statements by reiterating that Miss Vogel's condition was unchanged. They would not say whether it was satisfactory or unsatisfactory. Jill picked up the phone again to call Roger Miller in New York and ask why he hadn't told her Martha had had a stroke, then replaced the receiver in its cradle without dialing. There had to be a reason why Miller hadn't told her, a reason that had brought him rushing to Washington from New York on a day when the world was frantic. And if Miller hadn't wanted to tell her, it had to be a substantial reason. Jill was suddenly overwhelmed by misery. She looked at the dark November sky outside her window for a while and then she went home to her empty apartment so that she could cry. When the telephone rang, she didn't answer it, because she was sure it was Tom Roberts, her former husband.

She didn't want to talk to Tom, not because she was still angry with him, but because there was nothing left to say, and she didn't seem to be able to persuade him of that. Looking back on it, they had run out of communication long before he had slipped into bed with Caroline, and that probably wasn't all Tom's fault. They had married almost as a corollary to a relationship that had begun when Jill was in college and Tom was a budding political reporter on an Ohio newspaper owned by a national syndicate. She had learned from him, and almost at once outstripped him professionally. They were barely married before she had rushed to Washington to take a temporary, maybe permanent, job with PBS, leaving Tom to negotiate a post outside Ohio. When he had left, it had been for Chicago, to be a reporter with the WNN-owned station there, and it had been at the same time that

Caroline had taken her first upward step, becoming a talk-show co-host. The rest, Jill supposed, was inevitable, and she had been too busy at PBS to care. She had been mostly angry when he had told her about Caroline, exasperated that he felt he had to tell her, sickened by Caroline's disloyalty, yet, when she considered it dispassionately, far from devastated by the news. Her chief reaction had been to immerse herself in a difficult story and discover with pleasure that the pain of recollection faded faster than she would have expected.

Mike had helped, of course. Jill's wide mouth curled in a smile that was a mixture of joy and self-satisfaction. She wondered abruptly if it had been Mike who had called, then she dismissed it. He always called late, when she was in bed. They seemed to have spent a lot of their time in bed, she mused, and it had been so far an uncomplicated relationship in which they were grateful for each other. Jill looked restlessly about her apartment, which even Mike described as marginally comfortable. What Jill wanted most when she went home was a place to curl up, with a pile of books and magazines. Her priority in home decoration was a large, comfortable armchair. Her favorite chair was red, because she liked red, but the sofa was an undistinguished brown tweed, because she liked how it felt to sit on and hadn't wanted to wait until they could slipcover it to match the chair. Her rugs were what Tom had once called porridge colored, which meant they looked like the walls. Her bedroom was a mishmash of accumulated chests of drawers and bedside tables that didn't match, and the frequently unmade bed was concealed by a huge red down comforter. At least Mike never complained that the bed was unmade, she thought, and grinned, then remembered Martha and felt guilty.

She went into the kitchen to heat up some soup. She didn't feel particularly hungry, but she hadn't eaten all day and she wanted a drink, and she thought she'd better at least dilute it with Campbell's vegetable. Sitting on the drab brown sofa with a steaming bowl on a tray in her lap and a glass of Scotch on the table beside her, she wondered again about Martha. Wondered what had happened, and wondered how Caroline felt now. She turned on the television set, wondering if there would be anything said on the news about Martha, then chided herself. Martha wasn't dead. At least, Jill didn't think she was dead. She shivered and called the hospital again. They said Miss Vogel's condition was unchanged. Jill put down the receiver and thought that they made it sound as though Martha were frozen, and she supposed in a way that was true.

She remembered the last time she had seen Martha, when they had talked about politics and office problems and stories and even a little about Caroline. Martha had always been charitable about Caroline, perhaps because she knew better than most about the world in which Caroline would have to survive. What they had not talked about was Martha, Jill recalled. Martha rarely talked about herself, but in recent months, it had been as though Martha no longer considered herself a topic of conversation at all. She had lost interest in herself in a frightening way, and Jill realized only now how frightening it was, when Martha was lying in a coma in a hospital bed in a condition that had remained unchanged for hours. Would she be unchanged when she woke up? If she woke up? Finally, Jill began to cry softly.

4

IN HER nightmares, she was always in the beautiful room. It was bright and sunny, full of soft colors and textures. Its walls were patterned in a delicate filigree of ivory and pale peach. The thick rugs and the comforter were a warm, coppery peach. The room was the envy of every little girl in the town of Glayville, and Caroline Mitchell hated it. Her father had chosen almost everything in the room when he had it redecorated for her sixth birthday. He wanted it to be perfect for Caroline to remember when she grew up, he told his wife. Amy Mitchell admired the colors, although she detested pastels, and asked if the bed were not a little large for a small girl. Carlton Mitchell said it was economical to buy Caroline a real bed instead of one of those cutesy, frilly four-poster numbers.

"We do expect her to grow," he pointed out.

His wife went back to the room where she slept with Carlton, where the silk comforter was frayed, and the carpeting was a little threadbare, and thought about her husband in bed with Caroline. She had thrust away the suspicion at first. But when Caroline was barely five, Amy had walked into the bathroom, where her husband was bathing their daughter, and had seen his hands moving on the child's body. She never knew why she hadn't cried out in anger then. He had at once turned toward her, his face a careful mask, suddenly busy with washcloth and towel, explaining he'd thought he would help out with Caroline. Amy had said nothing, but she kept a vigil after that, a silent watch at doors and windows. And what she saw at first sent her into a dark rage against her husband.

She delayed only to make sure there could be no

question of her evidence against Carlton. Then she saw
the child climbing over her father, kissing him, hugging
him, and always smiling. Amy grew to hate Caroline's
smile. How could she smile? Why did she not come
weeping to her mother? And the thought crept into Amy's
head that Caroline could not smile so much if she were
not happy. If she were not enjoying what her father was
doing to her. Amy had been unhappy for a long time, but
now she was engulfed in despair. This was her baby, her
beautiful baby. And this was her husband, her handsome
husband. She sat staring blindly while Carlton took Caroline for sodas and to movies, and she listened to their
laughter as they came home. And Carlton would look at
her as she sat beside the empty cookie jar and grin at his
daughter.

"Mommy's getting fat, isn't she?" he would say.

Caroline's high-pitched laughter would echo that of
her father, and Amy would hate them both.

Slowly she retreated into the cave at the back of her
mind. Whereas she had once hoped for happiness, now
she renounced everything except hatred. She became
more withdrawn, rarely accompanying Carlton to social
functions—it was rare that he suggested it—and even
seeking excuses to avoid participation in school or PTA
activities.

Once, Caroline came upon her mother, lying on the
sofa, staring blankly upward. She did not move or smile
when she saw her daughter, and Caroline timidly touched
her mother's arm and saw her flinch.

"Mother?" She had long since stopped using the childish abbreviation.

Amy turned her head slightly and Caroline tried not
to retreat from the flat gray gaze.

"Mother? Do you hate me?"

The words filtered slowly into Amy's numbed consciousness. She sat up and looked at her daughter standing there, fragile as a flower in her pink skirt, glossy dark
hair falling around her shoulders, eyes wide smudges of
darkness.

"Why do you ask that?"

Caroline pinched a fold of her pink skirt between her
fingers uneasily.

"Sometimes you look at me as if you don't like me."

"Why would I dislike you, dear?"

Caroline stared at her white-sandaled feet.

"Why would I dislike you, dear?"

Caroline shook her head speechlessly.

Amy reached out and took her daughter's hand, which lay small and limp in hers. Like a mouse, she thought.

"Tell me what you mean," she said, and her voice was unusually gentle.

Caroline's dark eyes fastened with intensity on her mother's face, and Amy tightened her grasp on her daughter's hand.

"Try to tell me. Don't be frightened," she whispered and waited. It seemed as though hours passed, and still Caroline stood, lips parted. Now she was clutching at Amy's hand, her nails digging into her mother's fingers. Amy looked at the quivering, soundless mouth and struggled against a desire to shake out the words, to smash the silence surrounding the child even if she had to smash the child. And Carlton found them thus when he came striding through the door, calling for his little sweetheart.

"Mother?" said Caroline. But the word trailed off as she turned, smiling, toward her father.

"What's all this? Secrets?" cried Carlton. And Amy smiled to herself as she saw the uneasiness in his face. He scooped up the now squealing Caroline.

"Can't have secrets from Daddy, now, can you?" he adjured her, and nuzzled her neck. Caroline wriggled. For a moment, Amy thought she was struggling. Then Carlton was gone, with the child in his arms, leaping up the stairs, chattering loudly about the new pink jeans he had bought her at the junior boutique near his office.

"Try them on right now!"

Amy lay on the sofa, her fingernails piercing her palms, shaken by misery and supported by fury. Upstairs there was bumping and chuckling and a hysterically high-pitched giggling. Amy listened and thought Dear God, I am a monster, too. Yet she could not move, could not rush upstairs to accuse and rescue and save. She could have told me, Amy thought. She had a chance. She would not speak against him. She's worse than he is. Little bitch. Damn them both to hell. And the tears that slid down her pallid, fleshy cheeks were for herself.

She could not even salvage her usual bitter satisfaction

from the knowledge, or the lack of knowledge, of whether
Caroline was Carlton's daughter. In those dreadful months
after the shining bubble of a plan to save herself and her
marriage had exploded, Amy had taken comfort where
she could get it. Other men found the new Amy attractive, and she had sought reassurance in their arms. It
gave her something pleasant to think about when Carlton
paid his perfunctory and sporadic marital attentions to
her. When she became pregnant, she had no idea who
had impregnated her, nor did she care. At least, she
thought, she would have the child. And once she had the
child, Carlton would not matter so much.

She listened to Carlton making plans for the decoration of Caroline's room. It was done while Caroline was
visiting Amy's cousin. It was a big surprise. Amy was in
her bedroom when Caroline arrived, accompanied by Jill
Starling, her best friend, and she heard their excited
cries. Amy stayed in her room, although she wanted to
go downstairs and get something to eat. After a while,
she heard Jill leave, and when she finally went to the
kitchen, the door to Caroline's room was closed. She
stopped and listened, and heard Carlton's voice, very
low. Downstairs, Amy made herself a ham and chicken
sandwich and ate almost a carton of strawberry ice cream.

And Caroline never forgot the room that Daddy gave
her, never forgot what Daddy did to her there. Years
later, she would wake up moaning, her arms thrashing in
the darkness, again trapped in the horror of the room
where the delicate trellised design of the wallpaper reminded her of hands reaching for her. Hands haunted
her dreams as they tortured her nights, the fine, long-
fingered hands of her father, probing, pressing, seeking,
and sometimes striking. She could not remember how or
when hugging had changed to hands. She only knew that
when she was learning to read, she was also learning to
pretend she wasn't afraid. Her father told her repeatedly
there was nothing to be afraid of. How could she be
afraid of Daddy, who loved her? But she was. And
sometimes she screamed or cried in fright, and felt the
sting of her father's long fine fingers across her face.

Mother will hear, he warned, and Mother will be angry
with you. Why? she asked, hiccuping back her sobs. And
her father would take her in his arms and rock her and

explain she made him want to love her, that it wasn't his fault. Caroline made him do it, and Mother would be angry with her for doing this to Daddy. Mother would never love her again, if Caroline told her what she did to Daddy, he said solemnly. Caroline listened fearfully and believed him. Mother always seemed ready to be angry with her. Sometimes the expression on her mother's face frightened her almost as much as her father's hands did. She could not think what her mother would look like if Caroline told her about Daddy. So as she grew older, Caroline learned to hide, especially when her father crept into the lovely peach and ivory room when her mother was asleep and lay down beside his daughter. Caroline taught herself to think about something else, anything else that would blot out the hands and what they were doing. She recited poems to herself. When she managed to get through an entire poem, she felt a sense of pride and revenge. The hands had not really reached her.

She discovered she could also find comfort by looking at herself in the mirror, by talking to the pretty creature she saw in the mirror. The Caroline in the mirror had nothing to do with the frightened, rigid Caroline in the bed. She even sounded different. Caroline spent hours looking in the mirror, reading to herself, talking to herself, and slowly, Caroline in the mirror became the real Caroline. Caroline in the mirror was magic. She could enchant herself away from reality into a world where no one could hurt her because no one could reach her. Caroline in the mirror was safe.

By the time she was twelve, Caroline in the mirror had taken over. Jill Starling, who lived a block or two away, was Caroline's best friend, but it was only to the shining image in the mirror that Caroline really talked. Yet she liked Jill, partly because she couldn't imagine living the way Jill did. Jill's father had wanted a boy and what he had gotten was a girl who looked and acted like a boy. Nolan Starling, an affectionate and easygoing man who ran a successful sporting goods store, was amused and delighted to have a daughter who wanted to learn about fly casting and changing tires. His pretty, fastidious wife, Helen, was at a loss as to how to deal with a female who refused to wear skirts, wanted her hair cut like her father's, and exchanged punches with little boys. Helen

Starling watched enviously as Caroline Mitchell pirouetted by in her crisp pink skirts. Even when Caroline wore jeans, they were carefully pressed, and her long dark hair was brushed until it looked like black silk.

Helen kept telling Amy Mitchell she hoped some of Caroline's style would rub off on Jill.

"I keep thinking she has to turn into . . . well, a little *girl* sometime. And your Caroline is so lovely."

Amy Mitchell would smile that funny little smile of hers—Helen never felt close to Amy, although she had known her for years—and say yes, Caroline was very picky. Always taking baths.

"You'd almost think she felt dirty all the time," said Amy.

Helen laughed, a little uncertainly. "I have to practically throw Jill in the tub." She sighed. "Of course, after a day out with her father, they both look like they've been making mud pies."

"Nolan is a nice man," said Amy unexpectedly.

Helen glanced at her in surprise. "He really is," she acknowledged. "He has the nicest disposition you can imagine. In all the years we've been married, I don't think he's said a really cross word to me. And he's always bringing me little things—flowers, tiny presents."

"That's nice," said Amy.

"And he worships Jill," continued Helen. "But he acts like she's a boy. Of course, most of the time, she looks like one. Her hair gets any shorter, it'll be a crew cut."

"That's nice," said Amy.

Helen frowned a little. Sometimes it was difficult to make sense out of Amy, but then, she had always been inclined to be cryptic, even when she was young. Although then she had been funny, so it hadn't mattered so much. Now Amy seemed to keep more and more to herself. Helen felt sorry for Amy. It was a pity, Helen thought, that her attempts to improve herself had failed. She approved of people looking well groomed, and Carlton Mitchell was always immaculate.

"It's too bad about Amy," she said to Nolan one evening.

"What is?" asked Nolan, chewing on an ear of corn.

"That she's let herself go again. I mean, Carlton is so

. . . so distinguished looking, so charming. And Caroline's so pretty. You'd think she'd make more effort."

"I feel sorry for Amy," said Nolan.

"Why in the world?"

"I don't think you'd like to be married to handsome ol' Carlton, honey," he observed.

Helen frowned. "I don't understand."

"He's a bastard," Nolan said without rancor.

"Nolan!"

"Come on, Helen. Amy's got a lot to put up with. Everybody knows he runs around on her."

"Well . . . that was before Caroline was born, wasn't it? I mean, I know they went through a difficult period then, but . . . well, he seems to be home more now. He's certainly with Caroline a lot. He's always taking her someplace."

"Without Amy," noted her husband.

"Amy doesn't seem to want to go anywhere. Maybe she likes staying home."

Nolan shrugged. He was a kindly man, but he had reservations about the whole Mitchell family. Carlton seemed to him particularly unlikable because of his disloyalty to Amy—at the country club, he even bragged about his sexual prowess. Amy had a mad look in her eye at times. Not that Nolan blamed her for that. He had sometimes wondered why she stayed with Carlton. Even Caroline could set his teeth on edge. She was one of the prettiest children he had ever seen, but she reminded him of a mechanical doll. Caroline sounded as though she had been programmed, with her uncanny capacity for saying the right thing. At ten, his Jill would whine and wriggle through school musical recitals and church services. At ten, Caroline would sit raptly, and later charm the performers or the minister with her graceful little observations:

"I've always wanted to be able to play the piano/violin/harpsichord like that. You make it sound so easy, and so beautiful. Tell me how you came to learn and to be so good at it," she would say. Then she actually appeared to listen, nodding, interjecting a question.

The Reverend Mortimer Dagerman was enraptured by Caroline. Nolan occasionally watched him wait for her as she left the church with her father. She would be smiling, dark eyes bright, dressed in pale pinks or blues, and she would always have something to say about the sermon or the choir.

"Mr. Dagerman, the part about our responsibility to each other was so interesting," she would say. It was always the last few sentences of the sermon to which she referred, because that was all she had paid attention to. Mr. Dagerman would beam at her and be unaware he was talking to Caroline in the mirror, who was establishing herself.

She was not quite so successful in school, where teachers wanted to know whether their students understood what they had been listening to. At fourteen, not even Caroline in the mirror could win an essay contest without help, and Jill Starling could not give enough help.

Caroline and Jill were curled up on the peach rug watching television in Caroline's room. Jill was often invited to spend the night with Caroline, more often than Jill's father liked, but not as often as Caroline would have preferred. Jill was her buffer against her father, because Caroline in the mirror could not protect her against the hands. Jill liked staying with Caroline, whose mother served immense and gooey desserts and homemade chocolate chip cookies. And Caroline was never told which television programs she should watch. Her father said as long as she did her homework, he left that up to her judgment. Her mother didn't say anything. They watched some programs Jill knew her mother would have objected to, but what Caroline really liked to watch were news bulletins and talk show programs. Jill would munch apples and stare as Caroline took notes on shows.

"What are you doing? Why'd you want to watch *all* those news shows?" she would ask.

"I'm practicing," Caroline explained. "I want to do that when I grow up."

"Read news?"

"I want to be on television. An anchorwoman."

"Why?"

"I think it'd be neat. Everybody looks up to you and asks for your autograph."

"That's a movie star."

"This is better than a movie star. People think anchors are smart."

"My father thinks they shoot their mouths off too much about their own opinions," said Jill.

Caroline took a small, neat bite out of her apple and said nothing.

Jill considered. "Is that why you talk to yourself in the mirror?"

Caroline looked wary. "Well, I read in a book that's how they practice. It's called watching your visuals, or something like that. You have to know what you look like on camera. Television is sort of like a magic mirror."

Jill was impressed. "You'd be good at that," she said.

There was a light tap at the door, and Caroline's head jerked up.

"Yes?"

Carlton Mitchell's smooth dark head peered in, and his smile flashed at the two girls.

"Another pajama party, eh?"

"Jill is staying over, Daddy," said Caroline.

Her father chuckled. "I'd assume so, unless she's going home in her bathrobe. How are you, Jill, baby?"

"Fine, thank you, Mr. Mitchell," said Jill, who was uneasy around adults as formal as Caroline's father. She was used to Nolan, who ruffled her hair and made rude sounds at her.

"Fine, fine," said Carlton. "Caroline, come give Daddy a good-night kiss, sweetheart."

Caroline rose obediently and held up her face to be kissed. Carlton held her close, his hands caressing the slender neck. Jill watched with mild curiosity; her father kissed her on the forehead at bedtime, if he didn't slap her on the bottom.

"Sleep well, darling," said Carlton. "Don't chatter all night."

"Good night, Daddy," said Caroline, careful to keep the joy out of her voice.

"Where's your mother?" asked Jill.

"Downstairs in the kitchen, I guess."

"Cooking?"

"Eating."

Mrs. Mitchell never came in to say good night to Caroline, Jill noticed. Helen Starling made a point of coming into her daughter's room every night to tuck in the covers and smooth what was left of Jill's hair after she had cut it herself. Nolan thought Jill's haircutting was hilarious. Helen thought it was disastrous.

Jill chewed on her apple core. "I want to be an investigative reporter for public broadcasting," she said. "I've been reading all those books about the old political scandals. That'd be fun, showing up all those government crooks."

"You'd have to run around an awful lot," said Caroline doubtfully.

"That's the best part," said Jill. "You'll miss all the fun, stuck in a studio." She sat up abruptly.

"Hey, I forgot, I have to work on my essay for the contest."

"What contest?"

"The one at school. First prize is a trip to Lake Lodge. You get to spend a weekend there. Go boating and fishing and swimming."

"I guess I forgot. I should be doing something, too."

"Caroline," said Jill, "you know you hate writing."

"No, I don't. I just forgot." Caroline's mouth drooped. "Buck Jones doesn't like me," she said sadly, referring to their English teacher.

"Sure he does," Jill told her. "He just doesn't think you work up to your potential. Whatever that means."

She dug around in her canvas overnight bag and pulled out a sheaf of papers.

"I'm going to do mine on Glayville—you know, the history of the town and the people who lived here when it was founded."

Caroline leaned forward. "Can I see?"

"Sure." Jill tossed some papers to her. "These are just rough drafts. Just ideas."

Caroline read them carefully. "These are good."

Jill grinned. "I just want to get to Lake Lodge."

A week later, Buck Jones was surprised and pleased by Caroline Mitchell's entry in the annual essay contest of Glayville Junior High School. Like most of her teachers, he had found that Glayville's most beautiful and popular child had the attention span of a houseplant.

"She looks like she's hanging on your every word," he complained to a colleague, "but she's got no capacity for absorption. She'll recite what she learned one day, and two days later it's gone. And I mean gone. Some of her tests—you'd think she had never studied."

Dan Bly, who taught physics, was inclined to defend her. "Funny thing is, she's always trying to do something helpful in class. Always willing to help out. She's really a nice kid. And she does well in amateur theatrics: she's the standby of the Glayville Players."

"Except she keeps missing cues and forgetting lines."

"You're rough on her, Buck."

And when Buck read an essay that showed both style and observation, even if it did trail off into platitudes after a promising start, he wondered if he simply wasn't reaching Caroline. Maybe it was his fault. She was always receptive to advice and criticism, always apologetic. She was willing to please, to a fault, as a matter of fact. Maybe it was him. He gave the essay an honorable mention and noted without curiosity that Jill Starling had chosen the same topic. He knew the two girls were friends and it was not unusual for a similar subject to be chosen by students. They were an interesting study in opposites, those two, Buck mused. Jill was straightforward, a hardworking, perceptive student whose grades illustrated her capacity. Caroline was like shifting mist, ostensibly studious, with wildly fluctuating grades. Maybe Jill would be a good influence on her. Jill had been an easy winner of the essay contest, but he was encouraged by the fact that Caroline, for the first time, had entered.

Caroline didn't care about not winning, but she did care about not going to Lake Lodge. It would have meant several days away from home, and she was always eager to accept any invitation that would take her beyond the borders of Glayville.

Her father offered comfort. "Never mind. We'll go to a movie on the weekend to make up."

"I—Jill's coming over," Caroline said quickly.

"I thought you said the prize was a trip to Lake Lodge this week?"

Caroline nodded silently.

"So you'll have to make do with Daddy, won't you?"

Three days later, at the age of fourteen and two months, Caroline had her first menstrual period, and she had never been so grateful for anything in her life. She was even grateful for the cramps that sent her to bed in curled-up misery, clutching a heating pad provided by her mother, who was almost sympathetic. Her father did not come near her, other than to poke his head around her door and ask, rather stiffly, how she was feeling.

"Awful," said Caroline.

"Poor baby," said Carlton, and went to his club.

Caroline lay holding on to her heating pad as though it were a life belt, and felt blissfully happy. When her mother appeared with hot lemonade and aspirin, she observed that Caroline certainly looked cheerful, in spite of how she felt.

"I don't mind. I couldn't go to Lake Lodge anyway," said Caroline cryptically. Amy glanced at her sharply but said nothing. Caroline drank her lemonade, read a little, and lay drowsing. She woke once, roused by a familiar fear, as footsteps paused outside her door. Then she remembered, and renewed her grasp on the heating pad as the footsteps plodded on down the passageway. And Caroline slept deeply and soundly.

A line had been crossed, apparently. Caroline suspected it might be her father's fear of her pregnancy. But he was even tentative about touching her. It was as though she had suddenly become his daughter and he was uncertain what to do about it. At first her relief was so vast that she was almost grateful to him. For the first time in her life, her nights belonged to her. She slept well and she looked well, and she didn't talk as much to Caroline in the mirror, because the world around her had suddenly become more pleasant. She became more involved in school activities, and the specters receded a little in her mind. Until the night that a shy fifteen-year-old boy called Timmy Waring asked her to go to a movie with him. Caroline asked her mother, who gave approval with an evil joy, and made sure she told Carlton that Caroline was on her first date, and wasn't it sweet? When Caroline came home at eleven, she found her father waiting for her in the living room. On his face was an expression she hadn't seen since she screamed at his touch when she was five years old. She stood frozen in the doorway.

"Have a good time?" His voice was thick with anger and liquor.

"We . . . just went to a movie, Daddy, and Timmy . . . bought me a soda after."

He stared at her.

"Mother said I could go," she said desperately.

"Did she now?"

He took her by the arm and his fingers dug painfully into her skin. He pushed her upstairs ahead of him, and when they reached her bedroom door he stopped, looming over her. She glanced frantically toward her mother's door, and thought she saw it move slightly, but there was no sign of Amy.

Abruptly, she faced her father, trying not to flinch from him.

"I have to—Daddy, I need the heating pad . . .. Mother has to get me the . . ."

Her voice trailed away as his hand swung up, and she pressed herself against the door. Then the fury in his face subsided and it was as though his whole body sagged. As she stood there, shaking, he shouted toward the room he shared with Amy.

"Your daughter needs the heating pad again."

Her mother emerged so quickly from the room that she might have been standing behind the door. Her face was expressionless as she brought the heating pad to Caroline. She asked no questions, although Caroline was sure her mother knew she was lying.

That marked the end of Caroline's quiet time, of feeling safe. She spent the next three years avoiding her father, dating only when she was staying overnight with the Starlings, trying to speak to him as little as possible. But now the dreams came to torment her. The hands were gone, but she could not escape the memory. Sometimes she thought the dreams were worse than the reality had been, because in sleep, she moved into a realm of past horror. She locked her bedroom door hours before she went to bed, and sat down with Caroline in the mirror.

"You are going to be all right," said Caroline in the mirror.

"You will be going away to college and you will never come back. You will never see him again."

And Caroline in the mirror would smile, and experiment with cosmetics and hairstyles and practice reading the news from the local paper.

"This is Caroline Mitchell with the news," she would intone, carefully listening to her voice, watching her face, approving her face, studying it from various angles. She would practice what to say to people she knew. Expressions of sympathy, amusement, interest, concern would issue from her lips while corresponding emotions were reflected in her face. Caroline in the mirror never permitted self-pity. Neither Caroline ever cried. The closest they came was an expression of mutual blankness, as though an invisible lacquer had been applied to the delicately symmetrical features, and the dark eyes veiled.

Caroline graduated from high school, adequately if not with honors, and was commemorated in the *Glayville Gazette* for being named Miss Glayville, as well as being named Miss Teen Glayville and Miss County. Entering such competitions enabled her to get out of the house for hours and sometimes days. She and Jill Starling were both enrolled at *Glayville State College in Columbus,* two hundred miles away. She made a little song out of the words and put herself to sleep every night by murmuring, "Two hundred miles—*two* hundred miles—two *hundred* miles—two hundred *miles.*" The day before she left for college, Caroline looked up from packing her trunk to find her father standing in the doorway of her room. She went on bouncing on the trunk, trying to close the lid.

"You'll break the hinges."

He sounded like a real father, she thought. And felt anger.

He held out a small package wrapped in tissue. "A going-to-college present."

"Thank you, Daddy." Caroline took it without touching his fingers.

As she unwrapped it, she realized he was still standing on the threshold. He had not entered the room. The gift was a diamond, strung on a thin gold chain. Caroline held it to the light and swung the chain so that the diamond sparkled.

"Thank you, Daddy," she said again, and replaced the pendant in its blue velvet box.

"Aren't you going to wear it?"

"I'll keep it for special occasions."

She had gone back to tugging at the trunk.

"Don't I get a thank you kiss?" His voice was husky.

Caroline stood up, and realized she was almost as tall as her father. She forced herself to look directly into his eyes and held her gaze steady. It seemed like a very long time to Caroline, but only a moment or two passed before her father turned away and went quickly downstairs. So quickly that he stumbled, and almost fell. She heard the front door close and the car start, heard its wheels screech on the gravel of the driveway. Before she locked the trunk, she dropped into the bottom of it the blue velvet box in which lay the diamond pendant.

5

THE FOUR years she spent at Glayville State College were the happiest of Caroline Mitchell's life, not because she especially liked taking courses in communication, journalism, and drama, but because she never had to go home again. Less than a decade later, sitting in the softly lit burgundies and beiges of her elegant apartment overlooking New York's Central Park and brooding about her failure, Caroline remembered with desperate nostalgia the little yellow room she had shared with Jill Starling. Its window also had a view of trees, but the paint on the walls was faded, the rug was thin, and the two chairs had little to recommend them. Neither Caroline nor Jill had cared. They usually sat or sprawled on their beds anyway. The only tasteful piece of furniture in the room was the vanity Caroline had brought from her room in Glayville. She never wanted to see the room again, but it was within the graceful oval mirror, set in cream-colored lacquered wood, that she had escaped. Caroline in the mirror lived there. And the vanity had traveled with her to Chicago and New York, repainted, but still there. Except that in the end, Caroline in the mirror had failed her.

She remembered how Jill used to tease her about studying in front of the mirror, reciting to herself, memorizing, talking to herself, talking to the self-assured image in the shining glass. Caroline practiced so often and so long that she knew how she looked when she was cheerful, solemn, mischievous, or concerned, and when she added a tape recorder to her equipment, she knew how she sounded when her voice had to match her mood.

She pinned newspaper clippings on the wall and placed

them in a neat stack in front of her to simulate what she
had learned of a television studio's techniques. She had
read about teleprompters and the importance of not looking as if you were either reading or staring at your audience. So she read to herself in the mirror and tried to
assess her performance by comparing it to the professional news broadcasts she watched. She watched interview techniques too, but Caroline was good at talking to
people and getting them to talk to her. She was so
anxious not to betray anything of herself that she exuded
genuine interest in other people. Those were her real
studies. What she did in class suffered from the same
problem that had plagued her work in high school. She
would listen, almost frantically sometimes, but she did
not retain what she heard. "I think I have it all memo-
rized, then it's gone like fluff in the wind," she told Jill,
who was sympathetic but could only suggest that Caroline write down everything she listened to in class. Caroline said the trouble with that was that when she wrote it
down, it made her think she knew it when she didn't.
And certainly that had never changed, thought the older
Caroline, as she sat watching sleet fall on Central Park
and could not summon the energy to turn on the lights in
her darkening apartment, nor the courage to turn on
television to see someone else taking her place. Doing
what she should be doing.

She tried to think of pleasant memories, like discovering
that most of the male students on campus wanted to take
her out, and what made it especially enjoyable was that
she didn't care about any of them. She watched with
detached interest while Jill flirted and tried to make up
her mind whether to sleep with someone. Caroline continued to play her lifelong game of tag. Her father had
taught her well the art of evasion, and she did not know
how to stop. She never became involved in the undigni-
fied, puppyish sprawlings and strugglings that Jill enjoyed. Caroline could gracefully parry a lunge and slip
away from a caress. Yet she developed a style of delicate
disengagement that left her admirers all the more eager.
She refused to join in discussions about sex, and when
Jill stayed out all night and reappeared cheerfully dishev-
eled, Caroline retreated. Only once had Jill teased her
about the way she froze when masculine hands strayed

beyond her shoulder or her waist, flinching from even a casual gesture of affection.

"They're going to start calling you Caroline the Snow Queen," Jill had warned her, and backed away as Caroline turned on her a white and distorted face. Jill had been so genuinely distressed and sympathetic, without understanding what was wrong, that Caroline had almost told her. But she hadn't been able to get the words out in the end, like that day when she stood before her mother and wanted more than anything else in her life to ask for help. It was as though the hands lay across her mouth, condemning her to endure in silence. She couldn't even cry. She hadn't cried since she was six. She was frozen, and Jill could not have chosen a more painful analogy. After Jill left for her date, worried and apologetic, Caroline had sat down and looked miserably at Caroline in the mirror.

"I did that all wrong, didn't I?" Caroline in the mirror nodded.

She sat there for a long time, brushing her hair, looking at Caroline in the mirror, who looked so much calmer than Caroline felt.

"All I have to do is remember I never have to go home. Never have to see him again. And Peter Simmons is a very nice young man. Peter Simmons is a very nice young man and he didn't mean to upset me. I probably upset him, and that was silly so I won't do that again. I certainly don't want to be known as"—she made an effort, and smiled—"Caroline the Snow Queen."

As she looked into the mirror, it became easier to smile, and her eyes began to shine with a new glee.

"I don't have to be afraid anymore. All I need to do now is make people like me, so they'll want to help me. And I don't need to let anyone hurt me. I don't need to let anyone hurt me. Because people don't really want to hurt me. People like me, when I say things they want to hear and when I'm nice to them. So I'll be nice to people. Starting with Peter Simmons."

Caroline in the mirror was laughing, her wide-set dark eyes dancing, her head thrown back. And it was Caroline in the mirror who telephoned Peter Simmons and said she wanted to say she was sorry she had been such a bear, but she had been feeling sickie and she hoped he would forgive her and let her buy him a beer. Peter Simmons would and did, and Caroline, clinging to Caroline in the mirror, discovered that he was so surprised and pleased that she would let him kiss her and caress her, that he made no effort to go farther. Especially as she encouraged him to tell her all about himself and how he wanted to be an international lawyer.

She knew nothing had changed about the way she felt, but she also knew she could play the role she needed to play and be convincing. She had not reached the point where she could go to bed with anyone, but she assumed she would, eventually, and she didn't have to worry about it. That was the important thing. All she had to do was make people believe she was Caroline in the mirror, who was never ruffled or frantic and who always knew what to say and do, while looking as though she liked it. Caroline in the mirror wasn't real, but she certainly looked real, and she handled things much better than Caroline did. Talking to Caroline in the mirror was like watching herself on a television screen. Nothing uncertain or untidy or emotional—everything under control. She tested out her new public personality on Jill, who could be expected to detect chinks in her credibility.

"Caroline," Jill said, "I want to tell you that I don't know how you've done it, but you seem to be a lot happier with yourself. For a while there I was worried about you. I mean, you flipped out over the smallest thing. . . ."

"I know," said Caroline. "I guess I was going through early life crisis."

Jill grinned at her warmly, because she liked things to be simple and comfortable and it made her uneasy when she thought she was rooming with a neurotic. She'd said that. But no one could call Caroline in the mirror a neurotic. She was easygoing, funny, charming, and deliciously elusive, and she was there most of the time.

By the time Caroline was in her third year of college, she and Caroline in the mirror were indistinguishable and she only thought about Glayville and her parents when she'd had one of her nightmares. Of course, she never went home. She wrote polite letters explaining that she had vacation jobs, and on holidays she had invitations to go skiing or anything else that would serve as an excuse.

It puzzled Jill, who was always going home for weekends, but she knew better than to question her roommate about her lack of desire to see her parents. It was not Caroline in the mirror who reacted to probing about why she never went home, and Jill never did it again. Most of the time, Caroline was entertaining and fun to room with, and if she had a dark side, Jill didn't see it often enough to worry about it. She was more concerned about Caroline's demonstrated capacity to get what and whom she wanted without paying much attention to the consequences. Caroline acquired and discarded friends and acquaintances according to her use for them, lavishing them with attention as long as she needed them, and politely dismissing them when she didn't.

Jill occasionally shook her head over the increasing list of what she thought of as Caroline's casualties. Most of them were male, one or two on the faculty, bedazzled into believing that Caroline really wanted to understand what they were trying to teach her, subtly coaxed into grades that were just a little better than she deserved. Most were fellow students captivated by Caroline's beauty. She cultivated her resemblance to Jacqueline Onassis, because it brought her attention and she wanted people to remember her.

But Jill was used to Caroline, and in any case, she had her own life to plan. While Caroline flitted about the campus, Jill had settled into a steady routine that included intensive study and casual dating. Jill also knew what she wanted to do, but her methods of achieving her goal were different. She was as single-minded about becoming an investigative reporter for the Public Broadcasting System in Washington as Caroline was obsessed with becoming an anchorwoman. Jill studied political science, history, and journalism and worked as an intern at the local newspaper. She had strong opinions, and a well-developed sense of personal independence, and she wanted to feel she could rely on herself. Jill's father described her fondly as being strong-minded, but she was more than that. It was not until years later that she came to realize how little she needed other people, and how strong was her confidence in herself. It took even longer before she conceded that her self-reliance ran Caroline's self-absorption a close second.

They were both excited when they read an announcement on the bulletin board at Corby Hall that the journalism department was to be addressed by Martha Vogel, a Washington correspondent for World News Network in Washington.

"She might be very helpful to us." Caroline nudged Jill, who shrugged.

"I'd like to meet her. She's good on the air, and she's a professional."

"And she knows people." Caroline zeroed in.

Jill laughed at Caroline's vivid face, framed in silken black hair.

"Contacts, contacts. You and your contacts."

"Well, you need them. Even for your beloved PBS, you'll need contacts. But listen"—Caroline was speaking her thoughts—"we have to get her to ourselves. Maybe we could get her to have dinner with us?"

Jill was still laughing. "She wouldn't come here if she knew what was waiting for her. Okay, okay, yes, sure, it would be great if we could get her alone, but we're not the only ones in the class."

Caroline brushed that aside. And when Martha Vogel arrived the following week to address the class, Caroline and Jill were in the front row. Caroline, Jill noticed, was immaculately groomed, dressed in a soft, dark plaid wool skirt and dark cashmere sweater. Jill wore jeans and a bulky sweater. Martha Vogel was a tall, slender, dark-haired woman with lively eyes, a deep dimple in her rather square-cut jaw, and an easy manner. She was dressed simply but stylishly in a dress of fluid line, patterned in soft blues and purples. And her hair was tousled, which endeared her to Jill, whose hair rose above her head in a perpetually tangled halo. Martha spoke briefly about her own background and at length about her work. She compared newspaper and television handling of news, and told funny stories about things that could and did go wrong in both businesses. Several times she poked fun at herself and her work, and her humor was acerbic. Jill was sorry when she stopped talking, but Caroline, who had been fidgeting, was at once on her feet.

What advice, she wanted to know, would Martha offer to someone getting started in television? Martha nodded and said she would urge them to develop a solid background in news reporting and learn the techniques of camera work.

"A lot of newspaper reporters have found the transition to television difficult. It's a visual medium, and you have to adapt your writing skills, assuming you have any. You can't ramble on when you're on camera, and you can't ramble on if you're writing for television. You also have to remember that people are listening to the words, not reading them, when it's a television story."

"You found the transition difficult?" Jill asked, before Caroline could open her mouth. Martha nodded.

"I was too long-winded for a while. And I didn't pay enough attention to how I looked. You have to be prepared for the fact that in television you can't go on camera looking as if you just got out of bed with a hangover. You have to be on, in every sense of the word."

"What about being on camera when a story breaks?" asked a voice from the rear.

"Pray you won't make a fool of yourself and the station. That's when background and training help, when you have to ad lib and disentangle all the voices in your ear without looking as if you're listening to them."

"You mean the producers and director?" asked Caroline.

Martha nodded. "On a good day, they're telling you you're on too long, or a story's been moved, or speed it up—all kinds of things. On a bad day, they may not be there when you do need them."

"But that would apply only to an anchor, wouldn't it?" asked Caroline. Jill saw surprise and amusement cross Martha Vogel's face.

"You've been studying up, haven't you?" Her eyes rested sharply on Caroline for a moment. "Yes, that would apply mostly to an anchor. But anytime you're on the air live, you're subject to all this twittering from the bug in your ear."

"Do you regret leaving newspaper work for television? Is it as superficial as they say?" asked another voice.

Martha grinned, and the dimple deepened in her chin.

"Television is like newspapers in that it's as superficial as the people behind it. There's a stricter time element involved, and that puts considerable restraint on babbling, just as a good editor should restrain a reporter's overwriting. But no, I don't regret it, and one reason is that you can make much more money in television. I decided I might as well try to wind up financially comfortable while doing what I enjoyed doing."

A few minutes later, the question-and-answer session ended, and as Martha moved toward the door, chatting with faculty members, Caroline darted forward and gently touched Martha's arm. When she turned, Caroline said earnestly that she had been so impressed by what Martha had said, and it had so much bearing on what she wanted to do, that she wondered if Martha could perhaps have coffee with her and her friend Jill. Martha hesitated, while the staff looked on in amusement, and Jill poked her head around Caroline.

"You said you had to catch a plane. We could drive you to the airport."

Martha laughed. "Offer to buy me a drink while I'm waiting for my plane and you've got me," she said. Then, suddenly stricken by an afterthought: "My God, am I contributing to the delinquency of minors? Are they old enough?"

"Just," said the chairman of the journalism department.

In Caroline's car on the way to the airport, there emerged a Caroline that Jill had not glimpsed before. For fifteen miles, Caroline interviewed Martha with a skill and dexterity that astounded Jill and apparently took the subject by surprise. Within twenty minutes, Caroline knew more about Martha Vogel's life and times than, Jill suspected, she had meant to tell her. Martha indicated as much when she suddenly laughed, as though disconcerted, and told Caroline, "You do a good interview."

Caroline's smile glittered, and Jill nodded to herself. Caroline had indeed done one of the best interviews she had ever heard, perhaps because she was not trying to extract cold facts. She was gently drawing information from Martha. She managed to make Martha say what she felt as well as what she thought, and she did it as much by force of personality as by the quality of her questioning. Behind the simply phrased questions were the luminous dark eyes, warm and waiting, inviting an answer, promising understanding. Jill understood why Caroline had suggested she drive. It's difficult to fix your eyes on someone while watching the road.

"You know more about me than I do about you now," Martha told Caroline, with a teasing edge to her voice. "Tell me what your plans are—after you graduate, I mean?"

"Well, I'd like to get a job in a small station. People tell me that's the best thing to do."

Martha nodded. "They're right." She glanced over at Jill. "What about you?"

"I've applied for a job at PBS-in Washington, and I've got my fingers crossed."

"That's it? I mean, what if that doesn't . . . ?"

Jill's fingers tightened on the steering wheel, and Martha's eyebrows rose slightly as she watched her.

"That's what I'm aiming for. I've talked to people there, and they seem to think I've got a fair chance." She looked over at Martha for a moment and smiled disarmingly. "I guess I sound like I'm too self-confident, and I don't mean to. But that really is what I want. I've always wanted it."

"She has, always," interjected Caroline, who seemed to feel the conversation was getting away from her. Martha turned to her, and there was once more a note of amused curiosity in her voice.

"Caroline, are you as certain of what you want?"

"Well, I know what I'd like. I just hope I'll be good enough to get it." Caroline glanced through her eyelashes at Martha, who was sitting turned sideways in her seat so that she could watch both younger women. "I'd like to be an anchor."

Martha smiled. "So would we all."

"But you do anchor, sometimes, on weekends, don't you?"

Martha shook her head, marveling and mocking. "I feel as if I have no secrets from you. Yes, I do anchor sometimes on weekends. But that's quite an ambition, Caroline. I hope you make it."

"You want to be an anchor, don't you?" Caroline asked.

There was a pause.

"Yes, I guess I do," said Martha. "But it isn't entirely

up to me, obviously. There's a lot of competition, to put it mildly. Be aware of that."

"Oh, I know," said Caroline, with a certain blitheness.

"You might do very well on a talk show, with that kind of interviewing technique," Martha observed.

Jill smiled to herself. It had occurred to her that Caroline might make an excellent interviewer of celebrities. When she had been called on to conduct hypothetical interviews in class, dealing with specific subjects assigned by an instructor, Caroline's questions frequently had disappeared into the apparently bottomless depths of her famous memory gap. But when it came to coaxing out personal details, Caroline showed considerable skill. Martha Vogel was a stranger, or had been until an hour or two previously, and Jill suspected that for all her openness of manner, Martha did not betray much of herself. Martha's talk to the class had concentrated on what she did, not on who she was. Martha might be willing to open a gate in her personal wall, Jill reflected, but there was a wall, and within twenty minutes, Caroline had succeeded in scaling it. The many faces of Caroline Mitchell, she thought, as she pulled into the airport parking lot.

Casually, Jill asked if Martha was on her way to another assignment.

She hesitated, then smiled. "I'm meeting someone in Chicago."

"How nice," said Caroline politely.

"An old friend," continued Martha. "As a matter of fact, he's somebody you ought to talk to sometime about television, Caroline. He's an executive with WNN in Washington and he's the person who persuaded me to get into television. He's very good."

Judging from a certain warmth in her voice, Jill assumed that Martha was not speaking entirely professionally.

"Really? Who is he?" asked Caroline, her attention obviously caught.

"James Mellenkoff."

Jill watched Martha's face, and decided her earlier judgment had been accurate.

"That's a late date," Jill murmured, and Martha smiled at her.

"Yes. It is."

They said good-bye as Martha approached the security checkpoint, and to Jill's astonishment, Caroline hugged Martha. After a second's surprise, Martha hugged her back.

"I can't tell you how much help you've been," said Caroline softly. "And I hope you didn't think I was prying. I guess I get so interested in people I ask too many questions. Please forgive me if I did."

Martha's eyes were warm as she looked at the earnest, lovely face.

"Listen, you did a damned good job of asking. I haven't been interviewed like that in years. And I probably couldn't have done it as well!"

"Thank you very much," said Caroline. "That's a real compliment."

"Keep in touch," said Martha, as she turned away, "both of you. Let me know if I can help. I'll probably be seeing you both in Washington one of these days."

She shook hands with Jill, passed through the security barrier, and was gone. As she rounded a corner, she turned and waved, smiling.

Caroline was jubilant. "She said to keep in touch," she chirped.

Jill groaned. "I suppose you're going to write to her every week, reporting progress?"

"Don't be funny," said Caroline. "But if I have anything to report, I'm certainly going to take her up on it. Wasn't she just terrific?"

"You can drive back," said Jill, easing herself into the passenger seat. "Yes, as a matter of fact, she was. I liked her a lot, and I suspect she's very good."

"You suspect? Don't you watch her?"

"Occasionally. Remember, I watch PBS."

"Oh, yes." Caroline's tone was faintly dismissive. She had observed more than once to Jill that she had a low boredom point when it came to hour-long programs about the habits of water buffalo and discussions of budget prospects. Jill had observed that one of the virtues of PBS was that it didn't deal with substantial subjects in two minutes and three seconds, if that was what Caroline meant. Caroline said she was sure it was very educational, and they had left it at that.

On the way home, Caroline was quieter than usual.

"Martha going to be your model?" Jill asked lightly.

"I wish I could be like her," said Caroline.

"Maybe you will be."

Caroline shook her head. "She's different from me. She's nicer."

Jill glanced at her companion in astonishment. She had never heard Caroline admit that anyone was nicer than she. It was an uncharacteristic comment.

"What does that mean?"

"Well," said Caroline reflectively, "I'd never fly off to see somebody in the middle of the night, I don't think."

"They'd probably fly off in the middle of the night to see you!"

"That's not the point. I mean, I can't imagine wanting to see anyone enough to do that. She must really care about him."

Caroline's expression suddenly seemed vulnerable, and Jill did not associate vulnerability with Caroline.

"You just haven't met anybody you like enough to do that, despite that army of admirers that follows you around," Jill told her.

"It isn't that," said Caroline in a subdued voice. "I wouldn't want to do that. If she cares that much about this man Mellenkoff, that means he could really hurt her. She's letting him be able to hurt her."

Jill digested this, peering through a light rain. "If you're fond of anyone, I suppose that means he could hurt you, or you could hurt him. I mean, that follows, doesn't it? You have to take some risks with a relationship."

"I suppose you do," said Caroline.

"But you wouldn't?" Jill was curious. Caroline almost never talked about relationships. For that matter, she never talked about friendships. Jill assumed Caroline liked her, because she liked Caroline. But that liking had not so far been tested.

"I don't think I would," said Caroline, whose voice now sounded cool and withdrawn, as if she regretted an indiscretion.

"Then how can you be really fond of anybody?" Jill pressed.

Caroline shifted in her seat, turning her head to stare out of the rain-streaked window, and Jill knew the barrier was up again.

Nevertheless, she tried once again. "Suppose, Jill said, ignoring Caroline's uneasy fidgeting, "that you fall in love with someone. Wouldn't you fly to meet him in the middle of the night?"

Caroline considered this so long that Jill thought she had gone to sleep.

"If I flew to meet anyone in the middle of the night," she said finally, "it wouldn't necessarily mean I was in love with him. It would mean I needed to see him."

"Because you were in love with him, you needed to see him—right?" Jill was triumphant.

"No," said Caroline flatly. "Love would have nothing to do with it."

6

SETTLING INTO a window seat on the half-empty flight to Chicago, Martha Vogel ordered a Perrier, then fingered an unopened letter from her mother and asked for a martini. Sipping the drink, she adjusted her seat back and opened the pale green envelope, wondering for the hundredth time why Loretta Vogel, a woman of meticulous taste, chose green stationery. As usual, the letter began, "Martha dearest," and as usual, Martha dearest winced slightly. Loretta's letters followed the recipe of a cake frosted with endearments, sandwiched with compliments, and solid with complaints. She never wrote of having dinner; she invariably referred to "my poor lonely little dinner," although Martha knew her mother was invited out, or had friends in, three or four times a week. A cold in the head or a headache became "a recurrence of my old trouble," even though Loretta enjoyed admirably good health. The weather in the small Virginia town where she lived was always too hot or too cold or too damp, and a local burglary assumed the dimensions of a crime wave. Martha nodded as the letter followed a predictable course, and took a healthy swallow of gin as she reached the inevitable appeal to come home and settle down instead of racketing around. There was the customary subtle reminder of how much Loretta had given up for Martha, which made Martha finish her drink at a gulp. Her mother often caused Martha to remember how much she missed her father, who had died when she was twelve.

Martin Vogel was a lawyer who would have liked to have been a humorous writer. He had consoled himself by spending his free time reading, which annoyed his wife because it meant he could not always make up a fourth for bridge. And he had brought up Martha, his only child, to be able to laugh at what went on around her, which also annoyed his wife, who was suspicious that fun might be poked at her.

Yet until Martin died, Martha had had an unusually happy childhood because her father could usually flatter and tease Loretta out of what he called her "nonsenses." Martin was genuinely fond of his wife, content to trade her rigid conventionality of mind and shallow philosophy for her impulsive warmth and capacity to be funny without being aware of it. And Martin was always there when Loretta needed him, which meant that when he died, all she had left, she said, was Martha. The self-possessed twelve-year-old, driven deeper into introspection by the loss of a father who had been, in a real sense, a companion, found herself cast as her mother's only comfort, the axis around which moved the new world of Loretta, the lonely widow with only her child to live for.

It was a part Loretta played well, especially since her stage was her hometown of Colerton, a community with a substantial population of military retirees, with a small college to leaven its conservatism, and a lingering nostalgia for the days of magnolias. The town mourned Martin Vogel and sought to console his widow. Loretta in her early forties was an exceedingly attractive woman, delicately boned, with green eyes so bright that their blankness might go unnoticed, and a dimpled smile. She had loved it when Martin told their friends she was a reincarnation of Scarlett O'Hara, and had admitted coquettishly that Margaret Mitchell was her favorite author. Her only author, her daughter reflected. Like her heroine, Loretta had no shortage of suitors. Colerton bachelors, and some without that status, were paying court as soon as Martin was buried. Loretta told them all her only care in the world was poor fatherless little Martha, unaware that her daughter included in her nightly prayers the supplication that her mother would marry again, not because Martha wanted to replace her father, but so that she would not be suffocated by maternal attention.

Martha did not share her mother's passion for shopping or gossiping, and Loretta had no interest in walking in the woods and getting her feet wet looking for half-hidden flowers. If Martha disappeared into her room to read, Loretta fretted that she was moping about her father, and within half an hour, she would be tapping at the door with a milkshake or a plate of homemade cookies. Martha could not persuade her mother that she liked to be alone. She urged Loretta to go out to dinner, exerted herself to be friendly to her mother's suitors. But Loretta had decided that playing the merry widow was more to her liking than resuming the problems of marriage, and she made Martha a rationalization for that attitude. When the topic of marriage was raised, Loretta would lower her eyes, pensively shake her head, and murmur Martha's name. For the first five years after Martin's death, she said it was too soon. Then she spoke of the burden of getting Martha ready for college. Gradually she achieved her objective of establishing a small but steady escort pool, even if it was occasionally depleted by marriage or death. Its hard-core members remained perpetually hopeful, as a result of Loretta's skill at looking wistful, hesitant, noble, and pretty while hinting at how she hoped some day she would be able to think only of herself and what she wanted to do. She made it clear that marriage would be the only social state in which she would be interested, which ruled out premarital sex. Loretta had always considered sex rather untidy and did not miss it at all. Martha, to her amused exasperation, found herself the object of reproachful glances from the well-tailored men, bearing chocolates and flowers, who populated the Vogel living room.

She was even more exasperated by the reproachful glances of Loretta, who considered it a personal affront that Martha took after her neither in appearance nor attitude. Martha was tall, long-legged, and skinny, with a tumble of thick dark hair falling over the bright, dark eyes, which her mother referred to as her daughter's only good feature. The angularity of face and body, which later would soften into a careless elegance, made Martha look too much like a restless colt for her to fit into Loretta's concept of what her daughter should look like.

Martha's wardrobe epitomized the clash between mother and daughter. It consisted of blue jeans bought by Martha and silk shirts bought by her mother. Martha would have preferred button-down cotton, but she knew how much pleasure her mother took in choosing the rich silk blouses, and rebelled only when Loretta began buying silk pants to match.

What was worse, from Loretta's viewpoint, was Martha's social life. Boys are such fun, Loretta would say plaintively. Not if they bore you, her daughter would reply. Loretta was proud of Martha's grades, of her scholastic honors, her achievements in the debating society, and she assumed that eventually her daughter would become seriously interested in a man. When she did, it was another disappointment. Loretta, who had envisaged a handsome young student, preferably of a wealthy old southern family, was introduced to Wallace Hall, a divorced teacher at a nearby private school.

"He's as old as your father would have been," she complained.

"What's wrong with that?" asked Martha. "He's good company, he's bright, and he has a marvelous sense of humor."

"He's getting bald," wailed Loretta, and was mystified when Martha burst into laughter.

"Mother, give up on me," she said.

Loretta sighed and consoled herself that at least Martha wore a dress to go out to dinner with Wallace.

Wallace Hall was the first of a series of men whom Martha chose mostly because they reminded her of her father. It was a conscious choice on her part; she thought about it and found it logical that she should seek to renew the pleasure she had found in her father's company. She thought less about the likelihood that she would not be inclined to become as deeply involved in such relationships, as she might have with a man of her own age. That pattern was not broken until she met James Mellenkoff. After that, nothing was the same again.

Mellenkoff was part of what Martha considered the real world and what her mother considered the last straw. Loretta had always hoped that, women's liberation notwithstanding, Martha would eventually make what was once called "a good marriage" and settle into the kind of life-style with which her mother could feel comfortable. If she had to have a premarriage career, Loretta thought vaguely of something like interior decoration or a nice little boutique. When Martha announced she had a job with the AP bureau in Richmond, Loretta contemplated her child with despair.

"All that rushing around," she said so dolefully that Martha patted her mother's pale blue silk shoulder.

"Cheer up, maybe I'll wind up in television," Martha said.

"Like Phyllis George?" Loretta asked. She had approved of the way Phyllis dressed.

Martha said she was inclined to doubt that.

"You'd have to get some decent clothes," said Loretta, brightening.

Martha laughed and said a wire-service salary didn't stretch to designer clothes.

Seven years later, Martha had felt a sting of recollection as James Mellenkoff looked at her across a starched white tablecloth in an expensive French restaurant in Washington and said she had to do something about her clothes if she was going to be in television.

"Are you advising me?" Martha had asked.

Mellenkoff bestowed on her his famous smile, which softened the frozen blue of his eyes and offered a dazzling display of teeth. "That's not the kind of thing I advise you on, darling," he had said.

And Martha, who had cultivated a cool eye for men throughout her life, melted, as she always did with Mellenkoff.

She had met him at a party after she joined the AP bureau in Washington. It was their first official meeting, but Mellenkoff, who was bureau chief of WNN in Washington, and resolutely climbing upward, was always alert for unusually competent young reporters. He had been reading the by-line of Martha Vogel over major news stories for several years. Martha's coolness and quickness had early on distinguished her in fast-breaking news stories. Her coverage of a mining disaster, a spectacular plane crash, and an oddly poignant family murder won her awards and recognition in the news business. Her promotion to the Washington bureau of the wire service was a demonstration of that recognition, and at the time that she met Mellenkoff, Martha was enjoying a gratifying sense of being valued by the organization for which she worked. Her personal life was pleasant, but unexciting. Her work was what excited Martha most. She loved the challenge of deadlines, the pressure of time, the rush of accomplishment that followed the knowledge of a job well done. She was busy and happy and considering taking a foreign assignment. She was exactly the kind of acquisition that Mellenkoff was looking for. And, unfortunately, he was exactly the kind of man Martha had been looking for.

Mellenkoff was tall, heavyset, a little like a friendly, well-groomed bear. There were those in his business who held that he possessed more formidable ursine attributes, and that his geniality was assumed only on certain occasions. "Like before he eats you," as one WNN correspondent put it.

Martha met him and fell in love with him, and for years believed theirs had been a mutually conceived passion. He was only a few years older than she was, and unlike her father in every respect. Where Martin Vogel had been gentle, James Mellenkoff was ruthless. Where Martin Vogel had been unassuming, James Mellenkoff was immeasurably confident. Where Martin Vogel had worried about others, James Mellenkoff worried only about himself. And where Martin Vogel had been quietly appealing, James Mellenkoff was irresistibly and consciously compelling.

He had never had any doubts about where he wanted to go. Almost everything in the world was incidental to the Mellenkoff ambition, which would have done credit to Attila the Hun. Growing up as the son of an editor of a weekly newspaper, Mellenkoff had never understood why a man as intelligent and respected as his father should have chosen to remain in a backwater all his life. The writings of Daniel Mellenkoff were known and well-respected, far beyond the boundaries of the county where his newspaper was published. Daniel was content to be where he was, doing what he did. He used to say he wouldn't have done as well anywhere else, because he wouldn't have had peace of mind and quiet to think anywhere else. Both his sons wanted to enter journalism, but only the older, Thomas, showed interest in the family newspaper.

James, who had refused since he was six to be called Jamie, started his own newspaper at school and made clear his visions lay beyond his hometown, and had little to do with the kind of homespun wisdom purveyed by his father. James did well at everything, and if he didn't, he brooded. Where are you going to go after you get where you're going? Daniel would ask his son, and the boy would look at him with those fierce blue eyes and refuse to return his father's teasing grin. James knew where he was going, and that was what mattered to him. While Daniel worried that his younger son would burn himself out, James worried that nobody would hear about the conflagration. He never considered newspaper work. Television was where the money, the prominence, and the power were, and Mellenkoff aspired to all three. He took no shortcuts, knowing the value of experience in all aspects of the field he had decided to lead. He worked as an intern, as a reporter, as an assistant producer, as a producer, as a news director, as a bureau chief, and seared his way through each level. He bruised feelings and made enemies, but he also earned respect, albeit grudging, for his immutable resolve to get where he was going. Mellenkoff was the kind of employee who caught the eye of men who had once been like him and recognized their own toughness. And they were usually men at the top. With executives less certain of themselves, Mellenkoff was not above manipulation or deception. He did not seek to antagonize, and chose his confrontations carefully. By the time he met Martha Vogel, Mellenkoff had maneuvered his way through affiliate television into the more rarefied national levels, threading his way through the managerial maze. He wanted his success ultimately to be celebrated on the nightly news, but not as part of the anchor team. Mellenkoff had no wish to be part of the star system. He wanted to run it.

And he had already begun to acquire his own stable of reporters and correspondents indebted to Mellenkoff for their start on camera. They had all done well, because he watched them closely and eliminated those who did not live up to his uncompromising expectations of excellence. If Mellenkoff believed they could do it, then they would do it, or it reflected on his judgment. He gave few second chances, but those who earned his approbation also basked in the knowledge of his support. They were known in the business as the "bear cubs," and Mellenkoff was not displeased by the nickname. They were his cubs and he cuffed them or caressed them as he thought appropriate.

When he met Martha Vogel, he had already considered her as a potential cub. She was obviously immensely competent, hardworking, and intelligent, and with some grooming, she might do credit to his training. He interviewed her, studied her, assessed her, and during what he thought of as his training period, discovered Martha did not fit into any of his molds. It was partly because she was flexible but not malleable. It was also because she proved stubborn, unpredictable, and extraordinarily disarming. Mellenkoff discovered to his astonishment that he liked to listen to her even when she dared to laugh at him. He distrusted too much laughter, but he found he could not be angered by Martha's merry irreverence. There was a warmth about her, a gentleness pervading her strength, which at first intrigued him then endeared her to him. Because Mellenkoff thought he had no weaknesses, he viewed Martha as an aberration, and he was genuinely shocked when he realized how much he wanted to be with her.

Mellenkoff disapproved of personal involvement with his "bear cubs." When additional attention was required by men or women, he provided it, but it was carefully measured and did not demonstrate any favoritism on his part. He rarely slept with any of the women on whom his professional eye had fallen. When he did, he concluded it had been a mistake because they often proved to be professionally flawed. Martha, once again, was different.

On the night they met, they left the party to go to dinner, and left the restaurant halfway through dinner to go to Mellenkoff's apartment and go to bed. It was a departure for both of them. Mellenkoff was breaking his own rules about professional conduct, and Martha was breaking her rule that if she was going to go to bed with a man she hardly knew, it should at least be in her own apartment. With Mellenkoff she didn't care. By the time she reached home at dawn, she knew she was in love with him. For the first time in her life, a man had become her world. Her feelings for Mellenkoff went beyond passion and verged on obsession. She could not see enough of him. When she was with him, her attention was riveted on him, her eyes clung to his face. Mellenkoff was not unaccustomed to having such an impact on women, but he was taken aback by his own reactions to Martha. And in spite of himself, he was fascinated and pleased by her capacity to combine passionate devotion with at times uncomfortably candid assessments of his personality and his philosophy. It was as though she loved him in spite of what she thought of him, and that was something he had never encountered before, something even Mellenkoff could respect.

Martha was different, and she came to matter to Mellenkoff. For a time, he let himself share the enchantment, did not resist being drawn into a small, warm world where the touch of her hands and her mouth were more important than the threat of a merger. Mellenkoff knew then that he loved her, and probably would never love anyone else in quite the same way. He also knew that for him, Martha's world did not represent reality as he perceived it, or self-fulfillment as he conceived it. In another age, he might have seen her as a mistress, a highly intelligent courtesan who provided what a more appropriate partner would never dream of. When he let himself think about it, he realized that Martha could never be a "bear cub" because she would always be Martha, who was privy to his thoughts and habits as no other person ever had been or ever would be. Holding her in his arms, making love to her, feeling her cling to him, he would feel stirrings of fear that anyone should know him so well.

All Martha knew was that she was wildly happy. She had a new job as a reporter at WNN in Washington and she was imbued with a determination to succeed as Mellenkoff wanted her to succeed. She could not fail him in any way, and she worked harder than she ever had before. She studied her appearance, changed her hairstyle, learned to use makeup, bought the kind of clothes that went with Mellenkoff and her work, flung herself into the world of television, its technicalities and its intricacies. She learned from everyone and most of all she learned from Mellenkoff.

On one of those nights when they lay entwined in his king-size bed, he talked idly of the possibility that she might become the kind of woman anchor he envisaged. Not one of those prepackaged dolls who have to be fed questions, he said, ruffling her tangled hair. Somebody who can think, talk, and look good at the same time.

She listened, her eyes rapt on his face.

"Somebody like you," he said.

"Like me?" she asked breathlessly, and Martha had rarely been breathless about anything or anybody.

"Maybe," he said, caution reasserting itself. "There's a long way to go, my darling."

As long as she was his darling, Martha thought in uncharacteristic delirium, that was what really mattered. She told him that, and saw the smile glitter and felt him envelop her with his body as he had with his mind, and was happy. Mellenkoff permitted himself to be happy with her, although he was uneasy about it. He was especially uneasy when he found that he missed her when he was away from her. He could not afford to miss anyone, could not really afford to care for someone the way he cared for Martha, and could not bring himself to warn her of that. So he drifted with her, as on a vacation, and went so far as to arrange to see her even when it disrupted both their schedules. When he had to spend a week in Chicago at the WNN-owned station there and found that Martha had a speaking engagement a few hundred miles away, he urged her to meet him for the weekend. She was delighted at this demonstration of his need for her. It dispelled her own doubts, reinforced her blissful belief that Mellenkoff was indeed her friendly bear, that she alone knew the real Mellenkoff. Happily, she adjusted her schedule, and as she addressed the journalism students, she had nursed the thought of her rendezvous. She knew that her reference to him as she drove to the airport with Caroline and Jill had been an indiscreet spillover of an uncontrollable joy.

Martha folded the letter from her mother, tucked it into her purse, and went to the restroom to see what she looked like. She was not displeased by the image in the mirror. Her eyes were luminous, her face glowing. She applied lipstick and reflected happily that all she needed was a light bulb above her head. Once more in her seat, she ordered another martini and settled back to think about Mellenkoff while she drank it.

7

MELLENKOFF DID not meet Martha's flight. He hated waiting for people, especially at noisy airports. He had spent a taxing week assessing unused talent at the WNN-owned station in Chicago, and taking note of deadheads without being too obtrusive about it. Which had not been easy, for his visit had come but a few weeks after the takeover of WNN by Eliass Enterprises, a conglomerate built from scratch by Joel Eliass. Eliass was noted for his lean and mean methods of making profits by stripping away fat from business acquisitions. Eliass had made it clear in his first terse official comments to the network that its current status as number three in a field of three would not continue if he had anything to say about it, and he did. What he had to say about it so far in public had consisted of a warning that WNN would spend less and work harder, and if that didn't work, other measures might be expected. *Other measures* was a favorite phrase with Eliass, and it was already being translated to mean "Off with their heads." In private, Eliass had told Mellenkoff he wanted only the best in his network and he meant to have it, no matter what or whom it cost.

The talk had taken place at dinner at Eliass's sumptuous home overlooking Central Park, a residence reflecting the rewards of the financial acumen that had parlayed a modest family estate into a fortune close to half a billion dollars. Mellenkoff had been impressed and flattered, as Eliass had intended he should be.

Part of Eliass's success was due to his shrewdness in choosing the men who worked for him, and he had singled out James Mellenkoff as soon as he met him in WNN's Washington office. It was in its way a tribute to

Mellenkoff's efforts to scale the corporate ladder at a dizzying pace, but had he been aware of all of the reasons that lay behind the chairman's choice, he would have been less comfortable with such a mark of approval. Eliass had chosen Mellenkoff almost as much for his vulnerability as for his strength. To Eliass, Mellenkoff's tunnel-vision ambition was a flaw, because it made clear that there was almost nothing he would not do if he were assured the payoff would be worth it. And the carrot dangled, if not yet offered, by Eliass was presidency of the network. He had not suggested that such a prize would go to Mellenkoff, but he had indicated, obliquely, that Gordon Lansing, who had been president of WNN during the five years the network had scrabbled on the slippery slope of ratings, must be held at least partially responsible for the fact that the amount of money WNN spent on staff and stories was not commensurate with its popularity with viewers.

Eliass was not a man to move precipitately. His skill in manipulation of stocks and real estate had earned him the nickname "the Cobra," and he had smiled a little when he heard about it. What Eliass needed at WNN immediately was a brilliant hatchet man, and he had confidence that Mellenkoff would not fail him in that role. He was far from confident that Mellenkoff would be an equally brilliant president of the network, but Eliass was always willing to wait and see.

On Mellenkoff's part, the meeting with Eliass had left him shaken by excitement over what he believed was the fulfillment of all his hopes.

"I'm your man," he had told Eliass, his ice-blue eyes shining almost as brightly as his teeth.

Eliass's pouting button of a mouth had taken an almost imperceptible tilt upward at either side.

"I believe that, James," he had said in that dry, strangely highpitched voice that reminded Mellenkoff of clinking ice cubes. They had talked for several hours about potential changes in style and direction at WNN. Mellenkoff had exuberantly outlined cherished ideas for a more dramatic nightly news show. McNeil-Lehrer with sex, he described it.

Eliass, who often watched McNeil-Lehrer in preference to the network news shows, had regarded Mellenkoff thoughtfully and observed that he might have an interesting point there. Mellenkoff promised to work up a scenario of what he had in mind and have the chairman look at a test run. Eliass had nodded.

"But first," he had said, "I want you to take a look at the owned stations in Chicago and Los Angeles. There would seem to be problems at both. I want to know what's wrong and with whom. And I want you to take care of it. Or them. But I must sign off on all . . . arrivals and departures. Clear, James?"

Mellenkoff nodded, trying to conceal his exultation. "Clear," he had said.

It was the kind of assignment Mellenkoff knew he did well. The way he saw it, if everybody involved screamed, he knew he was doing it right.

They had certainly shown signs of screaming in Los Angeles and Chicago, where Mellenkoff had been the recipient of confidences, complaints, exhortations, applications, and compliments from those who saw him as Eliass's man. He enjoyed being unforthcoming about Eliass while leaving the impression that he had the chairman's confidence. But Mellenkoff was professional enough to know that feeding his own ego was no more than a pleasant supplement to the job at hand, which was to do what Eliass wanted. He was in no doubt about the consequences of Eliass not getting what he wanted. And he worked hard. He went over ratings, studied tapes, listened more than he talked, applying his own rigorous standards for what and who would work out and for a new improved WNN. Where he judged it necessary and useful, he offered qualified reassurance. In other cases, his silence had spoken for him. He was more certain of what Eliass would want pared away than of what he would want retained. Mellenkoff was prepared to take no chances with Eliass's good opinion. Where he was in doubt, he would await even a minute signal from the chairman. There was too much at stake, and not only for the network. Flushed with imminent triumph, Mellenkoff was still aware of the brittleness of the rungs on the ladder he was climbing. He suspected Eliass was handy with a saw.

After Chicago, Mellenkoff wanted to see Martha. He always wanted to see Martha when he was tense, because she was the only woman he had ever met who could soothe and stimulate him. He also trusted Martha as he trusted nobody else. He knew Martha's loyalty was of the type that could allow her to end her relationship with him if need be but could never let her betray him.

He was aware of what he should omit from his confidences to Martha, aware of how far he could test her devotion. And he needed her cool judgment as much as he needed her unfailing warmth, her capacity to give comfort. Martha was not the only woman in Mellenkoff's life, and she knew that. But she was the only woman he always came back to, and she knew that too. He was comfortable with Martha, and Mellenkoff was comfortable with few. She once told him that he spent much of his life with his head at a 180-degree angle, and he had chuckled and agreed. With Martha, he never needed to worry about who was behind him.

"Ours," he told her often, "is a strange and wonderful relationship." He sent her humorous cards with that inscription from everywhere he went, buying some of them when he was traveling with someone else. You're wonderful and I'm strange, Martha would say with that dimpled grin of hers. The first time she had said that, he had been puzzled by her definition of the joke, and she had refused to explain it.

"It's like trivia: you have to take months to work it out and then it isn't worth the trouble," she teased him.

"I'm not that wonderful," he had said defensively. It always made him uneasy when women paid him compliments.

"I know you're not," Martha had said. "That's what makes me strange."

It was the kind of small thing that once in a while made him wary of her. He could tolerate her laughing at him, in a gentle way, but cryptic comments exasperated him. Gradually, he stopped sending her the cards, and she never asked why.

The telephone rang, and Mellenkoff started, then checked his watch and smiled. He picked up the receiver on the second ring.

"Where are you, darling?"

"Room 512."

They always took separate rooms. For different reasons, they agreed it was more discreet and more convenient.

"You've eaten?" he asked.

"I had a few drinks on the plane."

"You've eaten."

Martha chuckled. "You could order some cheese or something from room service."

Mellenkoff glanced over his shoulder at the array of cheese, fruit, and smoked salmon the waiter had brought fifteen minutes earlier, and he smiled.

"I'll think about it. Come on up."

Five minutes later she was there, putting her arms around him, her face warm and fragrant against his. She looked at the cheese board and laughed, while Mellenkoff poured martinis.

"Not too heavy on the gin; I already had a couple," she cautioned.

"You had a letter from your mother?"

Martha toasted him with the frosted, stemmed glass. "You know me."

"Some things are predictable. And I've met your mother. I assume she is well?"

"Flourishing. Full of complaints and why don't I come home and settle down."

Mellenkoff nodded. "The day you get a three-line letter saying she's fine, you'd better fly home at once."

Martha put down her drink on the coffee table and forked up a sliver of smoked salmon.

"So how did it go in L.A. and Chicago?" She slipped off her shoes, tucked her legs beneath her on the sofa, and gazed at him attentively. Her attentiveness was one of the things he liked about her.

"Difficult."

"You expected that."

"Not quite as much as I found, though. There was a lot of paranoia around of course, and I had to take that into account."

"Having met Joel Eliass, I can't see how there wouldn't be. I mean, it's like having Eraserhead take over."

Mellenkoff winced slightly. "That's amusing, darling, but I hope it isn't going to be one of those great funny quotes from Martha around the office."

"I'm not that suicidal professionally, James; give me credit for a little discretion."

He sighed half humorously.

"Discretion isn't why I love you."

"It isn't why I love you, either," said Martha obliquely.

"Anyway"—he sipped his drink slowly—"There's a lot of dead wood out there, and Eliass wants it cut back."

"You're to do the cutting?"

"Oh, not necessarily. He wanted me to take a look, see what my advice was. I'm sure he's capable of doing his own hatchet work." Mellenkoff was careful.

"He might figure you'd be equally good at it."

He looked at her sharply. "What've you been hearing?"

Martha shrugged, biting into a section of apple. "The usual. People are worried. I heard Jim Burns was looking around, and that John Mayer might be moving up."

Jim Burns was the station manager in Chicago, a man whose charm was not equaled by his competence. Mayer was a friend of Mellenkoff.

Mellenkoff nodded, noncommittally. "They're really going to have to tighten up there. We're getting our socks knocked off by CBS, in political coverage especially, and in Chicago that's bad news. And the ratings—Jesus." He shook his head.

"Aren't there some good people in that bureau?"

"It's like a circus. There're a couple of good balancing acts, but they're dependent on a flawed foundation."

"And Jim's the foundation."

"Looks like it."

"You tell him?"

"Well, of course I was candid with him," said Mellenkoff untruthfully. "I told him with Eliass moving in as chairman and the takeover and all, we were all under scrutiny. Including me."

He sipped on his drink. "I mean, I tell you, Martha, it's no fun to be the messenger who brings the bad tidings. I don't enjoy that kind of thing."

Martha was silent a moment.

"But you aren't under scrutiny the way these people are—the way the rest of us are, James. You're being . . . sort of tested out by Eliass, aren't you?"

He eyed her narrowly. "What makes you say that?"

"Didn't Eliass send you and doesn't everybody know

it? I mean, how the hell can you pass yourself off as one of the boys? You're Eliass's boy."

Mellenkoff frowned. "Is that the word around?"

"Come on," Martha rebuked him. "You know damned well this is the word around. You're doing what you always do: you're testing the waters and using me to do it."

Mellenkoff's grin flashed. "Aren't you flattered? Assuming it's true?"

Martha held out her glass for a refill. "My life's ambition, my love, is to sit in a hotel suite at midnight and analyze your problems."

Mellenkoff poured the martini and concealed his exasperation. Martha was playing *him* rather than the other way around, and he disliked it. But he needed her as a sounding board, for himself and others.

"Stop sounding like the boys in the back room, darling. If Eliass wanted to send somebody to scout around, whom would he send—Roger Miller?"

"Hardly. Roger's too honest. He'd give away the play."

"Many thanks."

Martha grinned at him. "Don't get like that. If I'd told you anything else, you'd think I was stupid, right?"

Mellenkoff ignored the question, which was a statement. She was right about Roger Miller, who refused to be an interoffice gut fighter. Miller was laconic and outspoken to a fault, which was why he had remained a vice-president and probably would never rise any higher, assuming he continued to hold that position in an Eliass regime.

"What about Gordon Lansing?" Martha asked abruptly.

"What about him?" Mellenkoff knew that Lansing, the current WNN president, was unlikely to survive the takeover, but not even with Martha did he want to embark on a discussion of who might get the job. He felt her eyes on his face and deliberately kept his gaze on his drink, stirring the olive around with his index finger.

"Well . . ." Martha sighed and stretched. She knew when not to push, Mellenkoff thought, and was grateful.

He leaned over and kissed her lightly. "Perceptive, aren't you?"

She laughed. "You taught me all I know, darling."

"I'd hate to take responsibility for that."

This time their eyes met and understood.

"All I was trying to say," said Martha, "was that I assumed Eliass would pick the right man to help him build his new empire."

Mellenkoff smiled. "Flattery will get you seduced."

"Again?" Martha speared a piece of cheese.

"I like that dress."

"One of the results of your suggestion that I improve my wardrobe—meaning buy something that isn't blue and denim."

He hesitated. "You said something about people being worried about the takeover. . . ."

"Did I? Well, around the water cooler, it's your basic sounds of fear and loathing. Some are thinking of jumping. Some think it's the best thing ever happened to WNN."

"Who?"

She mentioned a few names, and Mellenkoff knew she made careful choices. Martha threw no friends to even a friendly wolf.

"They're casting you as hatchet man," she said.

He shrugged. "Let them. I'm like everybody else in the end. I do what Eliass wants."

"No matter what?"

"Come on, Martha, don't get pious with me at this hour of the night. I don't know what's ahead, either. And like everybody else, I have to look after my own skin."

"What about my skin?"

He was about to make a joke, when he saw the expression on her face.

"You think you're on the hit list too? Come on."

She smiled. "No. Not yet."

"What do you mean, 'Not yet'? You're in good shape. In more ways than one. You've done well."

She nodded. "You'd have told me if I hadn't. I know that, at least."

"You're right about that, my darling. It would've reflected on me if you hadn't done well." Her eyes flickered, and he ignored it and went on. "The only problem you still have is you tend to sound as if you're laughing at these titanic power figures you're talking about on the air."

"Maybe I am. Maybe I should."

"You shouldn't let your audience realize it."

"They might agree with me."

"Middle America tends to take its leaders seriously."

"Like Rolaids?"

"Like Eliass."

"Ah." Martha took a final sip of her drink and said gravely, "There's the crunch."

"There's the crunch," he agreed.

"You mean I'll never be an anchor because I don't sound respectful?" Her voice was only half mocking.

Mellenkoff ate a segment of apple to conceal the pause in which he reflected that Martha probably never would be an anchor, at least on WNN, because she was not controllable. If things went as he hoped they would, he wanted to be able to control the twinkling of that particular star.

"I mean you'll never be an anchor if you aren't nice to people who matter."

"Like Eliass?"

"Like me." He reached for her, burying the conversation and his face in her neck.

Later, Mellenkoff roused from a light sleep to search for a cigarette.

"Thought you'd quit that?" Martha said drowsily from his shoulder.

"Tomorrow."

"Uh-huh." She plumped up the pillow and pushed it behind her head. The flame of his cigarette lighter captured a cameo of her face; her eyes were warm and dark, her cheeks flushed. She looked lovely, Mellenkoff thought, and was sorry when the flame went out.

"I forgot to ask you—how'd the speech at the college go?"

"Glayville State? Okay, I guess. It was sort of fun."

"Don't we have a station there—in Columbus, I mean?"

"Yes, we do. There was a note of apology from the local news anchor. He wanted to be there for my speech but couldn't make it. Hathaway, his name is."

"Vaguely familiar."

"I saw the news show. He's very chatty-chatty. Full of good cheer. Very respectful about our leaders."

Mellenkoff grinned in the darkness. "You were telling me about the speech."

"Seemed fine. They were all enthusiastic. How do you know what they think? They mostly thought I'm doing what they would like to do and wondered how I do it. I met a couple of interesting students, though."

"Yeah?"

"One was a real beauty. Caroline Mitchell. Jackie Onassis lookalike. And she's a natural interviewer. Got me to tell her practically my life story."

"Really? That's unusual for you."

"I know it. She's got that sort of reaching quality. When you're convinced she really cares, and of course she doesn't. But she's really good at it. Especially for somebody at her stage."

"She wants to be an anchor, of course?"

"Of course. The other girl, Jill something, wanted to go work for PBS. Thought she wasn't the commercial TV type."

"Wise of her to acknowledge it, maybe."

"Hell, I thought I wasn't the TV type, either, James. You were the one who decided I was."

"And spent a hell of a lot of time persuading you of it, as I recall. You were determined to remain an ink-stained wretch."

"Sometimes I think I should have." Her voice was muffled, and Mellenkoff peered at her through the gloom.

"Why? You're making five times what you would have if you'd stayed at AP or even gone to one of the big dailies. And you're good at it."

"I don't always feel comfortable. I feel like I'm hanging on, always looking around."

"That's the name of the game in any business, once you get near the top, sweetie."

"I still don't like it."

He recognized a stubborn note in her voice that he had heard before, and pulled her over against his shoulder again.

"You sounded like you were really impressed by that Caroline kid."

"Yes. Yes, I was. And in a funny way, she bothered me. Couldn't put my finger on it, but it was as though there was something just a little strange about her."

His fingers traced the line of her neck and shoulder.

"How so?"

"I don't know. She was sort of like quicksilver. One minute she was there and full of questions and eagerness to know, and the next, it was as though she'd sort of retreated. But God, when she put herself out, she could get stuff out of you."

"She might make an interesting test some day."

Martha laughed. "Always on the lookout, dear."

"Always." His fingers continued their exploration, and Martha slipped closer to him.

"The casting couch for Caroline?" he inquired lazily, and waited for her attack. But Martha was unexpectedly quiet. He touched her gently.

"Hey?"

"I was thinking. I mean, maybe that's what was different about her. She was so pretty, so lively. But she wasn't sexy."

"She'll never make it."

His voice was muffled by her hair and then by her mouth.

8

FRANKLIN HATHAWAY was a gravely hand-some young man who, in another era, would have gone riding off to the Crusades, glittering with armor and verities. Unfortunately he had been born too late to be involved in the Watergate scandals, let alone the Vietnam War, and he grew up with a disconsolate sense of being misplaced in a generation more concerned with the mores of survival than the morality of insurrection. To make matters worse, Franklin's father, Mike Hathaway, was local news anchor of KRT, the World News Network television station in Columbus. It was not that Franklin was averse to the fourth estate or what it stood for. He considered the press the last best hope of those who sought new leadership and a world in which the Peace Corps was the only form of American intervention abroad. Franklin numbered among his heroes those who inveighed in prose against political and bureaucratic corruption, and sighed over the relative mundaneness of current controversies, compared with the days when the press could hope to topple a President. Franklin did not number among his heroes his father. He was fond of him, in a slightly patronizing way, but felt vaguely uncomfortable that the family income was derived from a source that he described as "news between commercial breaks." Franklin's ambition to be a reporter was a demonstration of his desire to show his father what he ought to be doing, instead of being paid substantial amounts of money for collating fragments of news somebody else had often written.

Yet Mike Hathaway had once been a reporter, covering politics for a local newspaper until he was persuaded that his affable manner and quick tongue could earn him more money in public relations work.

A few months later, Mike's friend Joe Moynihan, who was news director of KRT, had suggested that the combinaion of his background and his personality made him an appropriate candidate for television. Mike had been amused, flattered, and intrigued. He was a genial, easygoing man who wanted little more from life than a comfortable living doing something he enjoyed. So he tried out as a political commentator, and even Eric Kriss, the general manager of KRT, who had been less enthusiastic than Moynihan about Hathaway's credibility on the air, acknowledged the excellent public response. People liked Mike. He sounded as if he knew what he was talking about, but he didn't talk down to them. He looked like somebody with whom the male viewers might like to have a beer and the female viewers might like to dine.

Within eighteen months, he was anchoring KRT's six and eleven o'clock news broadcasts. He did not pretend to be an authority on world affairs or the global economy, but he kept well informed, his local contacts were good, and the station had two efficient writers who put together most of the stories on the broadcasts, while Mike added or inserted phrases of his own. And he did his homework, keeping up to date on current developments so that he would not flounder too much should he have to, as he put it, "ad lib doomsday." And he drifted happily along, marveling at how much money he made, and enjoying being a local celebrity.

He was unhappy about only one thing in his life, and that was his family, which was very important to Hathaway. His wife, Leslie, a slender blond woman with a patrician profile and a portentous manner, gave the impression he had let her down by giving up what she called bottom-line journalism for a career that allowed them to maintain a more than comfortable life-style but did not measure up to her standards of moral intellectualism. Mike was distressed and bewildered by her thinly veiled sneers at his occupation.

Leslie had been a college teacher when they met, a vivacious, high spirited young woman whose strongly held opinions were leavened by a sense of the ridiculous. But after her retirement from work, following the birth of their son—according to her conviction that children should have the full benefit of maternal attention—Leslie's capacity for self-ridicule and most of her once-exuberant sense of humor seemed to disappear. She became earnest, building a library of authors like Susan Sontag and Germaine Greer, participating in panel discussions of sociological trends at the university, and chiding her husband for reading spy thrillers, having beers with his friends, and displaying lack of what she called "awareness of totality." Her attitude toward his job had always been faintly amused, and as time went on, she indulged increasingly in little barbed comments about happy-talk time, a gibe at Mike's ability—much admired among his colleagues—to talk about anything on a minute's notice.

Mike nursed a growing sense of hurt and injustice. He had expected Leslie to be pleased and proud of his local prominence. He was proud of her; he loved it when network executives came to town and were entertained at one of Leslie's elegant little dinner parties. Her manner toward them was impeccable. She was beautifully dressed, amusing, hospitable. There was even the faintest hint of flirtation in her manner. The visitors were lavish in praise of Mike's bright and lovely wife. He was the only one who heard Leslie's sarcastic mimicry of his bosses. She and Franklin would giggle together, inviting Mike to join in mockery, although it was also directed at him. Mike was not a man who mocked people. He thought it was unkind, and it disturbed him that his wife chose to indulge in what he considered cheap malice. It disturbed him even more that Franklin seemed to be imitating her.

Mike remembered how Franklin had been a solemn little boy who laughed when he was with his father, and he was with him a lot. Mike and Franklin had gone bicycle riding together, fished in Lake Apurna, climbed hills, and munched on hot dogs at ball games. As Leslie seemed to drift away, Franklin was Mike's consolation. But as Franklin entered his teens, his mother decided it was time he devoted more effort to serious subjects, and the weekends with Mike became fewer. Franklin protested at first, but Leslie prevailed, partly by persuading

Mike that their son's barely adequate grades could be
improved if he spent more time in what she called intellectual pursuits. Slowly, Frankie who scuffed his feet turned
into Franklin, a tall, good-looking teenager with an air of
lofty condescension faithfully copied from Leslie. His
grades were still mediocre, but now Leslie blamed the
school and his teachers' lack of awareness of Franklin's
individualism. Mike kept hoping there was some Frankie
left in Franklin, but as the years passed, mother and son
grew steadily closer, and Mike was left out. Mike would
be greeted at the dinner table with a patronizing critique
by Franklin of the news show his father had anchored an
hour before. It was Franklin's voice, but the words were
Leslie's, Mike noticed. He would have an extra glass of
wine and try to change the subject. One evening, he
suggested gently that the solution was for Franklin not to
continue watching the news at six, if he had so many
complaints about it.

"I feel I must keep up with what's going on, Dad,"
said Franklin. "I just think it's ridiculous to dismiss the
budget or a presidential news conference in three sentences.
Surely you don't disagree?"

"That's a valid criticism, if hardly a new one. Unfortunately there are time limitations," said Mike wearily.

Franklin pounced, as his father expected. "That's because you have to do what those sponsors tell you. My
God, Dad, how can you stand the venality of it?"

Mike drank his wine. "Commercials pay for the show,
and it's not true that we do what the sponsors tell us.
There's simply a limit to the time we can spend on a
specific topic. That's why we have specials that go into
important areas in more depth."

"PBS manages to do that on the news," said Franklin
triumphantly.

"Then watch PBS," said Mike with such sharpness that
Franklin's jaw dropped.

"Use some of your allowance and buy a subscription to
WNQR. Put your money where your mouth is. If you
have enough money, that is."

"Why don't you subscribe?" Franklin was still on the
offensive, but his voice was uncertain now.

"It'd be my money paying for it whoever does it in this

house, since you've never had a job. Try to keep that in mind, too. Now get off my back and quit ruining my digestion."

Franklin had been seeking a major confrontation for a long time, his father thought grimly, and now he'd gotten one. Abruptly, he was tired of it all. As Franklin stared sullenly in front of him, Mike put down his knife and fork and walked out of the dining room. Leslie followed him angrily to his study a few moments later. Predictably, she thought he had been unkind and unfair. How could he deprive his son of "constructive disagreement," she wanted to know.

" 'Constructive disagreement' hell. He's just trying to twist my tail. And it isn't as if they're his own opinions. He's just aping you," said Mike, and poured himself a brandy. He would have drawn satisfaction from his wife's startled expression, had he not been so upset.

"You have to let him express himself," said Leslie, a little less firmly than usual. She was accustomed to dealing with a malleable, placid Mike.

"Look," said her husband, "this has been going on for years. And I'm tired of coming home every night to be hounded and twitted. Would you both be happier if I went back to the paper and earned thirty thousand dollars a year as a copy editor?"

"You're overreacting and being childish," said his wife.

"And you're encouraging that kid to be a mouthy brat. He spouts slogans, but he does damn little studying to back up his grand theories, judging from his grades. Why doesn't he do more homework and stop watching television entirely?"

It was one of the biggest fights the Hathaways ever had. Even Franklin, who had been more shaken by his father's anger than he had expected, stayed in his room and was noncommittal when his mother rushed in full of apologies for Mike's "nonconstructive attitude." That night marked the acknowledgment of the wall dividing mother and son from father.

Mike was not the kind of man who carried a grudge, and he patched things up so that there was a return to at least a veneer of domestic civility. He mourned the loss of the little boy called Frankie, and his anger against

Leslie slowly deepened. He still loved her, or he thought he did, but he began spending more time at the station and sometimes didn't bother to come home for dinner. Neither Leslie nor Franklin seemed to care.

When Franklin decided he wanted to make journalism his career, Mike was pleased, but he would have been more pleased had he not suspected that his son was motivated by a desire to show his father how it should be done. Franklin was less provocative about Mike's occupation than he had been previously, but his father judged that that was primarily because the boy was less certain of being able to get away with the mixture of taunts and sarcasm with which he had been accustomed to enlivening dinner-table conversation. Mike also thought Leslie might have suggested to Franklin that he was going too far, although there was nothing in her behavior toward her husband to confirm that belief.

Mike had said things during the domestic quarrel that had been simmering in his mind for years, and he knew some of them had struck home. When he suggested there were things they obviously needed to talk about, Leslie had turned a bright smile on him and said there was no need to apologize. He wasn't necessarily apologizing, he'd bristled. In that case, Leslie had said, with the same infuriating smile, she was sure his criticism was warranted, and she wanted him to know she realized he made a very good living for them all. Mike knew a stone wall when he saw one, and he retreated before the manicured politeness of her manner. He came to regret his outburst. Instead of producing any real discussion of family differences, it had divided them. Franklin became correct to the point of addressing his father as "sir." Leslie played the role of charming wife and conducted conversations that reminded Mike, ironically, of commercials for detergents. He knew they were punishing him, and he was increasingly unhappy. His only refuge was KRT, where people liked him.

And Franklin's grades did not improve enough for him to attract the interest of the kind of schools to which he aspired. Mike was conscious of the blow inflicted on his son's self-esteem when Franklin found himself going to school at Glayville State College. It was a small college with a good reputation, popular especially with parents who could not afford the well-known schools, but Franklin had had visions of Harvard, Yale, or Stanford. Leslie tried to bolster her son's ego, and her own, by talking about how much more thorough small colleges were, how there would be more opportunity for creativity and in-depth individuality. Mike said very little, because he knew what he did say would be misinterpreted by mother and son. Leslie accused him of indifference to Franklin's career.

"I'm pleased he's going into journalism, and I'm sure Glayville will do well by him. I've always said journalism is something you should learn by doing, anyway," Mike told her.

"Well, he has to go to college. He has to have a degree. But you know how disappointed he is."

Mike sighed. "I'm sorry he's disappointed. I know he wanted to go to Yale. There's nothing either of us could do about that, Leslie. That was up to Franklin. He knew his grades weren't good enough. Maybe he should have gone to summer school instead of white-water rafting."

Leslie's mouth tightened into a familiar line. "There are many ways of broadening your mind. I believe he learned a great deal about environmental problems in Idaho."

Mike was grateful Franklin decided not to live at home after he enrolled at school. His son's absence from the dinner table, which was where Mike had seen most of him, proved an incentive to Mike's digestion and an opportunity for occasionally satisfying conversations with Leslie. Sometimes Mike wondered if she too might not be relieved that Franklin was no longer living at home, if she might have wondered whether her efforts to intellectualize her son had created a half-baked pomposity.

After a few months, Franklin took to dropping in for dinner and talking about his journalism classes, casually and even entertainingly. Mike was delighted, especially when Franklin suggested once or twice they should go fishing or to a ball game. It was about then that Franklin made clear he wanted to be known as Frank. There was still constraint between them, and Mike never mentioned his job, but occasionally there were moments when they seemed to be able to talk to each other without being touchy about perceived underlying meanings. It was a tranquil period in Mike's life. He and Leslie remained at arm's length most of the time, but he dared to be encouraged about his son. He was pleased and interested when Leslie said Franklin was bringing a young woman friend home for dinner.

"Her name's Jill, and she's in journalism school, too. He said they've been dating a bit."

"Great," said Mike, who hadn't heard enthusiasm in Leslie's voice in years. "You doing something special for dinner?"

Leslie launched into a description of a special dish she wanted to try. "You and Franklin always liked curry," she said, and for a moment Mike felt unaccountably sad. "You'll be home on time?" Leslie asked, before she hung up the phone.

"Sure." Mike realized he couldn't remember when she had last shown interest in when he would be home.

Mike and Leslie sipped a drink together as they waited for Frank to arrive with his date. Mike thought how pretty she looked, in a soft, coral-colored silk dress, belted in black suede at her slender waist. Her hair was combed back in its customary chignon, but she was wearing more eye makeup than usual, and the flush on her cheeks was a becoming reflection of the color of her dress.

"You look terrific," said Mike, and toasted her with his glass. Leslie's smile was warmer than usual. She wasn't wearing what Mike thought of as her "porcelain princess" face.

"And you look very distinguished."

She leaned over to straighten his tie a fraction, and Mike thought fleetingly that maybe it was a pity they were having guests for dinner. It was a long time since he and Leslie had been this friendly, which he supposed was a commentary on their marriage. They both glanced up when wheels crunched on the gravel outside, and a few minutes later, Frank appeared in the doorway of the living room. By his side was a young woman with a glossy mop of short dark hair and a lively, friendly face.

"Mother, Dad, I'd like you to meet Jill Starling," he said.

Mike noticed that Jill had a vigorous handclasp and a vivid smile. She was not as pretty as Leslie, but she a scrubbed and shining look about her, from her obviously freshly washed hair to her crisp yellow linen dress. She was polite to Leslie, was quick to admire the bowls of fresh-cut flowers from Leslie's garden, but her face grew even more animated when she talked with Mike.

"I watch you most nights, Mr. Hathaway," she began.

Frank interrupted slyly, "But you usually switch to PBS, don't you?"

Mike saw a flicker of annoyance cross Jill's face.

"Not because I don't like the KRT news show," she said firmly. "Frank's probably told you I'm studying journalism, too, Mr. Hathaway. It's my hope to work for PBS after I graduate."

Mike nodded, wondering if his son were aware that he had been quietly put in his place by his date.

"I watch a lot of PBS myself. They do some terrific stuff," Mike said. He asked what each of them would have to drink.

"I'm afraid," said Leslie in her high, cool voice, "that we have a sort of friendly running argument in our household over television, Jill. Mike is sort of the champion of the commercial channels, and Franklin and I fight the often losing battle of the public service broadcasting."

Jill accepted a glass of wine and looked curiously at Leslie.

"My liking for public service broadcasting is mostly because they can do more lengthy characterizations of public figures and problems," she said. "Frankly, I'm also going into television because you can make a lot more money, even in PBS, than you can in newspapers. I've heard too many horror stories about good editors who live to starve unseen behind their typewriters, except now it's computers."

Mike handed his wife a drink and looked at Jill with approval.

"That's the reason I got into television myself," he told her.

"Really? Frank didn't tell me that."

Mike told her about it, relishing her attentive interest and conscious of the small smiles exchanged by his wife and son. Jill's interest was genuine. She found Mike

Hathaway engaging, unassuming, and funny—characteristics that were prized by his co-workers and frequently
overlooked by his family. As they ate dinner, Mike mused
that Jill had asked within an hour more questions about
his work and the operation of television in general than
his son had in ten years. Frank had liked to go to the
station with his father when he was small, when he was
still Frankie. But he had not been at KRT since he
entered his teens. And in the middle of Leslie's curry,
while Mike was regaling Jill with a lengthy anecdote
about an on-camera catastrophe, Frank's resentment
overflowed.

"Dad, I think you're overwhelming Jill with your stories of fun in your work," he said. His voice brought a
faint frown of disapproval to the face of his mother, who
disliked airing family grievances in front of strangers.
Mike stopped mid-sentence, surprised and shocked by his
son's rudeness. It was Jill who, after an exasperated
glance at Frank, stepped in.

"I think your father's description of his job is absolutely fascinating, Frank," she said sharply. "And this is
a very funny story. I don't know about you, but I find
what he's saying very informative, especially to someone
interested in his business."

Mike finished his funny story, Jill laughed immoderately, Leslie smiled politely, and Frank stared at his
plate.

The frozen silence that followed was broken by Jill's
compliments about the curry and Mike's urging that everyone have more wine. Everyone did, except Frank,
who continued to study his plate. Jill cast him a worried
glance, and Mike could understand why. He hoped she
wasn't too fond of his son, because he sincerely doubted
she would see him again, if Franklin had anything to do
with it. In an effort to mend matters, Jill completed the
demolition.

"Our journalism instructor—Dr. Bradley—had us study
that series that KRT did recently on the homeless. Remember, Frank?" she said hopefully.

"I didn't know that," said Mike.

Leslie felt called upon to say something.

"That was a good series, dear," she observed to Mike,
clearly for Frank's benefit. "I watched most of it. It was

especially good for commercial television." She couldn't resist adding that, Mike thought.

"I remember it," said Frank sullenly. "But that was their investigative people."

"But your father anchored it; at least, he did the introductory pieces. I thought it was fascinating," Jill persisted.

"Dad is what the British call a news reader, Jill. He doesn't exactly report," said Frank, with an edge to his voice.

Jill interrupted him, while Mike marveled. She was one of the most determined young women he had ever met, and he wondered how she and Franklin had ever gotten together. His son was notably opinionated, and he could only assume they shared a mutual passion for argument. Of course, he could hardly have foreseen that she would not have shared his mild contempt for his father, Mike thought bitterly.

"I think being able to anchor a news show is a real skill," Jill swept on, oblivious to the psychological debris falling around her. "I know there're still some airheads around, who can't read and probably can't write their names, for that matter. But you've got a real advantage over the rest of us, Frank, having your father an anchor who's so good at it. No, I mean it." She waved away Mike's modest murmur. "I wouldn't say it if I didn't. I remember that hostage story two weeks ago, in the bank? And that broke almost at the beginning of the show, and Mr. Hathaway did a lot of ad-libbing, and it was very smooth, very good. I watched it carefully and learned a lot."

Mike smiled his thanks and nervously watched his son from the corner of his eye. Frank was regarding Jill with an expression of growing dislike.

"I'm not interested in being an anchor, Jill," he said coldly. "I'm hoping to get a job on a good newspaper. Even if I can look forward to a prospect of starving, as you put it. I didn't realize you held newspapers in such low regard."

Jill's head came up and her jaw tightened. Mike looked down the length of the table at Leslie, who, judging from her expression, shared his feeling of being present at a potential volcanic eruption in the middle of her best crystal.

"You misunderstood me, Frank," said Jill.

Mike poured himself another glass of wine.

"It's unrealistic," she proceeded, "to think you can ignore television nowadays, whether it's public service or commercial. It's a major aspect of journalism, and we have to live with it. It's foolish to try to be lofty about it just because we can *see* its mistakes instead of merely reading them."

Mike finished his wine in a gulp and did not look at Frank, for whom he felt a faint, grudging sympathy. Jill was strong-minded, even by comparison with Leslie, who was more inclined to express opinion by small, sharp observations. It was ironic, he reflected, that Jill was expressing his own views, yet he was beginning to feel a trace of exasperation with her. He couldn't understand why she was challenging Frank at his parents' dinner table. Except Mike had a feeling that Jill would challenge anybody about anything on principle. She would, he suspected, be more intriguing ten years later, when she had mellowed a little. He saw Leslie's tense expression at the other end of the table and realized gloomily that she would probably accuse him later of egging Jill on.

Mike cleared his throat loudly and raised what he hoped was the safe topic of a new movie that he and Leslie had seen. Jill cheerfully entered into a discussion of that and other film-making, and Leslie chimed in with an enthusiasm suggesting her relief that the subject had been changed. Frank, however, remained silent. They exhausted the movie and moved on to coffee and desultory conversation about Jill's hometown of Glayville. And after half a cup of coffee, Frank looked pointedly at his watch and said he had an early class and they would have to be leaving. Mike said good-bye to Jill with the strong feeling that she would never set foot in the house again. For her part, Jill closed the lid on her relationship with Frank by asking Mike if she could visit the station and chat with him there.

"Anytime," said Mike, and deliberately was no more specific. His relationship with his son was fragile enough without encouraging acquaintance with someone who, he was certain, was about to be an ex-friend of Frank.

The door had barely closed behind them when Leslie turned on Mike.

"How could you have done that?" she demanded.

Mike knew better than to ask what she was talking about. He sighed.

"It's not my fault he's so damned touchy," he said, reaching for the brandy decanter.

"Touchy! She is one of the most aggressive creatures I've met in years. And you encouraged her."

"She wanted to talk about television, both PBS and commercial, for God's sake. How many topics are forbidden around this house?"

"But you know how Franklin feels—"

"It'd be nice if Franklin knew how I felt at times, when he joins you in sticking pins in me for working for money."

"Mike!" Leslie's voice was shocked. "That's ridiculous, and it's got nothing to do with that girl putting Franklin down the way she did."

Mike sipped his brandy and nodded. "I'm damned if I know how they ever got together in the first place," he said.

Leslie sat down, composing herself. "That occurred to me, too," she admitted. "She certainly wasn't what I expected."

"Me neither," said Mike, "and I grant you it wasn't an easy evening. I didn't like being put in that position, either, Leslie, but it was a dinner party, and while maybe Miss Starling was more forthcoming than she needed to be, Franklin didn't have to sulk like a ten-year-old, either."

Leslie hesitated, then smiled, and accepted a brandy.

"I know. I hadn't seen him behave like that in years. God, what an evening. Between her holding forth and Franklin staring at his curry . . ."

"It was great curry," said Mike firmly. "I ate two helpings, I hope you noticed."

She laughed. "I saw you tucking into the curry and the wine, and I wasn't sure whether you were hungry or you just wanted to take your mind off what was going on around you."

Mike grinned. "Sort of both, to be frank." He sighed. "Well, I'm willing to bet that's Franklin's last date with Jill."

"I certainly hope so," said Leslie stiffly.

"Not the kind of daughter-in-law you'd had in mind?" he teased her.

She finished her brandy and stood up.

"I have to finish clearing up."

Mike got up and put his arm around her fragile waist. "Why don't you leave it till morning, and let's go to bed?"

He kissed the back of her neck and felt her move away. Leslie didn't look at him as she went toward the kitchen.

"Leslie?"

She stopped, briefly. "What?"

Mike waited.

"What is it?" she asked sharply.

"Why do you have to finish the damned dishes or whatever now? It isn't important. Why can't we ever be together anymore? Why aren't you ever interested in going to bed with me?"

"Mike, for God's sake, it's been a difficult enough evening without your getting childish. I have a meeting tomorrow morning at the school, and I've a bunch of things to do around the house."

"That isn't what I asked you."

"It isn't—it isn't true I'm not interested in going to bed with you."

"Four and a half months ago was the last time you showed any such inclination. That's interest?"

Leslie flushed a little. "I don't want to get into this kind of argument tonight, please. We'll talk about it another time. All right?"

"We've talked it to death."

"In that case, let's drop the subject."

"Why the hell can't you tell me what's wrong?"

"Nothing's wrong!" Her voice rose suddenly and shrilly. "I just—well, I don't always feel the same way you do at the same time. You never think of that, do you?"

Mike stared at her sadly. "I don't think there's ever been a time I didn't take your feelings into account, Leslie. You can't be serious about saying something like that."

"All right, so it's my fault. Like everything else. Franklin sulks and it's my fault. I don't feel like making love after a dismal dinner and it's my fault. Is that what you want me to say?"

"None of it is what I want you to say, not that that

matters, either. Seems as if I haven't mattered, either, for a long time now."

Mike walked across the hall into his study and closed the door quietly behind him. He wasn't a door slammer. Arguments gave him a headache, and the slam of a door only made the headache worse. He didn't even feel like another brandy. He sat down heavily in his big leather armchair, leaned his head back, and closed his eyes. He noticed that Leslie had made no effort to follow him.

9

FRANK HATHAWAY never called Jill again, for which Caroline Mitchell was grateful, because she had come to the conclusion that she had no choice but to take him away from her friend. She was annoyed with herself for not making the link between Frank Hathaway and the Mike Hathaway who was the KRT-WNN anchorman in Columbus. Caroline had been looking for a high-level contact at the station, and the anchorman was an appropriate solution, although she would have preferred the station manager or news director, either of whom had hiring power. At this stage in her development, what Caroline needed was solid entrée to somebody who could give her the kind of job that could lead to the job she wanted. She was too shrewd to harbor illusions about instant stardom, but she was aware of the weight and value of influence at the right place at the right time. And when Jill related to her the course of the dinner party at the Hathaways' house, Caroline tucked away the information. Her memory was impeccable when it came to details like that. And she was glad that Jill hadn't really been involved with Frank. She was fond of Jill, although it wouldn't have stopped her from moving in on her in this case. Jill wouldn't have made the proper use of someone like Frank; obviously hadn't made the proper use of him, judging by her account of his taking her to meet his parents and then not speaking a word to her all the way home.

"I've no idea what I did wrong," Jill had told Caroline. "I told his father how much I liked his show and asked him some questions, and he was really nice and helpful. Frank just sat there all night, pouting. Hardly opened his mouth. And his mother wasn't much better."

"Maybe he's jealous of his father?" Caroline suggested.

Jill considered. "Maybe. Although Mike Hathaway doesn't seem to be on any ego trip at all. He told some funny stories, that was all. Frank seemed to be sort of gibing at his father for being in commercial TV instead of PBS, and that sort of irritated me. So preachy."

"You told him that?" Caroline had smiled.

"Not exactly. But well, maybe sort of."

Caroline could see why Frank had sulked all the way home. And she began to plan how to get to know Frank Hathaway. Once she did get to know him, what Jill had told her would be useful. It was sort of a list of things not to do, she thought. Making contact with Frank proved easier than she had expected, because in class next morning, she literally fell over his foot. Turning to speak to someone behind her as she walked toward a desk, she failed to see a large sneakered object in the aisle and went tumbling downward, with her books flying around her. Frank was mortified and remorseful. He leaped up and helped her to her feet, picking up the scattered books, awkwardly patting her arm.

"Caroline, I'm so sorry. Are you all right? My damn big feet."

Caroline laughed, then grimaced as she saw blood from a scrape on her knee seeping through the nylon of her panty hose.

"I'll get a Band-Aid. Or do you want to go to the infirmary?" Frank was frenzied with apology.

"No, no, I've got a Band-Aid in my purse."

Caroline dug around and came up with a gray and dusty oblong.

"That isn't clean," he objected.

"It's still got its backing on, so what's underneath is clean."

"Here, let me do it."

He peeled off the plastic and taped on the Band-Aid, then looked up in embarrassment as she broke into laughter.

"Frank, thank you. But maybe I should put it on the skin and not on top of the nylon."

"Oh God," said Frank, and suddenly laughed with her.

He's nice, Caroline thought, and was pleased, because

that made it easier. Frank waved at her to sit with him when she came back from doctoring her knee. After class, he invited her to have lunch with him at a café near the campus. There were two student hangouts for lunch and coffee and beer, and Caroline noticed that Frank chose the quieter, pleasanter of the two. He grinned at her over their sandwiches.

"You're not crippled, then."

She smiled back. "Not enough to get me out of drama class this afternoon."

"That's right, you take drama, don't you? I'm in political science."

"I know. I wanted to take that, but to be absolutely candid, I didn't think I was up to it."

"Of course you'd be up to it." Frank's voice was polite but she heard a faint reserve.

"Listen, I'm not fishing for compliments. You have to recognize your own limitations. I figure maybe I'll be a weather woman or something like that, to start with, and with television I thought I'd need drah-matic training!" Caroline struck a comic pose with her sandwich, and Frank's responding laughter was warm.

"Television has its own kind of skills." Now his voice was stiff again.

"You're going into newspaper work, aren't you? What field?"

"Investigative reporting. Or that's what I'd like to do."

"You're going to be pretty busy, aren't you? Especially when you get to Washington."

Her words and her admiring expression were calculated and effective. Frank bloomed. He launched into a lengthy dissertation on the corruption within the federal government, the failure of American foreign policy, and the lack of "idealistic individualism" on Capitol Hill. It was a speech Mike Hathaway was familiar with, having heard it first from Leslie. Jill's reaction had been to listen and dissect the flaws in Frank's theories, which had intrigued him the first time she had done it. But Caroline was genuinely impressed. She listened attentively, nodded, occasionally interjected a word of agreement, not so much because she agreed with him as that she hadn't given any thought to such cosmic topics before, and she had no basis for disagreeing with him. Frank felt he could talk to her forever, especially because he liked to look at her. He tried to turn an amusing phrase or two to see the bright, wide smile spread across her face and illuminate the wide-set dark eyes. She didn't interrupt, the way Jill Starling used to, he thought. He'd wondered why Caroline and Jill roomed together; they seemed so different in personality. Now he decided that Jill probably dominated Caroline, talked her to death, most likely. And Caroline was so sweet. She didn't chew on her fingernails, either, he thought, remembering the pulpy ends of Jill's fingers and comparing them unfavorably with the pale shining ovals at Caroline's fingertips. When they parted after lunch, they arranged to meet for dinner and a movie the next evening.

"I really enjoyed talking with you, Caroline," said Frank, whose enraptured expression left little doubt as to his sincerity. Caroline smiled her most brilliant smile at him over her shoulder as she walked away. It was an effective ploy, as long as she didn't fall over anything while she did it.

Jill was in their room, studying, when Caroline walked in. She looked up and grinned.

"I noticed you fell hard for young Frank this morning."

Caroline regarded her Band-Aided knee.

"Cost me a pair of panty hose."

"But was it worth it?"

"We had lunch together, and we're having dinner tomorrow night."

"Well! Another conquest for Caroline." There was a faint edge to Jill's voice.

Caroline glanced over at her. "You and he are all washed up, aren't you?"

"God, yes. He doesn't even say good morning to me. Whatever I did, don't do it. But you listen better than I do."

"Well, he does have a lot of opinions," Caroline acknowledged. "But I don't know all that much about politics, so I thought he was sort of interesting."

"I used to argue with him. I thought he was a bit pompous."

"Well, I don't know as much about these things as either of you, I guess, so I listened to him."

"You two may be made in heaven, so to speak," said Jill. "But he's so serious, Caroline. He'll bore you."

Caroline began to brush her hair, studying her reflection in her mirror.

"You're just picking on him because he isn't your type," she told Jill.

"Are you saying he'd be your type even if his father weren't the local news anchor?" Jill asked shrewdly.

"He never mentioned his father." Caroline brushed her hair with long smooth strokes and approved the blandness of her expression.

"And he won't. Now there's a point to be considered. What if he never takes you home to dinner? I mean, he may have been so discouraged by my performance . . ." Jill giggled.

"I thought he was sort of . . . comfortable to be with," said Caroline thoughtfully, and ignored Jill's mirth.

Over the next six weeks, Caroline and Frank were inseparable. They walked together, ate together, studied together, talked together, and laughed together. But they did not sleep together. Frank did not suggest it. He kissed her good night and sometimes put his arm around her shoulders, but that was all. Caroline was relieved. She was able to relax with Frank in a way she had never relaxed with anyone before. Sometimes she even hugged him spontaneously, and he seemed delighted, but did not try to turn the hug into something else.

Theirs was a joyously asexual relationship. Frank was the brother Caroline never had. He was a contradiction in terms of everything she had ever known about the opposite sex, and she became deeply attached to him, grateful to him for the discovery of gentleness. She refused to discuss him with Jill, who was openly curious. She didn't care if she never met his father, she snapped at her roommate when Jill twitted her about not having been taken home to Daddy yet. It was not true, of course, that Caroline didn't care whether she met Mike Hathaway. But she was content to steal a little time from a childhood she had never had, and Frank was in many ways her playmate. His father was something different, and Caroline fully intended to meet him. She was quite sure that Frank would do almost anything she wanted him to do, and she did not think she would have to ask him to take her to meet his parents.

She was right. Six weeks after their first date, Frank told Caroline he loved her. They were out walking near the lake on a mild spring Sunday, sitting beneath a tree eating apples.

"This is the kind of day that makes you want to stay outdoors forever," said Caroline, watching fleecy clouds move above the green latticework of the foliage. Frank touched her hand gently, and she smiled at him. "Hi."

"Hi," said Frank, and stroked her cheek. "I want to—tell you something," he said gravely.

"Something wrong?" Her eyes searched his face.

"No, no." He shook his head. "Nothing's wrong at all. I guess everything's right, and that's what I wanted to tell you."

Caroline waited.

"Caroline," said Frank. "I love you."

She sat quite still, not looking at him, and when she did turn toward him, he was watching her tensely.

"Caroline?"

She put her arms around his neck, and his responding clasp was as gentle as ever. Caroline took a deep breath and kissed him on the cheek.

"Frank, I love you too."

It was true, as far as it went. She did love him. He was the best companion she had ever known. He was kind, considerate, and intelligent and he thought she was wonderful, mostly because she liked to listen to him. Frank talked far more than Caroline, but most people talked more than Caroline. She was perfecting the art of conversation by response, injecting a few appropriate and encouraging questions into other people's monologues. She found she learned quite a bit that way, in addition to ingratiating herself to whomever she was listening. Now, Frank's thin, handsome face had broken into a wide grin. He kissed her mouth and her face and her neck, and Caroline, who always expected to be frightened when anyone touched her, found to her pleased surprise that she wasn't. They clung together, rocking in each other's arms. Settled against the tree, her head on his shoulder, Frank stroked her hair.

"You must have thought I was sort of strange these past weeks, darling."

Caroline looked up at him. "Why would I think that?"

His fingers tangled themselves in the soft dark curls.

"Well . . . I never made a real pass at you, did I? I thought maybe you wondered why."

Caroline looked at the distant lake shimmering blue under the sun.

"No," she said. "I never wondered."

Frank kissed her forehead.

"You're so special, Caroline. I mean, you never acted as if you . . . well slept around. You know, some of the girls—"

"I know what you mean," Caroline interrupted him.

"Anyway, I wanted you to know it . . . it certainly wasn't because I didn't want to go to bed with you; I mean—"

"Frank." Caroline sat up. "Please don't talk about that. You don't need to. I was happy with you the way we were. What you're talking about—it didn't matter."

"But it did. I mean, it does matter."

Caroline was very still. She calmed herself by thinking about Caroline in the mirror, who would have told her Don't get upset, he's doing just what you want him to do. Play your cards properly and you'll have no trouble with him. Get upset and you'll scare him off. He won't be your friend and you'll never get to meet his father. Smile a little.

Caroline smiled a little, trustingly, and Frank tightened his arms around her.

"Caroline, darling, what I'm saying is that I'd . . . I'd like to marry you. You're the only person I've ever met that I want to be around, I mean always."

"Oh Frank." Caroline kissed him and thought that Caroline in the mirror would have been proud of her. She snuggled her face into his shoulder and told him she was so happy.

"What does that mean?" He tilted up her chin, gazing adoringly at her.

"Frank, I'd like to marry you. If you're sure."

"Sure!" He pulled her close against him, and after a while, she was grateful to see another couple approaching, although a little distance away. She gently pushed him away.

"Darling, there's somebody coming."

He laughed. "Maybe we should just go to a motel."

Caroline was silent.

"Honey? I'm teasing, of course. Listen—" He tilted up her chin again.

"Should we go to Glayville so I can meet your parents? I mean, do I have to ask your father for your hand?"

His voice was light, but not even the memory of Caroline in the mirror could prevent her face from freezing.

Frank was bewildered. "What's wrong?"

"Nothing." She pulled away from him a little. "You don't have to meet my parents, Frank, unless you specially want to."

He was confused. "I thought you would want me to. I mean . . . won't they have to be at the wedding?"

"I thought we'd have a . . . a very quiet wedding, if that's all right with you. And no, they don't have to be there, Frank."

He had never seen this remoteness in her before. He wrapped her in his arms, seeking to break down the sudden barrier.

"Listen, darling, we'll do whatever you want. I didn't know there was a problem with your parents, and I don't need to know about it if you don't want to tell me. It doesn't matter. Hell, everybody has problems with their parents. I have problems with my parents."

"I thought you got along pretty well with them." Caroline relaxed.

"Well, I do, as a matter of fact. We've had our ups and downs, but nothing serious. They're both pretty nice, really. And I'd really like them to meet you. Would you like that?"

Caroline smiled. "I'd like that, Frank."

"Great. Because I know they're going to love you, and I think you'll like them. As a matter of fact . . . well, of course you know my father's the news anchor at KRT?"

Caroline nodded. "Yes. I've watched the show. But you don't talk much about him. You talk more about your mother. I thought maybe there was some difficulty and I didn't want to—"

"You're so sweet." Frank kissed her. "But to tell the

truth, sometimes lately I've wondered if I've been kind of hard on Dad."

"How do you mean?" Her eyes were at their widest and most attentive.

"Well, my mother's an English teacher, or she was. She still does some substitute teaching. And she's not very high on commercial television. So she and I—we've sort of given Dad a hard time about making his money out of something that can be that silly and superficial. And I have to say he's been damned nice about it. He's so good-natured, and he never seems to be upset. But I've thought maybe we've taken the . . . the teasing too far at times."

"Perhaps his feelings got hurt, Frank."

"You would think of that, and I should have. Tell the truth, Caroline, maybe I've been worried about living up to him in a way. I mean, I don't want to go into that kind of work, but he's got a good reputation. And he used to be in newspapers himself. Says he switched for the money—absolutely candid about it!"

"Well, I remember Martha Vogel from WNN in Washington said much the same thing when she spoke to our class," Caroline observed.

Frank looked sheepish. "I missed her speech, and I heard it was damned good, too. I guess I sort of took the position that she'd, well, that she'd sold out. Sounds pretty silly, doesn't it?"

"Sounds like you missed a good speech for the wrong reason, honey," she said lightly.

"That's true. You always put your finger on things, without worrying them to death, the way I do. The more good people go into television, the better it'll get, right?"

For the first time, Caroline glimpsed in Frank what had exasperated Jill, but there was no sign of her reaction in her face.

"Well, it doesn't really matter, darling." She patted his cheek.

"To get back to what I was saying about your meeting Mother and Dad," he went on, "maybe Dad could be of help to you. You were talking the other day about trying to get an intern's job at the station, weren't you?"

Caroline beamed at him. "Well yes, I was. But I cer-

tainly wouldn't want to impose on your father, darling.
He doesn't even know me."

"He's going to, and I'll bet he'll want to help. At least
you could go over to the station with him, get to know
some of the people. That'd be useful to you. I know I've
started spending time at the newspaper office, and it's
been a real help."

"That would be wonderful," said Caroline, and meant
it. As they strolled back, with their arms around each
other, she was smiling, and Caroline in the mirror was
smiling back.

10

"NOT CURRY," said Leslie, when she telephoned Mike at his office to tell him Franklin was bringing another girl friend home to dinner.

Mike chuckled. "Absolutely not curry."

They had been trying to be nice to each other since that dismal night. They had gone out more, tried to talk more, even made love, rather self-consciously, trying not to notice the shadow that never quite faded.

"I thought salmon, perhaps. Something light. Strawberries." Leslie knew Mike liked salmon and strawberries.

He smiled at the other end of the phone, touched. "That'd be terrific."

"And there's something else." She paused. Mike frowned. It was unlike Leslie to be coy. "You'd better bring champagne home."

"What?"

"He says he's going to marry this one."

"I'll be damned," said Mike.

"He says she's . . . quite different from anyone he's ever known."

"Familiar words, those," observed Mike.

"What's her name?"

"Caroline Mitchell. She's also a journalism student. And—wait for this, my dear—she's also going into television work."

"Well." Mike was enjoying being able to chat comfortably with Leslie about it. "Let's hope it isn't a rerun."

"If it's a rerun," said Leslie firmly, "you and I are going out to a movie after dessert."

Three days later, the Hathaway home was again prepared for a guest of Frank.. The rooms were fragrant with the fresh flowers Leslie prided on cultivating in her gar-

den. The lamplight was soft on armchairs and sofas
slipcovered in crisp, pale linen, and on the Monet prints
on the jade green walls. Leslie was regal in ivory silk and
heavy gold jewelry, and Mike was waiting with a mixture
of amusement and dread. He didn't want to live through
another evening of the kind he had spent with Jill Starling. He had barely seen Frank since. For that matter,
Frank had hardly been home for weeks. He assumed that
Caroline Mitchell was the reason, which was more reassuring to think about than the supposition that his son
was not speaking to him. A car door thudded, and Mike
grinned at Leslie.

"Here we go again," he said. She crossed her fingers
and held them up for him to see. Then he looked up and
saw Caroline standing in the doorway, with Frank looming protectively behind her. He remembered that moment for a long time, remembered the beautiful face
framed by a cloud of dark hair, the wide dark eyes with
their almost plaintive gaze, the flush on her cheeks reflected in the pale pink silken glow of her dress. Most of
all, he remembered her smile, which seemed to embrace
those on whom she bestowed it. It was not until Leslie
moved forward that Mike realized he had been standing
without speaking, gazing at Caroline. Frank, however,
appeared delighted at the entrance that Caroline had
achieved. He was grinning proudly, with his hand on
Caroline's shoulder.

"Mother, Dad—this is Caroline Mitchell," he said, and
with hardly a pause: "Caroline and I are going to be
married."

Leslie moved smoothly toward Caroline, her hands
gracefully extended.

"Caroline—welcome to our family. Franklin, what a
surprise, what a lovely surprise." She kissed her son.

Mike was behind her, also with hands outstretched. He
grinned at Frank and took both Caroline's hands in his.

"We're happy to meet you, Caroline. As Leslie says—
welcome."

She looked up and saw a tall, handsome man with
silvery hair and warm blue eyes set in a face tanned from
heavy golfing. His manner was as warm as his eyes, and
his voice was resonant without the tolling bell quality of
some of his colleagues on camera.

"It's wonderful to meet you both," she said. Her voice was low and clear, and she seemed perfectly composed, Mike noticed.

"Frank really has told me a lot about you both, and I'd think you would both be very proud if I told you all he said."

Leslie nodded approvingly. She was certainly an immense improvement over the last one, she thought. And a beauty, into the bargain. As Mike shook hands with Frank, Leslie took Caroline lightly by the arm and led her into the sitting room.

"We did have just a hint," she said, "so we're celebrating."

"Champagne, how lovely!" Caroline turned to Frank, her eyes shining. He put his arm around her. The fragile glasses were filled and toasts drunk. Frank and Caroline settled on the sofa so that he could keep her hand in his.

"Caroline dear," said Leslie, "we want to hear all about you, and all about the wedding plans."

She waited, and Caroline felt Frank's fingers curl warmly, reassuringly around hers.

"We haven't really set any date or anything yet. I mean, it's pretty new to us too," she said.

"Not that new though," said Frank. "Show Mother your ring, darling."

Caroline held out her left hand, to display a delicate ring of gold filigree set with pearls.

"Beautiful," said Leslie.

"I understand you're from Glayville, Caroline?" Mike asked.

She nodded, sipping her champagne. "I haven't really strayed very far from home so far."

"Your parents are still there?" asked Leslie.

"Yes."

"Well, we must have them here for a weekend."

Only Frank felt the stiffening of Caroline's slender body.

"I'm afraid . . . well, they don't travel," she said softly.

Leslie's eyebrows rose interrogatively.

"You see," said Caroline, "my mother has been . . . incapacitated, for some time now. She doesn't get around much at all. And my father . . . won't leave her by herself." She reveled in the words.

"But even for your wedding—surely some arrangement . . . ?" Leslie let her words trail off.

"I do hope so," said Caroline, conscious of the steady reassuring pressure of Frank's fingers. "But they haven't left Glayville since I was a baby."

"You aren't planning to be married there?" Leslie's voice made clear her surprise. Mike frowned at her. He had become aware of a slightly unnatural calm about Caroline's manner. Then Frank broke into the conversation.

"Caroline and I want a very quiet wedding," he said with a firmness that surprised his mother. "We don't want any fuss at all. And of course we'll let you know when we've got things firmed up."

His tone carried a faint admonition, and Mike saw Leslie react to it. She slipped easily onto another level, but her customary charm was still under the control of her curiosity. Leslie was not entirely comfortable at being confronted with a prospective daughter-in-law who was far prettier than she and equally self-possessed.

"You plan to go into television work, Caroline?" Mike asked.

Caroline nodded, and made a small, self-deprecating gesture. "That's my hope."

"What kind of reporting?"

"I'm still not sure. General assignment work, I expect." She laughed disarmingly. "Whatever I can get. There's a lot of competition."

"As a matter of fact, Dad," said Frank, astonishing his parents, "I was telling Caroline maybe you could show her around the station. She's looking for work as an intern right now, and I wondered if you might . . . offer her some good advice?"

Mike was briefly stricken speechless, and he could see his reaction mirrored in Leslie's face. Then he heard Caroline laugh again, looking directly at him.

"I told Frank I didn't want to impose on you, Mr. Hathaway, and I don't," she said easily. "But I certainly would appreciate your taking me around the station. I've been meaning to go over and see if they'd let me do some work as an intern, that's true, but I don't have any contacts at all, so anything you can do to help, believe me, I'd be grateful."

She was candid and she was charming about it, Mike thought. He nodded vigorously.

"I'd be delighted, Caroline," he said. "What are future fathers-in-law for?"

Caroline smiled at him, and then immediately transferred her grateful gaze to Frank, who slipped his arm around her.

"Thanks, Dad," he said. "I'd really appreciate it, too."

My God, Mike thought, the millennium. He raised his champagne glass in his son's direction and smiled.

"Shall we go in to dinner?" asked Leslie.

Later, Mike remembered that he had talked a lot during what was a festive meal, and so had Leslie and Frank. Caroline hadn't talked very much at all, that he could recall, but she had somehow directed the conversation. She wanted to know about Mike's job and the family background, but she also wanted to know about Frank's childhood and Leslie's days as a teacher and Leslie's gardening. Mike noticed that she frequently deferred to Frank's opinions, and often quoted him, yet there was no clinging quality about her. She accepted Frank's affectionate gestures, but initiated none. And she talked little about herself, beyond an amusing anecdote or two about a roller-skating contest she had won "entirely because I couldn't stop" and about some colorful characters she remembered in Glayville. She never mentioned her parents, and Frank appeared to know enough about that problem, whatever it was, to interpose himself between Caroline and any curiosity on that score. Caroline was charming, Mike reflected, because she said all the right things in the right tone of voice. She was one of the most composed young women he had ever seen. If she had rehearsed for the dinner, she could not have been more impressive. And he might have dismissed all of that as the veneer of a well brought up and self-confident young woman, had he not been conscious of something about Caroline that didn't match the rest of her personality.

As the meal progressed, he watched and listened with mounting interest and became convinced that what they were all seeing was the public Caroline. And he wondered whether it was the public Caroline whom Franklin wanted to marry. As long as Caroline was drawing out those around her, asking and listening and smiling and nodding and commenting, she was no more than an exceptionally pretty girl who knew how to make others like her. When Caroline talked at any length about herself, she threw up an instant wall of reserve. Her face lost its glow of interest and became oddly closed. The closest she came to revealing anything of herself was when Leslie, with what Mike suspected was a trace of malice aforethought, asked whether Caroline knew Jill Starling. For the first time, Mike glimpsed mischief in Caroline's face.

"She's my roommate. I've known her all my life," she said.

Leslie was slightly taken aback, and it was Frank who broke in, grinning.

"I'm sure Caroline heard about Jill coming here to dinner, Mother. In detail."

"Really," said Leslie.

Caroline laughed. "Both Frank and Jill told me about that. Jill said she managed to get into an argument with everybody at the table, practically. Jill has very strong views on most things. But she's my oldest friend. We grew up practically next door to each other and we were always together."

"You're quite different people," observed Leslie.

"They certainly are," said Frank, looking fondly at Caroline.

"I'm very fond of Jill," said Caroline firmly. "She's a very nice person, and she's very bright. She just likes to express her opinions. Her father's the same way, so I guess she comes by it naturally."

"Evidently you get along with her," said Mike.

Caroline smiled. "We get along fine. We don't want the same things, so we don't really clash at all. Jill has her whole life mapped out, knows what she's going to do and when. Or so she says!" She smiled at Frank.

"She hasn't met anyone yet who could change her mind."

Mike refilled Caroline's wine glass. "She doesn't talk you to a standstill?" he asked lightly.

"Oh no," said Caroline. "I say what I want to say. And I just tune her out occasionally."

Leslie laughed shortly. "I'm afraid we didn't handle Jill the right way, Mike."

He smiled, and his smile became wider when Frank again raised the subject of Mike's taking Caroline under his wing at KRT. Caroline took the opportunity to draw Mike out on his work, questioning him about stories she had seen used on the news and how decisions were made on their handling. He was impressed by how much effort she obviously had made to learn some background about television work, and less impressed by her apparent relative ignorance of what was going on in the world. She was unaware that the President was fighting a wave of unpopularity in the polls, which was considered an indication of the political shape of things to come in his battle for reelection. She was unaware of a new outbreak of racism, which had been well publicized. She was unaware of a mounting financial scandal about a well-known United States senator.

She admitted her ignorance, apologized for it, and was anxious to remedy it, but she did not explain it. Mike was wrong when he assumed that she was not aware; the problem lay in the fact that she could not remember what she was aware of. Caroline was hardly likely to acknowledge that inadequacy to a man she wanted to impress. And she had impressed him. She had done more than that: she had built him a bridge back to his son.

Mike chided himself for being too hard on Caroline, and, studying her, thought she might indeed do well in television. If her looks, her warm personality, and her smile transmuted into camera chemistry, Caroline might wind up with the kind of career that could confict with Franklin's dreams of domestic bliss, reflected Mike.

By the time they reached coffee and brandy, even Leslie was relaxed, which Mike considered a direct tribute to Caroline's diplomacy. They went outdoors to admire by moonlight the rockery, which was Leslie's pride and almost entirely her own work. Mike found Caroline standing beside him. She was taller than he had first thought, and she looked quite lovely. He felt a twinge of envy toward Frank as he smiled at his future daughter-in-law.

"I really would like to take you up on that invitation to visit the studio, Mr. Hathaway," she said softly.

"Caroline, I'll be delighted to show you around, introduce you to people who might be helpful. Maybe there's a summer job you could do around there. I'll talk to the station manager," he told her.

Caroline hesitated. "I'd be grateful for your help, but, to be candid, I don't want them taking me on because I'm engaged to your son."

Mike grinned. "That's sensible, and I'll make that clear. I'll provide the introductions and maybe a little background, and after that you're on your own. Okay?"

Her smile flashed. "Okay. More than okay. That's all I want, Mr. Hathaway."

"Good." Mike sipped his brandy. "So why don't we have lunch next week and I'll take you back to the station with me."

"That would be wonderful."

"What would be wonderful, darling?" Frank had appeared behind her.

"Caroline and I are going to have lunch next week, and then I'll introduce her around at the station. See if there's anything might be available for summer."

Frank beamed, and wrapped his arms around Caroline.

"Thanks, Dad, that's really nice of you."

"Isn't it?" Caroline smiled up at him.

"What's all this conspiracy?" Leslie was linking her arm through Mike's, a gesture so rare in her that he started. Told of the lunch plan, Leslie was almost coquettish.

"He never shows me around the station, Caroline. You see the effect you're having on this family already?"

Mike considered his wife with astonishment, and felt increasingly affectionate toward Caroline. She might turn Franklin back into a human being. He put his hand lightly on her shoulder as they went back into the house, and felt her flinch slightly.

"You're cold?" he asked.

Frank was instantly solicitous, hurrying her indoors, but it seemed to Mike that Caroline's reaction had been an instinctive withdrawal rather than a shiver. It was a little puzzling, because it was at odds with an otherwise outgoing personality. And as they said good night, Leslie again raised the subject of wedding plans.

"Caroline, dear, you and I must have lunch soon and see what I can do to help with arrangements. Even a small wedding has to be planned."

Caroline's smile was all-embracing. "Oh yes, we must," she said. "I'll call you soon."

But in her voice there was none of the eagerness with which she had talked of visiting Mike at the station, of having lunch with him, for that matter. He wondered if what Caroline had actually said to Leslie was Don't call me, I'll call you. But Leslie was oblivious to nuance.

"And I do hope we can work something out about meeting your parents."

Her words fell into a silence. Mike saw Caroline's smile fade.

"I hope so," she said noncommittally.

"Well"—Leslie was irrepressible—"I know you mentioned the problem about traveling. But we have to figure out some way to get them here for the wedding, since you don't want to be married in Glayville. And I assume you'll want them to be at the ceremony?"

Watching Caroline with rising curiosity, Mike saw her face seem to harden so that the skin resembled translucent marble. Her eyes, dark and blank, seemed fixed on something a foot to the right of Leslie's head.

"I really don't know, Mrs. Hathaway," she said with frozen politeness.

Mike realized that Frank was drawing Caroline within the circle of his arm and was glaring at his mother.

"Mother, we haven't put anything together yet. We just got engaged, for heaven's sake."

Mike had rarely heard his son speak so coldly to his mother. The line had been drawn, he reflected, and Leslie had just found out what happened when she crossed it.

As Frank's car left, Mike found Leslie wandering restlessly about the sitting room, moving flower vases a fraction of an inch, the way she did when she was nervous.

"What did you think?" she asked him, and he detected uncertainty in her voice. "That business about her parents was really strange."

"Why?" asked Mike impatiently. "Lots of kids nowadays don't talk to their parents. I mean, I expect you'll find out about it soon enough, and maybe it'd be damned awkward to have them at the wedding if she's not speaking to them. Why push it now?"

"You would take her part," said Leslie. Mike patted her shoulder and grinned at her.

"For once, my dear," he said, "it looks as if Franklin and I are on the same side."

Leslie did not return his grin. "I wonder what she's saying about us," she said.

What Caroline was saying about Frank's parents was predictably complimentary, and Frank was rapturous about how, as he said, they had instantly fallen in love with her. She suspected that was exaggerating the situation considerably, but she was not displeased with the way things had gone. She had accomplished exactly what she had hoped to accomplish, and she also had found Mike Hathaway immensely likable. If Caroline could have been attracted to a man, she was attracted to Mike, but she could hardly tell his son that.

"I liked the way you stood up for Jill," said Frank approvingly.

"Jill's my friend," said Caroline.

"You're so sweet," said Frank, and kissed her.

"Darling," she said, "we're going off the road."

"Jill really seemed pleased about our engagement," he observed.

"She was delighted. I think she felt she'd embarrassed you that night at your parents' house and she was sorry about it."

"Really?" Frank was pleased, because Jill *had* embarrassed him. She had done worse than that—she had humiliated him, and he was glad she was remorseful. He was of course unaware that Caroline had made up Jill's remorse because she knew it would please him. Jill still hooted about the disasters of that particular evening.

And Jill was still awake, studying, when Caroline came home. She looked up with a grin.

"How'd it go?"

"Really well, I think. You were right about Mike Hathaway. He's really nice."

"Didn't I tell you? And did you let Frank talk?"

"Of course."

Caroline sat down and looked at her reflection in her mirror. Caroline in the mirror smiled back at her. She

had done well. It had all gone well, except for that
moment when Frank's mother had kept nagging about
her parents. It would be a cold day in hell before Caroline would invite them to anything. Her mother would eat
them out of house and home, and her father—She saw
the gradual transformation of her face in the mirror and
reminded herself that she never thought about her father.
When she never thought about her father, she could
always smile.

Caroline had been a little worried about being so uninformed on some of the topics that had been raised at the
dinner table. She had to work on that. Sometimes reading the news aloud to herself helped, and she had been so
absorbed by Frank that she had let that practice lapse,
when she obviously couldn't afford to. Caroline in the
mirror was frowning now, in concentration. What else?
Nothing else. And next week she could have her entrée
to the station, sponsored, as it were, by Mike Hathaway.

"You look like a cat who ate a canary that disagreed
with it," said Jill, who annoyed Caroline by finding entertainment in what she called Caroline's "colloquies"
with herself.

"You look pretty smug, come to that," Caroline
countered.

Jill smirked. "You may not be the only one who's
getting married."

Caroline knew Jill had been seeing Tom Roberts, a
political reporter from the local newspaper. She was also
surprised. Tom was something of a romantic about women.
He had in fact shown some interest in Caroline until he
realized it was not reciprocated. Caroline thought he was
pleasant and intelligent, but a little wishy-washy. The best
thing about him was his looks, in her opinion.

"Tom?" she said, and was careful to keep the surprise
out of her voice.

Jill nodded gleefully. "He's such a love," she said
happily.

"Yes, he is, and that's wonderful," said Caroline, who
thought that was the problem with Tom Roberts, especially for somebody as keen minded as Jill. He was too
much of a love and he didn't have the kind of staying
power that Jill did. Jill would get to where she was going

or die in the attempt. Tom would stop halfway to get a beer.

"You like Tom, don't you?"

Caroline nodded vigorously. "Of course I do."

"Because he certainly thinks a lot of you."

Caroline glanced sharply at Jill, but there seemed to be no deeper meaning locked into the words. Jill didn't go in for subtleties much anyway. She came out and yelled at you if she was mad, which was probably a lot healthier than what Caroline did, which was brood. Or talk to herself in the mirror. Jill had never needed a Jill in the mirror to talk to.

And it was certainly true that Tom Roberts thought a lot of her, as Jill put it. Years later Caroline would remember the stepping stones. Frank and Mike had been the first. In a way, her engagement to Frank had been the beginning of her quest, which had been different from Jill's. Jill's determination to succeed professionally had been self-fulfilling, because she was capable and highly competent. To Jill, recognition and acknowledgment of her excellence were almost incidental as long as she met her own standards. Even when those standards reduced her personal life to rubble. To Caroline, recognition and acknowledgment of her as a person were crucial. Especially since she knew how tenuous was her hold on success. Caroline had no inner life to worry about, and since the time when she had been very small, had known she never would. When she let herself think about it, which was rarely, she believed she had died in the pretty peach and ivory room.

It wasn't that she didn't want to feel affection. She couldn't. Sometimes she thought of herself as hollow, which was why how she looked and sounded was so important. From the crushed child had sprung Caroline in the mirror—exquisite, charming, and unreal. Her biggest problem had been practicing to look real. She knew it wasn't enough to smile, but it was a start. She had fashioned other expressions from her smile, which gave her mouth a nice upward tilt while she was being serious. But no amount of practice could endow Caroline in the mirror with what Jill had. Caroline in the mirror had empty eyes when she did not remember to make them sparkle with pleasure or to make them brightly attentive or crinkled a little with concern. It was not easy, because Caroline in the mirror didn't care. That was how she had come to exist. She had been the child-Caroline's refuge from nightmare, and her comfort lay in the fact that she represented escape. Caroline in the mirror didn't care about anything, so nobody could hurt her.

Caroline couldn't remember when, as she thought of it, she had climbed into the mirror, but that was when she stopped feeling much except that steady flame of hatred for her father. She couldn't ask her mother for help, because all her mother wanted to do was eat. She also had never forgotten her father's prediction of her mother's anger if Caroline told her the truth. By the time she was old enough to realize he had been bullying her, it was too late, and what could her mother do anyway? She was more intimidated by Carlton Mitchell than his daughter was.

She never really knew whether she intended to marry Frank, yet she had not lied when she told him she loved him. He was her friend, her brother, and that was the only kind of love that Caroline could cope with. Anything else imposed the kind of emotional demand on her for which she had no response. She had no emotional resources on which to draw. She could only react with what she thought was wanted, needed, or required, and she would do that only when it coincided with her own needs. Sexually, she had no needs. Sexuality for Caroline was buried deep in horror. Sex had no meaning for her, even when she was a participant, because sex represented her father. She had come to endure, if not to accept, sex with him by willing herself into another dimension of thought. Later she came to accept sex, but without pleasure. She was only grateful that there was no physical pain, and as she became more confident of that, she learned to make sounds that were pleasing to her partner. She found that men who took pride in restraining their own emotions were uneasy with women who were silent in bed. Most of all, Caroline didn't care. She remembered thinking, rather sadly, that now that she and Frank were to be married, they wouldn't be friends anymore. She felt faintly resentful that he would want to spoil what they had.

Caroline smiled a little bitterly as she recalled that her

greatest pleasure in becoming engaged to be married to Frank had been in writing to her parents to tell them about it. She had lingered over that letter, carefully choosing words and phrases for their capacity to wound. She had rewritten it several times because she kept thinking of something she could say that would make her father even more miserable.

She wanted to leave no doubt in his mind that she was sleeping with Frank, wanted him to picture his little daughter in bed with someone else. Enjoying being in bed with someone else. Eager to be in bed with someone else. She wanted him to be able to conjure up that picture in his mind as he lay in bed beside the gross weight of her mother. Licking stamps for the envelope, she had reflected that perhaps he would be so distraught he would kill himself, and she smiled.

11

SHUFFLING THROUGH the mail, Amy Mitchell hardly paused when she found the envelope addressed in her daughter's handwriting. Sometimes she left Caroline's letters for Carlton to open. They were all he had left of his daughter now, Amy would think, and she would smile. She had not been surprised when Caroline had not come home for breaks, or even at Christmas, and she had not cared very much. Amy had long ceased to care very much about anything except her long dream of revenge upon her husband. Her feelings about Caroline had become a little warmer when she read the polite, uncommunicative letters with their occasional flimsy excuses for not coming back to Glayville on vacation. Amy knew how the letters hurt Carlton, and that gave her an almost physical pleasure. The fact that Caroline was contributing to Carlton's distress raised her in Amy's estimation. Sometimes there would enter Amy's mind the terrible possibility that she had misjudged her daughter, had inflicted upon her a dreadful betrayal. But it was easy for her to thrust away such thoughts and think about more cheerful things. Like losing weight.

Amy found herself bitterly entertained by the fact that, as Carlton steadily lost the looks that had made him admired for so much of his life, she seemed to be regaining hers. During the first months after Caroline left, Amy continued to eat. While Caroline had been at home, while her nightmare had been with her constantly, Amy's only comfort had been eating herself into emotional oblivion. It hadn't mattered what she ate: hamburgers, pies, milkshakes, peanut butter sandwiches, pasta, boxes of doughnuts, cartons of ice cream, pounds of cookies, loaves of bread. All had flowed down her throat as into a garbage disposal. She continued to eat out of habit for a while after Caroline's departure, until it occurred to her that if she were to look better while Carlton looked worse, it might heighten his misery.

Almost as an experiment, she drastically reduced her consumption. She went to her doctor, who was delighted and provided her with an appropriate diet. As the months went by, Amy lost eighty-five pounds. As she had more than twenty years earlier, she gained considerable satisfaction from watching herself visibly shrink, while Carlton's thick dark hair thinned and receded, his midriff expanded, and liquor sketched a crimson network around his eyes. Carlton increasingly sat at home and drank in the evening, while Amy went out with her friends, with Glory Swimmers or Helen Starling, who was lonely without Jill, with Nolan often on the road. Both were lavish with praise of the difference in Amy. Glory said she hadn't seen her look so good since before Caroline was born.

Carlton didn't say anything. They had long since ceased to say more than was necessary to each other. But occasionally, Amy saw him staring at her as she passed him with a new quickness and lightness in her step, wearing clothes bought to fit her trimmer body. When he asked her to buy some new slacks and underwear for him, she could not restrain her glee when she told him he needed two sizes larger.

Yet when she lay in bed at night, listening to Carlton snore, Amy found herself again deep in the dark cave of the past. Her memory was a procession of grim markers, tombstones commemorating her hopes, her marriage, her love, her child, and her compassion. She would give herself up to the hideous flashbacks—horrors glimpsed and imagined—and she knew all that stopped her from killing her husband was that she wanted to see him suffer. She rarely thought of Caroline. Her child had become a corollary to her obsession, to the point that Caroline was not so much Amy's daughter as an accessory to Carlton's guilt. Carlton rarely spoke of Caroline, which encouraged Amy to speculate frequently and casually on why their daughter never came home. You don't suppose she thinks she's too good for Glayville, do you? she would ask from time to time, and relish the expression in her husband's eyes. But Carlton did devour Caroline's occasional letters, and Amy would watch his eyes roam the neatly written pages, seeking for a sign of what? she wondered. But clearly seeking. Amy could hardly contain herself when she read the letter in which Caroline announced that she was going to marry Frank Hathaway.

She did not give any date for the wedding, nor did she share any of her plans in the letter to her parents. But she did, uncharacteristically, elaborate on her happiness. She had never dreamed, wrote Caroline in her careful script, that it was possible to be so happy with anyone as she was with Frank. They spent almost every minute they could together, she wrote, and it was never enough. She could not wait until they would be together for always.

As Caroline had intended, the letter left no doubt regarding the intimacy of her relationship with Frank, and Amy smiled as she read it. Yet she also speculated on why Caroline, who had never before hinted at any personal relationship with anyone, suddenly should have bestowed such elaborate confidences on her parents. Unless the letter was intended to hurt. The target, reflected Amy, was not Caroline's mother, which had to mean that Caroline hated Carlton as much as Amy did. In that case—The nagging dark doubt was back, and Amy found it more difficult to dismiss. Because if Caroline hated her father, then Amy's judgment of her daughter could have been totally unjust. How unjust, Amy did not really want to think about. In any case, it was still Carlton's fault, his responsibility, his guilt.

Amy picked up the telephone and called Glory Swimmers to tell her about Caroline's engagement. As Amy knew she would be, Glory was especially impressed by the fact that the pride of Glayville was going to marry a television anchorman's son. "Next thing you know, there'll be our Caroline on that screen," breathed Glory, taking frantic notes. When was the wedding? Would it be in the First Episcopal Church, where Caroline had gone as a child? she wanted to know.

"I don't think any of the details are final. I guess Caroline just wanted us to know first thing. And of course she sent her love to you," Amy lied.

"I always, always knew it," burbled Glory, pawing

through her substantial Mitchell photo file. "Is there a new picture of Caroline?"

Amy said there wasn't, but she expected one would be arriving.

"And of course you and Carlton will be going to Columbus to meet the Hathaways?"

"I suppose so," said Amy, who supposed nothing of the kind. "But this is all brand new, Glory, so we don't have any plans. Her father doesn't even know yet," she added, savoring the thought.

"Oh, I'm sure Carlton will be just thrilled. And maybe a little bit jealous too: I always remember how he was such a devoted father."

"He certainly was devoted to Caroline," Amy agreed.

"Well"—Glory was anxious to be off and composing more reverential twaddle about her favorite local heroine—"I expect the champagne cork will be popping at the Mitchell house tonight."

"You can put that in your story," Amy told her, and went to put Caroline's letter in a place where Carlton would be sure to see it when he sat down to have his evening drink before dinner. She took out steaks and dressed with care in a soft knit that displayed to advantage her weight loss. She wanted to look as attractive as possible, when she told Carlton Caroline's news. Amy laughed a small, unpleasant laugh as she brushed her hair into its new, becoming short flip. She did not think of calling Caroline. Her daughter had not written that letter in the expectation of receiving congratulations from her parents, and Amy knew it.

When Carlton's car pulled up in the driveway, the martinis were chilled, the steaks were defrosted, and the dining table was immaculate with pale pink linen and crystal candlesticks. Amy was sitting tranquilly on the rose-patterned chintz sofa, with a magazine on her lap, looking across the peaceful room to the garden, where her tulips were blooming in pink and purple regiments. On the stereo, Mozart was playing. On the little walnut reading stand next to Carlton's chair, lay Caroline's letter. Beside it, Amy had placed a small vase of pink azaleas. Pink was Caroline's favorite color. Carlton had always bought her pink dresses. The key clicked in the front door, and she heard Carlton's heavy step—much heavier than it used to be—on the polished parquet of the foyer floor.

"In here," Amy called cheerfully. She heard Carlton's steps hesitate, then turn toward the living room. He usually went into his den and drank alone there until dinner was ready, but Amy was determined that tonight she would not miss a moment of her husband's company. He stood for a second in the doorway, and she saw surprise cross his face.

"Hi. Did I forget? Are we having company or something?"

She shook her head and pointed to the martini shaker.

"No, nothing like that. I just thought we'd have a drink in here before dinner. I fixed steaks." She knew he liked steak. Carlton had no fancy culinary leanings.

"Oh. Well, fine." He was obviously taken aback, uncertain of how to react. He and Amy rarely troubled to pretend anymore.

Carlton walked over to his chair, and Amy noted with a stirring of satisfaction that a shoulder seam of his tweed sport coat had parted, and his tailored shirt was strained across his middle. As he lowered himself with a sigh into the leather easy chair, she picked up the shaker.

"Martini?"

"Sure." He peered across at her. "New dress?"

Amy smiled. "Not really."

"Nice."

"Why, thank you." She poured the icy liquid into the delicate, stemmed glass and reached over to hand it to him, making sure her fingers did not touch his.

"There's a letter from Caroline."

The glass stopped halfway to Carlton's lips, and his head swiveled abruptly to his left. Amy went on smiling and watched him take a quick sip before he picked up the envelope and pulled out its contents. Amy savored the sting of the frosted gin, toyed with her olive, leaned back into the soft cushions of the sofa, and never took her eyes off her husband's face. She had waited a long time for a moment like this. She hoped there would be many more like it. Carlton's eyes sped down the page, and Amy saw the muscles of his jaw clench and his mouth tighten into a lipless line. He looked up, and she saw pain and anger in his face.

"Isn't that wonderful news?" she chirped. "Glory Swimmers is so excited about it, I'm surprised she didn't call you to get your reaction."

Carlton stared at her; his face was contorted by emotions he was struggling to control.

"I've never heard Caroline sound so absolutely blissful, have you?" Amy continued. She couldn't remember when she had enjoyed herself so much. "Sly little thing that she is, not to give us a hint all this was going on. And she's obviously just wild about this Frank. They must have been—what's that term?—'shacking up' together for months and we never suspected a thing. Did we?"

For a moment, they gazed into each other's eyes with mutual hatred. Then Carlton picked up his glass and drained it.

"Another?" asked Amy.

He shook his head. He seemed almost paralyzed, and Amy wondered idly if he might have a stroke. She was glad she had remembered to mail the life insurance premiums.

"Glory was threatening to send over some champagne so we could celebrate. She was remembering how devoted you were to Caroline."

She poured another martini into his glass anyway and refilled her own. The icy liquid had never tasted better to Amy.

Carlton sat staring at his glass.

"Well," said Amy with calculated malice, "aren't you pleased? I mean, this Frank sounds like a good match for her. And I can't get over how happy she sounds. I've never heard her sound like that before. Have you?"

Amy tucked her feet under her comfortably. "I thought I'd write—or we might call her?—and invite her to bring Frank for a weekend. Wouldn't that be nice?" She giggled a little. "From the sound of that letter, I guess it'd be silly to put him in the guest room, wouldn't it? Oh well"—she sipped her drink—"you always did say she should have a big bed in her room, even when she was a little girl. Didn't you, Carlton?"

She leaned forward a little, looking into his face, and the malevolence in the quiet room was tangible. Carlton took a deep breath and drew back from the smiling face and the cold eyes.

"I . . . have a bit of a headache. Think I'll lie down for a while," he said.

Amy pouted. "You haven't said a word about Caroline's engagement! Aren't you pleased that your little girl is getting married to a nice young man?"

He stood up. "Yeah. Yeah, it's great. Great."

"Should we call her and tell how happy we are for her?"

For a moment, Amy was sure he was about to hit her, and that too would have given her satisfaction. But she knew, and he knew, that the travesty must be played out. He was trapped and tortured.

"You call her. Tell her for me," he said huskily, and hurried from the room.

Amy went on sipping her martini, and the pages of Caroline's letter lay where they had fallen from her father's fingers. Amy leaned over and picked up the letter and reread it, thoughtfully. She was beginning to feel the gin a little; Amy rarely drank much. She wondered whether Caroline had written the letter with the hope of producing precisely the kind of scene in which Amy had just participated. The phrases were unlike Caroline, who had never confided in her mother, nor, Amy was certain, in her father. She wondered whether Caroline really was sleeping with Frank. Amy put down her glass and walked into the kitchen to fix herself a salad. She left the steaks in the refrigerator; they had never been more than window dressing. Carefully, she chopped tomatoes, onions and celery and mixed a light dressing. Sitting down at the dining room table alone, she ate her salad, nibbling some melba toast with it, and felt at peace. There was no sound from Carlton's den, nor did Amy expect any. She assumed he would drink himself into unconsciousness and probably pass the night in a chair. She hoped so. On the nights that he slept in their room, she often made an excuse, wondering why she bothered, and slept in the guest room. She had never slept in Caroline's room: she avoided entering it as much as possible. The weekly maid cleaned it.

The telephone rang and Amy rose, waited long enough

for the sound to exasperate Carlton, and picked up the receiver. It was, as she had expected, Glory Swimmers.

"What did Carlton say? I'll bet he's high as a kite."

That was probably accurate by now, Amy reflected.

"Would you like to talk to him?"

"I'd love to."

Amy went over to the closed door of the den and knocked lightly.

"What is it?" asked a muffled voice from within, and she wondered if he were crying.

"It's Glory. She wants to talk to you. She wants to know how you feel about Caroline's engagement. Dear."

There was silence for a moment, then the door opened and Carlton presented a face sufficiently ravaged to evoke a smile of surpassing sweetness from his wife.

He picked up the receiver, swallowed, and spoke in tones of desperate jollity.

"Hey, Glory! How about this, eh?"

He listened, and looked faintly green.

"Absolutely. Thrilled. Absolutely. Indeed. You'll be the first to know, Glory. Absolutely. Yeah. Yeah, I guess we do know now why she hasn't been coming home. Great to hear from you, Glory."

He put the receiver down and stood staring at the telephone.

"Dinner?" asked Amy brightly.

He shook his head. "Headache. Think I'll turn in." He looked past her. "Sorry about the . . . steaks."

"That's all right. They'll keep."

He nodded, and turned toward the stairs, and she watched him mount the cream-colored carpeted steps with leaden movements. Standing there quietly, she heard his steps halt outside Caroline's door then the soft click of the handle, and the rage of twenty years swept over Amy, as she recalled other nights when his steps had halted and that door had quietly opened. Her face was stony; she waited until, after a moment or two, she heard the door to Caroline's room click again, and Carlton's heavy footsteps continued along the passageway to their bedroom. Amy began to clear the table, putting away the unused silver and crystal, pouring away the remains of the martini shaker, folding the unused napkin and the linen tablecloth. She felt suddenly drained and tired.

Once she would have gone straight to the kitchen and eaten everything she found in the refrigerator. Now she had learned that emptiness was enough. She looked at the telephone and for a moment wondered what it would have been like if her daughter's engagement had been an occasion for real joy. She realized she could not imagine experiencing joy. All she had to look forward to was vengeance.

12

IT HAD been a long time since Frank suggested to his father that they take a Sunday walk together, and it obviously was no coincidence that he did so on the day after he had brought Caroline to dinner. Mike didn't care. He was delighted that he and his son had found a subject they could agree on. Not even Leslie's amused sarcasm about their both being in love with Franklin's fiancée could diminish the mutual enthusiasm of father and son for Caroline Mitchell. Frank thought she was wonderful because he was in love with her. Mike thought she was wonderful because she seemed to be building a bridge between his son and himself. Leslie found her charming, an a vast improvement on Jill, but Leslie could contain her enthusiasm for any woman who was more attractive than she was. She noted with distaste that Franklin seemed to be wallowing in sentiment to the point that he put his arm around his mother and assured her that now they would have two beautiful women in the family. Leslie gently disengaged herself, retreated into the depths of the *New York Times Book Review*, and said why didn't Franklin take a stroll, since it was such a lovely day? Frank cast her a hurt glance and looked appealingly at his father.

"Dad? How about a walk down around the lake? Give us a chance to talk."

"About guess what," muttered Leslie. Mike winked at his son.

"That's a great idea," he said. "I'd like some fresh air."

"You think Mom's a little jealous?" Frank asked anxiously as they walked down the driveway.

"Maybe a little. She's used to getting all our attention, you know," said his father.

Frank looked unhappy.

"But Caroline was so sweet to her. I mean, she wants so badly for you both to like her, especially since . . . well . . ." He paused uncertainly, and Mike glanced at him, but said nothing.

A light and fragrant wind whipped blossoms past them as they walked toward the grove of trees overlooking the river where Mike used to take Frank fishing. The proximity of the river to the house had been a main reason for Mike's buying it. All his life he had loved to fish, finding solace in sitting peacefully on the bank of a river, only half caring if he caught anything. Leslie had gone fishing with him in the early days of their marriage, but she had done it to please him, not because she took pleasure in sitting and doing nothing except waiting for a tug on her line. Leslie liked to be accomplishing something and she did not consider waiting for fish a constructive pastime. Sensitive to her restlessness, Mike had not minded when she found excuses to stay at home, and had happily gone fishing alone until Frank was old enough to accompany him. He had enjoyed that probably as much as anything in his life, and now he felt a lightening of spirit as his son strolled beside him in the spring sunlight, heading for Mike's favorite spot on the riverbank. As they neared the water, Frank stopped and smiled.

"Boy, this is familiar. Our old fishing hole. We haven't been here for a long time."

"Maybe we should bring Caroline here?" his father suggested, and was rewarded by his son's grateful smile.

"That's a great idea! I wonder if she likes to fish? Well, anyway, we could make it a picnic. Except—" Frank's face clouded—"Mom isn't much on fishing. . . ."

"We could do it as part of a weekend," said Mike tactfully. "Come over here in the afternoon and have dinner later with your mother."

Frank agreed, and flopped down on the grass, watching the gently moving water with an expression of contentment.

"I gather . . . I don't want to pry . . . but I gather Caroline isn't too close to her parents?" Mike asked.

"You're right. As a matter of fact, she doesn't even

like to talk about them. I wouldn't be surprised if she hasn't told them we're engaged. When I suggested their coming here, or my going there to meet them, she just froze on me. I mean really froze. She got very upset."

"Well"—Mike chewed on a blade of grass—"sometimes a wedding brings a family together."

He felt Frank's quick look, but kept his eyes on the river.

"Sometimes, maybe. But I get the feeling with Caroline this is a real estrangement with her people. And she won't even tell me why."

"Better to let her tell you in her own time."

Frank hesitated. "I don't know how Mom's going to take this, but what Caroline wants is a really small wedding."

"Like a civil ceremony?"

"I'm afraid so. And the way Mom was talking last night . . ."

Mike chuckled. "Hell, that's how your mother and I did it—a civil ceremony, I mean."

"But you've got all those fancy wedding pictures—"

"That was the reception, and what we don't usually tell people is that was after the honeymoon! Leslie's parents were so disappointed at not being at the wedding that we let them give us a big party, and everybody got dressed up, and there was a wedding cake—the whole bit. Your mother thought it was silly, but she went along with it. Anyway, that's why I can't see her criticizing Caroline too much for wanting something quiet."

Frank was grinning broadly. "You know Mom never told me that?"

Mike did not say that the latter-day Leslie would have preferred an elaborate wedding. As Frank fell silent, Mike turned and saw his son lying relaxed on the grass, with a thick thatch of fair hair tumbled across his forehead. Even in repose, Frank's thin, handsome face was grave, a reflection of the solemn small boy who had taken his fishing seriously. Mike turned his gaze back toward the river and the trees beyond, thinking that had it not been for Caroline, he and Franklin would not be sitting in the sun on a tranquil Sunday morning. He determined that he would make sure she got taken on as a summer intern at the station. Maybe as an assistant to a producer, or as a reporter? And with those looks, she might try making a couple of tapes, see how she did. He grinned at himself. Next thing, they'd be offering her his job and she'd probably take it. He still had a feeling that there was steel beneath Caroline's sweetness, although if she wanted to make her career in television, she'd probably need it. He wondered idly what it was he had sensed about her. It might be accounted for by a childhood as unhappy as Frank seemed to think it had been. That could produce a certain wary reserve about people. But just now and then, he thought he had glimpsed a look in her eyes at odds with that warm and lovely smile. Mike mentally shook himself. Why was he spending so much time trying to analyze a young woman he had met only once, even if she was going to marry his son?

Observing that Frank seemed to be asleep, Mike lay back and gave himself up to drowsy enjoyment of the hour. He dozed a little, and through his dream floated a slender woman with long, dark hair, veiled in pink, waving to him, smiling at him, stretching out her hand to him. When he took her hand, it was icy, and when he raised his eyes to her face in concern, she was laughing, but she was laughing at him. He found himself following a pink-wreathed wraith who clasped his hand in her cold fingers, drawing him with her, and he followed without question, worried about her hand being so cold, and hearing her wild laughter at his worry. Then she was gone, and he was cold, colder than he had ever been in his life, and quite alone. Mike's eyes flew open, and he saw Frank's face grinning at him, and felt the wind suddenly cold.

"Hey, wake up," said his son. "I think spring just ended. It's starting to rain and I'm freezing."

Mike scrambled to his feet, groggily.

"You were really dead to the world," observed Frank.

"I was dreaming," said Mike, and did not say of whom. He chided himself for dreaming by day or night of Caroline, and put her firmly out of his mind for the rest of the day. By the time they got back to the house, Leslie had prepared brunch, and apparently was repentant of her earlier churlishness. They drank Bloody Marys and laughed a lot, and looked at the old wedding photographs, and it was a good day, Mike thought, for all of them.

*   *   *

As soon as he reached his office on Monday, he telephoned Caroline, having been assured by Frank that she would be waiting for his call.

"She's really excited about it," Frank had said.

Dialing Caroline's number, Mike reflected that Frank had not said a harsh word about the superficialities of television reporting for weeks, presumably since he began seeing Caroline. The voice that answered the telephone did not belong to Caroline, but it identified itself cheerfully.

"Hi, Mr. Hathaway? I recognized your voice. This is Jill Starling."

"Hi, Jill, nice to talk to you again."

Caroline was immediately on the line, her voice low and warm.

"Mr. Hathaway? It's so good of you to call so early."

Mike smiled at the telephone. "Listen, I thought if you were free from class, you could have lunch with me and come over to the station afterward. That way I could introduce you around and you could sort of see how things work."

"That would be wonderful."

"Good. Let's meet at the Coachman at noon."

He was at the restaurant a few minutes early, warmly greeted by the proprietor, who escorted him to his regular corner booth.

"How many, Mr. Hathaway?"

"Two," said Mike. "And this is sort of special, Peter. Franklin just got engaged, and his fiancée is interested in television work, so I'm going to show her around the station this afternoon."

Peter was charmed and said so. Mike noticed he was even more charmed when Caroline walked in a few minutes later. Standing with her dark hair loose on her shoulders, her face vivid, Caroline caught the eye of most of the diners, and Peter hastened to take her under his sleekly tailored wing, presenting her to Mike as though on a plate.

"Franklin is a very lucky young man," announced Peter, producing champagne glasses.

"You look lovely," Mike told her. She was wearing a light, loose, dark red raincoat over a black turtleneck silk sweater and skirt, and her pale skin had a translucent cast. Her eyes lit up at his compliment, and he remembered that she was young, younger than she looked.

"This is a really nice restaurant." She looked around, and returned the smile of Peter, who was assessing her appreciatively.

"I was going to suggest wine, but I think Peter is arriving with champagne."

Caroline laughed. "That's lovely, but I'd better not have much if I'm going over to the station with you. I mean, that isn't the kind of impression I want to create!"

Mike watched her face, watched its play of expression, listened to the vibrant voice, and knew why his son had fallen in love with Caroline. She exuded a certain magic; her personality became a tangible extension of herself. She fascinated him. When she flushed a little and began fidgeting with her glass, he realized he had been staring at her. He raised his glass.

"I seem to be doing this every other day, Caroline."

She smiled and sipped. "You've been very kind, Mr. Hathaway."

He resumed the role of prospective father-in-law, and began to talk about television. She immediately put down her glass, clasped her hands in front of her, and fixed her eyes on his face. Twenty minutes later, he realized he had hardly stopped talking, and Caroline had not moved. He had never encountered a more attentive audience.

"I hope this sort of sets the scene for you," he told her, as their lunch salads arrived.

She nodded emphatically. "I had no idea. You made it so clear. I feel as though I could go to work."

"It's not all that complicated. You just get used to how things work."

"How long have you been doing it?"

"A long time—about the time Franklin was born."

"Really?" Her eyes became dark pools of wonder, and Mike found himself telling her how he had wound up in television, how he felt about his work, and how his family felt about it—something he could not recall admitting to anyone before. Abruptly, he stopped, ate some salad, and laughed.

"You could get anything out of anybody, Caroline."

"Oh, no. It's just that I'm so interested. I mean, I've

watched you on the news so long, and in that job, you know, it's really like having someone come into your bedroom. Sort of."

She laughed, embarrassed, and Mike swallowed the response he would have made to anyone else. He glanced at his watch, and signaled to Peter.

"We should be getting over there, Caroline."

Escorting Caroline around the station proved to be even more enjoyable than Mike had expected. He knew what the staff gossip mill would assume as soon as he walked into his office with someone who looked like Caroline Mitchell, and he was entertained by the disappointed reaction to the disclosure that she was Frank's fiancée. Joe Moynihan, the news director, was one of the first to meet her, and responded in what Mike was beginning to view as a predictable manner by being admiring, polite, and intrigued.

Caroline was interested in everybody and everything, and Mike was pleased to note that she used what he had told her at the Coachman to ask intelligent questions about station procedures. He turned her over to an associate director and a tapes editor while he went to a scheduling conference, and from the glassed-in booth, he could see Caroline's dark head bobbing amidst a group apparently dedicated to giving her a crash course in television. After the tentative schedule for the newscast had been discussed, Mike stayed behind in Moynihan's office for a few minutes.

"Got something else, Mike?" asked the news director.

"We still taking on any summer interns this year?"

Moynihan's eyes flickered to Caroline, and he grinned. "You got somebody in mind?"

"Well, if we haven't settled on someone, I think she might be useful. Even if she is going to marry my son."

Moynihan studied what he could see of Caroline for a moment and looked reflective.

"We were planning on a couple of interns and we've got one. Caroline might be a thought." He looked at Mike quizzically. "Is it possible for you to be objective about her?"

"Try to."

"We might let her try out as an intern and if it works,

she might do a little street reporting. She's got terrific looks, and I'd like to see if she's got anything else."

Mike nodded. "Sounds great to me. And if it doesn't work out, Joe—"

"Don't worry," said Moynihan. "I'm not going to hire a turkey just because she's a ringer for Jackie Onassis and she's going to marry your son."

"Good."

"Have her come in and talk to me before she leaves, will you?"

Mike nodded again, and strolled back to his office. Scanning the cable-strung newsroom, he could see Caroline at the far end, talking animatedly to Alice Martinsen, a co-anchor of the five o'clock news. Mike observed that Alice, nicknamed "Alice Malice" by her critics, because of her inclination to be waspish under pressure, appeared receptive to Caroline's overtures. She had taken the younger woman over to her office and appeared to be explaining something to her. Caroline was a model of attentiveness, and Mike decided there was little more he could do to help. He suspected that Caroline probably didn't need more than a small push to accomplish an eighty-yard dash, and marveled gently at that kind of drive. Most of what Mike had accomplished, he had not really sought, which gave him a less competitive edge than some of his colleagues, but also gave him a quality of relaxation on the air that kept the station's ratings well above those of its competitors.

Sliding into his chair and flipping on his computer, Mike scanned the story schedule already put together by the station's editors, inserted a few phrases of his own, and checked them out with the writers. He read through wire-service copy, attended another prenewscast meeting with Moynihan and the two associate directors, and watched the five o'clock show. Shortly after it, Del Kelly, one of the associate directors, brought Caroline back to Mike's office. She was bright-eyed.

"Alice let me come into the studio to watch her, and she showed me how the teleprompter works, and she told me about how she'd made this awful mistake one day when she thought the mike was off and it wasn't. . . ."

Mike grinned, recalling that that was the time Alice had told a producer precisely what she thought of his

talents and his ancestry and inadvertently had passed on
those opinions to anyone who happened to be watching
television in the area at the time.

"Having a good time?" It was an unnecessary question, judging from Caroline's appearance.

"Mr. Hathaway, could I watch your show in the studio
too?"

Suddenly, she reminded Mike of a small child asking
for an ice cream cone. It was as though her personality
was split between her childhood and a totally adult concept of what she needed to say and do to get what she
wanted.

"Sure you can," he told her. "And since you're going
to be in the family, I think you can start calling me Mike.
Unless you want to call me Dad?"

The wide-eyed child instantly was transformed into a
remote young woman, and Mike could have bitten his
tongue.

"I'd like to call you Mike, if I may."

"You may." He put an arm casually across her shoulder as they moved toward the door of his office, and this
time, there was no doubt that she slipped away from his
touch. Mike sighed and held the door for her. At least
she didn't seem to take that as an insult.

In the studio, during commercial breaks, he was conscious of her intent gaze, saw her murmured questions to
producers and cameramen. She seemed utterly at ease
asking questions of strangers in a manner that endeared
her to them. It was the same knack she used to get
information of a more personal nature, Mike reflected.
After the show, she was waiting for him, careful not to
thrust herself forward, but standing where he could see
her. Not that she was easy to ignore, from any angle, he
thought.

"Ready to go home?"

"I called Frank and he's going to be a while. So I
thought I'd go back to the apartment and sort of collate
my notes on this."

"Some of us stop by for a drink on the way home; I'm
sure everyody'd be happy to have you come along,
Caroline."

She hesitated. "I'd really like to, but I want to write
some of this down while it's fresh in my mind. It—it's my

way of committing things to memory. That way I don't forget so quickly. And I expect Frank'll be along shortly. But thank you so much."

"Anytime. There'll be plenty of time when you come to work here—" Mike saw her startled look and laughed. "My God, haven't you talked to Moynihan yet? I thought you had."

She shook her head, her expression tense. This really matters to her, he thought.

"Moynihan wanted to talk to you about interning. Might even have you do a little reporting, if things work out. But you should go over and talk to him now."

Her smile seemed about to split her face. Even her hair seemed to glow. She took a step forward, and Mike thought for an instant she was going to hug him, but he hoped she wouldn't, given the circumstances.

"Oh Mike," she said, and her voice carried. "Thank you."

He saw two sets of neighboring heads swivel, and he sighed. There went his reputation for objectivity. The hell with it, he decided, and took Caroline's arm to lead her back to the newsroom and Joe Moynihan.

13

WHEN THEY talked about Caroline Mitchell's tryout at KRT-WNN later, it was with a mixture of awe and puzzlement. As Joe Moynihan said, it was rare when someone that inexperienced and that young did so many things right. She came in early, stayed late, worked hard, listened to what she was told, and clearly was anxious to learn. Mike Hathaway made a point of staying away from Caroline when she was at the station, lest she be tarred with the charge of favoritism, and Caroline asked for no favors. What astonished everyone was that her efforts to please Alice Martinsen succeeded to the point that "Alice Malice" took a liking to the younger woman and rarely snapped at her, even offered advice in a friendly tone instead of implying that only a fool would have to be told such a thing. Rudy Colling, the five o'clock co-anchor, was equally taken with Caroline, patiently coaching her in the tricks of keeping track of the teleprompter, the video, and the stream of miscellaneous instructions flowing into commentator's ear from his earpiece.

"She's such a great listener. She makes you feel like you're the brightest thing on earth when you're talking to her," associate producer Del Kelly told Mike. Kelly was more than a little infatuated with Caroline, but her response to him was so much that of a pupil to a teacher that he despaired of competing with Frank Hathaway. Moynihan and Eric Kriss, the general manager of the station, contemplated Caroline at first with amusement, then with increasing interest, especially when she performed well in some minor reporting assignments.

"You been training her?" Moynihan asked Mike.

Mike shook his head and laughed. "No, but just about everybody else has, I gather."

"She did real well on that stand-up last night. Voice was pretty good; still a little breathy, but she's good on camera. Real presence."

Moynihan kept a closer eye on Caroline than she realized, and, taking into account her inexperience, was not displeased by her performance. She was a quick study, rarely made the same mistake twice, and took criticism gracefully. Her memory was not all it might have been, and sometimes Moynihan and Kelly wondered why she didn't retain information to which she had given her apparently undivided attention twenty-four hours earlier. But she was exceptionally pleasant to work with, her voice emphasis improved daily, and on those occasions she had a chance to be on camera, she was not only at ease but unexpectedly authoritative.

"She might be a natural," said Kriss hopefully, "but let's wait and see how it goes. And make sure she gets told when she's screwed up. That's what she needs most right now."

Mike Hathaway, who had more or less stumbled into a happy career style, could never have taught Caroline what she learned from Moynihan. Mike did not know what Moynihan knew, had never needed to know. His ratings value lay in his personality, not in his writing skill or his command of domestic and foreign affairs. Mike had mastered the basic mechanics of anchoring, and because he was so popular with viewers, the station was willing to provide the journalistic reinforcement he needed.

Caroline was an egg that Joe Moynihan thought might be hatched into an exceedingly glamorous bird, and as the months wore on and Caroline spent more and more of her time at the station, Moynihan and Kriss became more sanguine about her potential. They suggested casually that she might try recording some tapes, to get an idea of her progress, and see where she was making her mistakes, as Moynihan told her. What would she do with such tapes? Caroline asked Mike. He concealed his pleased surprise at Moynihan's suggestion and said it was standard procedure for somebody new in the business to send out tapes to get reaction from television consultants, who kept talent banks of such material.

"This is important, isn't it?" she asked anxiously.

He nodded. "This is important, Caroline. If you do

well on those tapes, it can mean a lot to what happens to you."

She did the tapes, agonizing over them, calling on her friends at the station for help. She snapped at Jill and quarreled with Frank, who said he thought she was becoming hysterical about nothing.

"This is very important," Caroline told him. "Your father says so."

"He would," retorted her fiancé. "Dad's been on the boob tube so long, I sometimes think his values are shot."

"That's unkind and untrue," said Caroline coldly.

"When did you become an authority on my father? Although he certainly sees more of you than I do."

"You're being unreasonable, Frankie," said Caroline, putting her arm around him in an attempt to mollify him. Frank pulled back and glared at her.

"All you think about is that damned station, Caroline. You've been a different person since you started working there."

Caroline took his hand. "No, I'm not," she assured him. "I'm just trying to do well. I want you to be proud of me; isn't that all right?"

"I was proud of you before you became obsessed with camera angles and stand-ups and voice-overs and natural sound. I'm sorry, Caroline, but it's like you've gone crazy over this stuff. You couldn't even come to Mom's dinner party last weekend because of that dumb rally."

"You covered the rally, too," she pointed out.

"Yes, but I wrote the story and was through by dinnertime. You were at the station until nearly midnight. Or I assume that's where you were."

Caroline turned away. "I'll talk to you when you feel better."

She left him staring moodily at the dregs of a cup of coffee, and within ten minutes, she was no longer thinking about their quarrel or Frank.

At the station, she hung around Joe Moynihan's office, but he was in meetings and showed no sign of wanting to sit down and discuss his newest employee's career prospects. She buttonholed Del Kelly, who patted her arm reassuringly and said he was sure her tapes were fine, but he hadn't had time to look at them. She didn't dare bother Eric Kriss, so she decided to break her office-hours rule and ask Mike, who was sitting with his feet up beside his computer, reading the sports news. He looked up and smiled at her.

"Hey there, Caroline. What're you up to today?"

"Mike"—she had no time for platitudes—"have you seen my tapes?"

"Uh huh."

She looked at him expectantly. Mike sighed. He didn't want to be caught in the middle of this. She had to learn to get her information from Moynihan and not come running to him because she was engaged to Frank.

"You have to talk to Joe," he said gently but firmly.

"But—" Caroline looked so desperate that he relented a little.

"Joe and Eric looked at them and they'll talk to you about them when they get time. Come on, Caroline, settle down. The networks aren't calling yet."

She looked sheepish. "I know, I know I'm being childish. But I worked so hard on those tapes. . . ."

"I know you did, I know you did. But try to see this from my perspective, Caroline. I can't get too involved in what you're doing here, or it'll damage your chances. I mean, I'm sort of prejudiced where you're concerned, you know."

She looked worried. "I know the thing with Frank makes it awkward for you—"

Mike's eyebrows rose slightly. "The 'thing with Frank,' as you call it, isn't what I'm talking about."

She studied his face. "I don't understand."

"Well, quite apart from Frank, I'm very fond of you, Caroline, and I want to keep our friendship separate from work. I'm happy to talk with you or advise you, but since you got here, I've been trying to avoid any kind of nepotism. I'm not saying I won't discuss your tapes with you, for God's sake. I'm saying you have to get the word from Moynihan or Kriss first. Okay?"

His voice held faint exasperation, the first time that Caroline could recall hearing that from him, and she thought My God, I've managed to get on the wrong side of Frank *and* his father in the same day.

"Of course you're right," she said in a subdued tone, and turned to leave the office. Watching the slender neck droop, Mike felt sudden tenderness.

"Buy you a drink later?" he offered.

She turned her head and rewarded him with a small smile.

As Mike walked into his office after the show, his telephone was ringing.

"How about that drink?"

He smiled at the jubilation in her voice. "Meet me at the front door."

Sitting on the edge of her chair in the bar, Caroline scarcely touched her white wine. While Mike leisurely consumed one Scotch, she talked nonstop about what Moynihan and Kriss had said about her tapes. Should she be encouraged? What did he think? Now could he tell her what he thought? She thought they were pretty enthusiastic. Was that what they had told him?

Mike finally held up a hand, which the waiter translated as a call for another drink.

"Slow down, honey, will you? I think you've got reason to be pleased. For the length of time you've been at the station, those tapes are impressive. That's what they told me, and I agree with them. That does not mean you've suddenly become a star, but it does mean you show real promise. I think that's the appropriate term."

He accepted his second drink.

Caroline sipped some of her wine, closed her eyes blissfully, and put her head back on the black leather upholstered chair. Mike looked at the pure line of her neck and jaw, the happy tilt of the full red lips, and wanted to kiss her. That was the first time he had admitted to himself that he didn't want to be Caroline's father-in-law, he wanted to be her lover. And it wasn't just the Scotch. He realized bitterly that he was tired of playing what he had come to think of as "the Daddy game." Not that he could or would do anything to change the rules of that game. He was already guilt stricken by the kind of thoughts he had been entertaining about Caroline since the first time he met her, his son's wife, more or less. What an awful thing he was thinking. On the other hand, he reflected, had he met her before Franklin had, his unbroken record of fidelity to Leslie most likely would have been shattered. He stared into his

Scotch, then looked back at Caroline. She was watching him with warm and luminous eyes.

"Can I have another glass of wine?"

Mike signaled the hovering waiter and ordered the wine, savoring a certain happy recklessness.

"You seeing Frank tonight?"

Caroline's face clouded slightly. "We had a fight. I don't think he's talking to me."

Mike concealed elation. "About what? If I may ask."

"Of course you may. It was silly, anyway. He said I was paying too much attention to television and . . . well he was nasty. And I guess I shouldn't have mentioned you."

"How did I get into it?"

"He said something about television and your values, and I disagreed with him. That made him mad."

"I expect it did," said Mike, as the waiter brought more wine for Caroline. "But I appreciate your defending me. I'm afraid Franklin isn't too high on television as a means of communication."

"He's so condescending about it," Caroline said with exasperation.

"Tell me about it," said Frank's father, and they laughed together, comfortably.

Leaning forward, Mike took Caroline's hand lightly and was pleased by the responsive pressure of her fingers.

"I have an idea. Let's us go and have a little dinner to celebrate your tapes, and maybe by the time you get home, Franklin will have cooled off."

"That's a wonderful idea," said Caroline, "and you know what? I don't even care if he's cooled off."

They drove to a small, expensive restaurant outside the city, ate veal *piccata* and drank red wine. By the time they had finished the bottle, Caroline was a little drunk and Mike was amiably mellow, and they talked easily to each other. Mike told stories and talked about getting started in television. Caroline talked about what she wanted to do, and listened avidly to what he told her. They looked into each other's eyes and did not mention Frank, and when they left the restaurant, they went to its adjoining little dark bar for Irish coffee. Caroline licked the cream off the top of the mixture and reminded Mike of a coquettish kitten as he leaned over to remove a dab of cream from her chin and stroke her cheek at the same time. They did not leave the bar until it closed, and Caroline clung to Mike's arm as they walked to his car.

"Are you falling down or being affectionate?" he teased her. She laughed up at him, and he stopped there in the parking lot and kissed her.

Mike went on kissing her after they got into the car and he was pleased and a little surprised by the warmth of her response. So was Caroline. She had not gone to bed with Frank, which was another source of strain between them, because she didn't want to and it didn't matter to her. That it mattered to Frank didn't trouble her too much. But she had come to enjoy being kissed and caressed. Frank had done that much for her, and she was grateful to him. She simply had no desire to take the next step of sleeping with him, perhaps because Frank did not interest her that much. He had been her brother, and that was how she continued to see him. She had agreed to marry him mostly so that she could continue a cozy and comfortable friendship. She also did not care whether she never slept with a man again. She supposed she would, and she expected she would get used to it, as she had when she was a child, but she did not expect to enjoy it. Too many demons still haunted the darkness at the back of her mind. But she found Mike exciting. He was handsome, easygoing, reasonably sophisticated, and he was doing for a living what she wanted to do, and doing it well. Mike flattered her and petted her and made her laugh, and he never lectured her on her responsibility to society. He was also considerably more expert in his technique than Frank, and even when his hands began to move on her body, Caroline found the sensation pleasurable.

It was Mike who slowly, reluctantly, pulled back, although he kept his hand tangled in the thick dark hair at the back of her head so that he could hold her face close to his.

"What are we going to do?" he murmured.

Caroline's half-closed eyes opened wide. "About what?"

"Us."

A small frown appeared on her smooth forehead. "What is there to do?"

Mike regarded her quizzically. "You don't see any problems?"

"You mean Frank."

"I mean Frank."

Caroline sighed and was silent for a long time. Mike smoothed her hair away from her face and waited.

"I'm not going to marry Frank," she said at last. Her voice was unemotional, almost flat.

"Does he know that?"

"It's been pretty obvious we aren't getting along."

"So where does that leave us?"

Caroline raised her face to him. "I don't know, Mike. Where does that leave us?"

He kissed the top of her head.

"My God, what a mess. You're my son's fiancée and I'm"—he had been about to say "old enough to be your father" when he abruptly recalled her reaction to references to her parents—"years older than you."

Caroline giggled. "Anything else?"

"I'm also married."

She smiled a Cheshire-cat smile. "I know. I've met her. My once and future mother-in-law."

Mike winced a little. "Jesus."

Caroline's face became serious. "Listen. We can just forget this happened. I mean, you've got to think about your career, and I've got to think of—"

Mike shook her. "Always thinking, aren't you?"

"You don't want me to forget my career, do you?"

"Hell, no." Mike was laughing. "After all the effort KRT's put into you, we've got quite a bit invested in Caroline. You're a team effort!"

She snuggled against him.

"It'll work out, darling," he told her, and Caroline nodded comfortably, burrowing her head into his shoulder.

"Mmmmmm," she said.

It was almost dawn when she tiptoed into the bedroom where Jill was snoring gently. Hearing the soft movement, Jill stirred, muttered, and opened an eye.

"Caroline?" She roused crossly. "Frank's been calling all night, it seems like, and I might as well have slept beside the phone."

"I'm sorry."

Jill yawned hugely. "It's none of my business, but . . ."

Caroline groaned. "It isn't, but I need somebody to talk to."

Jill waited, noting the wreckage of Caroline's usually immaculate appearance. Her hair was a black tangle, her eye makeup seemed to have collided with her cheek blusher, and her blouse was partly unbuttoned. Caroline also seemed entirely unaware of what she looked like.

"I've got a problem," she announced.

Jill propped her pillow behind her head and waited.

"I don't think I'm going to marry Frank."

Jill restrained herself from saying she had suspected for months that Caroline was not going to marry Frank. Not only were wedding plans never mentioned, neither was Frank, except on rare occasions.

"You don't seem surprised," said Caroline.

"I'm not. I think all you're really interested in right now is KRT, and I can't imagine that's sitting well with old Frank."

"That's true, but it's not just that. It's—well, it's more complicated than that."

Jill realized gloomily that the sound she was hearing was that of birds chirping to announce a new day, and she tried to rub the sandpaper out of her eyes.

"You mean you've met somebody else?"

"Sort of."

Jill suddenly became irritable. Why was she lying here at dawn listening to her roommate babble about a new boyfriend when they could discuss the whole thing at a civilized hour? She never woke Caroline up with a recitation of her personal life—not that Caroline showed any interest in it. In fact, Caroline showed little interest in anything that did not affect her.

"Look," said Jill. "I've got a test tomorrow, I mean today. Why don't you go wash your face and get some sleep, and we'll talk about it later."

Caroline looked at her reproachfully. "You don't understand," she said in a hurt voice. "I have a real problem."

Jill raised her head from the pillow into which she had just dug it.

"A new boyfriend doesn't necessarily mean a problem, even if you are technically engaged to someone else, for heaven's sake. What happened, did you discover the joy of sex?"

She waited for an outburst, but none came, and Jill succumbed to rising curiosity.

"Who is it, anyway? Don't wake me in the middle of the night and make me drag out of you what you want to tell me."

"It's Mike," said Caroline, and began to undress.

"Mike, as in Frank's father?"

Jill took Caroline's silence as assent.

"My God," she said with feeling.

Caroline fumbled with her pajamas.

"It's just that it'll be so awkward at the station. I mean, a scandal would be awful for me right now, especially when things are starting to go well. Did I tell you Moynihan really liked my tapes? And I'm going to send them out to some consultants."

Jill interrupted her. "I'd think it'd be awkward for Frank too. Not to mention Frank's mother."

Caroline slid into bed, ignoring her usual routine of hairbrushing and bathing.

"I expect so," she said disinterestedly. "But I'm really worried about what might happen at the station. Jill"
—her voice became urgent—"promise you won't tell anyone about this."

Jill snorted. "You seriously think this'll stay a secret?"

There was a deep sigh from the occupant of the other bed. "I just don't want trouble at KRT. I'm sure Mike feels the same way."

"Frank isn't stupid."

"I know. And I'm sorry about Frank. I just can't help it. Anyway, he hasn't been very supportive lately."

"And Mike has."

"Yes, he has. He's been unbelievably helpful to me. I couldn't have gotten anywhere without him."

"And that's the key to your heart, isn't it?"

14

FRANK HATHAWAY called at seven in the morning. Mike Hathaway called at eight. Caroline ignored the insistent shrilling in the hall, and when a furious Jill got up and answered the phone, Caroline refused to get out of bed.

"Tell him I'll call back. This is a ridiculous hour," she said, when told that Frank was on the line, and she pulled a pillow over her head.

Jill wrenched the pillow away. "Go answer that damned phone. I've had enough of this nonsense," she said in a tone so sharp that Caroline blinked offendedly and groped her way to the telephone. Two minutes later she was back in bed.

"I told him I was too exhausted to talk now."

"Jesus," said Jill.

When Mike called an hour later, Jill was in the shower. When she emerged, the telephone was still ringing and Caroline was buried beneath two pillows.

"She'll be right with you," Jill shouted at a startled Mike Hathaway, and dripped her way back to the room to rip pillows and blankets off Caroline.

"I am not your answering service," she snarled, and began pulling clothes out of her closet regardless of color or coordination. Caroline stayed on the phone for twenty minutes and came back looking subdued. Jill ignored her, yanking a brush through her hair, slamming drawers, and slapping books together. When the phone rang again, Jill made no move to answer it, and Caroline, still in her robe, scurried down the hall. A moment later she reappeared.

"It's for you. It's Tom," she said meekly. Jill tried to remind herself none of this was Tom's fault.

"Hi," she said.

"What's wrong?" asked Tom.

Jill smiled in spite of herself. "How can you tell that much from 'Hi'?"

"You sound as though you have a mouthful of nails."

"I didn't get much sleep."

"How come? Last I talked to you, you were dug into the books and set to go to bed early."

"That was B.C. Before Caroline."

Tom laughed. "Are you going to be up for dinner after all this?"

"God yes. If I don't I'll probably have to play Mother Superior to Caroline."

"Bring her along," said Tom wickedly, and chuckled as Jill swore at him.

She felt better as she hung up and went back to pick up her sweater and books. Caroline was sitting at the window, still tousled. She looked up as Jill came in.

"Listen, I'm sorry. I didn't mean to ruin your sleep and make a fool of myself."

"You don't make a fool of yourself," said Jill, "you make fools of other people."

She left before she had time to regret her words, because she knew that Caroline would eventually explain how none of this was her fault and Jill would wind up feeling she had been cruel to a child.

And Caroline barely heard Jill's caustic comment. Jill always simmered down, and if she didn't, Caroline would explain and apologize, if necessary. But Caroline was having the kind of morning when even Caroline in the mirror was of little help. For one thing, she had never before seen Caroline in the mirror with last night's makeup still smeared on her face and her hair looking as though it had been in a wind machine. Caroline sat down, brushed her hair, cleaned her face with cream, and contemplated her reflection with more tranquillity.

"I have to call Frank back," she told Caroline in the mirror. "But I have to be very calm and very gentle. I have to look as if I am really upset."

She drew her brows together, let her mouth droop, and decided not to wear any blusher. Her eyes were faintly shadowed, and that was the right look. She had to look as if she were as upset as she anticipated he would be. Mike had been warm and loving on the phone, but he had made it clear she had to get things straightened out with his son. He obviously felt guilty about it all, which Caroline thought was unnecessary, but she knew better than to say that. It was the kind of situation she disliked most, where only she could carry out a disagreeable task. What she really wanted to do was go back to bed. She thought about it, then yawned and stretched and headed for the bathroom. Half an hour later, she was blow-drying her hair and trying to decide between blue and green pants when the phone rang again. As she had feared, it was Frank, tenser than ever.

"We have to talk, Caroline."

She sighed. "We could have coffee. I have a class and then I have to be at the station."

"I'll meet you in twenty minutes." She opened her mouth to protest, but he had hung up.

Disconsolately, she poked at the blue and green pants and pushed them both aside. She didn't feel cheerful blue or green, she felt black. She pulled on a black denim skirt and her favorite black silk turtleneck sweater, and tied a pink wool sweater around her shoulders. Inspecting her face, she noted with satisfaction that a combination of makeup and excitement had erased nearly all the traces of a hectic night. Her eyes were faintly shadowed, but she decided that made her look more dramatic. She picked up her purse and left with a light step. She had to talk to Frank, but then she would see Mike.

The meeting with Frank was as bad as Caroline had thought it would be. They met in the same café where he had first taken her to lunch, and she assumed that it was deliberate. Why did Frank always have to make her feel bad? She tried to be warm and friendly, kissing him on the cheek when she met him, and noticed that he was about as receptive as the statue of a Civil War general on the campus outside.

"I tried to reach you most of last night," he said. Caroline knew this was her cue for repentance and conciliation.

"I know," she said. "I got home late."

Frank waited, and she sipped her coffee and avoided the hurt blue gaze.

"Is that all?"

She went on sipping her coffee. "I guess so."

Frank was staring at her now, increduously. "Caroline," he said, "we're supposed to be getting married."

She was silent.

"Aren't we?"

"Frank," said Caroline. "Maybe we should just be friends for a while? I mean, we don't seem to get along as well now, and I have to spend so much time at the station, and that upsets you. I mean, why don't we just go back to the way we were? I mean for a while, anyway, until we get things sorted out."

She felt rather than saw him stiffen, and when she stole a glance, his face had hardened and his eyes were angry.

"Where were you last night?"

"Frank—please. Don't let's fight. I mean, we used to be such good friends."

"You were with someone else, weren't you?"

She was silent.

"I can't believe how much you've changed," he said slowly.

Caroline played with the snap on her purse. "I haven't changed, really," she told him.

"That makes it worse. I guess I didn't really know you."

"We're beginning to sound like a letter to Dear Abby," said Caroline tartly.

Frank was stung, as she knew he would be. He hated being compared to any stereotype. With relief, she saw him dig into his pocket for money to pay for their coffees. She would have offered to contribute, as she often had, except she was certain that on this occasion he would take it as an insult. She watched as he figured the tip; he was one of the few people she knew who calculated everything to the nearest penny. Mike tipped lavishly and casually. She looked at Frank and wondered what his reaction would be if she told him whom she had been with. She shivered a little, and Frank glanced quickly at her. Once he would have been instantly concerned, tucking her sweater around her shoulders. Now she saw his eyes, recollecting, grow bleak.

She stood up, searching for something to say that would not deepen his anger. Caroline hated scenes. It was always possible to block out the unpleasant, if you tried hard enough. That was something she knew about. You couldn't get anything done any other way. And she really did want to go on being friends with Frank. She couldn't understand why he was being so stony and difficult.

"I'll see you again soon?" She looked up at him appealingly, warmly.

Frank looked at her despairingly. "Not for a while, Caroline."

He stood for a moment as though disoriented, then turned and walked out of the café, leaving her standing there. Caroline picked up her purse and smiled nervously at the waitress, who had been an interested observer. Outside she hesitated, pulling her sweater around her against a crisp breeze. In the distance she could see Frank's rigidly erect figure walking quickly and determinedly, although she suspected he had no firm idea of where he was going. She felt adrift, abandoned, and suddenly resented Frank's failure to understand. She had been reasonable and honest. And she wasn't saying they couldn't be friends. She wanted to be friends. It was Frank who was being cruel, who was making her unhappy, and Caroline didn't want to be unhappy. She wouldn't let him make her unhappy.

Impulsively, she walked to the nearest telephone kiosk and telephoned Mike's extension at the station. He picked up the receiver on the first ring, as though he'd been waiting for her, she thought. The thought pleased her.

"Caroline? Darling—" She noticed his voice dropped discreetly on the "darling." "Are you all right?"

Caroline's voice wavered a little. "I guess so. I just talked to Frank."

She heard Mike take a sharp breath. "And?"

"I said we should just be friends for a while."

"I'll bet that went over well."

"He isn't speaking to me, I don't think. And that's so unfair, Mike. I really do want to be friends with him. He was my best friend!"

"It's hard for him too, you know."

"But I was making it so easy for him."

Mike sighed. It was one of those moments when he was reminded that Caroline was afflicted by tunnel vision.

"I'm sure you felt you were."

Caroline looked at the receiver with faint irritation. Whose side was he on?

"He asked who I was with last night."

"Did you tell him?"

"Of course not."

This time, Mike's sigh was heavier. "It's going to be hard to keep anything a secret between the campus and the station and the fact that everyone knows me here."

"But they don't really know me," said Caroline with faint regret in her voice.

"But they will," said Mike firmly, and for the first time that morning, her spirits lifted.

"By the way," he said in a more businesslike tone, "some of the shakeups that happened in the network are filtering down to the affiliates, apparently. I may have to go to New York to talk to the new president of WNN."

"Really?" Caroline was all attention. "Who is it?"

"Mellenkoff. He's apparently Joel Eliass's boy, and I understand he's very tough. They're on a ratings rampage, and they're also looking around for new talent. So maybe your tapes will do you some good."

Caroline was almost dancing with excitement.

"Listen, remember I told you I met Martha Vogel, the WNN correspondent, when she gave a speech here? Well, she was flying out to meet Mellenkoff that night. He's her special friend."

"I'd heard that on the grapevine. Goes back quite a way, I understand. I think it was Mellenkoff gave Martha Vogel her first chance at the network in Washington. He was bureau chief of the station then. But since the Eliass takeover, Mellenkoff's been the man to watch. And apparently it's paid off for him. He and Eliass sound like two of a kind, from what I hear."

"Martha said he was very, very good."

"May well be. He's been playing hatchet man for Eliass around the country, firing and hiring. Mostly firing."

"Why do you have to go see him?"

"He's not to come see me. I'm pretty far down the pole in network terms, honey. But they're apparently having sort of a get-together of anchors and types like that, running us in and out on a conveyor belt to see if the network is interested in us. And I assume they've taken a hard look at the ratings."

"You're not in trouble, Mike?"

"Not as far as I know, which isn't very far in this kind of situation. The ratings are good, and we're still ahead of the competition. But you never can tell with a new team, especially one that is going to get exactly what it wants, as I think is the case here. Between you and me, I think Alice could be in trouble at KRT."

"Why? I thought she was popular."

"She's been dropping lately. And she's so damned difficult to get along with. I mean, I know she's nice to you, but you're the exception. She's hell for everybody else, from the camera crews to the producers and directors. And she's got a temper that won't quit. That's a bad reputation to get, because it means if things don't go well here, she might have trouble other places."

"Is she going to New York, too?"

"I don't know. I don't even know that I'm going. Mellenkoff was just named president day before yesterday, although a lot of people seemed to think it was coming."

"It's so exciting."

"It's a little nerve-racking too."

Caroline looked at her watch. "I have to get to class. Will I see you later?"

His voice softened. "I certainly hope so. At least we can have a drink. I . . . ah, may have to get home reasonably early."

"Leslie?"

"I think she's curious. I don't know how much she cares, frankly, but it's a situation that has to be dealt with."

"Why?"

"What d'you mean 'why'?"

"Well, why tell her anything? I mean it . . . it's not as if you're moving out or anything. And it'll make things so . . . so unpleasant."

"Caroline," said Mike patiently, "sometimes things are unpleasant, whether you like it or not. As you've just found out with Franklin. And if we're going to see each other, obviously it will cause problems, and maybe changes."

"Mike," said Caroline tautly, "please don't do anything because of me. I mean, I don't want you to. It'll be awful. And you don't need to."

"It's not because of you. Well, not entirely. I haven't been exactly blissful at home for a long time, Caroline, and that's got nothing to do with you. The only thing I'm really sorry about is the business with Franklin. God knows, he and I have gotten along better since he got engaged to you, and I suppose that's over, too."

Caroline fidgeted. "Let's not worry about it for a bit," she suggested.

"That sounds like you. All right, we'll talk later. Go on to your class."

She put the receiver down and walked away slowly. What Mike had told her about the changes at WNN had set her mind churning. She wondered about sending her tapes to Mellenkoff. Maybe not; she would have to ask Mike. But he'd said they were looking for new talent, and you never knew. If only she could go to New York with Mike, then she could meet Mellenkoff in a way he'd notice her. But she couldn't very well show up as Mike's traveling companion. There was still Leslie to take into consideration. Although—Caroline's mind was racing and twisting—Mike had been saying how he hadn't been happy with Leslie for a long time. Maybe she should encourage him to leave, because that way there would be nothing to stop him from taking her with him to New York. On the other hand, it would be better if she could arrange it herself somehow. Except she didn't know Mellenkoff, and from what Mike had said, it would be difficult to fool him. She had to be there for a legitimate reason. Wanting to see him was all right, but showing up as Mike Hathaway's girl friend was different. It could put her in an unfavorable light, make them think she was just a groupie.

It had begun to rain lightly, but Caroline walked on under the trees, absorbed in her thoughts. She was convinced that a New York opportunity could be important to her, far more important than getting to a communications class.

There had to be a way, and abruptly Caroline thought of one—Martha Vogel. She had been so nice, so helpful. Caroline had been watching her as often as possible on television, and although Martha's style was not hers, she was in awe of the self-possession and assurance exuded by the older woman. One of the rare times Caroline had dared to differ with Alice Martinsen had been when Alice criticized Martha for being so patronizing to politicians.

"I think she offers a different perspective," Caroline had volunteered. Alice had cast a scornful glance on her.

"You don't let the assholes let you know you think they're assholes. That's bad office politics," she said.

"I don't think Martha plays office politics."

"What makes you such an authority on Martha Vogel?" Alice had asked.

Caroline had backed off. She could not afford to antagonize Alice, who could and did make life miserable for those who took issue with her, on topics ranging from a camera angle to the angle of a story.

"I just met her once. She seemed nice," Caroline had murmured.

"She isn't going to be any help to you, my dear," said Alice waspishly. "Wasn't for Mellenkoff, she wouldn't be on the air as much as she is."

"You don't think she's good?" asked Caroline meekly.

"She's a wire-service hack who got into television because of her boyfriend—that's what I think." Alice was living up to her nickname, and Caroline was silent. Now she wondered if Mike was right that Alice could be facing problems of her own.

Alice Martinsen was a striking, attractive woman of thirty-seven who had climbed the ladder from weather woman to general news reporter to talk show host to anchor, and when she reached anchor, all of the anger and resentment pent up during previous years apparently had spilled over. She had become temperamental, quick-tempered, argumentative, and downright abusive with anyone beneath the level of associate director. She had fought her way through her last contract negotiations and won only because her counterpart in the competing station was so good that viewers still watching KRT were liable to switch if Alice disappeared. But since then, the other anchor had been lured to Chicago; Alice's bargaining position was weaker. There was also the matter of the new management. Eric Kriss had decided that the thing to do with Alice was bide his time. He too had access to the network, and when he deemed it appropriate, he planned to take advantage of it.

Meantime, Alice cut her devastating daily swathe through the studio, and even Rudy Colling, her easygoing co-anchor, often was hard put to hold his tongue in the face of her tirades. Alice had been of considerable help to Caroline, perhaps seeing in her a younger Alice, and Caroline had been grateful. But she was not so grateful that she was prepared to accept Alice's opinions without question. Especially on Martha Vogel. Alice might be right about Martha's style; she knew more about that than Caroline did. But the fact remained that Martha was close to Mellenkoff, and that might be the key to success at WNN nowadays. Caroline mounted the steps to her apartment building, having given up on even making a pass at attending class, and nodded to herself. Martha could get her to Mellenkoff. She opened the door to the room she shared with Jill and sat down at the window, shaking raindrops off her pink sweater. Suddenly she smiled and reached into a drawer of the desk for writing paper. The simplest thing was always the best. She would write to Martha and tell her how she had been doing, tell her about the tapes. She might even tell her about her broken engagement, because she was pretty sure Martha would be sympathetic. And she would say she might be visiting friends in Washington and New York. There was no way to prove whether she was or she wasn't, and she did know some people who had moved to New York, although she certainly didn't know them well enough to make a special trip to see them. That didn't matter, thought Caroline, outlining the letter in her head. What mattered was that Martha almost certainly would invite her to have a cup of coffee or visit the studio, because Caroline worked for a WNN station. All Caroline needed, she decided, was to get inside. She had developed enough confidence in herself to believe she could take it from there. Moreover, she could tell Mike that Martha had invited her to visit and that would give her an excuse for being near him.

Walking in the door half an hour later, Jill was surprised to hear the sound of a busy typewriter.

"Well, hard at work?" she inquired in a faintly conciliatory tone.

"I'm writing a letter."

"Oh."

Jill hesitated.

"How'd it go with Frank—did you talk to him?"

Caroline nodded distractedly. "Oh yes. We're . . . we're just going to be friends."

"That was all there was to it?"

"More or less."

"So how'd you feel? That must have been sort of hard."

Caroline turned her shining smile on Jill. "I feel terrific," she said.

15

THE FIFTH floor office with a view of the Capitol was beginning to look unoccupied. The photographs that had lined one wall were gone, as were the books that had lined another. The fake palm tree with a frantic little man scrambling up it, a gift from staff, also was gone, and Martha suspected that Mellenkoff would not put that in the corner of his office on the fortieth floor in the New York headquarters of World News Network. She knew he was leaving his desk behind. He had always said he needed a bigger desk, and now he would have one. Martha stared out of the window at the white dome of the Capitol shimmering in the noonday sun of the nation's capital, and wondered why she was so depressed. Mellenkoff couldn't understand why she was depressed at all. He had just told her she was to be the chief White House correspondent for WNN, which wouldn't have depressed anyone else who worked for the network, she was sure. But she had always been disturbed by change in her personal life, and for several years, Mellenkoff had been her personal life. They did not live together, but she was either in his apartment or he was in hers, and they lived only a few blocks apart. She had always assumed that eventually they would set up house together, perhaps even get married, although Mellenkoff had made clear his disapproval of what he called "interoffice nepotism." And the present had been so pleasant that Martha had given little thought to the future.

That was something Mellenkoff had lectured her about. She didn't look out for herself enough, he warned occasionally. Martha had laughed and pointed out that she had done fairly well. And might have done just as well without his help, she added tartly. No, she wouldn't have done as well without his help, he contradicted her, because she had no idea of how to handle office politics. She never looked over her shoulder, never inspected her back to see if there was a knife in it. He reminded her, as she knew he would, that she had refused to distrust that son of a bitch who had spread a calculated lie about her in an effort to save himself from the results of a story on a security leak. That was the exception, Martha insisted. It was the rule more often than she knew, said Mellenkoff, and it had been he who confronted that particular son of a bitch and broke him down. My knight in shining armor, Martha teased, and Mellenkoff had shaken his head. She had to learn to look after herself. He might not always be there. And now he wouldn't be there. Now he would be in New York, president of the network, running with that monster Joel Eliass, separated from the world by layers of secretaries and bureaucracy.

"You're making too much of this," he told her. "What's going to change? There's the shuttle to New York; you're going to be up there a lot anyway, and I'll be down here from time to time. And you've got a great new job. You're going to be too busy to do any moping, let me tell you, especially with this President. You're going to be on the road about sixty percent of the time."

She knew all that, and it was true. What nagged at her was the growing realization that she and Mellenkoff had what she could consider no more than a floating permanent relationship, which might last forever but would never be any more than it was now, and might very well become less. Or to put it in more old-fashioned terms, she was a lot more in love with Mellenkoff than he was with her.

She did not doubt his affection for her, but Mellenkoff's personal relationships were jigsawed into his life so that no sharp edges protruded to impede the progress of his professional life. Martha had fit in. That was why she was so much a part of his life. She had been happy enough to fit in. They had a warm, comfortable, adversarial relationship, with affection and respect on each side. She was aware of his failings and he of hers, and they had both adjusted. Which had been easy enough to do when he was in Washington and they were considered one of the capital's more interesting dinner-party couples. Martha was less fond of the party circuit than Mellenkoff was, but she was aware of its importance in terms of contacts, and it also amused her. That was something else she had been scolded about when she was told about the White House job. Her "anointment," she had called it, and Mellenkoff had observed that not too many Americans found the President of the United States an appropriate butt for sarcasm on the national airwaves. Not too many Americans, including Joel Eliass? she had asked, in an attempt to make light of the discussion.

"Damned right, including Joel Eliass, and keep in mind that ultimately he controls the purse from which springs your not inconsiderable salary, darling," Mellenkoff said coldly.

"You're beginning to sound like the president of the network, darling," said Martha.

"I am the president of the network, and neither of us can forget it," said Mellenkoff.

"Brrr," said Martha. But there was only the faintest softening of the frozen blue eyes.

Martha roused from her gloomy reverie as Mellenkoff strode through the door.

"What're you doing here? I thought we were going out to dinner?"

"Lucy said you were tied up with a couple of people, and it was quieter here. Especially since there's nothing left in the room, practically. Has your stuff all been moved?"

He nodded, glancing around the walls where pale patches were the only clue to what had once hung or stood there.

"The interior decorators are descending on both my office and my apartment in New York, even as we speak."

Martha had helped him decorate his Washington apartment, but she had sense enough not to mention it.

"Your official move is next week, isn't it?" she asked as they prepared to leave.

"I may be up there part of this week and I'll probably go up on the weekend, try to get settled in. Eliass wants me over for a dinner party Sunday night. Very fancy, I understand. At least I was given to understand by his secretary that it was black tie, for God's sake."

But Mellenkoff was smiling, and Martha knew the

signs of his satisfaction. She was silent, and he glanced at
her and read signs of distress in her face.

"Sweetie, why don't you plan to come up the weekend
after this, if you aren't traveling, that is? This is really
settling-in time, and I'd be rushing around and be bad
tempered if I had to think about somebody else. You
understand that."

Martha tried to look cheerful. "I know that, James, I
know. But you know how I am about disruptions in my
little routine."

He took her arm and pressed it gently. "I know, and
I'm sorry about this. Well, hell, Martha, I'm *not* sorry
about any of this, but I don't want you to feel left out or
anything."

She *was* left out, she thought, but did not say so. She
would also be curious to see if she were as popular with
Washington's voraciously power-hungry society hostesses
without Mellenkoff at her side. A network White House
correspondent still carried cachet in such circles, but she
had always suspected that Mellenkoff had the real clout.
If she had said that to him, he would have berated her
for underestimating herself, and he might have been right.
But she also knew that her occasionally sarcastic humor,
combined with her customarily sardonic turn of phrase
did not always endear her to those who worshiped the
proprieties. What would be much more difficult to deal
with than the loss of an invitation or two would be
finding herself alone in her apartment, with no other
apartment to consider as a second home. Even if there
were quite a few of Mellenkoff's clothes in her closet,
and he had shown no inclination to move them. Martha
shook herself mentally, chiding herself for assuming what
Mellenkoff referred to as her "doomsday posture."

She smiled at him. "Listen, I'm not going to be left
out. You think you're going to get away from me this
easy?"

He grinned. "What makes you think I want to?"

As they passed the newsroom, Martha paused.

"Let me get my mail or see if there's anything interesting. I have to pick it up when I can, now I'm over at the
White House all day."

She took a bundle of envelopes from a tray labeled
with her name, and flipped quickly through them while

Mellenkoff chatted with one of the correspondents. It
was rare for him to be seen in the newsroom with Martha. Their relationship was no secret, but Mellenkoff
tried to avoid, as he put it, reminding the staff that the
bureau chief was sleeping with one of their kind. Martha
was aware of how potentially awkward the situation was,
and how much effort he had put into ensuring that it led
to no charges of favoritism. That was one of the few
consolations about his move to New York. It could—it
might—be easier now. She had to hope for that. A pale
green envelope caught her eye, and she wondered why
her mother was writing to her at the office. But when she
glanced at the address on the top left-hand corner, she
saw the name of Caroline Mitchell in neat, small writing.
Martha frowned, for the name teased her memory, then
she remembered: the pretty student who had interviewed
her. She opened the envelope, scanned the page-long
letter. Caroline had decided, wisely, that a short letter
was best.

"Ready?" Mellenkoff was at her elbow.

Martha nodded, and tucked Caroline's letter into her
purse.

"Remember I told you about that student in Ohio—
the one who got me to tell her more about myself than I
thought I knew?"

"Vaguely. Was that the one you said was gorgeous but
wasn't sexy?"

Martha smiled. "You would remember that. Yes, that's
the one. Well, she's working part time at our station in
Columbus now, and apparently doing quite well. She's
done some tapes"—Mellenkoff groaned—"and she's going
to be visiting friends here and in New York—"

"And she wants to visit the studio." He finished her
sentence and hailed a taxi as they stepped into the street.

"How prescient of you."

"They all want to visit the studio. I'm sure she'll want
to send you her tapes, too. Or worse yet, send me her
tapes."

He helped her into the taxi and told the driver to take
them to the Cantina d'Italia.

"As a matter of fact," said Martha, who had been
trying to recall what it was that had impressed her about
Caroline Mitchell, "you might be curious to see her tapes."

"Another overnight success story. Another blond air-head makes good?"

"She's a brunette, and she's no airhead. And since when did you have anything against helping talent get ahead?" She grinned at him.

"Difference is that I don't do it unless I think there is talent."

"Well, I'll take her to lunch or something and show her around. And if she's in New York, maybe your secretary can set up a tour for her."

"You always were a pushover," said Mellenkoff amiably.

Settling into a booth in the restaurant and ordering antipasto, Mellenkoff looked reflective.

"Columbus—that's KRT and my old friend Moynihan, isn't it? We've got some ratings trouble with one of the anchors there, it seems to me."

Martha sipped on her Scotch. "I don't think little what's-her-name is quite ready for that—"

"No, no, I don't mean that, don't be silly. But I think it's a woman anchor. Real prima donna bitch type."

Martha grimaced.

"And there's another anchor who's doing well in the ratings, except the research shows he's not considered authoritative enough. Somebody called Hathaway, I think. We're having some of them come up to New York for a chat."

"You can always have him out on the street more, if it's just a matter of authority on the air," Martha suggested.

Mellenkoff nodded.

"We certainly don't want to have to spend money buying out what can be salvaged. I've seen his stuff. He's very warm, personable. People like him. He's comfort-able, chatty. But a shade light-weight."

"Chatty," Martha reflected. "Maybe I saw his show when I did that speech a year or so ago."

"May have been you who described him that way. Anyway, that's where your little protégée is working, eh? Too bad she isn't sexy."

Martha grinned at him. "Maybe she just didn't appeal to me."

Mellenkoff touched her hand. "Let's not talk about her. Let's talk about you. Tell me your honest opinion of me."

It was their traditional joke, the result of an evening when Mellenkoff had talked about himself for two and a half hours without stopping and without being aware that Martha was taping his monologue. She had always thought it spoke well for him that he thought it was funny when she played it back. She wondered if she could play the same trick on him now. Mellenkoff's ego had kept pace with his career climb, she had noticed, and although he still liked her to poke fun at him, he was not as ready to find himself ridiculous as he once had been.

"You want me to discuss the professional you or the personal you?" she asked.

"Both of them. They're both lovable, aren't they?"

His eyes were a warm, sunlit blue now, and Martha had no wish to look anywhere else.

"I think they're pretty lovable. Most of the time." Her expression belied her light tone. "I'm going to miss you, James."

"Don't say that. I'm only a shuttle away; think of it like that. And why will you miss me more than I'll miss you?"

"You're going to be in the middle of a whirlwind. You won't have time to miss anyone."

Mellenkoff stirred his drink meditatively. "You know, Martha," he said, "why do you always assume you're the only one who feels anything? The only one who suffers doubts?"

Martha sputtered. "Darling, you haven't had a doubt since you were six." She sobered at his expression. "I don't think I'm the only one who feels anything. But you're going to be pretty remote, whether you mean to be or not. And you won't be able to show it if you do feel anything. Even if you want to. Even if it's me."

"Martha, we aren't going to change."

"It isn't going to be the same. How can it be?"

"We've gone round and round on this. This is a tremendous deal for me, you know that. I'll have to work at it. Eliass can be a bastard. But I'm still going to need you."

"I won't exactly be next door," said Martha in a voice so low he could hardly hear her.

Mellenkoff hesitated.

"I gave you the White House job because I thought

you deserved it, and you wanted it. If you hadn't deserved it, I wouldn't have done it, because I couldn't have justified it. It's better than anything you can do in New York right now."

Except anchor, she thought. But she didn't bring it up again. Mellenkoff read her mind.

"I know what you're thinking, and there are no changes planned for Roy Chelter as anchor. He's doing okay. Frankly, I don't understand what you're unhappy about. Who knows what may happen in the next year or two?"

"I might move to New York?"

"You might. It would depend on what opens up."

"At WNN."

Mellenkoff finished his drink. "At WNN."

Martha was silent. He picked up the menu and abruptly put it down.

"Martha, for Christ's sake. You don't expect me to carry you off and stash you away in my penthouse in New York, do you? Remember, you're the original independent woman. That's why I love you."

She grinned. "That's me, all right."

She disappeared behind the menu. "How about some veal?" she asked.

Mellenkoff was visibly relieved, as she knew he would be.

"And how about some red wine?"

They ate, they drank, they laughed, they went back to Martha's apartment and made love, and three days later, Mellenkoff moved to New York.

16

SALLY ELIASS had always hated her Uncle Joel. She remembered how he had bullied her father, Ronald Eliass, who was seven years younger than his brother Joel and, as Joel said, seven times as naïve. The Eliass family was in real estate in Southern California, making a comfortable living, but nothing like the kind of life-style that Joel had in mind.

"Joel wants to own the world," Ron Eliass used to say, and Joel would respond that his little brother would be lucky if he wound up owning his own socks. It wasn't so bad when Ron's health held up, but it didn't. When leukemia was diagnosed, Joel said nobody in the Eliass family had ever had *that* before, but he would do his duty by poor Ron. Rebecca Eliass, a vague, gentle little woman who viewed feminism as akin to a social disease, was grateful to Joel.

"He's our security," she told Sally, when her daughter railed at Uncle Joel's domineering ways.

"Be nice to Uncle Joel, honey. He'll take care of mother and you," Ron Eliass told his daughter.

Sally found it difficult to be civil to Uncle Joel, let alone nice to him. He liked Rebecca because she listened to him and waited on him and asked his advice. Rebecca was Joel's kind of woman in that she knew her place. Had she been more of a jeweled accessory of a woman, he would have married her. Instead, he negotiated a suitable match for himself with Julia Puzio, daughter of an exceedingly rich Italian banker. Julia was a lot younger than Joel, very beautiful, and her passion in life was collecting sapphires, which she wore with great style. She attracted a lot of attention in restaurants, which Joel liked, and didn't talk much, which he liked even more.

Joel's passion in life was collecting corporations, which he did with cold-blooded relish, using a fortune accumulated from several shrewd and unscrupulous land deals, combined with a deadly eye for stocks and bonds. At fifty-three, Joel Eliass was an enormously wealthy man, and at forty-six, Ronald Eliass was dead. His estate barely covered his funeral expenses, and had it not been for the substantial life insurance that Joel had insisted he take out, Rebecca and Sally would not have been able to go on living in their rambling ranch home on the edge of Emerald Beach, fifty miles from Los Angeles. Nor could they have continued to live there, given Rebecca's casual attitude toward bank balances and Sally's expensive habits, had Uncle Joel not stepped in. Rebecca was lavish in extolling the glories of Uncle Joel, constantly inviting him to come and stay with Sally and her so that she could fawn on him and listen to him tell her what would have happened to her had it not been for him. In fact, Rebecca didn't hear most of what Joel said, and she didn't care. She simply tuned him out and enjoyed living in a manner that Ron could never have provided for her.

Since Julia Eliass liked to go home to Italy by way of world trips, and Joel rarely could take that much time away from making money, he accepted Rebecca's hospitality more often than Sally found tolerable. At twenty, Sally had other places to go and other people to see, and she did both while Uncle Joel was sprawled in her father's favorite chair, watching the sun set over the Pacific and sipping gin and tonics brought by her mother.

Sally was the kind of young woman everybody thought of when people talked about a California type. She was tall, blond, and blue-eyed, with a deep, golden tan, and legs that, as a boyfriend said, seemed to go on up to her neck. She had been expensively if not thoroughly educated, and had dropped out of college because it bored her, and because Uncle Joel did not approve of her ambition to be a photographer. All of her life, Sally had been popular. In a society overflowing with golden girls and boys, Sally had always been the center of the larger cluster of species on the beach. Her telephone at home (her father had insisted she have one of her own when she reached the age of ten) rang so constantly that her mother had Pacific Bell make an adjustment so that it buzzed instead of shrilled. Sally took it all for granted. She tried various drugs and was bored by them. She tried various young men and was bored by them. She tried a few jobs and was bored by them. The only time she was not overwhelmed by ennui was when she was taking pictures, and she didn't do that very well, because Uncle Joel had told Rebecca the photography course she wanted to take was a waste of time.

"She can take her little snapshots without all that," he said, and bought his niece an expensive camera and lot of equipment because he did think she was a very pretty young woman, and because he wanted her to be as grateful to him as her mother was. Joel liked people to be grateful to him; it gave him a warm sense of power, like sitting in a hot bath full of liquid gold.

Sally was not grateful, but she was aware that she owed her comfortable way of life to her detested uncle, and she had no illusions that what Uncle Joel gave, Uncle Joel would have no hesitation in taking away. Her mother warned her that all they had was dependent on Joel's savagely successful reading of the stock market.

"If it weren't for your Uncle Joel, we'd be on the street. We'd both have to go to work." said Rebecca, shuddering at either alternative.

Sally shrugged. "He feels so guilty about what he did to poor Daddy, he'll fork out," she said, inspecting the two-inch-long scarlet nail wrap she had had done for seventy-five dollars that morning.

"Don't push him too far, Sally," Rebecca warned, and Sally yawned, until the day she did push Uncle Joel too far.

Joel considered himself a reasonable man, especially when it came to his family. He felt he had proved that by his generosity toward Rebecca and Sally. And he felt the least Sally could do was go settle down with some rich and solid stockbroker or lawyer, with whom Joel could chat in the evenings when he came to visit, instead of being stuck with his niece's sulking or his sister-in-law's servility. When he saw Sally kissing someone good night one moonlit night, he paid little attention to the two figures wrapped in each other's arms in the expensive foreign car at the end of the driveway. Not until he realized the object of Sally's affections was female.

Joel thought briefly that his eyesight might be failing
him, so he picked up his late brother's binoculars and
focused them on the front seat of the car. What he saw
there was his beautiful blond niece passionately kissing a
beautiful brunette woman. There was no question about
the passion. Joel had never before seen any of his female
relatives or acquaintances fondling the breasts of another
woman, and he devoutly hoped he never would again.
Joel was conservative and controlled when it came to sex,
as Julia could attest. He was aware of the existence of
what he considered deviate practices, but he had been
unaware that they were being practiced within the bosom
of his family, as it were. He was not about to put up with
it.

He poured himself a brandy, Rebecca having long
since retired, and waited until Sally opened the front
door. She regarded him without enthusiasm; he had been
staying with them for two weeks, and she kept hoping
she would come home to find him gone.

"Hi, Uncle Joel. G'night," she said.

Joel raised a hand in a manner that brought his office
subordinates running. Sally paused, puzzled.

"Just a moment, Sally. I want to talk to you," he
intoned in a voice resembling the tolling of a bell. Joel's
voice normally was high and dry, and Sally barely recognized it. Hesitantly, she crossed the room and sat down
on the pale peach linen sofa opposite him.

Joel did not believe in wasting time or words.

"Who was that you were with tonight?" he asked bluntly.

Sally stared at him.

"Karen, Karen Ward. She's a friend of mine. Why?
Do you know her?"

"I do not," said Joel, "and you will not."

Sally gaped at him. "What are you talking about?"

Joel brandished the binoculars at her. "Disgusting.
Disgusting," he said.

Sally was taken aback. She lived her own life, but she
had never advertised her sexual preferences, and she
resented her uncle's awareness of them.

"Uncle Joel," she began bravely, "I really don't think
my friends are any of your business. I mean, Karen is a
very nice woman. She . . . she's older than I am, and
she's sort of . . . like a mother to me—" Sally stopped.

Why was she denying Karen, with whom, to her own astonishment, she had developed the only personal relationship she had ever found exciting or enjoyable?

Joel glared at her. "I have never seen you indulge in that kind of conduct with your mother, miss."

Sally was grateful that she had never been known to blush and also that the farewell in the car had gone no farther than it had. Otherwise Uncle Joel might have had a heart attack, which was a delicious thought.

Sally could think of nothing to say, and it was just as well, because her uncle was not prepared to listen.

"It seems to me," he began, "that you would benefit from being away from this—this place, for a while. I think you should come to stay with Julia and me in New York. I am sure your mother will have no objections."

"But I don't want to go to—"

Joel cut her off. "I am quite sure your father would want me to step in, as it were, and help you, as his only child and my only niece."

"I don't want to be helped, and I'm happy here," said Sally with quavering defiance.

"You will either do as I say, and you will keep this matter confidential—it would kill your poor mother if she knew—or I shall withdraw my financial support forthwith. Do you feel competent to support Rebecca and yourself? Because I assure you, that is what you will have to do. And I doubt that your earnings will support living in such a house as this."

Sally felt as though she had entered a time warp. She hadn't heard anything like this since she read the Brontë sisters.

"You—I mean—what's so awful about—?"

The magisterial hand was raised again to silence her.

"There will be no further discussion of this. Now or ever, Sarah."

Nobody ever called her Sarah. Not even Uncle Joel. Sally tried to collect her scattered thoughts. She wished she could call Karen, and decided that Uncle Joel would probably pull the phone out by its roots if she tried.

Then it occurred to her that Karen, a wealthy divorcée, spent a lot of time in New York. She had even mentioned an apartment there that she and her former husband still owned jointly. Theirs had been a friendly divorce.

en had discovered she preferred women at much the
me time that her husband had disclosed to her his
preference for men. Sally thought that was pretty funny.
Things were beginning to look brighter, although she
realized that she ought to look both guilty and miserable
if she were to appease even partially her uncle's outraged
sensibilities.

"I'll do anything you say, Uncle Joel," she said, bow-
ing her head and hoping she wasn't overdoing it.

Joel, who had not made a fortune by misjudging the
human race, studied her and speculated on why she was
not protesting more. Staying with Julia and himself at
their vast house in New York was not to his niece's
liking, he was sure. But she was his niece, after all, and
aware of the value of money. Especially money she lived
on and might be about to lose. She was a practical young
woman, unlike her parents. Perhaps she took after her
uncle, at least from the viewpoint of pragmatism.

"We shall leave tomorrow," he told her. "I'll tell Rebecca I have to be back in New York for business, and
that I'm taking you for a vacation."

"So soon?" Sally was clearly distressed, and Joel decided that the reaction was appropriate.

"The sooner the better. Good night, Sarah."

He assumed she would call her—that woman. He did
not care about that. He doubted that they would run
away together. Joel rose and retired to his room, leaving
his niece sitting disconsolately in the dark, listening to
the distant pounding of the surf. Joel was right about the
call. Sally waited for more than an hour before she went
to her room, put a pillow over her head, and put the
receiver to her ear. Karen's voice was sleepy, and Sally
smiled affectionately.

"What is it?" murmured Karen.

Sally told her. There was a brief pause, and Karen
laughed a little bitterly.

"Binoculars, eh? That's wonderful. Well, don't worry
about it, sweetheart. He's not going to keep us apart."

"That's what I hoped you would say," breathed Sally.

"I get to New York from time to time, as I told you.
We have my apartment. There'll be no problem. We'll
just be cool until the old bastard forgets about us. He'll

produce some dullards for you to date and figure that'll take care of all this wickedness. You so young and all."

Sally giggled. "I wish you were here," she whispered.

"Me too. But hang in there, honey. The apartment's listed under William Ward, in the east eighties. Very private." Karen laughed her low, warm laugh, and hung up.

Sally buried her head in her bedspread and cried angry tears. Damn Uncle Joel.

Sally bought some paperbacks for the flight from Los Angeles to New York and was glad she did, because her uncle did not address a word to her during the entire flight. They ate and drank in silence, while Sally clutched her book and Joel dissected the *Wall Street Journal*. As far as she knew, the only time he looked at her was when he cast a disapproving glance at her paperback, the cover of which showed bloodstained lingerie on black satin sheets. The contents of the book, dealing with a fairly sedate series of murders in a theater, did not live up to the jacket illustration, but Sally knew there was no way she could tell her uncle that. She wondered what she would do for money in New York. Her clothes were strictly Southern California, and apart from being brief and casual, they would probably cause her to catch pneumonia. But in the limousine from JFK airport to the Eliass mansion, her uncle opened his tight little purse of a mouth.

"I assume you will need something to wear, Sarah. Something more ah—appropriate for the eastern climate. I shall have my secretary open accounts for you at Bergdorf-Goodman and Henri Bendel."

"Thank you very much," said Sally, and meant it.

"Be sure to purchase some dresses appropriate for evening. I shall be having a dinner party at the end of the week and I shall expect you to attend."

"Yes, Uncle Joel," said Sally, repressing a sigh. She could imagine what her uncle's dinner parties were like. But Karen wouldn't be in New York for at least two weeks, so she might as well make the best of it. At least she could go shopping and cost the old goat some money. Sally began to feel a good deal better. Her lodgings wouldn't be bad either. She had stayed with Uncle Joel before, and his home reflected immense amounts of money and lesser amounts of taste. But there was no question that it was comfortable.

Sally slept until noon the next day, then went to the stores, clutching one of Julia's coats around her. New York was undergoing what the weather forecasters called unusually cool summer weather, and what Sally called freezing cold. She spent several happy hours prowling the designer labels, and found that the use of her uncle's name ensured an instant and warm welcome.

"How is dear Mrs. Eliass?" purred what evidently was Mrs. Eliass's pet saleswoman at Bergdorf's.

Sally said dear Mrs. Eliass was fine and in the Greek islands at that moment, but expected home within a month or so.

"We miss her," said the saleswoman sincerely.

Sally beamed at her. "Well, now you have me," she told her. The woman's expression suggested it wasn't quite the same.

Joel was out for dinner, so Sally ate alone, in as solitary splendor as was permitted by the presence of a maid and a butler who appeared to have been chosen because their personalities reflected that of her uncle.

The days passed slowly. Sally missed the beach, and she missed Karen, but she hesitated to call her collect, and she knew that Karen could not call her at the Eliass house. She was sure Hames the butler had been alerted to keep an eye on her and she wouldn't have been surprised if Taylor, the housekeeper, eavesdropped on her. She shopped some more, went to two matinees, and spent the evenings in the company of Uncle Joel, who apparently was satisfied with her demeanor to the point that when he did speak to her, which was rare, he addressed her as Sally. She reached the point where she was looking forward to the Sunday-night dinner party. She asked, timidly, if she could do anything to help, and Uncle Joel bent on her a glance in which there lay a smidgen of approval.

"Well, you might discuss the menu with Taylor, although I'm sure she's perfectly competent, and I don't want you interfering, Sally. But you might make arrangements for the flowers; Julia does that when she's here.

Sally was grateful to have something to do. She discussed the dinner so animatedly that even Taylor unbent somewhat and confided that Mr. Eliass tended to be very meat and potatoes when Mrs. Eliass was away, and if Miss Eliass thought they could try something a little imaginative . . . Sally was delighted to say she thought they could and should. She telephoned florists, studied place settings, and felt a little like a Victorian ghost.

Sally had bought a lacy black dress for her uncle's dinner party, and she was pleased with the effect. Its asymmetrical skirt accentuated her height, and the scanty bodice showed off her tan and how far it extended. On her feet were high-heeled black silk sandals, her hair was a flow of gold silk down her back, and the whole thing had cost a sum well into four figures. Sally smiled at herself in the mirror of her pale blue bedroom and thought that Karen would like it too. Then she went downstairs to play hostess for Uncle Joel, whose guests were just about what she had expected. They were mostly bespectacled, balding, and given to discussion of high finance, while their wives were diamonded according to their husbands' financial stature and given to discussion of society and children. Sally sighed while she put on a display of polite small talk that would have astounded her mother, and wrung an approving glance or two from Uncle Joel. All the child needed was a good example, he thought complacently.

The cocktail hour was almost over and Sally was about to signal to Taylor when another guest was ushered in. He promptly went to Joel to make anxious apologies for almost being late.

"Problems at the studio?" Joel asked.

"Nothing serious," the new arrival said. "Just like to make sure."

Joel nodded approvingly. He had no objections to lateness as a consequence of conscientiousness. He looked around and waved at his niece.

"Sally? Come here, my dear, there's someone I want you to meet."

As she walked across the ornate drawing room, Sally was conscious of a penetrating blue gaze. What stood before her was one of the most ruggedly handsome men she had seen. He looked a bit like a polar ice cap, she thought wildly, with his eyes glittering blue and his teeth glittering white.

"Sally, I'd like to introduce you to James Mellenkoff, the new president of World News Network. James, this is my niece, Sally, from California. She's staying with Julia and me for an—an extended visit."

Mellenkoff said he was delighted to meet her, and looked as though he meant it. Sally offered him her congratulations and expressed her pleasure at meeting him. She meant it too. Had he not been there, she would have had nobody to talk to at dinner who interested her even remotely. And Mellenkoff was certainly interesting. He was. also a little chilling, although she could not have explained why. She suspected he might be a little nervous beneath all that self-assurance. But she would have liked to get Karen's reaction to him. Karen was very perceptive about men. Of course, being perceptive was easier when you were able to be objective about them, and Sally reflected happily that she appeared to have reached that plateau. She could look into Mellenkoff's blazing blue eyes, aware that Uncle Joel was watching slyly from the other end of the table, and think about Karen.

17

"YOU'RE KIDDING," said Joe Moynihan. "Hathaway's crazy about his wife."

"I tell you, he's moved out. Susan at the switchboard told me he's given them a new number," said Del Kelly.

"So they had a fight."

"Furniture people called about delivery at an apartment on the other side of the lake."

Moynihan didn't give a damn whether Mike Hathaway had split up with his wife, but he was a close friend of the anchorman, and he was a little hurt that he had to find out through office gossip. He shrugged and went back to critiquing the five o'clock news. "It's Mike's business." His tone was dismissive, and Kelly changed the subject.

Peering over Moynihan's shoulder at the computer screen, Del observed, "It wasn't just my imagination about Martinsen then."

"Damned right it wasn't. It's bad enough when she mouths off when she's off the air, but that little dig at Colling on the air—that kind of thing's got to stop. You know we had six phone calls asking why she was 'being nasty to that nice Mr. Colling,' as some little old lady put it."

"What the hell is it with her, anyway? She's getting worse."

"Probably nervous. Hathaway's going to New York later this month. So's Kriss. Summit talks," said Moynihan.

"Mellenkoff?"

"I assume so. And from what I hear nobody's head's sewn on too tight."

"Mike's in good shape, isn't he?" asked Kelly.

"Pretty much, except for that last survey that showed viewers don't think he's very knowledgeable. I mean, they're very high on his personality, but not on his credibility. Colling does better there. Less casual manner, I guess."

Moynihan grinned reminiscently. "God knows, when Kriss hired Mike, it wasn't because he was an authority. He was just a great storyteller, and it caught on with people."

They both glanced up as Caroline Mitchell put her head around the door of Moynihan's office, and both smiled.

"Hey, Caroline."

"Hey there." Her smile encompassed the whole office. "You got anything for me today, Del?"

He thought a moment. "Yeah, how'd you feel about being nice to an old lady who has fifty cats and is fighting to keep them while the neighbors are fighting to get rid of them?"

"Make sure you get some good catfight shots. Heh, heh," said Moynihan.

"Viewers love these," observed Kelly.

"I'm gone," said Caroline cheerfully, and disappeared in search of a cameraman.

"Speaking of gossip . . ." said Kelly.

"Jesus," said Moynihan. "Maybe we should put you on the air with dirt from all over."

"Okay." Kelly turned away.

"I might as well know what you're going to tell everybody else."

"Mitchell isn't engaged to Mike's kid anymore."

"The switchboard tell you that too?"

"Mitchell did. I had a drink with her the other night, and she said the wedding was off. Temporarily, she said."

Moynihan looked up at the associate director. "You gonna tell me now that she's engaged to Mike?"

"Come on, Joe. You know you love to know everything about everybody. You're just pissed that you didn't get it first."

Moynihan growled to himself and went back to work at his computer. He was more worried about Mike Hathaway than he would have admitted to Kelly, whose competence at his work was exceeded only by his curiosity. There had been a two-point drop in ratings, which was a

source of concern, and at first Moynihan, discussing it
with Eric Kriss, had attributed it to the problem of Alice
Martinsen. But Martinsen's popularity had never been
that high. Viewers seemed to sense the sharp edge to her
personality and to be uneasy with it. Like inviting someone in and having them read you a lecture, as Kriss
observed. But the uneasiness with Hathaway, once dubbed
"the Cronkite of KRT" because of his local stature,
seemed to run deeper. It was a new generation with new
worries, and the easygoing Hathaway lacked a decisive
ring to his resonant voice. Kriss had shown Moynihan
one letter from a male viewer who asked why Hathaway
seemed more comfortable in chitchat about how the fish
were biting at Lake Apurna than discussing tax increases.
One letter like that would not have mattered. But there
had been enough similar complaints for Kriss to watch
Mike Hathaway's performance with increasing vigilance.

"We would put him on some reporting assignments.
That usually helps with credibility. But it's been so damned
long since Mike was a reporter . . ." Kriss told Moynihan
worriedly.

"How about a series? Abroad?"

"Budget won't stand it this quarter."

"Drugs? On campus? That's always good for some
compliments on our civic responsibility."

Kriss's brow was furrowed as he lit another of the
cigarettes nobody could get him to stop smoking. He told
them they could take their pick: if he didn't stop, he'd
probably die younger; if he did stop, it would make life
miserable for everybody else trying to work with him.

"Drugs might work. We've got another backup for
that, and it wouldn't cost anything much more than over-
time for the crews. He'd probably do well talking to the
kids," said Kriss.

It crossed Moynihan's mind that Mike didn't seem to
do too well talking to his own son.

"I'll have people poke around on the drug thing, Eric,"
he said.

"Probably a good idea to have Mike able to tell New
York he's involved in something like that when he's
seeing Mellenkoff."

A year earlier, Moynihan reflected, he would have

laughed if anyone had told him he would be having a worried conversation about Mike Hathaway. He sighed and looked enviously at Kriss's cigarette. Moynihan had stopped smoking five years ago and still missed it. But he had made a conscious choice between nicotine and bourbon.

"I'll talk to Mike," said Kriss. "But he's no fool. He's seen the research that came in last month. He'll do whatever he needs to do. He's a professional."

He looked at Moynihan through a cloud of smoke. "Mike say anything to you about his split with Leslie?"

Moynihan again felt a sting of resentment. "No. He didn't. But Kelly's spreading the word. Came from the great god of the switchboard, I understand."

"Well, he didn't tell me either, I assure you. All I know is I called his home, or my wife did, rather, to check on something social, and Leslie said in no uncertain terms that Mike no longer lived there but could be reached at another number. Mary said she was very cool and polite about it."

"Fits," said Moynihan.

Leslie, however, had been neither cool nor polite when Mike announced he thought they should have a trial separation. That was ten days after Caroline had broken her engagement to Frank. Mike and Caroline had spent half a dozen of those intervening evenings together, and he had emerged unthinking and uncaring about anyone else, including his wife. Those who had watched the progress of the Hathaway marriage, in stages from friendly to frozen, were not surprised when Mike finally rebelled against the woman nicknamed "Princess Leslie." Even Leslie's friends had squirmed over the way she treated Mike. Wives wished their husbands were like Mike, and husbands were grateful their wives weren't like Leslie. Even Mike, enraptured as he was with Caroline, was aware in cooler moments that she had played only the role of catalyst as far as his marriage was concerned.

When Caroline had announced she would not marry Frank, it was as though a door had opened in Mike's mind, and it led at least to freedom, if not to happiness. It had taken Leslie three days to notice he was coming home even later than usual, and when she did mention it, it was in the course of a conversation about Frank.

"I assume he's told you the engagement is off?" she asked.

"Barely," said Mike. Frank had hardly spoken to him since the split with Caroline, although as far as Mike knew, his son didn't know the identity of Caroline's new love interest. Mike was pretty certain he would have heard about that from Frank. But he and Caroline had made a point of discretion. So far as he knew, the only person who was aware of the situation was Jill Starling and she apparently had kept their secret.

"I think it may be for the best," said Leslie. "I thought she was a bubblehead. Pretty, but cloying."

"Is Frank very upset?"

She shrugged. "Well, I expect it's mostly pride. He would have realized sooner or later that he wouldn't want to live with someone who wanted to—ah—" Leslie paused.

"Be in television work?" prompted Mike.

"Well, not just that, but I don't think she's on the same intellectual level as Frank. So I expect he'll get over it soon."

"He seemed pretty fond of her."

"Oh well," said Leslie. "I expect he was sleeping with her. I mean, what else, with someone like that?"

Mike took a deep breath.

"Leslie. There's something I want to talk to you about."

She looked at her watch. "I have to be at the Mensa meeting in twenty minutes, so make it fast."

"I think we should separate for a while. Is that fast enough?"

Leslie stood quite still, her eyes fixed on her husband's face.

"Separate?"

Mike made an impatient gesture. "Don't look so stunned, for God's sake. For years I haven't thought you cared whether or not I was around. I can't see it'll make any difference in your life. Certainly not in your bank balance."

Anger flickered on Leslie's face. "You would bring up money, as though I've ever cared that much about that."

"You don't exactly reject it, though." Mike waved at the relative opulence of the room in which they were confronting each other.

"What . . . brought this on?"

"It's not male menopause, before you haul that one in. I've been pretty unhappy for a long time, although I don't think you've noticed."

"No. No, I guess I hadn't."

"Well, I guess you didn't pay enough attention. You were too busy with the snide remarks about happy-talk jobs."

As though she were hearing it for the first time, Leslie reacted to the bitterness in his voice.

"You took that seriously? I mean, I was teasing—"

"Maybe you were, maybe you weren't. But it was damned cruel teasing, and you put Franklin up to the same gig."

"I certainly had no idea you took it so literally—"

"Maybe not all the time. But it went on all the time. I came home to the Leslie and Franklin Show—snickers at Dad's expense."

Leslie sat down abruptly in the nearest armchair.

"What will you do? Where will you go?"

"I've checked on apartments over at Lakeside. There's one available now."

"When . . . ?"

"I thought as soon as I got my stuff packed. Don't worry, just my clothes and some of my books and fishing gear."

"Mike, please, don't suggest that I'm one of those women who worries about . . . division of property, if it's come to that."

"I don't know, Leslie. I don't really know which of those women you are. We haven't communicated for a long time. On any level."

Leslie regained her control, smoothing back her smooth hair, straightening her skirt.

"Have you told Franklin?"

"I thought I should tell you first. You can tell him. It'll just confirm what he's always heard about me, I guess."

"You—you hate me, don't you?" Her voice was genuinely puzzled.

Mike shook his head. "No, I don't. I never have and I probably never will. I'd like to love you, but you wouldn't let me."

"That isn't true! I've always—I mean, I guess I just assumed things were fine. I—we've been married a long time. I don't know what I've done."

"Then I can't tell you. And that's the problem," said Mike, and his voice was tired. "I just know I want some time to think. I'm not going to spend the rest of my life . . . being laughed at. You can be just as intellectually superior alone, Leslie. You don't need an old television hack like me."

"Mike, for heaven's sake, this is ridiculous! I had no idea—" Leslie spread her hands in a supplicating gesture, but Mike made no move toward her. "Can we . . . talk some more?"

He sighed. "Sure. I've wanted to talk for years, but you never had time, or you never wanted to listen to anything I had to say."

Leslie's mouth tightened. "You've obviously made up your mind."

Mike was silent. She picked up her purse and searched for her car keys, and he noticed her hand shook slightly.

"I'll pick up some stuff tonight. Try not to get in your way," he said.

"Don't worry. You won't."

She walked past him, with her slender shoulders rigid. Mike watched her and thought she had always had beautiful posture, and he supposed this kind of crisis put that kind of thing to the test.

"Leslie."

She stopped instantly and her head came around. He thought he glimpsed hope in her eyes, and ignored it.

"I—don't worry about anything. I mean, if you need me, or anything like that."

Her eyes were cold again. "Very kind of you, Mike. Should I assume I'll be hearing from your lawyer?"

"We haven't reached that stage. All I said was I wanted a trial separation."

"So I wait while you decide whether or not you want to go on living with me? While you pass judgment on me?" Leslie was more comfortable being angry. "Has it ever occurred to you that I might have had some problems, too? And that your making this great big salary—at least in terms of this place—didn't solve everything?"

"I'd have been happy to try to talk about things anytime. I tried. Several times, if you recall. You said we didn't have any problems."

"And you went and shut yourself up in your study and had another brandy."

Mike looked at her steadily. "You never seemed interested in doing anything else after dinner, for that matter. And when I came to bed, you were usually reading Susan Sontag and couldn't be disturbed."

"That's a cheap shot. There were times I didn't feel well, either, as you well know."

"You mean you really did have a headache?"

Mike raised a hand as Leslie seemed about to launch into a tirade.

"Look, what's the good of this—this awful lacerating conversation? This is why I think we both need time off from each other. We can talk some more. If we've still got anything left, maybe this is the way to find out. Let's take a break, Leslie. Please."

She brushed past him. "You know where to find me, Mike."

The front door slammed, and her car, on its way down the drive, almost decapitated a rosebush. Mike sank into a chair and lit the first cigarette he had smoked in months. He thought of calling Caroline and decided to wait until he got to the office. She had been nervous about his separating from Leslie. She didn't want to be the cause of anybody's trouble, she kept saying, which he found rather endearing. Caroline hated trouble. She was as warm and affectionate as a kitten until the subject of Leslie and Frank came up. She seemed to have blotted Frank entirely from her mind, and she seemed determined not even to think about Leslie.

"That's the other part of your life, and I'm separate," she had insisted.

"But I'm going to be separated, and then you won't be separate," he had told her, holding her tightly.

She had stiffened a little, urging him, "Don't do it for me, please. Not for me." She was a stubborn little creature. But after Leslie, it was wonderful to envision going home to Caroline with her enthusiasm and her energy and her embraces.

Going upstairs to pick up his briefcase, Mike paused suddenly and smiled bitterly as he thought of the one thing that Leslie had not mentioned during their recent conversation. She had not asked him if there was anyone else. It had probably never occurred to her.

18

DRIVING TOWARD the lake, Frank wondered if he should have called his father to tell him he wanted to talk. He slowed down as he neared a telephone booth, then drove on. Mike was just getting settled in. He could say he'd thought he would drop by and give him a hand. Maybe they could go out for a beer and he could tell him what Leslie had said. Frank was close to admitting, at least to himself, that he was as tired of his mother's rationalizations about why her marriage had collapsed as he was of her calling him Franklin. He'd always despised the name and suspected she had chosen it solely because of her admiration for Franklin D. Roosevelt. He was unimpressed by her complaints about being lonely sitting at the dining table by herself and not enjoying a glass of wine when she was alone. Dad had always said they didn't need a dining table big enough for a banquet hall, even if it was Italian workmanship.

Frank suspected Leslie was getting a bad time from her friends who liked Mike. Now that he came to think of it, just about everybody liked his father. He'd started watching him on the tube recently; with Caroline gone, he'd had more time on his hands in the evening. Mike was pretty good. As he used to say, there wasn't an awful lot you could do in two minutes and twelve seconds, even if you were describing the Second Coming. Frank sighed. He'd rarely seen his mother cry the way she had cried that afternoon when he was leaving. She hadn't even seemed to care that her hair was a mess and her makeup was wrecked. For a minute, he'd thought she wanted him to ask Mike to come back to her, and he had been so sorry for her he'd offered to do it. That, of course, had straightened her up. She'd found Kleenex and a mirror and her composure, more or less all at once, and he'd been relieved.

"By all means, tell your father I hope he's happy in his new life," she'd said, and Frank had relaxed. He didn't want to start feeling sorry for his mother, because he wasn't. But he was looking forward to talking to his father, and now that Leslie wasn't around, maybe they'd get to know each other. He still thought television was pretty shallow, but he was beginning to see Mike's viewpoint. Mike had never taken it that seriously, and Frank was beginning to find it harder and harder to listen to his mother. She sounded as though she were saying what she thought she was expected to say as an enlightened liberal intellectual, and he realized he'd never known what she really thought.

He sighed again. It was bad enough that his personal life was falling apart, without his parents splitting at the same time. He still felt miserable when he thought about Caroline, and he wondered sometimes if he should have been more patient with her. Maybe she'd felt he let her down the way his father felt Leslie had let him down. Maybe he should call Caroline. She had said she wanted to be friends and she was such a strange, remote little creature. On the other hand, Frank reflected, he didn't want to get into the kind of marriage his father had. But he'd thought his life was laid out in a neat pattern, with Caroline fitted in, and now it was in pieces and Caroline was gone. Depression swept over him again as he remembered how he had missed her. Maybe it had been his fault, although he'd tried to be what she wanted him to be, and God knows he'd made no demands on her. Sometimes he wondered if she'd ever go to bed with him. She had sort of turned into a lump of ice in his hands, and it wasn't the kind that melted.

He saw the apartment building ahead and found a parking space a block away. At the front door, he hesitated, checking the list of occupants. The building was new, set in a parklike complex. He found the name *Hathaway* opposite 1220, which was the penthouse. Dad did himself well. He shrugged. Why not? Stepping out of the elevator, Frank heard music faintly from the end of a short, carpeted corridor and tracked it to 1220. He pushed the buzzer and waited. There was a lengthy pause. Maybe

Mike was in the shower. He pushed the buzzer again, firmly. The door opened, and his father stood there in jeans and a plaid shirt, his hair rumpled. Behind him, Frank could see cartons stacked. He grinned at Mike.

"Hi, Dad."

Mike seemed a little taken aback, but he hadn't been expecting him.

"Frank! Great to see you." He hesitated a moment, his hand on Frank's shoulder.

"You going to invite me in? I thought I'd see if you needed any help or—or anything."

"Yeah, yeah, come on in. This is nice of you, son."

The room was a little bare, but comfortable, with a big tweedy sofa and a leather chair that looked like a newer version of one Mike had at home. Frank looked at it a little sadly.

"Hey, sit down," said his father. "How about a beer?"

"That'd be great. But let me get it; don't wait on me, for God's sake. I just want to see what you're hiding in the refrigerator!"

It was an old joke between them that went back to Frank's childhood, but now it seemed to fall flat. Mike stood in the doorway of the kitchen, embarrassment and anxiety mingled on his face.

Frank stopped. "What is it—?"

"Hello, Frank," said Caroline, and she stepped out of the kitchen.

Frank stared at her. "What're you doing here?"

"I came to help your father get moved in."

They obviously had not come from the studio. Caroline was also wearing jeans, which was unusual for her, and a pink cashmere sweater. She looked a little flushed, and less immaculate than usual. Frank wished he were anywhere else in the world. Why hadn't he phoned? Why had he come over? He wished he were a thousand miles away from Caroline's cool, dark gaze. His father was scrabbling in the refrigerator.

"Caroline, you want a beer, too?"

She shook her head. "No, thank you." She looked around for her purse. "I'd better be going, Mike. I have an early class."

"Listen, thanks for coming over. I'd never have gotten the stuff arranged without you."

Caroline nodded. "I'll see you at the studio."

She looked at Frank with a trace of a smile. "Nice to see you again. Everything going well?"

Frank felt as though his jaw were unhinged and his mouth flapping loose.

"Fine, fine. I—Caroline, you don't have to leave, you know. I—"

"I know. But I have to study. I'm late now. Take care, Frank."

The door clicked behind her, and Frank was alone with his father, who was still holding a beer toward him.

"Sit down, will you?" said Mike, and Frank had a sense of sudden relief emanating from his father. He sat down, accepted the beer, and drank gratefully.

"Sorry about your encountering Caroline like that. Sort of awkward," said Mike.

"I guess I . . . should have called first," said Frank, watching his father's face. Mike was not a good liar.

"No, no. I just . . . didn't want you to be upset. That's all."

"Well, Caroline said she wanted to be friends."

Mike nodded, but said nothing.

"I went by the house," said Frank.

"How's your mother?"

"Not too good. As a matter of fact, she was crying."

"Leslie?"

Frank appreciated his father's astonishment.

"Yeah. She's pretty upset about your leaving. I mean, I think she really is."

"I'm sorry she's upset," said Mike gently.

"Do you think you'll be talking to her?"

"Sure."

"Well"—Frank gestured with his beer can toward the room around them—"is this—this separation really permanent?"

Mike stared out of the window at the distant hills.

"I don't know, Frankie. I really don't."

Frank realized how long it had been since his father called him by that name, and again was struck by sadness.

"This has been a long time coming," said Mike slowly.

Frank sighed. "I understand that."

"Do you?" His father's expression was grim.

"Well, I guess I didn't until recently. But I sort of do

now. Funny, I was thinking coming over here that the way things have worked out with you and Mother, maybe it was as well that Caroline and I found before it was too late that we didn't . . . well, that it wouldn't . . ."

"Maybe so." Mike spoke carefully.

"Are you—how's Caroline doing at KRT? She was talking about tapes—"

"She's doing pretty well. Her tapes were quite impressive, so Moynihan and Kriss said, anyway. They're the experts. But she's just getting started."

Frank nodded. "Everything okay with you?"

"I guess so. I'm going to New York to talk to the network people. There's a new president, rumors of changes, that kind of thing."

"What does that mean for you?"

Mike drank his beer. "Hard to tell. I think I'm all right, but it's an unpredictable business. Everybody's expendable."

He changed the subject. "How's school?"

Frank shrugged. "It hasn't been easy, recently, what with the problems with Car—" He stopped, and realized he was unwilling to utter her name in front of his father now.

Mike nodded. "I understand that. All of this has been hard on you, Frankie."

His son stared at the beer can in his hands and was silent, and Mike realized he wished Frank would leave. He wanted to be alone in the apartment, sip a brandy, savor the peace and quiet. He didn't even want Caroline around at this point, especially as he found himself inclined to worry about her. There were times when he felt he hardly knew her.

He was not sleeping with Caroline, although he assumed he would. He had detected only nominal reluctance on her part. Where their relationship would lead, he was uncertain. He was in love with Caroline, yet it was as though he saw her as the first installment of a serial he wanted badly to follow despite a feeling it might not turn out the way he would prefer. He had been shaken by Frank's arrival in the midst of a scene with all the trappings of domesticity. Yet what Frank had seen had been precisely what was going on. Caroline had come to the apartment to help Mike arrange kitchen items they had bought together. And the delay in opening the door had been the result of Mike's being on top of a ladder and Caroline's reluctance to play what she called the "wife role" for the benefit of the building supervisor, who was expected to arrive to fix the refrigerator door. Now he found himself oddly lacking in any desire to reassure his son. It was as though the deeply rooted disappointment of his marriage was irrevocably associated with Frank. He was part of the pain, and by now, it didn't really matter whose fault it had been. All that was left was disillusionment in Leslie, and somewhere in Mike's mind, Franklin—not his little Frankie—had become her accomplice.

He knew he felt a tiny, mean flame of satisfaction when Frank had found his former fiancée in the apartment of the father he used to jeer at. Mike had let him read into the scene whatever he chose, standing back and watching disbelief, confusion, and misery mingle in Franklin's face. He was pleased by Caroline's composure, but not surprised by it.

She had been jubilant that day because she had received a letter from Martha Vogel. She had been bubbling with enthusiasm about it, telling him how nice Martha had been to her, how she had invited Caroline to visit her in Washington. That had intrigued Mike to the point of questioning Caroline about this hitherto unsuspected friendship with WNN's new White House correspondent. Caroline had hesitated only briefly before acknowledging that the letter from Martha had been in response to Caroline's note of congratulations on the White House job. What mattered, she had rushed on, was that she could be in Washington at the same time Mike was in New York talking with the new network president. She had been so crestfallen when Mike had frowned at the indiscretion of her plan that he had soothed her, told her he could work it out, ignoring at the back of his mind a nagging, warning voice that suggested that Caroline always got what she wanted. He was in no doubt about the extent of her ambition, which far exceeded his own. When it did not worry him, it amused him. He tried to banish from his mind the occasional fleeting thought that Caroline at times behaved as though her ambition were the only controlling factor of her life. He reminded himself how very young she was, how excited she was. And how exciting she was.

Mike became aware that his son was watching him, and roused himself guiltily from his thoughts.

"How about another beer?" His voice rang falsely hearty to himself.

Frank shook his head, and Mike thought with a pang that he looked suddenly, painfully young and awkward.

"Dad?"

Mike tensed a little. "Uh-huh?"

"What—why was Caroline here?"

Mike thought Frank sounded as if he were five years old and wanted to be reassured that there was still a Santa Claus.

"She told you. She was helping me stow stuff in the kitchen. I'm not very domestic, you know that."

"Why Caroline?"

Mike shrugged; his face was expressionless.

"Well, why not Caroline? She was going to be my daughter-in-law, and we've become friends. Does that have to end because you're not going to marry her?"

Frank looked stricken at the challenge. He shook his head.

"No, no of course not. But I guess I was pretty surprised to see her. I didn't expect it, that's all."

"I didn't expect to see you, either."

"No," said Frank, "I know you didn't."

Mike sighed. "You're sure about that beer? I ought to get back to cleaning up this place."

Frank shook his head again. He opened his mouth to offer help, and closed it again. He felt a little sick, and to distract himself, he gazed around the room, which had the characterless cream-colored walls and anonymous draperies of most rented apartments. It reminded him of what Mike had left, of Leslie's carefully chosen color coordinations and objets d'art bought on trips abroad. He looked at the beer can in his hand. His mother would have insisted they drink from English tankards, an insistence that had always exasperated his father. Frank looked at Mike as though trying to see beyond the noncommittal expression on the handsome, genial face.

"You've got a nice place," he forced himself to say.

Mike laughed. "It's your usual one bedroom with balcony. But you can see the lake from the balcony, so that's a plus. See my old fishing hole?"

"*Our* old fishing hole."

"Yeah." The word came out as a sigh.

"Remember the last time we were there?"

"Yes."

"We were going to take Caroline."

Mike was silent.

"You could take Caroline, couldn't you, Dad?"

Frank felt as though he were holding his breath for a long time, waiting for his father to reply.

Mike drained his beer and tossed the can into a trash basket.

"Yeah, Frankie," he said evenly. "I could take Caroline there."

19

THERE WERE only two people in the world whom Martha Vogel wanted to hear from that rainy Friday, and Roger Miller was one of them. His call fortunately followed that of James Mellenkoff, who wanted to let her know that Eliass had him tied up again for the fourth weekend since his departure for New York.

"It's a settling-in period," he explained. It sounded familiar.

"Settling in with gorgeous Sally, as Liz Smith calls her in the column?" Martha couldn't resist it, but she knew it was a mistake as soon as she saw frost forming on the telephone.

"Sally Eliass is the chairman's niece," said Mellenkoff after a pause. "She's in town from California, she doesn't know anyone, and he wants her to be entertained. What do you expect me to do?"

"Entertain her," said Martha. "You're good at that."

"I don't expect this kind of jealous wife nonsense from you, Martha."

"I know you don't. Should I revert to my role of house masochist and apologize?"

This time the pause was so long she was sure he was going to hang up. When he did speak, his voice was expressionless.

"You may not believe this, but I have enough to cope with right now without your having a tantrum because I can't spend every weekend with you. Isn't the White House keeping you busy enough? Maybe you should do more travel, keep your mind on the job."

Martha sighed and gave up.

"I'm sorry" she said wearily. "Is it all right if I miss you?"

"Not to the point of irrationality," said Mellenkoff. "I'll talk to you next week."

He hung up, and Martha sat staring at the telephone for a moment or two before she replaced it in its cradle. She wasn't surprised, but it still hurt. Every time he called now, it hurt, because she still remembered too keenly how much she looked forward to the sound of his voice. The worst of it was that not only had she sounded like a jealous wife, she felt like one too, and that she hadn't expected. And he was right; it wasn't doing much for her interest in her work. She was grateful that the day was over at the White House press room and people were drifting home. Terry Steiner, her fellow correspondent for WNN at the White House, poked his handsome dark head around the door of their booth and asked if she wanted a ride back to the office. She shook her head.

"I've got a couple of calls to make yet, thanks, Terry."

"You look a little peaked, Marty. You all right?"

That was wonderful; now it showed on the face she showed on camera. She made an effort and grinned at him.

"Just lack of oxygen in this place. That, and waiting for calls that always come when you've gone to the john."

He nodded. "God, I know. Well, take care. See you tomorrow? I'm going to do that damned prayer breakfast he's got."

She made the sign of the cross over him.

"Bless you, Terence. Yeah, I'll probably stop by."

He left laughing.

Martha had no calls to make and expected none that mattered. She shuffled through some notes halfheartedly, peered into the small mirror glued to the wall beside the door, and sighed. She did look peaked. The telephone rang, and she hoped, unreasonably, irrationally, that it was Mellenkoff calling back to say he was free after all. Cherishing that possibility, she let it ring five times before she picked up the receiver.

"Martha, my love, how the hell are you?"

She frowned, then smiled. "Roger?"

"Of course it's Roger," said Roger Miller. A former newsman, Miller was a tall, soft-voiced Texan possessed of quiet charm that had taken him almost as far in success in his work as it did with women. He was cheerfully irreverent about his work, but pragmatic enough to be appreciative of its pecuniary rewards. It had been said of Miller that were he not so shrewd, he would not have survived the internal network politics to become a news director, let alone part of the executive team, because his tongue had a serpent's sting. When the remark was quoted to him, he had smiled his slow, easy smile and taken issue only with the reptile.

"Rattler," he had said.

Miller was as close a friend as Martha had, and he was more than a little in love with her, but he was too sophisticated to sacrifice friendship for an unpredictable relationship. In many ways, he and Martha were remarkably similar in temperament. Miller once observed that they shared a stubborn determination to cling to hopeless situations, and he spoke from experience. He had married a woman who almost at once fulfilled previous signs of psychiatric and physical frailty.

"It's reached the point that when she breaks a leg, it's an improvement on her depressions," Miller once commented cynically to Martha, who had chided him mildly for callousness while inwardly sympathizing with what was generally conceded to be a marriage that had achieved new dimensions in misery. She knew Ella Miller, a porcelain figurine of a woman, who had been an exquisite twenty-year-old when she married Roger. At twenty, her psychological unpredictability had taken the form of what Roger called Ella's whims and foibles. He had humored her, laughed at her, and been entertained by what seemed no more than a tendency toward eccentricity. But he had assumed she would grow up. And Ella at forty was a wire-strung specter of Ella at twenty, a demonstration of psychosomatic ailments at their most advanced level. Her troubles were compounded by what her current psychiatrist called an uncontrolled anxiety complex. Ella went to psychiatrists the way other women shopped sales; her medicine cabinet was stocked like a pharmacy, and nothing helped. Roger Miller came to view his wife, as he once admitted to Mellenkoff around midnight in a bar, the way Mr. Rochester in *Jane Eyre* might have viewed his mad wife in the attic.

"She's there and there doesn't seem to be much I can do about it. All I can do is try to live my own life.

Separate but equal, you might say," said Miller, and if
there was a certain bitterness in his voice, there was no
self-pity. He had discussed divorce with Ella, assuring
her of lifelong financial support, but she had collapsed in
abject terror at the mere suggestion. He couldn't leave
her, she had sobbed. He was all she had. Roger had to
concede that was probably true. Ella's family had long
since ceased to offer more than long-distance expressions
of affection and sympathy at Christmas. Her widowed
mother and brother told Roger bluntly they could not
tolerate Ella's barrage of alternating recrimination, abuse,
and mawkish sentimentality. They left no doubt that if
they had to cope with Ella again, she would almost
certainly wind up in an institution. Roger did not blame
them, and over the years, he had come to see his wife's
pitiable psychological state with a certain amount of cool
objectivity. As long as she could assure herself of his
continuing, if sporadic, presence as her husband, Ella's
fragile self-control seemed strengthened. More time elapsed
between suicide attempts, which had become legend at
WNN, where heads shook sympathetically as Miller made
one more ambulance ride to wait while his wife's stomach
was pumped out. But gradually Roger built a life of sorts
for himself. There was no shortage of women willing to
comfort the gently drawling Texan with the dry sense of
humor, and it said much about Miller that most of those
women remained his friends when they were no longer
his lovers. The way it had worked out, he related with a
grin to Mellenkoff, was that he had accumulated not only
a harem but a sibling extension service.

Yet Miller was lonely, and that he never talked about.
It was when he was at home with Ella that he was most
alone, sitting in their lavish apartment listening to her
weeping in the next room, or sitting across a table, watching her darting blue eyes and hearing her sparrow's chatter. They had had separate rooms for years, and a live-in
maid, Emma, was devoted to Mr. Miller and dedicated
to the care of Mrs. Miller, whom she treated like a
difficult six-year-old. Occasionally, Ella was enough in
command of herself that she would dress up, excited as a
child on Christmas morning, and attend a formal dinner,
making the kind of small talk that made those who did
not know her think what a refreshingly different ap-

proach she brought to dinner-table conversation and wonder why she was so rarely visible on the social circuit. But she always left early. If Roger could not leave with her before her charm dissolved into paranoia, the faithful Emma arrived to take her charge home and hear an account of the evening that would have astounded those to whom Ella had talked.

Martha Vogel was one of the few women about whom Roger Miller permitted himself to be wistful. Beyond that, he worried over her the way some of his friends worried over him. He had followed the progress of Martha's relationship with Mellenkoff almost since it began, had predicted it before it began, and he had never stopped worrying about her. Miller was one of the few people in the world whom Mellenkoff trusted. They had been friends since they first met, when Mellenkoff was an associate producer and Miller was a correspondent. In those days, Mellenkoff had still been human enough to sympathize with Roger's pathetic marriage, although he was unable to understand why anyone would not rid himself of such an albatross.

Miller often joined Mellenkoff and Martha for drinks and dinner, and years later, all three remembered those evenings as some of the happiest and most carefree they had spent. But Miller was far more conscious than Martha of Mellenkoff's consuming ambition, and what haunted him was the fear that the fire that drove Mellenkoff would in the end consume Martha. Over the years, Miller and Martha shared their troubles, grumbling, commiserating and always grateful for each other. When Mellenkoff was named president of WNN, Miller saw with grim clarity what lay ahead. He read in Martha's face confirmation of his concern. He did not question that Mellenkofff was genuinely fond of Martha, but he was aware of the limitations Mellenkoff imposed on himself in personal relationships. If necessary, Martha would cease to exist for Mellenkoff, and Miller suspected that their relationship was already too close for Mellenkoff's comfort. The days when Mellenkoff would permit closeness to anyone were over, in Miller's assessment. All of the legendary energy and ambition would now be focused on keeping Mellenkoff at the pinnacle he had attained, and enhancing that position. Martha's role, Miller feared, might be coming to an end.

Almost from the day Mellenkoff arrived in New York, his demeanor and schedule had confirmed Miller's theory. As Joel Eliass's man, Mellenkoff left to chance nothing that might displease the chairman. He worked long days, and made sure Eliass concurred in his thinking. And if escorting Eliass's glamorous blond niece were part of the scenario of success, Mellenkoff had no scruples or doubts about that either. It didn't even occur to him to think of Martha. In a similar situation, he wouldn't have expected her to think of him.

Miller read the gossip columns. He had also seen Sally Eliass. When she arrived to visit her Uncle Joel at the WNN offices, every heterosexual male on the premises, and a few who weren't, sought an opportunity to see "the Silver Girl," as somebody dubbed her after seeing the palomino tresses streaming down her back and the endless golden legs flashing beneath a brief skirt. She had come to see Uncle Joel, but she had left with Mellenkoff, after the chairman asked him as a personal favor to take his place and escort his niece to a cocktail party. They made a striking couple as Mellenkoff assisted the shining Sally into the chairman's limousine. Miller sighed, and as the days went by, decided he ought to provide support for Martha who, he assumed, remained in comparative ignorance of the speed with which events appeared to be moving in New York. He was curious about Eliass's pointed encouragement of Mellenkoff as an escort for his niece, but assumed it was part of the chairman's general inclination to nail down the loyalties of those whom he had chosen to elevate. He arranged an excuse for a visit to the Washington bureau of WNN and shortly after he arrived there, telephoned Martha at the White House. She sounded about as he had expected, and he assumed that meant she knew Mellenkoff was staying in New York for the weekend.

"I am so glad to hear your voice," she told Roger, and meant it.

"Where are you?"

"I'm in Washington. Officially on network corporate business. But what I'm really here for is to have you make me one of your well-known martinis, after which I shall take you to dinner."

"It's a deal," said Martha, and was grateful she didn't have to pretend.

When he reached her apartment, she met him at the door with a chilled glass in her hand and threw her other arm about his neck.

"I'm so glad to see you," she told him.

"Enough of this. That's an empty glass," said Roger, and hugged her back.

Sitting opposite her a few minutes later, he noted she was visibly thinner, though she had never been fat. The faint hollows beneath her cheeckbones probably photographed well, but she would have to be constantly smiling to belie the mournful dark eyes.

He raised his glass. "Here's to us, but mostly to you."

"And to James." Her eyes were watchful now. Roger drank.

"To absent friends."

She sipped briefly, then turned her glass carefully in her fingers.

"How is James?"

"Doing well. Doing everything Eliass wants him to do, so he's doing well."

"How's his apartment?"

"Just about what you'd expect when you turn loose an expensive interior decorator with a penchant for purple."

Martha grinned. "Purple?"

"Well, it varies. The rugs are sort of pale lavender and the sofas are sort of pale gray. But generally speaking, the theme is purple."

"Eliass recommended the decorator, of course?"

"Of course."

"How is James taking it?"

"Stoically. But he did confess he was having nightmares about purple people-eaters."

Martha's laughter was so close to shrill that Miller wondered when she had laughed last. He refilled her glass.

"What else?"

"Well, the usual gossip. You get that in Washington—it's a short grapevine."

"I mean what else about James, Roger."

"You haven't talked to him?"

"Not really. He's called four times in four weeks to tell me not to come up for the weekend and that he can't get down. He's entertaining Eliass's niece, he says. All in the name of business."

"I think Eliass did give him that assignment personally," he said carefully.

"Roger, don't play games. Did you come down to give me the bad news?"

Miller was silent for a few minutes, staring unseeingly at a watercolor of beach dunes hanging on the wall opposite.

"I don't have any 'bad news,' as you put it," he said finally. "But I think you're going to have to recognize that James isn't going to be the same. Hell, what am I saying? He's going to be exactly the same, but you aren't going to get any sugar coating the way you used to."

"I don't think James pretended with me."

"That's not what I'm saying. You chose to see him the way you wanted to, although you knew there was another James. You've always known what he was; you're too bright not to."

"That's not fair, not even true."

"I'm not going to argue. We've had this discussion before. James'll do whatever he has to do, no matter what it costs or whom it hurts. Now the whom is you. Or something like that."

"Did he tell you to tell me that?"

Miller stared at her and her gaze dropped.

"I'm sorry. I know he didn't. Know you wouldn't, either. But does he know you're here?"

"No."

"And you think it's over. For me, I mean."

"I'm not saying that, because I don't know that. James would say we're both making a fuss about nothing. But knowing you, I'm suggesting, probably out of turn, that you're going to have to face some unpleasant facts of life, like he's got a new life-style and it's what he's always wanted. He's finally made it. James Mellenkoff, success. And Eliass is the key to that success. I don't know where you'll fit in. James may not even know. But I'd be surprised if you saw much of him until the dust settles, as it were."

Miller took her hand and leered at her exaggeratedly. "That is really why I'm here, my dear. Drink up, and let me wine you and dine you and all that."

Martha looked for a while at her untouched second drink.

"I can't even say I'm surprised," she said softly. "I guess it's just been a long time coming."

She played with the heavy silver bracelet on her wrist.

"I should get myself back into circulation, right?"

Miller shrugged. "Don't do anything you don't feel like. But keep busy. That's probably one way to get his attention, as you know. Don't sit home and polish up your memories, my love."

"That's all very well for you to say," said Martha sharply, and checked herself.

Miller smiled thinly. "My problem is that I can go home to my memories any night of the week. That's why I don't recommend it."

Martha reached over and took his hand. "Roger, I love you."

"I wish you did. What's second prize?"

Her wide mouth curled in a smile, and the dimple deepened in her chin.

"Name it."

Miller lifted her to her feet and held her close for a while, feeling her burrow her head into his shoulder. When she put her arms around his neck and kissed him on the mouth, he was tender with her, caressing her gently, until she made clear that gentleness was what she didn't want.

Roger raised his head and considered Martha's closed eyes.

"Stop it," he said. "If I'm going to make love to you, I'm damned well going to make sure you know it's me."

When her eyes opened, they had a hard brightness, but there was no filming of tears. She traced his mouth with her fingers.

"I know who you are, Roger."

"But you'd rather I was somebody else."

She smiled and pulled his head down to hers again.

"How about tomorrow?" he said against her mouth.

"Are you asking me if I'll still love you in the morning?" He didn't smile and the mischief faded from her eyes. "Yes," she said. "I will."

They made love slowly at first, almost tentatively, then with unexpected fierceness, their hands moving over each other in passionate discovery. And later, lying still locked against Roger's body, Martha brushed back tangled gray hair from his damp forehead and smiled at him warmly.

"Now there isn't anything we haven't done together," she said softly.

He contemplated her through half-closed eyes.

"And now?"

She kissed him lightly. "Now you take me to dinner, of course. Haven't I earned it?"

He grinned at her, then grew serious. "That simple, my love?"

She hesitated. "No."

"Has anything changed?"

"No."

"Then why?"

"Because you're my best friend. Because I do love you."

"Which?" His arms tightened around her.

"Both. It has to be both."

"Does it?"

His gaze was steady, and she looked away, over his shoulder.

"No. Not always. But maybe it should be," Martha said.

She stirred and pulled gently away, and she was smiling when she looked at him again.

"What's important is that nothing's changed for us. We're still friends," Martha said.

He was silent.

"Aren't we?" she asked.

Roger sat up and stretched, and ruffled her tangled hair. "You know that. On that you can rely, my dear."

Martha hugged him and slipped from the bed, reaching for a robe as she did so. Roger glanced away as she belted Mellenkoff's blue velour robe, and lit a cigarette as she disappeared into the bathroom. Almost at once, she turned on the shower, and when she emerged, glowing and cheerful, there were no traces of her tears.

20

LYING ALONE between his purple sheets, James Mellenkoff tried to concentrate on the eleven o'clock news on the television set in the corner of the bedroom, while uneasily wondering if he should take antacid to rid himself of the taste of the lobster sauce that had drowned the Dover sole and now coated his palate. He finally got up, shook an Alka-Seltzer tablet into a glass of club soda, and drank it in one gulp. He still felt a little queasy, and he tried to remember whether his escort duty of Sally Eliass was to continue on Sunday. It wasn't that he minded escorting Sally, who was, in addition to her spectacular looks, possessed of a wicked sense of humor. She was even irreverent about her Uncle Joel, although not, Mellenkoff noticed, in Uncle Joel's presence. He sighed. He had come to New York prepared to work eighteen hours a day in the corporate offices of WNN, where the interior decorators favored black and white instead of purple. He had found himself caught up and spun around in a social maelstrom over which he had no control. That troubled him more than he cared to admit to himself. Obviously he could not decline to do the chairman of the board a social favor. But during the past two weeks, he seemed perpetually to be leaving the office early in order to keep Sally entertained. Eliass was evidently on the list of every upwardly mobile hostess in Manhattan's Upper East Side, and he appeared to feel it incumbent on him to make sure his niece spent no moment unoccupied.

"With Julia out of town, and so many things on my plate, I would be most obliged to you, James, if you would make sure Sally isn't too lonely," Eliass had said, contorting his little round mouth into a parody of a smile.

Mellenkoff hadn't said that Eliass's wish was his command, but it might as well have been. The only time, so far as he knew, that Sally was alone was when she went to bed at night, and he was pretty certain her uncle would draw the line at her entertaining anybody there. Joel had in fact hinted that he was keeping an eye on his poor dead brother's girl because of a little bit of a wild streak, as he called it. So far, Mellenkoff had seen no sign of any wildness in Sally's behavior. She was an enchanting creature, and he enjoyed being seen with her, but she was a model of decorum, if he didn't count her occasional sotto voce derision of the New York social scene. When he took her home, she kissed him politely on the cheek and thanked him, while her huge blue eyes danced with mischief. He didn't know what the hell was going on, and apparently neither Sally nor her uncle was about to enlighten him. He assumed she had been in some escapade in California and had been whisked out of harm's way by her avuncular protector. And he was just as happy that she offered no more than a kiss on the cheek. All he needed was to be offered an opportunity to seduce Joel Eliass's niece, thereby finding himself in a classic no-win posture. One way or another, he hoped the whole thing would settle down soon, so that he could get back to the real world and his job. He knew the gossip columns had taken note of his arrival on the party circuit, undoubtedly because of the company he had been keeping. And God knows, Martha had to be aware of it. He put Martha out of his mind, where she already had been relegated to the corner labeled "good old."

He didn't want to think about personal problems. He never wanted to think about personal problems, because they weren't, in Mellenkoff's opinion, as important as professional problems. If Sally weren't Eliass's niece, he would be delighted to go to bed with her because she was the kind of woman he found most entertaining—beautiful and bitchy. And she didn't try to crawl inside your mind. He avoided comparisons and began to contemplate the series of meetings he would have in the week ahead with station managers and anchors from various WNN affiliates around the country. The meetings had grown out of a casual suggestion by Eliass that they examine potentially commercial talent. Mellenkoff had expanded that into calling in anchors, because some were beginning to look a little shaky, according to research and ratings, and the network thought a New York pep talk might be worthwhile, getting across to station owners who valued the affiliation that the network was concerned. Eliass had suggested Mellenkoff apply his discretionary powers to the situation. It was a matter of walking a fine line with the affiliates, as usual, indicating that a new order was at hand, but also making clear that WNN standards were being raised. It was not the kind of task that Mellenkoff wanted to have to put his mind to while attending to the social requirements of Sally Eliass. Maybe Julia Eliass would be back to take over the care and feeding of her niece. Or maybe Sally would go home to California. Mellenkoff was mildly surprised to discover he would prefer Sally to stay, although not under the chaperonage of her Uncle Joel.

The eleven o'clock news was over and he could still taste lobster. He sighed, flipped off the bedside lamp, and buried his head in his purple pillow. Where was Sally now that he needed her? he thought drowsily.

The next morning brought Mellenkoff no comfort for the headache he woke up with. Eliass summoned him to his office at nine o'clock, urged him to sit down, and looked at him with an alarming cordiality.

"My dear James," he said, "I'm afraid I have presumed upon you both socially and professionally these past weeks, and I must tell you that I feel you have performed admirably. Admirably."

"Thank you, sir," said Mellenkoff, and wondered what in hell was coming now.

Eliass lowered his bulk into his oversized executive chair, upholstered in black leather set in rosewood, leaned forward, and placed his small pale hands together tent-style. His cheeks shone ruddy, giving him the appearance of a ripe tomato. Sitting in the ornate office with its stained-glass inset at the top of a peaked window, Mellenkoff felt as though he were trapped in the sanctum of the Antichrist.

"I hope you will bear with me further, James," Eliass continued, "although what I have to say is of a personal nature, and of course I would never place any pressure of that kind on one of my people."

Like hell he wouldn't, Mellenkoff thought.

"I am not wrong, am I, in assuming that you are compatible with my niece, Sally?"

Mellenkoff felt his eyes bulge. "Compatible?" he echoed hollowly.

Eliass nodded, and uttered the strange twittering sound that meant he was chuckling.

"I have been watching you two young people, you know"—Oh, my God, thought Mellenkoff—"and I think I may have played the role of Cupid."

He's crazy! This is obscene. Why don't I get up and leave? I've got to be having a nightmare. All these thoughts raced through Mellenkoff's mind as he sat frozen in the overstuffed black suede chair Eliass reserved for his special visitors. Mellenkoff had wondered why he was being offered it. Now he knew.

Eliass actually seemed to be winking at him now. Mellenkoff decided he had to say something.

"Well, you know, I don't really know Sally that well, and while she's a lovely young lady, I don't—"

Eliass held up a hand.

"I know what you're about to say, James, and it's what I would expect. Of course Sally is very young, and, well, I think she's been swept off her feet. Not for the world would I try to force things along. I just wanted you to know that, well, should you and Sally become fonder of each other, nothing would make me happier."

Eliass's horn-rimmed eyeglasses flashed. "I would be delighted to welcome you into our family, James," he said silkily. "Our personal family."

Mellenkoff opened his mouth and found he had nothing to say. He suddenly visualized himself as a fish with a hook firmly embedded in its mouth.

"I—ah—arrmph—I'm—flattered, sir," he gasped.

Eliass nodded his rotund pink head. "Not at all, James."

The chairman rose from his seat, and Mellenkoff knew he was dismissed. He stood up, felt perspiration on his brow, and made as dignified a departure as the occasion permitted.

After he had gone, Joel Eliass went to the window and looked down at Manhattan far below, permitting himself a grunt of cold satisfaction. He was not displeased with his morning's work, following a conversation he had had with his niece the night before. When Sally had abruptly replaced the telephone receiver as he walked into the library, her uncle assumed correctly that she had reestablished contact with what he thought of only as "That Woman." At that point, what had been an idea clicking in the oiled mechanism of his mind had become a working proposal. He had hoped the knowledge of his disapproval and the threat of financial embarrassment would suffice. Now he believed more far-reaching steps had to be taken. He did not doubt that Sally could and would be cured of this hideous aberration. But he did not have the time to devote to the cure, and what seemed to be the solution was an alternative interest. A substitution, in other words. Casting around, Eliass had come up with the obvious choice. Mellenkoff was eligible, acceptable, and worked for him.

Sally had sat on the velvet sofa, her silk dress displaying an indecent amount of thigh, if you were affected by that kind of thing, and the blue eye that wasn't hidden by her hair had become saucerlike as she listened to her uncle.

"I had hoped never to raise this subject with you again, Sarah," he began, and she knew she was in deep trouble.

"But I fear that the—ah change of scene has not had as salutary an effect as I had assumed it would."

She was silent. There was nothing she could tell him that he would believe, and she dared not tell him the truth. Karen was in New York, and Sally was going to see her the next day. She was so excited that not even Uncle Joel could entirely quench her joy. What could he do to her? She didn't think he wanted to cut off money for her and her mother. It wouldn't look good, and Joel Eliass liked to look good, even in his own eyes. His cruelty was of the type that was veneered in goodness toward others.

" . . . in your own best interests," he was saying, and Sally dug her long nails into the palms of her hands to stop herself from screaming at him. Why didn't she get up and run away, run away to Karen? Because she wasn't certain of that either, and if she were to be entirely honest, because she didn't want to lose the damned money. Karen couldn't keep her; she didn't know if Karen *would* keep her, for that matter, and she couldn't keep herself.

Certainly not in the style to which Uncle Joel had accustomed her. She had to hang on, tough it out. That's what Mellenkoff would have told her. Mellenkoff. Uncle Joel was talking about Mellenkoff.

"Absolutely ideal," he was saying, tenting his fingers and bobbing his head.

What was absolutely ideal? What had she missed? He was looking at her as though he expected her to say something.

"I'm sure you're right, Uncle Joel," she volunteered, and pushed her hair back to get a better look at the expression on his face. He was smiling. Now what had she said?

"I knew you would feel that way. Now I think you should just take things as they come, don't force things with James. But I'm sure if you just enjoy each other, then it will all come about naturally and all this . . . this . . ."—he could not bring himself even to refer to the horror——"will seem like a bad dream."

He had Sally's full attention now. She heard her own voice, and it sounded squeaky.

"Uncle Joel," she said. "Are you saying you want me to marry James Mellenkoff?"

"In time, in time. If you should want to, I think it would be very suitable. Very suitable," he told her judiciously.

"What about him? What does he have to say about this?"

"I'm sure he will agree with me, my dear Sarah."

The pursed mouth snapped shut, and Sally looked at her uncle in horror.

"But I don't—I mean, I don't know him, and I don't love him and I don't want to marry him and I—I don't want to marry anybody."

She regretted her outburst instantly. Eliass regarded her stonily.

"I suggest," he said, "that you let yourself be guided in some things, Sarah. Believe me when I say that I have only your happiness in mind, and I have a great deal more experience of the world than you."

He paused, ominously.

"I would hate—nothing would distress me more than—to lose you from our family circle, Sarah. You know how fond I was of your father, how fond I am of your mother. But I have my principles—my morals, old-fashioned though you may think them—and I shall make every effort to prevent your becoming more—ah—mired in perversion. Make no mistake about that, Sarah. I mean what I say. I assume you have not forgotten our conversation in California."

She shook her head.

"Then I suggest you give considerable thought to what I have said."

Eliass had risen and walked from the room. Watching his back view and hating him, Sally thought no tailor could make him look anything but grotesque. How could Julia bear him? And the answer came to her instantly, because the thought of Julia Eliass immediately conjured up the image of sapphires glittering in the sun. Sally had fled to her room and flung herself across her silk-canopied pale blue bed. She lay tense and sleepless most of the night, watching the hours tick by on the gold digital clock, wanting desperately to talk to Karen. In the morning, she waited until she knew her uncle had left in his limousine for the network offices, then picked up her telephone. She didn't care if Taylor was listening. Karen answered on the second ring.

"It's me. Karen, I must see you now. It's awful."

"All right, all right." Karen's voice was warm and sleepy and slow. "So come on over. Or do you have to unlock the fetters first?"

Sally pulled on jeans and a sweater, brushed her hair, and waited until Taylor was in the kitchen before she slipped out the front door and hailed a taxi. Karen's apartment was nine blocks away, in a sedate and mani-cured security building where the doorman requested Sally's name and business, pushed a button, relayed her message. She stood fidgeting until he told her Mrs. Ward said she could come up. Fifth floor. Karen was waiting in the doorway, smiling, dark hair smoothly brushed, her dark gray wool pants well tailored, her raspberry silk shirt uncreased. She always looked so cool, Sally thought. She scampered through the door and flung her arms around Karen.

"You don't know how much I've missed you," she wailed.

Karen patted her back gently, and rubbed the back of her neck.

"My, we are tense, aren't we."

Sally flopped into a chair. "Karen, what am I going to do?"

Karen poured coffee and handed her a cup. "You're going to explain what all this uproar is about, my darling, that's what you're going to do."

"He wants me to marry James Mellenkoff!" Sally's tears spilled into her coffee.

"Begin at the beginning."

Sally blew her nose into a tissue Karen handed her, and began at the beginning.

When she finished, Karen had consumed two cups of coffee and was looking thoughtful.

"So what do you want to do, Sally?"

Sally stared at her. "How can you ask such a thing?"

"Well, that's what you've got to decide. Obviously, you don't want to turn your back on Uncle Joel's money, do you?"

Sally looked sheepish.

"I thought so. And frankly, you can't very well move in with me at this point. I mean, we aren't at that stage yet, Sally. You're still butterflying around."

"Karen, I'm not, I'm not."

"But you are, you are. You have to know what you want, and right now you don't."

Sally was silent, and another tear splashed into her coffee cup.

"You don't want me," she said miserably.

"On the contrary. I want you very much. But I want you to be sure of yourself as well as me. And your uncle is the kind of man who could make things very difficult for anyone who defied him. And I expect that would include your mother. He's sort of your classic ogre."

"So what will I do?"

Karen shook her head, smiling at the lovely tear-stained face turned toward her.

"Let's consider Mr. Mellenkoff," she said. "What's he like?"

Sally shrugged. "He's all right. He's very good-looking in a rugged sort of way. Very smart. Very, very ambitious."

"And Uncle Joel owns him too?"

"I suppose. He made him president of his network."

"And he could fire him equally quickly. Mellenkoff is in a fix, too."

Karen poured herself more coffee and propped her feet up on the coffee table.

"Do you know whether Eliass has talked to Mellenkoff about this?"

Sally shook her head. "He sort of indicated that Mellenkoff wouldn't object."

Karen laughed. "He might not at that. You're a real catch, darling. I mean, he gets the top job and the chairman's niece too? I'd think an ambitious man would jump at it. I mean, didn't you tell me your uncle married that Italian woman because she was the daughter of a rich banker? That was an arranged marriage, wasn't it? And how much does Julia see of Joel?" She raised her eyebrows quizzically at Sally.

"What are you suggesting?"

"Well, let's be really cold-blooded and pragmatic about this. Suppose you do what Uncle Joel wants and marry Mellenkoff. So what?"

"So what!" Sally exploded. "How can you of all people suggest such a thing?"

"Settle down."

Karen sat down on the sofa beside Sally and drew the tangled blond head to her shoulder, lightly kissing her forehead.

"Listen. to me. You'll hold all the cards. You marry Mellenkoff, and you're home free."

Sally sobbed. "But I'll have to sleep with him!"

"Not necessarily. You can just tell him you're not interested in sex. Now it's true you have to hope he's not a rapist, but if he's as good-looking as you say, I suspect he already has at least one and probably several women around, and he may not give a damn if you don't sleep with him. You might snoop around, see what you can find out about his personal life. Maybe he's equally upset right now—you thought of that? I mean, you're both Uncle Joel's prisoners, in a way."

Karen was rocking Sally gently in her arms as she spoke, and she felt the younger woman's body gradually relax against her.

"I hadn't thought of that," said Sally in a calmer voice.

"Now you have, though."

"We might have one of those—what do they call them?"

"A marriage of convenience," said Karen.

"But would you be here?" She looked anxiously into Karen's face. "Would I see you?"

Karen threw back her sleek head and laughed. "What's to prevent your taking a plane to California to see your mother? I mean, when I'm not in New York."

Sally's smile was brilliant. "Oh, Karen." She put her arms about the other woman's neck.

"Now all that's settled," said Karen, smoothing Sally's hair back from her face. "Let's think of something more pleasant."

21

LOOKING BACK long afterward, Martha Vogel associated the beginning of the nightmare with the arrival in Washington of Caroline Mitchell. She knew it wasn't fair, but there remained vivid in her mind the image of Caroline—beautiful, bright, and new—bouncing into the WNN office, confident of being welcomed and helped. As Caroline had been welcomed and helped.

When Martha got back to the office from the White House to take her visitor to lunch, Caroline was ensconced in the office of an associate director, Jim Jakes, who was another old friend of Joe Moynihan. Caroline of course, carried with her a letter of introduction from Moynihan, who was amused and intrigued at what he understood to be her friendship with Martha Vogel. Martha, who felt a little tired and hung over from a weekend spent chiefly in the company of Roger Miller, felt even more tired as Caroline leaped up to greet her with a warmth that was flattering, but scarcely justified by the extent of their acquaintance. But Martha knew how excited Caroline must be, and how important all of this must seem to her, so she opened her arms and welcomed Caroline to Washington.

"Everyone's been so wonderful to me. They took care of me and showed me around until you got here," Caroline burbled.

"That's great. Thanks for looking after her, Jim," Martha told Jakes with a smile.

"It was my pleasure, believe me," said Jakes, who was eyeing Caroline appreciatively.

"Listen, I brought my tapes. I hope you don't mind, but I'd so value your opinion, and maybe you can tell me what's wrong with them." Caroline's dark, limpid eyes fixed themselves beseechingly on Martha, who was beginning to feel slightly smothered.

"Sure, I'll be glad to look at them, Caroline. Although Jim there is probably more of an expert than I am. We'll get him to run them later today. Now how about some lunch? Jim, you want to come along?"

Jim came along, which was a relief to Martha, because he could take on some of the burden of coping with Caroline's vast reserves of enthusiasm and curiosity. Caroline wanted to know who everyone was, where everything was, and everything about everyone. Jakes, a normally phlegmatic young man, was clearly enamored of the glamorous newcomer who paid such rapt attention to every word he uttered. Martha noted that by the time she arrived in the office, Caroline had drawn from Jakes most of his life history and could already contribute little remarks tying what he was saying to what he had already told her about himself.

Dispiritedly forking up salad, it occurred to Martha that Jakes might be able to take over the role that Caroline apparently had in mind for her, at least until she went to New York. Martha had, with a certain malice aforethought, set up an appointment with Mellenkoff for Caroline, and had called him to tell him so. That was why she had been late coming back from the office. He had sounded tired, strained, and strange. Almost uncomfortable. She had asked him why, and he said sharply that he didn't want to be analyzed long-distance, he just wanted to get his schedule in order and get some sleep at some point in the near future. As she made no reply, he hastily apologized, saying it had been a bad day and seemed to be getting worse. She had made no further inquiries.

He had volunteered that he had to see Hathaway, the KRT anchor from the Columbus station where her protégée worked, and he wasn't looking forward to it.

"Going to suggest the station fire him?" she had asked casually.

Mellenkoff said not necessarily, but he had already met the man briefly, and he appeared to be one of those hearty types full of the milk of human kindness.

"You never know, you might learn something, James," Martha had observed acidly. He had not hung up, but she knew he had come close. And she had felt miserable after the conversation, which had widened the rift between them. And now she had Caroline to cope with, Caroline who was as full of hope and optimism as Martha had once been. Well, she qualified that, looking across the table at Caroline's glowing face. She had never been that hopeful or that optimistic. Or maybe she had never appeared that hopeful or optimistic. She was beginning to see that with Caroline, it was difficult to separate what she actually thought from her command of the right things to say and do. She did look quite a lot like the young Jacqueline Kennedy, Martha mused, but there was no reticence about Caroline, at least not over the lunch table. Something else that was different was her physical demeanor. Martha realized that was what had struck her when she walked into her office and saw Caroline sitting there in her pale pink silk shirt and trim black skirt, exuding a paradoxical mixture of self-confidence and breathlessness. Caroline had acquired a sexual confidence now. Martha smiled to herself. Evidently the broken engagement of which she had written so sadly had taught Caroline something.

Caroline was regaling Jim Jakes with a merry account of her beginning errors at KRT, including warm references to his friend Joe Moynihan. Jakes's eyes were full of amused approval, and Martha saw an opportunity to avoid an entire afternoon filled with the joy of Caroline.

"Why don't you have Caroline spend the rest of the day with you, Jim?" she suggested. "She could make comparisons with the system here and get a feel for that. And she could meet some more people, and—" she dropped the hook—"you could run her tapes. Maybe Sullivan would take a look at them."

Sullivan was the news director in Washington, and Martha suspected he would politely not have time to look at Caroline's tapes, but you never knew. She was beginning to think that when it came to Caroline, you didn't know at all. She had Jakes eating out of her hand, and God knew who'd be next to succumb. She would be curious herself to see those tapes, to see whether Caroline was all charm and an inch deep, or whether there was something solid in there. Not that the tapes would tell all that much, but if they were good, it would be unusual for someone of Caroline's age and experience.

"I understand Caroline's going to New York," said Jakes.

"Who's she seeing there?"

"Grrrrr," said Martha merrily, and Jakes chuckled.

"Himself?"

"Of course."

Caroline looked from one to another, wide-eyed.

"You're going to meet James Mellenkoff. Briefly," Martha told her.

"Oh, my God," said Caroline in awe. "The new president of the network?"

She looked at Martha and opened her mouth and then closed it. Martha nodded approvingly. At least Caroline had learned to be careful in reference to what she knew from her first meeting with Martha was a close personal relationship with Mellenkoff.

Jakes was obviously amused. "That's who you should get to look at your tapes, Caroline."

"Well, I think she'd better play that by ear," suggested Martha. "It'll depend what mood he's in and how busy he is."

"Mostly the former," said Jakes.

"Okay," said Martha, "I have to get back to the White House. Caroline, Jim'll take good care of you, I know."

Caroline looked a trifle downcast. "I can't go to the White House with you?"

"It's going to be a very dull afternoon. There isn't even a briefing today, and the President has no public events on his schedule. And I have some appointments with staff people, so you'd be sitting in a stuffy booth by yourself. You're a lot more likely to do yourself some good by sticking around the office and learning things."

Caroline nodded. "Of course. I'm delighted to do that. If Jim doesn't mind putting up with me hanging around. I'll try not to get in the way."

Jakes beamed on her. "Be nice to have you. And I'm sure Moynihan's trained you well enough so you know when to stay out of the way."

"Will I see you back at the office?" Caroline's question was so wistful that Martha relented.

"What are your dinner plans, Caroline?"

"Well, I don't really have any—"

Jakes interjected himself cheerfully into the conversation.

"Let's us all go to dinner."

"Fine."

Martha regretted her offer as soon as she left the restaurant, but as the afternoon wore on and she waited in the outer office of the White House special assistant for domestic affairs, she decided it might be an amusing evening. She'd have the feeling she had done something useful, a feeling she rarely had anymore. Martha was not especially enjoying covering the White House. It was a beat that ranged from the dramatic to the dull, and often there was little in between. Daily briefings had to be attended, with the knowledge that any real information came from painstaking cultivation of presidential aides and not from the perfunctory responses of the press secretary. Presidential events had to be covered, the speeches analyzed for substance amidst the platitudes. Presidential travel was the way Martha visualized life in the army. The White House press followed *Air Force One* in its own chartered jet, with departure usually in the dawn hours from Andrews Air Force Base, often arriving at another military base near the site of the presidential speech. Security had become tighter, even for the hard core of those assigned to cover the White House, most of whose faces were familiar to the Secret Service. But the agents were suspicious of everyone. There had been too many presidential assassination attempts for them to relax their guard with the press and drink with reporters occasionally, the way they used to.

Martha disliked the regimentation of the coverage, and the fact that almost the only people she saw were other members of the press corps covering the White House. It was a classic example of pack journalism, she had complained to Mellenkoff.

"We all get fed our news rations daily, and if we're lucky, we can scrape up some dessert to titillate the viewers, but that's about as far as it goes. We all get the same damned backgrounders, and if one of the White House people crosses the line, the White House reams them out. It's like being in a fancy cage."

"You're also on the air every night, just about. Have you forgotten that?" asked Mellenkoff unsympathetically.

"I know," said Martha. "Pinnacle journalism, is that right?"

"Would you rather be on the Pentagon and never get on the air, or general assignment and wind up with the feature ragbag?"

"You know what I'd rather," Martha had said.

"Nag is what you'd rather," Mellenkoff had told her in a warning voice, and she dropped the subject, but he knew she would raise it again. Martha believed she could be a good anchor. She had the background, the experience, and the ability. She knew the ratings on the current anchor were flagging, and she also knew that this was a time when WNN was going through massive changes. Eliass had made that clear when he took over, and had followed through with a series of arbitrary firings, promotions, and demotions, culminating in the naming of Mellenkoff as president of the network. That in itself had caused a flurry of reaction among the staff. It was a spectacular leap even for Mellenkoff, leaving him at once brilliantly successful and precariously balanced.

She had never been able to pin Mellenkoff down on whether he considered her a possibility as an anchor. As the first solo woman national anchor, for that matter. She knew Mellenkoff's fondness for setting precedents, and that he had in mind revamping the seven o'clock news show with the hope of overtaking their competitors. WNN was still trailing, and Eliass wouldn't tolerate that for long. He had sunk not only money but his reputation for backing winners into his investment in WNN. Martha wondered if Mellenkoff was aware of what a tightrope he trod, and whether that accounted at least in part for his irritability and his remoteness.

Now that he was gone, Martha had more time to think about what she had and what she hadn't. From a material and professional standpoint, by any standards, she had done well. She was extremely well paid, especially by journalistic standards; she was liked and respected; and she enjoyed her work. From a personal standpoint, her uncertainty was such that without Mellenkoff as the basic focus of her life, she found herself adrift and frightened. She was thirty-four years old, and when she looked in the mirror, what she saw was Martha Vogel, television correspondent. Sometimes she thought there was no Martha

Vogel, there was only the television correspondent. With that thought there came an eerily empty feeling, a question of her own existence. She had dismissed it as depression over Mellenkoff's leaving, but it stayed with her, nudging her in the night and when she sat listening to music alone in her apartment. What was that song—"Is That All There Is?" When she asked herself that question, Martha found herself wanting.

She could begin a new relationship, accept the invitations she had been turning down, ask for a transfer to a foreign bureau. Her options were varied, but they were transcended by her feeling of hopelessness. She went to her doctor, had her first medical checkup in six years, and came out several hundred dollars poorer and just as healthy. She had no excuses, no excuses at all. Yet she had the feeling that she had taken a step too many into quicksand, and she had no idea how she could extricate herself. In her darkest moments, all she could think was that she would wait and see what Mellenkoff did next. Or wanted her to do next. She knew they would never marry now, and she would not have cared about that if they could still be together. But that seemed to be lost to her too, and she could not take her troubles to him. He had never been a man who offered a shoulder to cry on. The kind of women Mellenkoff respected cried in private and kept their snuggling for his shoulder. He would listen, attentively, and offer pragmatic advice. There was nothing he could tell her that she didn't know, and nothing that she wanted to hear.

Martha heaved herself out of the overstuffed chair, in which she had been slumped for forty minutes, at the news that Donald Kingsburgh would see her now, and arrived in his office two minutes later with a series of crisp questions designed to deflect mushy answers. She had always been able to compartmentalize her mind, and for that she was devoutly grateful. Otherwise she could never have concentrated on the carefully measured opinions of Mr. Kingsburgh on how the President was solving his problems with minorities. Mr. Kingsburgh, who was pale and balding and oval-shaped, reminded Martha irresistibly of an Easter egg.

Thirty minutes later, Martha emerged with a dozen pages of notes and the conviction that the White House had no idea at all what to do to solve the problems with minorities. She would try to work that impression into the piece she was planning on administration soft spots. Looking at her watch, she realized Mr. Kingsburgh had wasted a fair part of her afternoon, and she decided to call and find out what fresh fields Caroline had conquered.

"How's our protégée?" she asked Jim Jakes when he took her call.

"Swept through the place like a forest fire. She even got to Sullivan."

Martha was impressed and asked if Sullivan had been impressed.

"Let me say he didn't throw her out, and that's not entirely because of her looks. He's got a low tolerance for the cutes."

"Did you take a look at her tapes?"

"They're interesting. She needs a lot of polishing, but I tell you, Marty, she's got something. For her age and the little she's done, she's really got something. She's a natural."

That was something of a magic word in the business, Martha knew, and while she respected Jakes's opinion, she would want to hear that from someone less entranced by Caroline's charm.

"Oh, by the way," said Jakes, "Caroine wants to know if she can bring someone else along for dinner. Apparently the anchorman from KRT in Columbus—Mike Hathaway, I think it is—is seeing the brass in New York tomorrow and he's flying in here tonight." He chuckled. "I suspect Caroline's the reason he's flying in tonight. She was a bit too casual about the whole thing."

Martha raised her eyebrows slightly, said that was fine with her, and as she touched up her makeup in the restroom attached to the press room, wondered why the name *Hathaway* rang a bell. Applying lipstick, she suddenly stopped and saw her eyes widen slightly in the mirror. Unless she was mistaken, Caroline had been engaged to someone called Hathaway. When she wrote about her broken engagement, she had mentioned a name, and Martha was sure that was it. Not this Hathaway, she assumed. Another journalism student, she recollected. She wondered if they were related. At least the introduction of the anchorman might make the evening more interesting. She wondered how he would get along with Mellenkoff. It was none of her business and Mellenkoff would tell her that.

Dinner proved more interesting than Martha had expected. She liked Mike Hathaway immediately.

"Mike's taught me a lot," said Caroline gravely, and Martha caught a quick glance between them that suggested that what Mike had taught Caroline might not have been entirely during office hours.

Martha's curiosity was roused. Whom had Caroline been engaged to, and which Hathaway was this? She couldn't very well ask, but as the meal became merrier, with Mike and Jakes exchanging anecdotes, and as the atmosphere became more relaxed, Martha saw enough to convince her that Caroline's mentor probably was also her lover.

"I hear Caroline's going to New York tomorrow, too," said Mike. Martha, who suspected he had known all along, nodded.

"She has an appointment with Mellenkoff at two."

"I'm so nervous," said Caroline.

"You should be," said Jakes, and sputtered into his third vodka tonic.

Martha frowned. "No, she shouldn't. He likes to encourage people," she said. "He certainly encouraged me," she observed, and noted the pause that followed her words.

"Do you think I should ask if he'd like to see my tapes?" asked Caroline.

Martha hesitated. "I suppose you could mention them. But I wouldn't push it, Caroline. You may spend a very short time with him, you know."

"Hell, go for it, Caroline honey," said Jakes. "What've you got to lose?"

"Her head," said Martha.

22

IT WAS almost midnight when Mellenkoff called Martha at her apartment. Martha was lying in bed reading the latest book on what was wrong with the American presidency. It had been written by a friend, and she felt called upon at least to skim through it. Knowing that he had held a position in the White House for two years, she assumed the book would in large part relate what he had told the President, and she was right. At least it was a short book. Some presidential advisers appeared to feel that any tenure at the White House made their life history of deathless interest to the public. She picked up the receiver and felt the old joyous lift of spirit as she heard the familiar "Hey there."

"How are things, hey there?" she asked.

"Frenzied," said Mellenkoff. His voice was deeply tired.

"I wish you were here."

"God, Martha, so do I."

"Well?"

"You know I can't, right now. I can't get down there."

"You mean you're still baby-sitting Sally."

There was the kind of silence that, from long knowledge of Mellenkoff, meant he had something to say and didn't know how to say it. Martha pushed her fingers through her already tousled hair and wondered drearily how she would cope with more bad news.

"We need to talk," Mellenkoff said thickly. "And not on the phone."

"But you don't want me to come to New York this weekend either, right?"

"It won't work out right now." His voice was harsh.

"James," said Martha as gently as she could, "why

don't you just tell me the truth? Why is that so difficult? Or are you practicing pulling the wings off flies?"

"You don't know what I'm going through."

She sighed. "Last I heard, you were closeted in your office with Caroline Mitchell."

There was a chuckle on the other end.

"There's a little tiger!"

Martha smiled. Leave it to Mellenkoff to recognize his own kind.

"What'd you think of her?"

"Very interesting. Don't laugh, but I even took a look at her tapes."

Martha wasn't laughing; she wasn't even surprised.

"And?"

"She's going to be good. Very good. She's a natural."

A clanging sound outside sounded to Martha like a lid slamming on a coffin.

"Did you tell her that?"

"Don't be silly. She's got a long way to go. But we'll get them to give her more responsibility at the station. Maybe try her out as a weekend anchor, see whether she hangs herself. If she doesn't, at this stage, she might be a real find. But we'll take it slowly."

Martha heard the words and felt suddenly cold. She pulled the blue comforter up and tightened her blue velour robe around her. Then she remembered, it wasn't her robe, it was Mellenkoff's robe.

"I'm wearing your robe," she said childishly, and fought back tears.

He waited a moment or two before he spoke.

"Listen, Martha. You know I care about you."

"Yes."

"You don't doubt that?"

"No."

"There's—Jesus, how can I explain this?—there's something very odd here. Something involving Eliass. I can't go into it now."

"Is Eliass tapping your phone, too?" Her voice was acid enough that Mellenkoff could relax.

"Martha, I am sitting here in the middle of a purple bed, surrounded by surrealistic paintings, trying to cope with the most difficult situation I've ever faced, and you're not helping."

She sat up in bed, torn between misery and amusement.

"James, how in hell can I help when you won't tell me what your problem is, how I'm involved in it, or why you have to tell me in the middle of the night that you care about me. The last is the one I care about, anyway."

"That's right," he snapped. "All you want to hear is that I love you and you can come to New York for the weekend."

"Goddamnittohell!" Martha shouted. "That's contemptible, even from you."

Mellenkoff laughed. "Feel better now?"

Martha hung up and put two pillows over the telephone, thought about pouring herself a Scotch, decided he wasn't going to drive her to drink as well, and sat glaring at the jangling mechanism. On the fourteenth ring, she picked up the receiver. "Proud of yourself?"

"What's that again?" asked Roger Miller. Martha giggled helplessly.

"I thought you were someone else, Roger. I'm sorry."

"I've been trying to reach you for a while. Your line's been busy."

"Maybe you should all move in with me and we could play railroad station."

"Are you cheerful or merely hysterical?"

"I don't know," said Martha, suddenly wary. "Should I be either?"

"I assume you've been talking to Mellenkoff?"

"Right."

"How'd he sound?"

"Pretty much the same as usual. Why?"

There was a long sigh from Miller.

"Martha, I don't want to be the bearer of gloomy tidings, and I don't vouch for the truth of any of this. But there have been rumors around the office tonight, and there's an item in one of the gossip columns I thought you might have seen."

"And you wanted to save me that. Dear Roger."

Martha wished she had disconnected her telephone when she went to bed. Bad news was always worse at night, because you had those wonderful dawn hours during which to brood upon it and work yourself into a pulp over it.

"I think James was trying to tell me something, but wasn't up to it," she said.

"I don't know that he was," said Miller quickly. "Maybe he was trying to talk something through with you."

"Look, for God's sake, what is all this?" demanded Martha exasperatedly. "Is he sleeping with Eliass?"

"The rumor is that he's going to marry Sally Eliass."

"He's not only robbing the cradle, he's raping it."

"Martha," said Miller gently.

"Is it a rumor, Roger?"

"I honestly don't know. The whole thing's bizarre. I've heard Sally was in some trouble in California and Eliass wants her settled down and out of his hair, and he's picked Mellenkoff as the man to settle her down."

"I can't fault him on his taste."

Miller's voice sharpened. "That's about enough of the sophisticated cynic bit, Martha. I'm telling you this only so you wouldn't be taken by surprise by reading it, and also because I don't know that there's any truth to it. I think he'd have told you himself if there had been. Christ, he's only known her a month or so."

Martha felt sick.

"Roger," she said, "thank you. And I'm sorry about the wisecracks, but what else do I say? But thank you. And now I must go, because, no kidding, I think I'm going to throw up."

She replaced the receiver carefully, and went into the bathroom, where she threw up. Afterward, she crouched beside the toilet, shivering, wrapping herself in a bath towel, and resting her damp forehead against the cool porcelain. The telephone rang insistently in the bedroom, but she was shaking too much to move. After a while, she pulled herself up by leaning on the side of the bathtub, and splashed her face with cold water. When she tried to brush her teeth, her hand was shaking too much to hold the toothbrush, and she settled for mouthwash.

"What the hell is wrong with me? I'm acting as if I'm coming apart!" she scolded herself, and made a conscious effort to focus on the mundane, such as the fact that she had to be at the White House at eight the next morning to interview the national security adviser.

Cautiously, she let go of the towel rail, frail support that it was for her five-foot-eight-inch frame, and walked slowly back into the bedroom. She was thirsty, and she wondered if she could make it into the kitchen and get herself some club soda. She decided not to risk it. Reaching the bed, she relaxed her control over her wobbly legs, and slid gratefully beneath the sheets, clutching at the comforter. She lay quite still for a long time, letting her mind meander. Then she got up, quite purposefully, and threw up again. After that, she felt surprisingly better. The whole thing was something I ate, she thought, and managed a weak chuckle, which sounded oddly loud in the quiet room.

She looked at the clock, which said two o'clock, and thought wearily that she had to be up in four hours. She couldn't ask Terry Steiner to do the Kephardt interview on that short notice, and she disliked canceling such appointments because they often were not easy to set up. Of course, if she were dead, they would have to make some other arrangements. This time, her chuckle was stronger. The telephone rang again, and she counted twelve and lifted the receiver. As she had expected, it was Roger Miller.

"Hi. I feel better," she said.

"Are you sure? Shouldn't you call somebody?"

"Roger, I'm fine. I promise I'll wait until you're here to have my nervous breakdown."

His voice was perceptibly relieved.

"You sound better. Try to get some sleep and I'll talk to you tomorrow. Maybe I'll come down this weekend again."

Martha said good night, smiling, and slid down on her pillows. She felt numb, but at least she didn't feel sick. She hated to feel sick, hated to feel out of control.

She slept sporadically and dreamed about her mother. At six her alarm went off, and she stumbled out of bed, showered, washed her hair, dressed in a crisp dark green linen suit, and went to work. It was a busy day, with a presidential press conference in the East Room of the White House in the afternoon, and an announcement of what might or might not, according to which pundit you listened to, be a variation on administration policy toward the Soviet Union. It was eight at night before Martha reached her office, and she was almost too tired to think. On her desk there was a basket of flowers,

fragrant and cool, and she closed her eyes and held them
to her face for a few seconds before she detached the tiny
ivory envelope wired to a stem.

"With gratitude and affection," it read, "from Caroline Mitchell." Martha smiled, and riffled through her
mail. There was a pale green envelope with Caroline's
name in the top left-hand corner. Martha opened it.
Caroline had written a short, graceful note full of enthusiasm for her trip.

"I'm especially grateful," she wrote, "for your arrang-
ing an appointment with Mr. Mellenkoff, who was really
very gracious, and was kind enough to look at my tapes.
He offered me very constructive advice, and I have to
admit that he really raised my hopes as to the future."

"You get a letter from Caroline too?" asked the voice
of Jim Jakes behind her.

Martha looked up. "You too?"

"Sure. So did Sullivan. God knows what Mellenkoff
got."

"She probably sent him more tapes," said Martha dryly.

Jakes chuckled. "I heard he was quite taken with her—
professionally, I mean."

"That's a real possibility. You can't fault her for lack
of effort."

Martha had a headache and she didn't feel like discussing Caroline Mitchell's future when she was so depressed
about her own.

"How about a drink?" suggested Jakes.

She shook her head. "Not tonight, Jim. I didn't sleep
much last night and today seemed to last about forty-
eight hours."

"Looked good on your stand-up."

She smiled at him and wondered if she was imagining
that he was regarding her with unusual solicitude.

"Sure you won't just have a quickie? Cheer you up."

She put Caroline's letter into her purse.

"I look like I need cheering up?"

"Yeah," said Jakes. "Frankly, you do."

Martha paused.

"By any chance," she said, "have you been talking to
Roger Miller?" Jakes grinned.

"My little Band-Aids," said Martha and patted his
cheek.

At home, she fixed herself soup and a sandwich, drank a glass of wine, and munched an apple. She wrote a note for her cleaning woman, checked clothes that needed to go to the dry cleaner, and accepted four invitations for the next two weeks.

Sitting at her desk, she went through some tax records, wrote herself a reminder about a friend's birthday, and threw away some ancient receipts. In the kitchen, she inventoried the refrigerator, made a list of what she needed, and noted that her liquor supply was low. Walking into the bedroom, she removed what was left of Mellenkoff's clothes from the closet and hung them at the back of her coat closet in the foyer. She hesitated over the blue bathrobe, then tossed it into the laundry hamper to be washed and put away. His shaving gear and lotion she removed from the medicine cabinet and put away in a drawer. She was pleased to note that she felt no particular depression while she did these things. She was putting Mellenkoff on hold, in her mind and in her closets. It didn't mean she was throwing him out. Someday she might, but not yet. She looked with disapproval at the rumpled bed, a departure from her firmly held belief that there were few things more depressing to come home to than an unmade bed. She stripped it, dumped the sheets in the hamper, and neatly remade the bed, fluffing up pillows, turning back the comforter.

Then she called Roger Miller, who was still at his office, as she knew he would be, and invited him to come down to Washington again for the weekend.

"I'd love to," he said. "How are things?"

"Better," said Martha.

"You sound tired."

"I am. What I put myself through last night would have tired anybody. And I had Kephardt this morning at breakfast. But I've been cleaning house, sort of."

"Throw out anybody I know?"

Martha chuckled. "Not yet, Roger, not yet." She hesitated, then asked the question. "I assume you have no update?"

"Yesterday's rumors are still flying. He was moodier than usual, but that may be because he spent quite a bit of time with our chairman. You haven't heard from him?"

"No, and maybe it's as well if I don't for a bit. I don't

want to go through a frontal lobotomy daily. Anyway, I'm glad you can come down, Roger. There's a party at the French embassy you might like, or we can just mush around."

After she had put the phone down, Martha went into the bathroom, put out fresh towels, and ran a hot bath into which she poured an extravagant amount of bath oil. She found a murder mystery on her bedside shelf that she had begun the previous week, and took it with her when she slid into the tub. She stayed in the perfumed hot water for half an hour, and was pleased to find she could also immerse herself in the problems of guests in a snow-bound lodge who were being murdered one-by-one by a killer in a ski mask. By the time she padded off to bed, she had guessed who the murderer was, confirmed her guess with a peek at the final pages, and slipped into a dreamless sleep. When the telephone rang, she stirred, muttered, and turned over, but she did not answer it.

23

WHEN MELLENKOFF had picked up his telephone and told his secretary to delay his next meeting for twenty minutes, Caroline knew she had taken a first small step down a long road. She had been warned by Betsy Cooley, the impassively polite guardian of Mellenkoff's door, that he had allotted her no more than ten minutes.

"His schedule is just unbelievable today."

Then Caroline knew how much time she had to sell herself. When she walked into the black and white office, her face was serene, her carriage erect and graceful, and she waited until he looked up from the papers on his desk before she smiled at him. It was a transcendently radiant smile, and Mellenkoff, who was no slouch at using his own grin as a weapon, was mildly impressed. He shook hands with her, waved toward a black leather armchair, which Caroline correctly gauged as designed to test the stamina of visitors. She perched herself lithely on the edge of its overstuffed seat cushion.

"How's Joe Moynihan?" asked Mellenkoff.

"He's fine. He's been taking me in hand," she said.

"Good. Moynihan's a good teacher. You can learn a lot from him. And I gather you think you've learned something, or you wouldn't be here."

She nodded. "It was Joe who thought I should make tapes."

"Was it Joe who thought you should persuade me to hear them?"

She smiled again, and saw a flicker of a responsive grin. "That was my idea."

"What made you think I'd look at them, Miss Mitchell?"

She hesitated only briefly.

"Martha Vogel told me you were the best in this busi-

ness. She said you'd helped her. And"—her hands came
out in a charming gesture—"obviously you could help
me."

He was not displeased. "Only if I thought you were
any good."

"I understand that. But I'm sure you'd tell me if I
weren't."

He nodded. "You're entirely right about that."

Mellenkoff leaned back in his chair.

"I took a look at your tapes." He looked at her, and
Caroline tilted her head interrogatively to one side and
hoped that the tension didn't show. "You show promise."

Caroline smiled again, this time out of sheer relief, and
to her surprise, Mellenkoff grinned back at her.

"You've got a great smile," he told her, "and you're
good on camera. Voice, manner—both relaxed. You've
got to get rid of those teleprompter eyes. You still look
too often as if you're reading aloud. Think of it as if
you're talking to me. When you're not afraid of me."

"Do I look like I'm afraid of you?"

"No, you're not a bad actress. But if I'd told you those
tapes were lousy, you'd have crept out of here in tears."

"No," said Caroline with unexpected firmness, "I never
cry."

"Never?" Mellenkoff sounded dubious.

"Not that I can recall."

"In any case, you're apparently getting good solid training and it shows. Kriss told me Moynihan had been
keeping tabs on you. Tell him from me he's doing a
decent job."

Caroline was rigidly attentive.

"Go on back to Columbus and work hard. Work harder
than you ever have before, and don't let anything interfere with it. Kriss'll be in touch with me from time to
time. After a while, maybe we'll see just what you can
do."

Caroline hesitated.

His eyebrows rose. "Yes?"

"That tape you saw—I have another. A later one. I
think it's a lot better."

He glanced at his watch, looked back at her, then
laughed and picked up the telephone.

"Betsy? I'm going to be a little delayed. Yes, I know, I

know. No more than twenty minutes. We'll try to catch
up by changing that lunch timing, okay?"

He ran the tape, which was brief. She watched his
face, surreptitiously, but it was uncommunicative.

"You're right. It is better. Not as much better as you
think. But you're moving in the right direction."

He looked at her with some amusement. She was certainly not lacking in confidence, and her appearance was
spectacular. She had taken him by surprise with her
request that he look at a new tape. Martha had been
right: there was something different about Caroline
Mitchell.

"It's my hope," she was saying now, "that I can work
in New York some day. Maybe for WNN."

"A lot of people hope that," he observed. "But you
certainly seem to have a lot of determination, Miss Mitchell. We'll talk again someday."

She could hardly wait to tell Mike when she reached
the New York hotel room where he was waiting for her.
They had carefully taken separate flights to New York
from Washington after their dinner with Martha and
Jakes. Caroline had been anxious to maintain the façade
of discretion, especially as she wasn't sure what she would
do without it. But she was so excited about her talk with
Mellenkoff that she poured out the details before she
recollected she hadn't even asked Mike how his meeting
with the network president had gone. Guilt-stricken, she
clutched at his hand.

"How did it go for you?"

Mike patted her hand reassuringly. "It's okay. They're
going to ask the station to have me do more reporting.
Apparently it's almost entirely a question of some of the
younger viewers feeling I'm too cheerful. I mean, life is
grim and full of apartheid and foreign policy fiasco and
starvation and why am I so goddamned happy about it
all? Why do I never get out there and find out what's
going on? So I told them, after all, I had started out in
the newspaper business and I didn't think I'd forgotten
how to do an interview. So we're going to have me
leading an investigation into drugs on campus—your campus, for that matter, darling."

"But you'll still be anchoring."

He nodded. "Mellenkoff apparently told Kriss, and

indicated to me, that a breakdown on the market research shows a need for some repairs, but not a general overhaul."

"What about Alice Martinsen?"

Mike frowned. "I don't know. Obviously Mellenkoff didn't discuss anyone else in front of me, and Eric is pretty closemouthed about that kind of thing. I still have the impression she's in bad shape."

"That's too bad," said Caroline mechanically. Mike looked at her and laughed, pulling her into his arms.

"I can see your mind working from here."

Caroline hugged him excitedly. "Oh Mike, I can hardly believe it. I mean, he actually seemed to think I was good!"

"You didn't believe us, hmmm?"

He kissed her, and she kissed him back. But as he made love to her, Caroline's mind remained in Mellenkoff's office. She didn't mind Mike's lovemaking. He was tender and very gentle, and he seemed to worry about whether she was enjoying it, so out of gratitude, she tried to behave as if she were enjoying it. She made pleased sounds and clung to him at what she hoped were the right times, and he seemed happy. She never felt very much. It was as though her mind and her body were separate, and if she did not keep them separate, then she might find herself back in that peach and ivory bedroom, rigid and full of hate. But she was very fond of Mike, and when she told him she loved him, she meant it. It disturbed her occasionally when he talked, as he had, of marriage. He seemed to take for granted that he and Leslie would be divorced. That was up to Mike. But Caroline hoped that he did not assume his divorce would necessarily be followed by marriage to her. Especially now that she had met Mellenkoff and after what he had said to her. He had told her to work hard, and that was what she had to do. Nothing else mattered as much as pleasing Mellenkoff, because, as everyone told her, he was the man with the power.

And she lay in Mike's arms, planning happily. She didn't know whether she was going to graduate from Glayville or not. She probably would, but it would be a close thing, given all the classes she had cut so she could work at KRT during her senior year. Moynihan had suggested she might be able to claim some credits for on-the-job training, as it were, and she had to check on that. But unless it would affect her chances at the station, she didn't really care. And from what Moynihan had said, she didn't think it would. It was helpful that Moynihan was the kind of news director who adhered to the old-fashioned belief that you didn't learn to be a reporter in a classroom.

"You'll never be a good anchor unless you're a good reporter, unless you know how to cover a story. I'm not bringing you up to be one of those airheads," he told her over a beer one night, while she sipped a little wine and absorbed advice.

She speculated about Alice Martinsen. Suppose she were out as co-anchor? Caroline wriggled ecstatically at the thought, then quieted herself as Mike's arms tightened around her. She wanted to be able to think in peace. Realistically, she could not expect to snag Alice's job, although she'd always gotten along very well with Rudy Colling, and she knew Alice drove her co-anchor crazy. But Alice did anchor the weekend news a lot, and that might be a possibility. She would have to find out what Kriss told Moynihan, and work on Joe. Caroline snuggled her head into Mike's shoulder and fell contentedly asleep.

Their mutual contentment was only slightly dented by the mixed reception that awaited Mike and Caroline on their return to Columbus. They might as well not have taken the trouble to fly back on separate flights, because, as Jill had predicted, both Frank and Leslie Hathaway had added two and two and come up with four, as had most of the KRT newsroom. There was a letter from Frank awaiting Caroline. It was full of reproach mixed with bitter condemnation of his father. There was a letter from Leslie awaiting Mike. It said he would be hearing from her lawyer. The two letters were the result of an evening spent together by Leslie and her son, in which they had discussed the situation in what she termed an open-minded way, which meant they blamed Mike for everything and dismissed Caroline as a seducer's victim. Frank was not quite certain that Caroline fitted that role, but he was so deeply angry at his father that he was willing to acquiesce in his mother's cold contempt. It was

after finding out from a classmate of Caroline—not from
Jill, to whom he rarely spoke—that Caroline's visit to
New York and Washington coincided with that of his
father, that Frank told his mother about finding his ex-
fiancée in his father's apartment. But he knew his father
was in New York, and the suspicion had become painful
certainty in Frank's mind.

Leslie had shown little emotion. She had seen Mike
only once before he left for New York, and as she had
told her friends, he might have been a stranger.

"Maybe you should try your luck," she had told Linda
the divorcée, who was shaking her head sympathetically
while her eyes gleamed.

"You sure there isn't someone else?" Linda had asked,
and Leslie had shaken her head.

"Mike? Heavens no. That was one thing I never had to
worry about. For one thing, he knew I'd never put up
with it. No, I think this is worse. It's all in his mind."

"Really," Linda had said.

Listening to Frank a few days later, Leslie burned with
the knowledge that she had made a fool of herself. She
was especially bitter over the tears she had shed; even
breaking down in front of Frank over a man who at that
very moment—*at that very moment*—was having a tumble with a teenager, or the next thing to it. Leslie's rage
consumed her embryonic feelings of guilt about her marriage, and left only a residue of self-pity. It was bad
enough that Mike had left her. It was unforgivable that
he had humiliated her. And what was unforgettable was
that he had sought solace, if that was what it was called,
with the young girl whom his son had been planning to
marry.

"Obviously, I'll divorce him," Leslie told Frank, who
nodded miserably.

Where his mother could console herself in righteous
fury, Frank was obsessed by loss. Suddenly, he had been
stripped of father and sweetheart. Was this what Caroline meant by being friends? He tortured himself by
picturing her with his father, smiling at him, kissing him,
making love to him. As she had never made love to
Frank. He barely listened as Leslie fulminated against
Mike, and tossed in a few barbs about Caroline for good
measure. He could hardly defend either of them. Yet he

was strangely lacking in sympathy for his mother. Sitting in her elegant sitting room, there crept into Frank's mind the thought that had his mother been different, his father might have neither left nor given Caroline a second thought. He remembered hearing his parents discuss friends who were being divorced, and his mother observe coolly, "Well, it takes two, of course."

His father had smiled an odd little smile and said, "No, it took three."

Perhaps Caroline had played the role of the third party, straying into territory occupied by a couple drifting toward estrangement. But how could his father have become involved with Frank's Caroline? That was what really hurt. His father must hate him even more than he hated Leslie. Mike had called him once or twice since coming back from New York, and Frank had hung up each time. He wasn't angry so much as he wasn't ready to talk to his father. He needed time, and he was beginning to think he needed a lot of distance. He needed to be a long way from Columbus.

He made some calls to friends; he noted with satisfaction the level of his savings account; and he found himself a job on a newspaper in a suburb of Los Angeles. He told nobody in Columbus. But the day after he graduated, a ceremony attended by his mother and father, carefully sitting on opposite sides of the auditorium, Frank packed his clothes and his tennis racquet and his running shoes, and bought a one-way ticket to California. He left his mother a brief note saying he would be writing to her, that he had a job on the West Coast, and not to worry, that he had to get things sorted out in his mind.

Leslie blamed Mike for that too. He had driven away their son, she told her friends. She hoped he was proud of himself for ruining two lives. She reacted angrily to the friend who suggested that Frank was only doing what he probably would have done anyway, and Leslie's life wasn't much different than it had been before Mike left. Materially, she meant? Leslie had snapped. The friend shrugged. Leslie had considered returning the substantial check Mike sent to her monthly, but went on depositing it, while alternately berating herself for doing so and rationalizing that there was no reason she should suffer any more than she had already. Mostly, Leslie spent her days being angry, the kind of anger that spilled into her lunches and dinners with friends and embittered the promise of any other relationship. She roamed the empty house, where the floors and furniture didn't shine the way they once had, and she didn't trouble to make sure there were fresh flowers in the living room anymore.

She telephoned Mike one night, uncaring whether he was alone or not, and poured out her pent-up fury at him and her frustration at not being able to do anything about it. He listened until she had raged herself into exhaustion, grateful that Caroline was not there. Into a simmering silence, Mike suggested, "Why don't you go back to teaching? You used to love it. I always thought you were good at it. It'd give you something more worthwhile to worry about than—than me."

"Who'd want me?" asked Leslie bitterly.

"That's silly," Mike reproved her. "You've got a lot of good friends in the university, not to mention the college. I expect they've been waiting for you to bring it up."

"Maybe I could teach a course for Caroline."

"Look," said Mike, "we've been over that ground for the past twenty minutes. Why not see what's available that you'd enjoy, and try it out. You don't need to, Leslie, but I think you're bored. You're far too bright not to be busy. And you know you always ran that house in half an hour a day. That's no occupation for you."

It was the kind of subtle flattery that Mike knew would appeal to his wife. Leslie was bright, she had enormous reserves of energy, and he had always admired her capacity for organization. She knew that. And judging from the quiet at the other end of the telephone, she was not rejecting what he had just said.

"Let me know," said Mike.

"Why would you care?"

"Leslie," he said patiently, "I do care. I always shall."

She hung up, but quietly. And Mike felt a small degree of satisfaction. He was finding it difficult to adjust to his new life, and not one of the smaller problems had been the ultimate bitter estrangement from both his wife and his son. Frank had not left him a note when he left town, nor had he called. Mike had accepted that he had to wait until Frank could come to terms with the pain for which he blamed his father.

Meantime, Mike was beginning to realize he had exchanged one set of problems for a new set of problems. He did not want to live with Leslie again, but he had to admit that after twenty-five years, she at least had been predictable, even if the predictability was often unpleasant. Caroline remained in many ways an unknown quantity, with wild emotional mood swings that he had learned to try to fend off before they gathered force. During her darkest moods, she simply disappeared, psychologically, if not literally, and he did not dare touch her. When she was happy, she was as affectionate as a kitten, and as pliable. But her happiness frequently seemed linked to what was happening to her at KRT as much as to her relationship with Mike. She would talk for hours about how to improve her on-camera delivery, whether her visuals were better, how she had blown that interview with the police chief. But she would hardly talk at all about what lay ahead for the two of them. When Mike pressed her on the subject, she fixed huge reproachful eyes on him and lapsed into silence. If she had cried, it would have been easier, but Caroline never cried. She walled herself off. Her work performance was improving; there was no doubt of that. Eric Kriss and Joe Moynihan had both commented to him on it. Mike suspected that Caroline was maneuvering for the weekend anchor job, as Alice Martinsen's stock continued to descend in the ratings as well as in the newsroom. He had noticed with wry amusement that not even Caroline's formidable charm could distract Alice from the fact that the young woman she had befriended had become her chief rival. Alice lost no chance these days to gibe at Caroline, who wisely kept her cool and her temper.

The day that Moynihan told Caroline they were going to try her out as weekend anchor was the day that she danced in Mike's living room, spinning in joyful circles, singing to herself while he watched, smiling at her.

"This is the happiest day of my life," she caroled. She paused in mid-spin. "No, not quite. That's yet to come."

Mike pulled her down onto his lap, felt her brief resistance, and thought it was like capturing a wild thing. But she immediately nestled against him, scattering kisses on his face.

"So what would be the happiest day of your life, darling?" He looked into her face, fondly, and yet anxiously.

She kissed him and laughed. "That would be up to Mellenkoff."

"Mellenkoff?"

She tapped his face lightly with her warm fingers.

"You can't have forgotten Mellenkoff knows I want to work for him. He knows I want to be a national anchor."

"You told him that?"

"Of course not. I didn't need to. You know, Mike" —she curled herself into a ball on his lap—"I think maybe Mellenkoff and I understand each other."

He looked at her, his eyes searching the lovely face, and found nothing there except glee. Later, Mike would decide that that was the day he lost her.

24

IT WAS front page news in the *Glayville Gazette* when Caroline Mitchell was named weekend anchor on KRT-WNN, and everybody in town tuned in for her first appearance, or at least those whose television antennae were powerful enough to pick up the Columbus station, and they invited people in. Glory Swimmers considered it her best story of the month, fulfilling all of her prophecies about the success in store for Caroline. She was a little put out that the Mitchells had not rushed to tell her about Caroline's new job, but Amy wasn't quite sure how to explain that they hadn't known about it. They had not heard from Caroline since the letter in which she announced her engagement, the year before. Amy occasionally wrote a short note to her daughter, heavy on information about the weather, the garden, and how her old school friends were. Whether Carlton wrote, Amy didn't know and didn't ask. They had almost stopped talking at all after the arrival of the engagement letter. Carlton stayed home more, drank more, and had begun mentioning early retirement. Amy went out more—she was president of two local clubs on flowers and new books—and didn't care what he did. She had moved into the guest room, and in a strange way, was almost happy. She might have been living alone; Carlton was a sagging, graying ghost who occasionally passed her on the stairs. But Amy liked to maintain the façade of being the mother of the star of Glayville.

"That Caroline," she said placatingly to Glory. "This must have been the surprise she said she had in store for us. Said we might be seeing her soon, and I expect this is what she meant."

"That's something else I've been wondering about, Amy," said Glory. "Why hasn't Caroline ever come home?"

Amy allowed herself to look wistful.

"Well, just between us, Glory, I think things may have gone to her head a little bit. I know Carlton's quite upset about it. But it's probably just a phase."

Glory sniffed. "You and Carlton certainly gave her everything a girl could want, I know that, and it saddens me to hear you say that. Not that I haven't wondered—I mean, she hasn't written a line to me, and we were such good friends. But of course I haven't said a word to anyone," she said untruthfully. Caroline Mitchell's ingratitude had provided many a happy hour of gossip in the Glayville Inn, but it was Caroline's climb to success that filled the columns of the *Gazette*.

"Well," said Amy, "I expect to hear from her about all this, and I'll have her get in touch with you."

"She needn't trouble," said Glory petulantly. "I called the television station and talked to the news director, and they're all very high on her, apparently. He gave me some nice quotes and would have put her on the line but she was out on a story, he said. And I have my files on her."

Glory frowned. "Whatever happened to her engagement? Wasn't she engaged to the son of the anchorman at the station?"

Amy hadn't the faintest idea. She suspected Caroline never had been engaged or had made the whole thing up to annoy her father, but she had no intention of admitting that to Glory. She decided to waffle, which would let Glory interpret for herself.

"I'm afraid that doesn't seem to be in the picture anymore. That poor young man; I'm afraid Caroline may have left him by the wayside. Just like her father and me. I shouldn't say this about my own child, but when I see that nice Jill Starling coming in and out to see Helen and Nolan, it really breaks my heart sometimes."

Glory patted her on the arm to encourage her. There was about a week's worth of gossip in this.

"Doesn't Caroline room with Jill anymore? What does Jill say?"

"Not much," said Amy truthfully. "Jill would never say a word against Caroline, no matter what she thought. But sometimes she'll stop by and say hello to Carlton and me, and I can tell she feels for us."

This was pure fiction, culled from the fact that Jill waved as she drove by, if she saw Amy in the garden. But Glory's well-coiffed head was nodding vigorously. Amy did occasionally speculate on what Caroline might be up to, but it wasn't anything that dominated her thoughts. She was glad Caroline was gone, because it meant that Carlton would be alone forever. Sometimes Amy felt she had been reborn with a new purpose in life. She now had it in her power to make Carlton suffer as he had made her suffer. That was why she called Caroline at college that night, making sure Carlton was within earshot and that she was standing where she could see his reactions. She noticed that Caroline's voice was guarded.

"Mother? Hi, what a surprise. How are you?"

"Well, I wondered how you were. We were all delighted to hear about the job."

"I'm sorry. I meant to call. Things've been crazy, really, and it was a surprise to me too. I mean, it's just a tryout, it may not be permanent, so I'm not getting too excited about it," said Caroline untruthfully.

"Well, I understand. But Glory Swimmers has it all over the front page of the *Gazette* of course—'.

"Oh God," said Caroline.

"Your old friends are interested in you, dear," said her mother.

"That's nice," said Caroline.

"Tell me," Amy continued, watching her husband's stony face across the room, "what about your wedding? I mean, you wrote and said you were just head over heels in love and that was the last we heard. Or are you just living together, the way you all do nowadays? I heard Jill's getting married—I mean, Helen told me."

There was a brief pause.

"My engagement's off," said Caroline tersely. "We—we both decided it wouldn't work out."

"I'm sure there'll be lots more along, dear. I've always said to your father that you could have your pick of young men, and I'm sure you have them on a string, don't you?"

Amy laughed her high, brittle laugh, and saw Carlton flinch. At the other end of the line, Caroline was tense.

"Mother, I have to run. I have an assignment. I'm late. I'll call back."

She hung up. Her mother put down the receiver and turned cheerfully toward her husband.

"Well, I was going to put you on the line, Carlton, but I guess she was just too busy. . . ." But Carlton Mitchell was gone, and the door of his study closed behind him. Amy heard the lock click, smiled, and made herself comfortable on the sofa to study her seed catalogs. She was so engrossed in varietals, she hardly noticed when Carlton made his unsteady way upstairs.

Caroline's mood was dark as she walked back to the room where Jill was writing wedding invitations. Jill looked up, raised her eyebrows, and inquired, "What's wrong?"

"Nothing," said Caroline, "except my mother called to congratulate me on a job I may not have much longer."

Jill put down her pen. "You mean the flap over the secretary of state story?

Caroline nodded.

"What does Mike say?"

"He tries to be sympathetic. He's more interested in whether or not I'll marry him than whether I'll keep the weekend anchor job."

"And you're more interested in the job."

Caroline made a gesture of frustration. "It was my fault. I know it was my fault. But I tried to explain. I guess I did screw up, but I mean, I learned. I wouldn't do it again. I told Moynihan that."

"What did he say?"

Caroline's mouth twisted. "He said I was damned right I wouldn't do it again; he'd see to it."

She did not tell Jill what else Moynihan had said about what he had described as her "total fuck-up" on coverage of a story that, for a brief shining moment, she had thought would make her nationally recognized and respected. Moynihan had had doubts about Caroline's capacity to cover major news, and those doubts had been confirmed in an ominous way. The question in the news director's mind, and in the minds of others, was whether what had happened could be at least partially excused on the grounds that it was Caroline's second weekend on the job; she was still a novice, despite her aplomb on camera, and it might have taught her the kind of lesson others did not have the opportunity to learn until it was too late for excuses.

One thing it might have taught her, Moynihan reflected, was the importance of reading the papers and keeping up with what was going on in the world instead of relying on other people to tell her. Had Caroline been reading the local newspaper attentively, or even listening to network news, she would have known that the secretary of state's recent comments in defense of stockpiling nerve gas had incensed the radical element in most college towns, of which Columbus was one. The station had, however, decided not to cover the secretary's speech live when he addressed the state Foreign Relations Council. There was a camera crew and a reporter, and the speech was carried by the university radio station, which meant it was heard by the crowd of hostile demonstrators outside the hotel where the secretary was speaking. Moynihan had been alerted when the reporter on the scene noted unusually heavy police security, because of the presence of protesters. When the demonstrators broke through police lines and rushed through the hotel lobby toward the ballroom where the cabinet officer was shaking hands, Moynihan had assigned Caroline to anchor what had become an unpredictable story. KRT was the only station with a live picture from outside the hotel. Caroline had been equipped with her earpiece, handed some wire copy, and put in front of a microphone with the task of telling the town and possibly the nation what was happening to the secretary of state.

It had become painfully obvious that Caroline had not listened to the secretary's speech and was only sketchily aware of the controversy surrounding his arrival. She read the wire-service copy again and again, while Moynihan growled into her ear from the control room. He didn't growl too sharply because he didn't want things to get worse.

But things got worse anyway. The KRT reporter didn't know where the secretary was. All anybody seemed to know was that he had disappeared. Caroline, struggling to gain control of herself and the story, suddenly had begun to interpret the scraps of wire-service information as suggesting that the government official might have been kidnapped or taken hostage. To his sorrow, Moynihan passed on to Caroline a tip from one of his own sources in the police department that there had been a threat to the life of the secretary of state, information passed to them by the Secret Service. Which accounted for the heavy police security at the hotel. Caroline pounced on this potentially sensational report and breathlessly passed it on to her audience, making it sound as though assassins were chasing the secretary of state through the hotel lobby. That, of course, got everybody's attention, from the wire services monitoring the television coverage, to the networks. And Caroline had run with it, seeing her name mentioned in a fresh piece of wire-service copy, seized by sudden elation at seeing herself at the center of a national tragedy. She had begun to embellish, soar, and float in her own rhetoric, which, as Moynihan later assured her, captured the essence of sophomoric.

It had all ended, quite abruptly, with an official announcement by the State Department that the secretary of state was airborne on his way back to Washington, after being quickly and quietly escorted from the hotel as soon as police lines were penetrated by protesters. Caroline was disconcerted, even disappointed, and looked it.

"You sounded like you didn't believe what the goddamned State Department said because it made you look like a fool," Moynihan yelled at her ten minutes later in his office.

"It seemed logical to me, from what the wires were saying—" Caroline had protested weakly.

Moynihan shouted her down. "If it hadn't been for the fucking wire services, you wouldn't have been able to tell them who the secretary of state was. As it was, you could barely identify the governor. You didn't know why somebody might be after the secretary. You hadn't done any goddamned homework at all. What the fuck do you think is expected of you on the air? We don't need another stupid talking head; this business has been cursed with them and I'm not going to contribute to idiocy on camera. You made yourself look stupid and you made this station look uninformed. Maybe you're in the wrong line of work, Ms. Mitchell. Maybe you should go model hairstyles or learn to do happy talk. Because at this point, you sure as hell aren't a news reporter, let alone an anchor."

He was faintly impressed by the fact that she had not broken down into tears. She turned white, but she had stood there and taken it until he had stopped for breath and simply sat glaring at her.

"I know you're right. It won't happen again," she said in a surprisingly firm voice.

"You're goddamned right it won't happen again!" And he had begun to scream at her again, but he knew and she knew that that was a matter of relieving justifiable anger. What mattered to her, and he knew it, was whether she would get a second chance, whether Eric Kriss, the general manager, would be even more angry than Moynihan.

It had not been a day when Caroline needed a telephone call from her mother. Jill had not seen the performance that had brought wrath on her roommate's head, but from what she had heard about it, she was inclined to agree that Caroline had brought it on herself by not knowing what she was doing. She had seen Caroline reading the newspapers, and her eye appeared to skim at top speed across national and foreign news, searching for the feature section. Jill sighed. She wanted to say something sympathetic but she didn't feel sympathetic.

"Why don't you talk to Mike about it?" she suggested. She wanted to get her wedding invitations finished, and she'd never accomplish it if Caroline sat there like a thundercloud all night. Caroline looked at her plaintively.

"I've been trying to read more," she said. "I just don't seem to remember things."

She had learned a lot. Moynihan would have conceded that. She had learned how to cope with the pressure of reading stories while not looking as if she were reading, while keeping an eye on the video so that she wasn't describing something different from what was on the screen. She had learned to listen without looking as if she were hearing the staccato directions emanating from her earpiece, transmitted from a producer in the control room. She had shown herself capable of enough concentration to use the equipment surrounding her because she knew it could make her look good on camera. She wanted desperately to succeed. It was the most important thing that had ever happened to her. Sometimes she fantasized about Mellenkoff seeing her on the air; now she was afraid he might have.

Once she had dared to ask Moynihan if he thought Mellenkoff might remember her, whether she should write to him or send him new tapes. He had looked at her over his battered horn-rimmed glasses and smiled sardonically.

"No one can predict Mellenkoff, Caroline," he said.

"He said I had promise," Caroline ventured.

"I suspect he says that to a lot of people. He told you to work hard too, didn't he?"

She nodded.

"Well, that's what you have to do. And I wouldn't hold my breath waiting to hear him tell you he's going to make you a star, not that I think you're stupid enough to fall for that line, which has been just about worn out by airheads who not only don't know what camera to look at but don't have the common sense to find out. This business is growing up, and you should be glad you're getting into it at a time when you're not getting assignments because you're a good-looking woman. Though I have to say it still doesn't hurt on camera."

But that was before she had made a fool of herself. Before the secretary of state fiasco, the worst thing she had done on the air was mix up videos of the mayor and a man who had been indicted for drunken driving. But Moynihan, while annoyed, had noted that she had done the right thing in realizing her error almost at once and apologizing for it to the viewers. He did not tell her that her self-possession and the graceful way she had handled the correction of the mistake had impressed Kriss and himself. It had also been of considerable assistance in mollifying the outraged mayor.

Caroline picked up her purse.

"I'm going to see Mike," she said abruptly. Jill heaved a sigh of relief and reflected that Mike had her sympathy. He was such a decent, kindly man, she thought, as she licked stamps. Why didn't he see through Caroline?

Mike was full of tender understanding when Caroline moped into his living room. He enveloped her in his arms, stroked her back, smoothed back her unusually rumpled hair.

"Anything more from Moynihan?" he asked. She looked at him anxiously.

"Has he said anything to you?"

Mike shook his head. "Not really. Give him time to simmer down, honey. I don't think they're going to chop your head off."

"Just take me off the air. Make me an assistant producer, where I can't get them in trouble."

Mike kissed her and poured her a glass of chilled white wine.

"Drown your sorrows, darling."

She smiled at him. He was so good-natured and patient, and she really was very fond of him. But he didn't understand how she felt about her job. Maybe because he'd never felt that way about his. It had come easily to Mike. It didn't come easily to her, and that was why she couldn't ever let up, if someday she were to ask Mellenkoff if he thought she had fulfilled her promise. She sipped her wine and tried to calm herself. Mike mixed himself a martini and sat down beside her, slipping his arm around her shoulders.

Caroline fitted herself accommodatingly into the curve of his arm. She liked to sit there in the twilight, where it was quiet and she could think about what she ought to do to get herself out of this scrape.

"I talked to Leslie today," said Mike. His voice was cheerful, and Caroline tried not to stiffen.

"Oh? How is she?"

"As a matter of fact, she's doing better. Teaching a class in English and planning a trip to Europe. Maybe she's got a friend. She's also going to get the quickest divorce she can, she says. Says she wants to get it behind her."

"That's wonderful for you," said Caroline disinterestedly.

He kissed her forehead.

"It's wonderful for us, darling. Now we can make some plans."

Oh God, thought Caroline, and took a large sip of wine to forestall a more comprehensive embrace from Mike. He looked at her quizzically.

"You're not exactly full of enthusiasm."

"Mike, I really am pleased about the divorce, because I know this has been hard on you. I mean, I really want you to be happy."

She knew it was a mistake as soon as she said it. He tilted up her face.

"Then marry me."

"Mike . . ." She pulled away a little and curled her feet beneath her. "I love you, I really do. But why do we have to—I mean, why is it so important we get married right away? We have time."

"Well, sure we have time, darling. I don't mean to rush you. I just thought you'd want to . . ."

Caroline was conciliatory. "Oh, but I do. It's just I'm so frantic and worried right now, Mike. It's no big deal to you, but it's a great big deal to me, and I—half the time I can't think of anything else, I worry so much about it."

There was so much truth in what she said, and she was so earnest, that Mike began to laugh.

"Poor baby, I'm sorry. You've got a lot to think about right now and I'm being selfish. We don't have to worry about doing anything, Caroline. I understand what you're saying, and you set the pace. You let me know, okay?"

She threw her arms around him, enchanting in her triumph.

"Mike, you're such a love. You're so good to me."

This time she did not pull away from his embrace, even when his fingers gently unbuttoned her blouse.

"We're going to have our before-dinner drinks in bed?" she purred in his ear.

"I'll even carry you there." He picked her up easily, and Caroline nibbled his ear, because he seemed to like that, and reflected contentedly that she could do a lot of thinking in bed. Moynihan had said it was all a matter of disciplining yourself when you were on camera. Lying in Mike's arms, she methodically checked off in her mind precautions she might take against erring on the air. Now and again, she remembered to make little sounds of pleasure.

"You're wonderful," Mike whispered.

25

CAROLINE DIDN'T quite understand why Jill wanted to marry Tom Roberts, who seemed like a young man of limited ambition, but she was so immensely relieved that KRT had elected to let her continue as weekend anchor that she was disposed to be charitable to everyone. She was genuinely fond of Jill, whom she considered perhaps the only friend she had ever had. She did not entirely trust Jill, but then Caroline trusted nobody. She insisted on helping with preparations for Jill's wedding, set for the fall after they graduated—Caroline to her own surprise. It was a fall that began crisply, with the air full of bright blowing leaves, and turned dank and dark before November.

Caroline and Mike gave a dinner for Jill and Tom in a private room at the Coachman, inviting not only friends of the bridal couple, but people whom Caroline considered useful at KRT, such as Eric Kriss, Joe Moynihan, and Del Kelly, the associate director who had remained one of her most devoted and hopeful admirers. Not invited was Alice Martinsen, Caroline's former mentor at the station, who was grimly trying to renegotiate her contract. Alice had stopped speaking to Caroline, although she talked *about* her a good deal.

Caroline was working hard to mend her fences at KRT. She spent part of her morning not only reading the newspapers, but taking notes that she carried in her purse so that she would not be caught short again. Jill sometimes wondered if Caroline understood much of what she was taking notes on, but conceded that she was making an effort. And her concentration on the job provided Caroline with a reason for seeing a little less of Mike, who was divided between amusement, exasperation, and grudging admiration at her dedication to her career.

But they were together at Jill's party, rousing the curiosity of Jill's parents, Helen and Nolan Starling, who were storing up gossip for the Glory Swimmers mill back in Glayville. Jill's mother could not understand why Amy and Carlton Mitchell were not invited to the wedding. It had been the talk of Glayville that they did not attend Caroline's graduation.

"You spent so much time in the Mitchell house when you were little, I do think it looks strange," Helen Starling had said to Jill in mild reproof. Her awareness that the Mitchells were not invited had deprived her of discussing the wedding with Amy because of the awkwardness of such a conversation, but it had not stopped her from speculating with Glory Swimmers about why Caroline Mitchell wouldn't have anything to do with her parents. Helen was also determined that this time, the *Glayville Gazette* would not ignore Jill. Glory had spent a lot of time glorifying Caroline Mitchell in print, which had not been lost on Helen. She remembered the outpouring about Caroline's engagement to a young man whose name she recalled as Hathaway. Nothing more had been heard about a wedding, and here was Caroline as glamorous as ever and being fawned over by somebody called Hathaway, although he looked old enough to be her father. For that matter, he was old enough to be the father of the young man Caroline had been engaged to, and Helen realized she might have uncovered a nugget of delicious gossip with which to regale Glayville. She supposed Jill wouldn't tell her anything, as usual, but she could draw her own conclusions. She was a little tired, anyway, of seeing Caroline get all the attention when everyone said Jill was so much more intelligent. Maybe not as pretty, but she was certainly pretty enough that night in her pale yellow chiffon dress, with that nice young man she was going to marry.

"Honey, don't meddle," said Nolan Starling, when Helen confided her suspicions about Caroline's escorts. He didn't know what Caroline's problems were, either with her parents or her men friends, and he didn't especially care. He had always disliked Carlton Mitchell. A warm-hearted man, Nolan had been sorry for Amy, the

dowdy, dull-eyed woman who had eaten her way through
a life spent in the shadow of a debonair husband and a
beautiful daughter. But in the years after Caroline went
to college, Nolan had felt even more uneasy around
Amy, as she dieted herself into sleekness and habitually
wore the soulless smile of the Cheshire Cat. Sometimes
Nolan hoped Caroline wouldn't take after either of her
parents. He hadn't seen Caroline for more than three
years, and he was slightly disconcerted to discover she
had blossomed into an exotic blend of her father's dark
good looks and her mother's smile. Nolan looked fondly
at his daughter, who was bright-eyed, a trace tousled
about the head, and giggling uncontrollably over the
zipper that had come apart at the back of her dress.
Caroline was beside her, laughing up at Tom Roberts as
she produced a safety pin and led Jill away to be fastened
back together. Nolan's eyes narrowed as he saw Tom's
gaze follow the filmy pink vision of Caroline as she glided
along beside Jill.

"Caroline is gorgeous, isn't she?" said Helen with a
sigh.

"Pretty fancy," said her husband, who had been impervious to Caroline's winning ways when she was the
most beautiful baby in Glayville. He liked her even less
at dinner, when Caroline, sitting next to Tom Roberts,
captured the attention of the prospective bridegroom with
an entertaining account of her misadventures in the television business.

Jill, seated between her father and Mike, listened with
considerable amusement to the expurgated version of
how Caroline felt about her work. The gay anecdotes
floating across the table were far removed, she reflected,
from the frantic intensity with which Caroline had approached her job since the day when, as Moynihan had
put it, she killed off the secretary of state. Jill noticed
that this was not among the amusing descriptions now
being given by Caroline.

"She's feeling better," Mike murmured to her. Jill
smiled at him warmly. She liked Mike Hathaway and
wouldn't hurt him. Dealing with Caroline, she suspected
he had enough of that in store.

"She looks lovely," she responded. She saw a faint
glint in Mike's eye and wondered if he were really as

blind to Caroline as he appeared to be. He was so much more interesting than his son, Jill wondered why Caroline could not see Mike as more than a means to an end. She also wondered if he had any suspicion that Caroline would never marry him.

"How's Frank?" she asked. Mike looked slightly surprised, then pleased. "I hear he's doing well in California, working on a newspaper there."

His face darkened a little. "His mother hears from him," he said quietly. Jill was silent. There was nothing to say that could soothe the hurt on his face. She suspected Caroline never asked about Frank at all, and maybe she was right.

Abruptly, she realized that Caroline was offering Tom advice on getting into television, and Tom was saying he hadn't given it any serious thought.

"I didn't know you'd given it any thought at all, darling," said Jill lightly.

"Oh, but you should talk to Mike about that," chirped Caroline. "I think you'd be terrific on camera with your profile and the way you tell a story."

Jill choked slightly on her wine, and was aware of a responsive grin from Mike and a frown from her father, who appeared to feel Caroline was talking too much to his future son-in-law.

"Well," she said cheerfully, "it'd put us both in the same business if I get that job with PBS, wouldn't it, sweetie?"

Tom looked vaguely uncomfortable, and Jill felt a twinge of exasperation that he did not appear to share her perception of Caroline. Like many men she had known, he had a habit of referring to Caroline as "little" despite the fact that she was almost as tall as Jill. That reaction, Jill had decided years earlier, was probably due to what she thought of as Caroline's "meltdown look," which she was capable of using to good effect even when she was in the middle of eating a hamburger with ketchup and onions. It made most members of the opposite sex think of Caroline as fragile, which Jill knew to be entirely erroneous. Yet she derived a good deal of entertainment from watching the psychological interplay, and marveling at how often Caroline's ploys worked. Jill didn't grudge her them, because she was aware she could never have succeeded with the same mannerisms. She would have laughed instead of cast down her eyes.

"Have some more wine, honey," said her father, and Jill realized he was being protective. He had always resented it when Caroline had the center stage and never realized that his daughter was unperturbed by the maneuverings of her roommate. She grinned at him reassuringly, and picked up her glass.

"It's probably not etiquette for the bride to do this, but I'd like to propose a toast to the two people who made this dinner possible, and especially to the one who made it possible for me to get to the table fully dressed!"

She raised her glass to Caroline, and Nolan Starling's face broke into a pleased smile. Mike touched his glass to Jill's.

"I'd like to drink to you, Jill," he said softly. "I don't know what Caroline would do without you."

Jill smiled. "Perfectly fine, that's what," she assured him. "But I'll accept the toast anyway."

Mike's gaze was curious, suddenly intrigued.

"Frank made a real mistake about you," he said.

Jill laughed. "No, he didn't. He didn't make any mistakes, in the end," she said, and her eyes were cool. Mike frowned and fingered his napkin.

"I'm not sure I understand," he began.

Jill shook her head. "Listen, I didn't mean anything. Forget I said it. I've always talked too much." She smiled at him. "It's the wine," she said.

"Perhaps we should talk sometime, Jill," Mike said slowly.

"Perhaps. Perhaps not, on the other hand." She turned to chat with her father, and remained aware of Mike's interrogative eyes. She reproached herself for implying criticism of Caroline. It was no excuse to feel that it was time somebody warned Mike Hathaway. She had noticed that when Mike suggested that he and Caroline might be following in the footsteps of Jill and Tom, Caroline instantly launched a new conversation. And she suspected that Caroline's sharp reaction was linked to an exchange with Del Kelly that Jill had overheard before they sat down to dinner. Kelly had taken Caroline aside as soon as he arrived.

"You hear about the Chicago opening?"

"You mean on 'People Are Asking'?"

He grinned at her. "I heard a rumor that a friend of yours in New York was interested in taking a look at those new tapes you sent out."

"Who?" Caroline's voice was tense.

Kelly said, "I'm not sure. But if something like that were to go anywhere, it would probably have to come from the top."

"You mean Mellenkoff?"

"I honestly don't know." Kelly was telling the truth there, and he had in fact embroidered the exent of his knowledge. What he had heard was Joe Moynihan's end of a conversation in which Caroline's name had been raised in connection with the search for a new co-host for the talk show.

What Kelly suspected was that Moynihan might be pushing Caroline because he wanted to get rid of her by getting her what she wanted. He knew Moynihan had doubts about Caroline, intensified by her poor showing in a crisis situation. He also knew Moynihan was worried about Mike Hathaway, partly because of his recent problems with ratings, mostly because of his infatuation with Caroline. Before Caroline had fallen from local corporate grace, Eric Kriss had hinted that one day she might succeed Hathaway. It was after that that Moynihan had encouraged Caroline to prepare more tapes, to demonstrate her improvement, he said. He had also been engaged in some long-distance calls with friends in the Washington and New York offices of the network. It was Moynihan who had trained Caroline into what he described as the beginnings of something good. It was also Moynihan who remained worried about her basic inadequacies, some of which had recently been dramatically demonstrated. Over a few drinks, the veteran news director would confide his doubts.

"It's as though there's nothing there in Caroline," he had said once, looking like a distressed owl. "I mean, when you start to dig, you stub your toe."

"She's young," Kelly had protested.

Moynihan had shaken his balding head. He was fond of Caroline, but he had no illusions about her.

"Staying power," he said judiciously. "She's got no staying power."

Kelly's interest in Caroline was less professional. He had made a play for her as soon as she arrived at KRT, her engagement to Frank Hathaway notwithstanding. Her rebuff had been graceful but unequivocal. Caroline was interested only in men who could be of professional assistance, and Kelly accepted that. He figured that passing on a tip about the talk show opening might qualify him as a source. And he wondered whether Moynihan, who was discreet when he chose, had deliberately allowed him to overhear his conversation about the Chicago show, and that now he was doing precisely what Moynihan intended him to do. He noticed with amusement that Caroline's eyes were brilliant with excitement.

"What should I do, Del?"

"Sit tight, probably. Or if you've got any contacts, use them."

She reflected, a faint frown appearing between the heavy dark brows.

"I know Martha Vogel in Washington, but I don't know if she'd—'.

"She's got access to Mellenkoff, doesn't she? Is that still going on?"

Caroline hesitated.

"Well, it was when it—when I last saw her."

She had no idea whether Martha was still involved with Mellenkoff, but she had no intention of admitting it to Kelly.

"Didn't you talk to Mellenkoff in New York?"

Caroline nodded. "Yes, but I don't know if he remembers me."

"You don't know that, and what've you got to lose?"

"You think I should call him?"

"Maybe you could sound out Vogel. She's a good sort. Maybe she'd go to bat for you."

Caroline's smile was radiant.

Kelly looked past her abruptly and greeted Mike Hathaway, and Caroline turned at once, speaking before Kelly could say any more.

"Honey—Del and I were just wondering where you'd got to."

"Parking," said Mike, and Kelly suppressed a grin. It was obvious that Mike was one person whom Caroline did not intend to ask to help her check out the Chicago job. Mike put his hand on Caroline's shoulder, and Kelly drifted away, feeling a twinge of compassion for the older man. He would have liked to sleep with Caroline but he couldn't see her as a longtime proposition.

Kelly's information buzzed in Caroline's head for the rest of the evening. She veered between jubilation and fright. This might be her chance, and what if she blew it? What if she had already blown it? Moynihan could finish her with Mellenkoff with a few words about the secretary of state story. She might never even get a chance to try out for it.

"Are you all right, darling?" It was Mike, his arm about her waist, his eyes worried. Even as she nodded and smiled, she was disengaging herself from his grasp and dissolving into the group, leaving him with an indefinable uneasiness. Later, she insisted on returning to the room she shared with Jill instead of going back with him to his apartment.

"It's Jill's last night, and she might be nervous, or need some help with packing," she said.

"Oh come on," said Mike, and she patted his cheek and told him she would see him in the morning at the church.

Mike found himself standing alone outside the restaurant as Caroline drove off in her car. Moynihan strolled up beside him.

"Need a ride?"

Mike shook his head.

"Kriss really liked your drugs-on-campus series."

"Thanks."

Moynihan eyed him. "Something wrong?"

"Just a little tired, I guess."

Moynihan nodded. "We're all getting old."

"Not all of us." Mike said it so quietly, Moynihan barely heard the words.

Caroline remained distracted throughout Jill's wedding, quieter than usual because she was constantly turning over in her mind what to do to advance her cause in Chicago. After the wedding, she went back to the television station, evading Mike's anxious solicitude, assuring him she'd be over later and knowing she wouldn't. She sought out Kelly, asked his advice.

"All I hear is that they're going to be trying people out in a few weeks." He smiled at her expression. "Tell you what," he said. "Why don't you call Washington about that film we need? You're going to be working on that story, aren't you? So it's logical you'd call."

Caroline beamed at him.

"Buy me a drink if you get it," said Kelly.

"Anything," said Caroline, and did not back away from his expression.

She asked for Jim Jakes as a pretext to reaching the correct department in Washington, and Jakes was delighted to hear from her.

"You coming our way again soon?" he asked.

"I hope so," Caroline told him sincerely. "How's Martha?"

There was the faintest pause before Jakes answered.

"Oh, she's pretty good. Busy as hell at the White House."

"I know. I watch her every night."

"Maybe you should talk to her. She's done her stand-up; probably pretty quiet there right now. I know she'd like to chat with you. I'll put you through to the tapes editor and he can switch you to the White House."

"Wonderful, I'd love to talk to her for a minute if you don't think she's too busy."

"No problem," said Jakes. "Matter of fact, she told me she had a note from you about your getting weekend anchor there. That's great!"

"Thank you." Caroline's gratitude was genuine, because that meant Martha had enough interest in her to at least mention her note to Jakes. A few moments later she was transferred to the WNN booth at the White House and heard Martha's low, clear voice on the line.

"Martha, this is Caroline Mitchell. I just wanted to say hi, because I was talking to your tapes people anyway. Wondered how you were."

Martha's voice was warm. "Caroline, it's nice to hear from you. I was really pleased about the weekend anchor job. How's it going?"

"Pretty good. I've made some howlers."

"We all do," Martha assured her. "It's marvelous they're letting you do that so soon."

"I put together a new tape," Caroline volunteered.

"Good idea. Let people see what you can do. And it lets you see the difference between earlier tapes. They're very useful."

"Well, as a matter of fact"—Caroline took a deep breath—"I heard a wild rumor here that somebody in New York had been interested in my tape—in connection with the Chicago talk show job?"

"Oh, yes, I heard Barbara Guess was moving to the West Coast. Really, Caroline? Are you going to have a tryout?"

"I've no idea. This was just a rumor somebody told me. But I'd love to know if there's any truth to it, as you can imagine."

"Maybe I can find out for you. Who looked at the tape? Chicago or New York?"

"I'm not sure. My friend here thought it was New York." Caroline hesitated.

"Would it be your friend, Martha? I mean, who looked at the tape?"

There was silence, and Caroline closed her eyes.

"My friend? You mean Mellenkoff?" Martha laughed briefly. "I rather doubt he'd be the one, but I suppose with him you can never tell. About anything." Her voice had lost its usual warmth.

"I—I just thought if anybody would know, you might. . . ." Caroline's voice trailed off miserably.

Martha sounded tired when she spoke again. "Listen, I know how important this is to you, Caroline. I can remember—well, anyhow, let me check it out for you. Don't get your hopes up, but at least you'll have an idea one way or the other and not have to agonize. I think I can find out. And I'll let you know."

"Martha, I can't tell you how much I'd appreciate it."

"I know. I know how it feels. Nothing's worse then uncertainty. Nothing."

Martha's voice seemed to break suddenly, and Caroline tapped impatiently at the telephone.

"Did we get cut off? Martha?"

"I'm here," said Martha. "I have to go now, Caroline. But I'll call you as soon as I know something."

She hung up while Caroline was still giving voice to her gratitude. Caroline leaned back in her chair and wondered whether she felt better or worse. She still didn't know anything, and there was no assurance that whatever Martha discovered would be welcome news. She heaved a sigh and looked up as Kelly came hurriedly into the office.

"You got Vogel yet?"

She nodded.

"Jesus," said Kelly, "What did she say? Did you bring up Mellenkoff?"

Caroline stared at him. "Yes, yes I did. And she was really nice."

"She say anything about Mellenkoff?"

She shook her head. "No. Well, she was a little odd about that, but—"

"I'd think she would be odd about it."

"Why?"

"I just heard this minute, so maybe she doesn't know. But Mellenkoff just got married to Joel Eliass's niece."

Caroline's mouth dropped open. "Eliass the chairman of the board?"

"That's the one."

"Oh my God."

"Well, I don't know that Vogel and Mellenkoff were still an item anyway, so maybe it's no big deal. But I thought I'd try to catch you so you'd know before you called."

Caroline was staring into space. What awful luck. If Martha had known about Mellenkoff's marriage, she certainly would not have appreciated Caroline's reference to her "friend." That would have opened up the wound. And if she didn't know then, she certainly knew now. That might be even worse for Caroline, because Martha probably wouldn't even remember to check out the Chicago deal for her, and if she did, she'd hardly go to Mellenkoff.

"I have the damnedest luck," said Caroline bitterly.

Kelly looked at her and shook his head a little. "Martha Vogel probably isn't feeling too lucky either," he observed drily.

26

THE MARRIAGE of James Mellenkoff and Sally Eliass was performed quickly and quietly by a New York judge on a rainy October afternoon, and was never consummated. Mellenkoff, who hardly considered his nuptials the natural consequences of a romantic attachment, nevertheless was disconcerted and disbelieving when his bride made clear that she had no interest in sharing the same bed with him, let alone making love with him. Sally was polite about it, even faintly apologetic, but firm. They had taken a suite in a small exclusive hotel before flying to California for their honeymoon the next day. The California trip was at Sally's request; she explained that she was homesick for the sun, and Mellenkoff had no argument with two weeks in Malibu. So he was waiting with chilled champagne in the sitting room of their suite when Sally emerged from the bathroom, firmly belting a pale blue silk robe about her slender waist. Mellenkoff eyed her appreciatively and rose to embrace her. It had occurred to him during their somewhat unconventional courtship that Sally's unswerving observation of the proprieties was at odds with a sense of humor even bawdier than his. She had permitted him to kiss her good night, but briefly. And since he was dealing with the niece of Joel Eliass, Mellenkoff had not sought to force any attentions on her. He had never had any reason to doubt that he was attractive to most women. So he assumed Sally, who had indicated her family's financial dependence on her uncle, was reluctant to endanger her economic security by behavior that, should it be discovered by Eliass, would arouse his disapproval.

Mellenkoff understood that rationale. It was similar to the reasoning that had impelled him to marry Sally in the

wake of weeks of heavy hinting by Eliass. He might in
any case have considered her as a marital prospect, given
her money and her connections. Mellenkoff had few illusions about the tenuousness of his hold on Eliass's approval, and he was aware that marriage to a member of
the chairman's family might strengthen that hold, especially in view of Uncle Joel's stated desire for such a
union. But Mellenkoff had assumed that once he was
legally wed to Sally, then events would take a course
that, in his view, would have been normal weeks earlier
with any other woman in whom he was interested. So
there he stood, prepared to enthusiastically if belatedly
embrace his delectable Sally, whose skin was enameled a
soft gold by a lifetime in the sun, her hair a pale shining
fall of silk. And there was Sally, dexterously evading his
extended arms, seating herself in a chair on the other
side of the coffee table, and calmly pouring champagne
for them both.

Mellenkoff's eyebrows rose slightly, but he accepted
the delicately frosted glass and courteously proposed a
toast.

"To us, my darling."

"To happiness," said Sally, and sipped.

She did not speak until she had finished her first glass
of champagne and poured a second. By that time,
Melienkoff had concluded charitably that she was simply
nervous. Surely she couldn't be a virgin? It was so long
since he had encountered one of those, he thought the
species was extinct.

He also had understood, rather vaguely, that Eliass
had been concerned about some "escapade," as the chairman had put it, that his niece had become involved in on
the West Coast. It was apparently at that point that
Sally's future had become a matter of avuncular decision.
Mellenkoff sipped his champagne, and reflected that this
might be more interesting than he had thought. And it
was. Halfway through her second glass, Sally explained
that she was sorry, but she was not in the least interested
in sex, and she hoped he didn't mind too much.

Mellenkoff found himself almost bereft of speech.

"What do you mean, do I mind? Of course I mind!
What the hell is this, Sally?"

"That's the way it is, I'm afraid, James."

Her manner was serene. She might have been apologizing for a minor social indiscretion.

Mellenkoff gestured helplessly.

"I don't understand. I mean, is there some physical problem, or what? Or did you have some bad sexual experience, is that it? Because you know you can certainly tell me about it, and you can rely on my understanding, honey. This—well, frankly, I'm at a loss."

Sally shook her lovely head. "Nothing like that, James. I just don't like sex."

"You have tried it, I assume?"

"God, yes." She grimaced faintly, and Mellenkoff swallowed the rest of his champagne.

Sally had given thought to telling Mellenkoff the truth, but had decided against it. She suspected Uncle Joel had not revealed what would have been hardly conducive to persuading Mellenkoff to propose marriage. She also guessed that a mysterious distaste for physical intercourse might be more acceptable to Mellenkoff than an admission of preference for her own sex. As it was, he was looking at her with an expression that suggested she had sprouted another head.

"But—why didn't you tell me—I mean, before?" he asked almost plaintively.

Sally looked at him levelly. "What difference would it have made? Uncle Joel wanted us to get married."

"Well, I know"—Mellenkoff found himself foundering in the face of such candor—"I know your uncle approved, but—"

"Approved? He orchestrated it. You know that as well as I do. We might as well face it, James. We're stuck with each other, at least from the standpoint of appearances."

Sally smiled sweetly at him, and Mellenkoff had a sudden angry desire to rip off the expensive robe and throw her on the floor. He restrained the impulse. He was beginning to realize that Sally would be a better friend than an enemy, and in any case, he had no wish for her to go running to Uncle Joel with charges of marital abuse. He suspected that Eliass could bring about an annulment as efficiently as he had arranged the marriage. And Mellenkoff's mind was clicking along its oiled tracks again.

Watching his face with secret amusement, Sally offered him more champagne.

"Have another drink," she said cordially. "When you really think about it, James, we may have the best of all possible worlds. You may do as you please, and so may I."

That was what Julia Eliass had told her. Apprised by Joel of what he called "the problem with Sally," Julia had agreed that it probably was time her niece was married to someone suitable. Julia had been married to Eliass when she was nineteen, a year younger than Sally. It had never occurred to Julia, a carefully raised Italian daughter, to question her father's choice of a husband. Although she viewed her prospective spouse with distaste, he was a rich man, likely to be a great deal richer, and appeared perfectly willing to keep her in style and sapphires. When Joel told her, with great awkwardness, what the problem with Sally was, Julia had expressed the kind of shock he expected from her, but mentally had shrugged. She preferred men herself, but on the other hand, she had gone to bed with Joel a few times, and what could be worse than that? Julia and Joel had occupied separate bedrooms and led separate lives for years, and she found the arrangement left her with a luxurious life-style and freedom with which to conduct it. She indulged in discret dalliances in other continents, but was a model of decorum in the United States, where Joel displayed her at his side the way she displayed her magnificent collection of sapphires.

Julia had taken Sally to lunch and tried to explain to her that things were not nearly as bad as she seemed to think. Julia had sounded a good deal like Karen Ward, which made Sally sit up and pay attention, especially when she realized that her aunt was trying to give her the benefit of her own experience.

"My dear"—Julia waved a sapphired hand at her niece—"James Mellenkoff is handsome, a presentable escort. He is your uncle's current favorite. Your uncle wants you to be married; he has chosen this man for you. Your uncle gets what he wants."

"It's medieval," said Sally, poking at her shrimp.

"I haven't finished. One must look at all sides. You will be this man's wife, but you will still be the niece of Joel Eliass. What could be better?"

"But—" said Sally.

Julia's charmingly accented voice flowed over Sally's protest. "You are like me, my dear. You like the good life. If you didn't, you would not have let Joel bring you back to New York with him. Because you knew he meant it when he said there would be no money." She shrugged. "So it was unfortunate that he found out about you. But Joel is an old-fashioned, stubborn man. And he did not have to find out, Sally. You were indiscreet—you and your friend."

That was as close to a reproof as Julia came, and Sally felt a lightening of her spirits. It was one thing to hear support for the idea from Karen, but Karen was biased, while Julia's logic was as cool as her jewels. Sally regarded her aunt with new respect, and Julia smiled at her.

"You could always go to California for your honeymoon," she said.

Sally gasped, then burst into laughter. "But what about Mellenkoff? James, I mean?"

"What about him? He is is a sensible man. He will do anything to keep Joel's favor, otherwise he would not have been so accommodating in this matter of marriage. I am sure he will find plenty to keep him amused while you are . . . otherwise engaged."

Sally nodded thoughtfully. She had tried to find out as much as she could about Mellenkoff. After seeing an item in a gossip column referring to his "on again, off again" romance with Martha Vogel, a White House correspondent for WNN, Sally had used the pretext of a California acquaintanceship to have lunch with one or two of the network's correspondents. What she had culled from those conversations had diminished her sympathy for Mellenkoff and aroused her compassion for Martha Vogel. Looking into Mellenkoff's sea-blue eyes, Sally thought about Martha and wondered why a woman like that would become obsessed by a man like this. She had even gone so far as to comment favorably on a story Martha had done one night, and Mellenkoff had actually seemed pleased.

"She's an old friend of mine. In fact, I hired Martha," he said with obvious self-satisfaction.

"She's a superb reporter."

As an afterthought, he added, "You might tell your uncle how good you thought she was in that piece, Sally. Couldn't do her any harm."

"I shall," said Sally, and he smiled at her.

"Good girl."

He might have been discussing a stranger, she thought.

She noted that Martha appeared popular with other members of the WNN staff. She heard about how competent Martha was, how decent Martha was, how loyal Martha was, how Martha had been screwed over by those bastards—excuse me, Sally!—when she should have gotten an anchor job. Mellenkoff's name was never mentioned, understandably, in view of Sally's association with him. But she occasionally had the impression there was an unspoken warning in what she was told. Sally had listened, absorbed it, and reported it to Karen, as she would tell Karen what Julia was saying to her.

"And you're worrying about this guy?" Karen had asked, raising her head from her pillow to look mockingly at Sally lying beside her.

So Sally had accepted the proposal she received from Mellenkoff after an outrageously expensive dinner in the golden gloom of one of New York's most fashionable restaurants, and they had gone back to the Eliass mansion to show Uncle Joel and Aunt Julia the emerald ring on the third finger of her left hand. Julia had inspected the ring critically and nodded cryptically at Sally.

"Emeralds may be your jewel, my dear," she said.

Mellenkoff, looking at Julia standing there iridescent with sapphires, could only hope she would not impart a similar passion for emeralds to her niece. The ring had cost more than he could afford, but he had consoled himself with the thought that it was an investment.

"Very nice, James," Eliass had said in a jocular croak. "A very nice little ring."

Sally and Julia had exchanged smiles.

"And when," continued Eliass, "is the happy day, my dear Sally?"

Sally hesitated, and Eliass's froglike eye fell on Mellenkoff. He wanted to have this family irritant disposed of once and for all, and he considered that he had displayed remarkable patience with all this adolescent delay.

"We thought—just a quiet civil ceremony. Sally doesn't want a big wedding."

Sally was entirely in agreement on that point.

"I hate big weddings, Uncle Joel. So ostentatious," she said.

"In that case," said Julia gently, "there's no reason for any delay at all, is there?"

A sapphire steamroller, Mellenkoff thought.

It turned out, as Mellenkoff had suspected it would, that Eliass was the old friend of a judge whom he knew would be just delighted to perform a quiet, dignified little ceremony. Later that week, perhaps. That would give Julia time to arrange a nice dinner party. And to buy Sally some clothes, of course.

"This week?" said Sally on a rising note. Her uncle's expression became uncompromising.

"I'm afraid I have conferences all next week, and I have to be in London on the twentieth. No, this week would be the most convenient, Sally."

He bestowed a chilly smile on her.

"You have no other plans, do you, my dear?"

She shook her head speechlessly, and saw that Mellenkoff also wore a faintly stunned expression. Julia had swept them both off for brandy, chatting gaily about guests and menus.

They had been married, with Uncle Joel smirking with satisfaction in the background, and Julia wearing her most inscrutable smile. And now it was all over, and Sally could only hope that both Karen and Julia were accurate prophets of Mellenkoff's reactions to her description of the terms of their future living arrangements. Looking at Mellenkoff, sitting there in his tailored robe, she saw in his face incredulity, astonishment, and exasperation, but no distress. Mellenkoff sighed, cast a glance of regret at the shapely body in the silken robe, and began to reorganize his thoughts.

Obviously, he had little choice but to go along with this strange young woman's conditions for marriage. Having gone this far, he was not about to confront Eliass with a complaint about his niece's sexual problems. And when he came to think of it, Sally was an amiable and entertaining companion. She simply didn't want to sleep with him, unlikely as that sounded to his ears. Didn't want to sleep with anybody, from the way she put it, so it had nothing to do with him. Not that he'd thought it had.

So now what? Mellenkoff considered his options and found them wider than he had half an hour earlier. He was in no danger of either loneliness or celibacy. He had as his wife the niece of Joel Eliass, with all the professional and social perquisites. He also had retained his personal freedom; it had in fact been officially conferred upon him by his bride. Which meant—Mellenkoff sipped his champagne with increasing enjoyment, and Sally, watching, smiled to herself—that he was at liberty to make other attachments. He had not talked to Martha since that night she had hung up on him. He had been unable to bring himself to tell her he might marry Sally Eliass, and he certainly had not expected the event to take place as soon as it had. He had thought about Martha when the announcement was made; he had thought about calling her. But what could he have said? He could not have told Martha why he was marrying Sally, because she would have reacted with scorn and disbelief. But now he could tell her. Joyfully, he thought, he could tell her the truth, more or less, describing his infatuation with this glamorous California blond. Martha wouldn't like that, but she would understand it. And since it was Eliass's, niece, there he was in over his head, and the next thing you know, he's married to her, and then what does he find out? And of course the whole thing was a terrible mistake, but now what's he to do? He's trapped. Eliass will fire him if he divorces his niece, and anyway, the poor girl's crazy.

The scenario began to take shape in Mellenkoff's mind. What he was certain of was his ability to arouse Martha's sympathy, and after this fiasco tonight, he hoped that wasn't all he could arouse. But Martha would be sympathetic. Martha was always sympathetic. In a world full of Eliasses and Sallys, there was still Martha. Thinking about her, Mellenkoff smiled, the twinkling smile that had captivated Martha and that even Sally had admired.

"Well"—he looked across at Sally—"I guess you're right. We just have to make the best of things, don't we?"

He looked around the suite. "Flip you who gets the bed."

Sally laughed with genuine relief and poured him another glass of champagne. It had all worked out so well. And tomorrow she would see Karen in California.

27

IT WAS the kind of Washington party where it was too noisy to hear and too crowded to be able to escape anyone. Jill Starling Roberts was there because she didn't want to go home to an apartment where the only sound was a ringing telephone with an unhappy husband at the other end of it. She sometimes felt she was married to someone she probably wouldn't have dated, had she met him later. The good-humored, knowledgeable Tom of her Columbus days had been transformed into a constantly complaining young man who seemed to have lost his sense of humor. He had thought it was wonderful when she was offered a job as a reporter on PBS, even if it didn't pay a lot of money and it was still on a probationary basis. He had been so proud of her, he said, when she left for Washington as soon as they got back from their honeymoon. There was no trace of pride in his voice nowadays when he called several times a week to tell her what a rotten newspaper company he worked for, and had she heard of any openings in Washington for him? Jill had suggested he move with her to Washington and look for a job, but he had refused. It was a matter of principle, he said rather stiffly. Jill said he could view it as a loan against their buying a house, if that would make him feel any better. She just thought it was crazy for him to be in Ohio, doing a job he didn't like anymore, while she was in Washington, when they both wanted to be in Washington. She knew that he had been deeply disappointed when the syndicate he worked for refused to put him in its small Washington bureau. His self-esteem never recovered from that, especially since he was considered a senior and experienced newsman in Columbus. From the standpoint of their marriage, Jill knew, it would have been better had she not been offered or taken the Washington position until they could go together.

She hadn't wanted to do that, and when he accused her angrily of caring more about the PBS job than being with him, Jill had admitted, if only to herself, the justice of his anger. He had come to Washington once or twice for a few days, and they quarreled constantly, mostly because he did not at once find a job, but even over such minor disagreements as her housekeeping arrangements. Why did she need a maid? he wanted to know. Jill said it was hardly a matter of high living, it was mostly that if she didn't have a maid, she would live, as her father put it, like a medieval peasant. The maid cleaned up once a week and organized the apartment, and in between Jill tried not to demolish the orderliness Mrs. Dill created. Tom had waxed sarcastic. Of course, he forgot, he said. She'd made it. She was big time now. Jill made allowances for his battered ego and forebore to point out that she was a long way from making anything, including a good salary. Her current situation was dependent on budget expansion and, she suspected, how well she did. She had been willing to accept a minimal salary so she could show she could work harder and better than anyone else. Tom's absence at least left her free to concentrate on her work, and she could thrust her marital frustrations to the back of her mind when she was busy. The last visit from her husband had left her relieved when the door closed behind him. She had tried to persuade him that what mattered was that they should be together. He said all that mattered to her was that they should be together at her convenience. That was when a real quarrel had started. Since then, their telephone conversations had been civil but terse. Jill was reluctant to ask him how things were going, because it seemed to trigger hostility.

She had begun to go out more in the evenings, stopping for a beer with friends on the way home, occasionally going out to dinner, although so far she had accepted no dates. But she was finding that she didn't even want to think about Tom anymore. When he told her he had lunch with Caroline Mitchell and she had been so sympathetic, Jill said that was nice. He instantly retorted that Caroline was more interested in what was going on in his life than his wife was. Not that he'd seen his wife since their honeymoon, and she'd spent most of that worrying about her big job in Washington, he'd added acidly. Jill had hung up that time and he had called back to apologize. He was now talking about investigating opportunities in television work, which she assumed was the result of his lunch with Caroline. She wished him luck, and sometimes she thought that was about all she wished him. She was tired of being whined at. Perhaps she was self-centered, as he said. But she was tired of thinking about his problems, while he never conceded she had any. Increasingly Tom was relegated to the recesses of her mind.

Jill was grateful when she sighted Martha Vogel across the bar. She had had lunch with Martha several times since coming to Washington and liked her a great deal, even if Martha had initially remembered her as Caroline Mitchell's friend. Jill was not so egotistical that she could not find humor in her taking offense at the connection. People always remembered Caroline, but not always for the right reasons, she reminded herself.

She waved at Martha, who grinned and beckoned to her. Jill slowly threaded her way through the crowd and was so absorbed in keeping some sense of where she was going that she bounced off a waiter and into a man maneuvering in the opposite direction. They both stared at each other.

"Jill?" said Mike Hathaway.

"Mike?" She smiled at him warmly. "What're you doing in Washington?"

"Having career talks," he said casually.

She looked around. "Where's Caroline?"

Mike's genial smile disappeared, and Jill's eyebrows rose slightly.

"Forget I asked," she said.

He shrugged. "It probably won't come as any surprise to you," he said with a faint trace of bitterness.

Jill sighed. "Why don't you ask me where Tom is?"

Later, she wondered why she had said it, perhaps known why without acknowledging it. His eyebrows had risen in turn.

"You just got married," he said mildly.

"I know," said Jill. "Here comes the bride, there goes the bride."

"You don't sound too distressed about the problem, whatever it is."

"I'm drifting, you might say, or that's what it feels like. We don't seem to be able to get together here, there, or anywhere." She began to laugh. "My God, what a conversation. A real reunion!"

Mike's face creased in his warm, easy grin, and Jill remembered what an attractive man she had always found him. She and Caroline had some tastes in common, she reflected. They had both dated Mike's son, and they had both found the father more attractive than the son.

"Can I get you a drink?" he asked.

"If we can find the bar. I was trying to reach a friend somewhere in this mob, Martha Vogel—you know Martha?"

He nodded. "Caroline introduced."

Jill's laughter became uncontrollable, and after a moment of apparent annoyance, he began to join in.

"I'm sorry," she sputtered, "it's just that everywhere we step, there's Caroline. I mean, my husband tells me, in between yelling at me, what a nice lunch he just had with Caroline. I run into you out of nowhere and probably the only person we both know at this awful party is a woman whom we got to know through Caroline. She's our nemesis, or something."

Mike was laughing as hard as Jill by now. "In between my yelling at her about how she's ruining our relationship, she tells me about the nice quiet lunch she had with your husband."

Jill leaned her head against his shoulder and shook.

"Hey, are we interrupting something we shouldn't, or are you just holding each other up?" Martha's voice sounded from behind Jill.

They turned, and Jill met Martha's amused gaze. Behind Martha was Roger Miller. He held out his hand.

"Jill, nice to see you again."

Martha had focused on Mike.

"I didn't know you were in town," she told him, patting his arm. "How's Caroline?"

They looked bewildered as Jill and Mike again dissolved into helpless mirth.

"Look," said Martha, "laughs are hard enough to come by nowadays. You have to let us in on this one." She looked up at Roger. "God knows I need it." She moved a little closer to him, and his hand rested gently on her shoulder.

Jill dug in her purse for a tissue to wipe her eyes. "It's just that—well, it's hard to explain." She looked to Mike for help.

"We're haunted by Caroline," he said solemnly.

"Is that right?" said Martha. "I thought she was doing rather well at KRT in Columbus."

"All true," said Mike. "It's just that Caroline would appear to be the link that binds us all together. Whether we like it or not. Without her, none of us might ever have met."

He began to laugh again.

Martha and Roger exchanged quick glances.

"Is there some reason you two don't have a drink?" Miller asked, contemplating his empty glass.

"There's a good reason why we *should* have a drink," declared Mike. "Stay right there, all of you."

"We can't move. This was a major expedition to get to you," observed Martha, who was nursing a glass of wine. As Mike began to heave his way toward the bar, she looked searchingly at Jill.

"I didn't know you two knew each other this well."

"We don't," said Jill cheerfully. "There's nothing like shared misery to cement a friendship."

There was a faint pause.

"How true," Roger drawled. "How very true, Jill."

Martha grinned in spite of herself.

"You see?" said Jill. "It's catching."

"Roger," said Martha, "I'm sorry, I didn't introduce you to Mike Hathaway. He's—'.

"I know who he is, my love," said Roger. "I make it my business to know who quite a few people are when they are connected, even remotely, with World News Network. I believe I ran into Mike some while back when he was in New York for inspection."

"The celestial summit," murmured Martha.

Jill studied them, and wondered what was going on with Martha. She had read about Mellenkoff's marriage, and she was afflicted with curiosity. She also knew she

could not raise the subject in front of Martha, and doubted
that Martha would ever discuss it. For that matter, she
seemed very cozy with Roger Miller, who was the kind of
man who could be funny by raising an eyebrow. She
suspected he also would be interesting to sleep with, and
was faintly surprised at herself. She didn't usually react
to men like that, especially since she got married. She
sometimes wondered if she had married Tom so she
wouldn't have to take her mind off her work by worrying
about her personal life. She hoped the same thought had
not occurred to him. Mike Hathaway reappeared, clutching drinks.

"Why are these parties so popular in this town?" he
inquired. "I've been to less crowded Superbowls."

"Everyone thinks they'll come for a few minutes, then
they can't get out, so they try to get to the bar and on the
way they meet somebody they once knew and they start
to laugh and then they can't stand up. . . ." said Martha
mockingly. Jill grinned appreciatively.

"To old friends," said Roger, and raised his glass.

"To old friends," said Jill, and found that her eyes
clung to Mike's as she toasted him.

Martha smiled, and touched Roger's hand.

"We have to begin the long march to the door, because Roger has to catch a plane," she said. "Jill, I'll call
you for lunch. Mike, nice to see you."

Jill hardly noticed their departure, and was suddenly
faintly flustered.

"You don't want to stay at this party either, do you?"
Mike asked. She shook her head.

"Would you like to have dinner?"

She nodded, and wondered why she had become
tongue-tied.

"Then if you'll hang on to my arm, I'll try to fight our
way out."

She stood looking at him, and he put his arm around
her and began to propel her forward. She was sharply
conscious of the warmth of his hand through the thin silk
of her blouse, and when they finally reached the exit, she
knew it was not her imagination that his fingers briefly
caressed her shoulders as he helped her on with her coat.
She knew too that if he wanted to come home with her
and make love to her, she would have no objections. As

they climbed into a taxi, she glimpsed Martha and Roger
walking along the sidewalk. Miller's arm was lightly across
Martha's shoulders, which, even from a distance, seemed
to droop. She realized Mike was talking to her.

"There's a nice little restaurant next to my hotel. Why
don't we get a bite there and maybe have a drink after
somewhere else? So we can get caught up, as it were."

His eyes were merry in the dimness, and his face was
close to hers. It seemed entirely natural for him to kiss
her; and they were still in each other's arms when they
reached the restaurant.

Martha Vogel was in no mood for romance. She refused Roger's suggestion of dinner or even another drink.

"Just drop me off on your way to the airport," she said
quietly. "It's been a bad day, Roger.

"I assumed that. You sort of glow in the dark when
you've heard from him."

"I didn't answer the phone," said Martha defensively.

"He called last night?" Even Roger was surprised.

"A pause in the midst of marital bliss, or so I assume."
Martha's voice was bitter. Roger waited patiently, but all
she wanted was to go home, where it would be quiet and
she would be alone. She had only gone to the party with
him to avoid telling him anything, which she suspected he
was aware of.

"Roger," she said tightly, "I'm not falling apart. Take
that look off your face. I just don't want to talk tonight."

"Going out more and enjoying it less, darling?"

"Don't lecture me," she said with sudden sharpness.
"He's married. You don't have to go on telling me I have
to get out. I'm out. Or he's out. Either way, it's over and
you can stop worrying about me."

"Stop that damned nonsense," said Roger. "Get in the
cab and I'll drop you off."

In the taxi he held her hand gently, and she was
grateful. She could feel him watching her with those
shrewd eyes networked by tiny lines. She had always
loved Roger's smile, because it made his face a series of
upward swoops, like seagulls upside down. He did not
speak again, and when they reached her apartment door,
she kissed him and closed her eyes briefly against his
cheek.

"I'm sorry. I'll call you." He nodded and grinned, and in spite of herself, she grinned back.

As she let herself into her apartment, the telephone was ringing.

"The hell with it," said Martha, dropping her coat on the sofa and heading for the kitchen to heat up soup. While she waited, she went through her mail, scanned a magazine, and ignored the insistent sound. She made a sandwich and ate it, and spooned up her soup. Then she padded into the bathroom and turned on the hot and cold faucets. Sitting in a tubful of warm water always soothed her, and she had just begun to relax when the phone rang again. On the eighteenth ring, Martha reached for a terrycloth robe, wrapped herself in it to blot up the moisture from her wet body, and snatched up the receiver.

"Martha," said the familiar voice.

She replaced the receiver, went back to the bathroom, and got back into the tub. She was shivering, but she suspected it was fatigue and not the impact of the voice. The news of Mellenkoff's marriage had done little more than deepen her sense of numbness. She had been seeing other people, refusing to let herself think. She supposed sometime she would, but she didn't think it would be the end of the world when she did. She had almost cracked when her mother called and asked how she had let that gorgeous man get away.

"Blondes have more fun," Martha had said. Loretta Vogel said she didn't know how Martha could joke about these things. Martha had even managed to laugh when she repeated the exchange to Miller, who had snorted with glee. She had been so determinedly cheerful and sardonic at the office that people had stopped tiptoeing around her. She hadn't even thrown out Mellenkoff's clothes and books, although she still kept them tucked away. She knew they were there, but she didn't look at them, and that way, she didn't think about them. She stayed busy and made herself tired and surprised herself by occasionally enjoying herself. There's life after Mellenkoff, she assured Roger.

The telephone rang as she got out of the bathtub, subsided after fourteen rings, and jangled into life again as she slipped into a restless sleep.

"Jeeeesus Christ," said Martha and picked up the receiver.

"What the hell do you want?" she asked it, and didn't care if it were Joel Eliass on the other end.

"I have to talk to you," said Mellenkoff.

"Why?"

"I know you're angry."

"Perceptive."

"But I must talk to you, Martha. Please. Please."

She could count on the fingers of one hand the number of times she had heard Mellenkoff say please.

"Aren't you on your honeymoon?" she asked.

"Supposed to be."

"What's that mean?"

"Martha, for God's sake, listen. This is the worst mess I ever got into and I know it's my own fault. I don't expect you to be anything but angry, but you've always let me explain."

"It's a little odd," said Martha coldly, "to describe your marriage to the niece of the chairman of the board as a mess. Have you mentioned this to Uncle Joel?"

"I can't talk about this on the phone," said Mellenkoff.

"Why?" asked Martha. "Is Sally on the extension?"

"Listen. Aren't you coming out to the coast with the President next week?"

"So?"

"He's going to be holed up at his beach place. I've got to see you. For a drink. For half an hour. Give me that chance. Please."

"Look," she said. "There isn't anything to talk about, James. It's over and you ended it. Whatever problems you've got with your new wife, those are your problems, not mine. It's outrageous you should try to involve me in this."

There was a brief pause.

"I had a message—I guess it must have been before I—I left—that you had called me," he said in a subdued voice.

"Called you?" Martha paused. "Yes. Yes I did. As a matter of fact, my little protégée, Caroline Mitchell, called me. She's weekend anchor in Columbus now. She'd heard somebody in New York had taken a look at a new tape of hers and obviously she was praying it was the great god Mellenkoff. She's after a tryout for the Chicago talk show."

Mellenkoff thought for a moment.

"I remember something about that," he said. "That news director at KRT, the one who's pushing Mitchell. I think he sent me the tapes. I wondered why he wasn't trying to keep her instead of trying to get rid of her."

"Altruism."

"Anyway, I did see them, and I can't remember, but they weren't bad. I suppose she could try out. Wouldn't hurt."

"Will you set it up with Chicago?"

"Sure." He was unusually obliging. "She'll probably bomb, but she can test."

Martha was silent and Mellenkoff was grateful she was still on the line.

"Look," he said. "What harm can it do to talk to me for a few minutes?"

"James," Martha said with finality, "you're married. What the hell else is there to say?"

"But I'm not."

"Not what?"

"Not married."

"You've changed your mind after a week?"

"I've been alone. She—Sally's at the beach with friends. I haven't seen her since we got to California."

"Come on," said Martha.

"It's true. She doesn't want to be married to me. Said she never did. Eliass made her marry me."

"Who made you marry her?"

"I—Christ, Martha, I didn't want to get into this. So I had the hots for her and she wouldn't go to bed with me unless I married her, or so she said. It was one of those idiotic things. Then when we got married, she said she hated sex and wanted nothing to do with me. Said she just wanted her uncle off her back."

"So to speak," said Martha, and laughed harshly. Three thousand miles away, Mellenkoff listened with relief to the sound.

"You could say I deserved everything that's happened," he ventured.

"Yes, you could, James," said Martha. "There's a solid element of justice in everything you've told me."

"I've never been so miserable in my life," said Mellenkoff. "And I don't know how to get out of it."

"I'd say you can't," said Martha, "unless you want to sever connections with WNN, and knowing you, you don't want to do that."

"Martha, I don't have anyone else in the world I can talk to. Please."

She hesitated, and was lost.

"I could maybe have a quick drink when we get to L.A. You can call me at the hotel. I think the press is staying at the Century Plaza. But, James—"

"Yes?"

"I don't want to be seen with you. I'll meet you somewhere quiet and you can cry on my shoulder, as usual. But that's it. You remember that old saying about a worm, and I'm in the process of turning."

"You're not a worm. You're wonderful. You always were."

He knew he was taking a chance, and when she did not respond, he thought he had gone too far. But propped up on her pillows, Martha was pressing her fingers against her eyes to stop herself from crying.

"I said I'd see you, James. But that's all," she said, and hung up, but not before he had heard the break in her voice.

Mellenkoff replaced the receiver, leaned back in the chaise on the balcony overlooking the Pacific, and smiled. He hadn't even had to lie, or not much. The story was in itself incredible enough that it required little embroidery. And he was delighted at her determination not to be seen with him. He preferred discretion, for a while.

He lay down on the huge bed in his suite, again feeling a surge of perplexed anger at Sally. Where the hell was she anyway? She'd called him once to say she'd meet him at the airport before they went back to New York. He had heard laughter in the background and had hung up. To make the situation more ludicrous, he had been keeping in touch with New York and had to put up with the coy comments of Eliass, who had once or twice asked to speak to "Mrs. Mellenkoff." He had to make the excuse that she was surfing. He couldn't wait to get back to New York, and then Sally could go about her business, whatever it was, and he'd go about his. With Martha, he hoped. Now and again, when he let himself think about it, he realized how much he missed her. Mellenkoff drifted into a light sleep, and when he roused, he glanced at his watch and put in a call to New York. This was no time to break his promise to Martha that he would okay a test in Chicago for the Mitchell woman. After he had hung up, he thought for a moment, then put in a call to KRT in Columbus and asked for Joe Moynihan, who sounded pleased and surprised.

"Mitchell can do a test for Chicago," Mellenkoff said with his customary terseness.

"I thought you might like those new tapes. Showing promise," said Moynihan.

"Glad you sent them," said Mellenkoff, trying to remember the Mitchell woman's first name. The computer of his memory did not fail him.

"Tell Caroline I wish her luck," he said, and hung up. He knew the first person Caroline would call with her good news would be Martha.

28

MIKE HAD found out from Eric Kriss, the KRT station manager, that Caroline was going to test for the co-host job in Chicago.

"Are you serious?" he'd asked, as he and Kriss stood in the passageway outside Joe Moynihan's office.

Kriss stared at him. He had been annoyed that he had to be told about any developments regarding station talent by Moynihan, the news director, whom Kriss outranked. Especially as Moynihan had casually mentioned Caroline's forthcoming test in the middle of a meeting. It was strange that Hathaway didn't know, thought Kriss, in view of what was supposedly his close relationship with Mitchell. He felt a momentary pang of regret for mentioning it and breaking such news, then decided if Hathaway had taken the chance of becoming involved with as volatile a package as Mitchell, he should have been aware that ambition was her dominating characteristic. Kriss rather liked shooting stars like Caroline. It was always interesting to try to figure out how far they'd get before they self-destructed. If they self-destructed.

"I thought you knew," he told Hathaway lamely, and tried unsuccessfully to slip away when he saw Caroline tripping toward them, wearing the smile that Kriss sometimes thought looked as if the ends of her mouth were taped to her ears.

"What's going on?" she caroled. She stopped as she saw Mike's grim expression.

"That's what I'm wondering," said Mike.

"What are you talking about?" asked Caroline, and directed a perplexed glance at Kriss.

"Have you talked to Moynihan?" asked the station manager brusquely.

Caroline shook her head. "He just called me and told me to come to his office, that he had something to tell me."

Kriss was partially mollified; at least Moynihan had talked to him about the test before telling Mitchell. He still wondered how her tapes had reached Mellenkoff's rarefied level, but Moynihan had been less than communicative about it. According to the news director, Caroline was friendly with Martha Vogel, whose friendship with Mellenkoff was well known, and he assumed Vogel had brought the tapes to Mellenkoff's attention.

"She's quite an operator, little Mitchell," Kriss observed sourly. He had assumed that if anyone gave Mitchell a break, it would be he. For that matter, why had Mellenkoff called Moynihan about the tapes instead of him? He wondered how much of a hand Moynihan had in this. Kriss was aware that the news director was unhappy about Mike Hathaway's infatuation with Caroline.

"She'll eat him alive," was the way Moynihan had described his reaction to the relationship. On the other hand, having a test didn't mean she'd get the job. And it was probably true that Mellenkoff would set it up as a favor for Vogel. If the network gossip was accurate, he owed her one, after up and marrying somebody else. However, Kriss took it on himself to tell Caroline what it was that Moynihan wanted to talk to her about, and made sure he gave the impression he had had a hand in it.

Caroline's face was luminous with joy.

"Oh my God, really? Really? Oh, that's terrific."

"It could be a good opportunity," Kriss told her.

"I can't believe it," she said. "I just can't believe it. Excuse me, I'd better see Joe."

She darted into Moynihan's office without glancing in the direction of Mike, who was standing stony faced and silent. As her excited voice rose in Moynihan's office, Mike turned and walked slowly toward his office. Kriss sighed. He hoped Hathaway's worries wouldn't show on his face during the broadcast. He was not as high on the anchorman as Moynihan was. Moynihan was an old drinking friend of Mike, and Kriss belonged to a breed of television executive whose chief interest in anchors, whether male or female, was that they maintain or raise the ratings and not make fools of themselves and the station on the air. He assumed Hathaway was enough of a professional to keep his personal problems under control. Ironically, he would have been less concerned about someone like Mitchell in a similar situation, because her emotions clearly were firmly under the control of her ambition. He sometimes wondered if intelligent robots might not be the answer to such a situation. When millions of dollars were tied up in somebody's personality or lack of it, it was a fragile reed for people like him to lean on. No wonder television had a high burnout rate, not to mention a high risk factor, for those who pulled the strings that controlled the puppets.

It was not until Caroline had left Moynihan's office that she remembered the look on Mike's face. Sighing, she walked down the hall to his office and found the door closed, which was unusual. She knocked gently.

"Yes," said Mike.

"Mike? It's me."

There was a pause.

"I'm sort of busy now. I've got a couple of things to finish off. I'll see you later." His voice was polite, impersonal.

"Sure," said Caroline, with a sense of relief over a delayed unpleasantness. She had not mentioned the possibility of a test for "People Are Asking," precisely because of what was now happening. She knew that if she went to Chicago, it would cause problems with Mike, whether she got the job or not. And she didn't want to worry about Mike. She wanted to concentrate all her energy on the possibility that she might test, and that she might win out. If she hadn't been asked to test, Mike would never have known. If she were asked to test, she had decided she would worry about that when it happened. Now all she wanted to think about was the test, and she was going to have to go through some dismal discussion with Mike of why was she doing this to them. Damn, she thought, then her smile flowered again as she saw Del Kelly waving and grinning across the newsroom. She'd much rather go out and celebrate with Del, who had her career interests at heart.

Behind the closed door of his office, Mike was sitting staring out the window at the rain. The weather matched his misery. She hadn't even told him she was trying to get a test for the PAA show. In all their interminable discussions of her career, in which she so anxiously had sought his advice, counsel, and encouragement, she had not mentioned that; although, knowing Caroline, and judging by her reaction to Kriss's announcement, it must have been heavily on her mind. She obviously had not told him because she knew he would be puzzled and hurt. Their relationship was just beginning to settle. He had been thinking, albeit tentatively, in terms of marriage, especially since Leslie had become amenable to a quick divorce. He suspected her cooperation might be linked to the fact that her new part-time job at the university apparently had led to a friendship with a member of the faculty who had a distinguished reputation for his studies in English and French literature, and who had recently become a widower. Mike had seem them together, having dinner in the Coachman, and he had waved cheerfully at them. He was still sorry about the collapse of his marriage, but if it had to end, he preferred that it be concluded in a civilized fashion and not in the kind of emotional brawl in which he had seen too many of his friends embroiled. And he was so wrapped up in his joy in Caroline, his lovely, mercurial Caroline, who could be so adoring and attentive. Except when she was negotiating her way up.

Grimly, he turned his attention to his computer and the day's story schedule. The President was complaining about Congress and vice versa. A local legislator had been arrested while patronizing a well-known cathouse. Poor bastard, Mike thought. He would pick a night when they were raiding it. Toxic waste was seeping from a disused dump outside town. There was another uprising in the Middle East. He forced himself to concentrate on what he didn't care about. He knew he had to talk to Caroline, and he wanted to put it off as long as possible, but he knew he wouldn't, because he was angry. Mike didn't get angry often, but when he did, it was a slow burning ember. He managed to avoid Caroline for most of the day, and after the show, he took a deep breath and dialed her extension. She picked up the phone immediately, and her voice was a little breathless. She was either nervous or excited. Probably excited, he thought bleakly.

"How about a drink?" He kept his voice as casual as possible.

"Sure." He wasn't certain, but he thought he detected a note of resignation.

She met him in the parking lot, and Eric Kriss shook his head as he saw them leave together. Hathaway had looked like hell on camera, while obviously trying to be his usual genial self. He hoped this thing would get straightened out, or Hathaway was going to find that doing more reporting on the street wasn't going to be enough if he looked depressed and tired on the air. Robots, thought Kriss. That had to be the answer.

Moynihan wandered past his door, and Kriss regarded him with mild dislike. He held the news director generally responsible for Hathaway's poor performance that night. Moynihan stopped and looked in at him.

"Not too good, hmmm?" he said, peering over his glasses morosely.

Kriss shook his head. "Hathaway had better watch it, Joe. He's not home free by any means."

"Well, things may take care of themselves," said Moynihan.

"You mean Mitchell's test, I assume? I thought I saw your paw prints all over that."

Moynihan shook his head. "Not really. I think it was Kelly who told her about the opening, and she didn't need any encouragement. She used everything and everybody she knew."

"Except Hathaway."

"Come on now."

"You think Mellenkoff's backing her?"

"That I don't know. Nobody knows. But it can't hurt her chances, that's for sure. Especially with the trouble they've had getting a woman to work with Josh Henry."

Kriss smiled evilly. "I'll back Mitchell against Henry."

"She could do very well," Moynihan acknowledged, "as long as she doesn't get into a situation that plays to her weaknesses."

"As a matter of fact," said Kriss, "she's come a hell of a long way in a short time. I've got to give her credit."

"She's a very fast study," said Moynihan. "But there's still that problem of retention. It's as though she skates very fast but she's always on thin ice. However, a talk show might be just the thing for her. She can turn on the charm better than anybody I've ever seen, and that'll go a long way on that kind of show."

"Not to mention with Josh Henry." They both grinned.

Sitting in a bar a few blocks away with Mike, Caroline tried to look solemn. She had spent most of the day in the kind of joyful haze that had evoked a tart admonition from Moynihan not to look so happy when she was on the air with a story about a group of elderly being evicted by a landlord with visions of condominiums floating in his head. In the postshow critique, Moynihan had observed sharply that Caroline had to learn to concentrate on what she was working on and not let anything interfere with it. "Remember, people can see you, and what they saw tonight was a silly grin in the middle of a serious package," he had told her. Caroline had been chastized, but not much. Nothing could ruin this day for her, not even her current gloomy dialogue with Mike, who was acting as if she'd committed a murder.

"Why the hell couldn't you have told me you asked Vogel to intervene for you with Mellenkoff? Why did you have to leave me with my face hanging out in front of Kriss and Mellenkoff?"

"I didn't ask Martha to intervene. I told her about the tapes. Maybe I mentioned the PAA opening. But I didn't ask her to go to Mellenkoff," she said in defense of herself.

"Who else would she go to? That was who you knew she would go to, if she went to anyone. Don't fudge, Caroline. You were playing your own game. And you were playing it with me."

"I knew you'd get mad if I told you." She stared sullenly at her white wine. Why was he spoiling her lovely day?

"But you didn't care if you hurt me, did you?"

She looked at him in surprise. Mike had never used that harsh a tone to her before.

"I didn't want to hurt you, Mike," she said honestly. "I really didn't. It was just something I wanted to try for, and I didn't expect to hear anything back. So what would have been the point of upsetting you?"

"But you knew it would upset me. For God's sake, Caroline, we've been talking about our future. What would something like this do to it? What *will* something like this do to it?"

He had been talking about their future, Caroline thought. She certainly hadn't.

"I didn't mean to hurt you," she insisted, and drank some of her wine. She was hungry. She wanted to go out and have a drink or two and have fun with someone like Kelly. She didn't want to brood about Mike's dream of domesticity. She didn't want to dream about domesticity at all. All she wanted to think about was the test, and how she should handle it. She had to call Martha when she got home, and thank her. God, Mellenkoff himself calling the Chicago station about her tape—she still couldn't believe it. Maybe she would send Martha a present— flowers or candy. Or she'd wait, and if she got the job, she'd send her champagne. Abruptly, Caroline realized she hadn't heard anything Mike had said for the past five minutes, and he was staring angrily at her. She wished she could get up and leave, but she couldn't afford to antagonize Mike at this point, either. She hadn't got the job in Chicago yet.

"Mike," she said, and fixed him with her most appealing look. "I know you're angry, and you've a right to be. I didn't think of anyone but myself, and I'm sorry. I just got so carried away about the whole idea, and it was sort of a fantasy in my head. I never thought it'd come to anything. I really didn't. But all this is new to me. I mean, you're a star and you've been in the business a long time, and little things don't matter so much to you. . . ."

That was wrong. His face had darkened again.

"This isn't a little thing," he said tightly. "If you get that job, and you may, if Mellenkoff is behind you, where does that leave us? Or me, rather. I guess I know where it leaves you."

"Why would it be the end of the world if I moved to Chicago? I mean, just supposing I got that job. Wouldn't you be pleased for me—that I'd got it? Doesn't that matter at all?"

Mike was silent for a while, turning his Scotch glass in his hands.

"I know I'm being selfish about you, Caroline," he admitted. "And I know this could be a terrific chance for you. I'm pleased about that. I'm pleased you're doing so well, believe that. It's just that . . . well, I feel so . . . left out."

She was touched. She remembered how fond she was of him.

Caroline put her hand over his. "You aren't left out, Mike. You aren't. I need you."

He nodded. "Yes, you still need me, Caroline. But if you go to Chicago, you won't."

That was so close to the truth that she flinched a little.

"You make me sound like a real user," she said.

Mike glanced at her and smiled wryly. "My darling," he said, "surely it's occurred to you that you are a user. I mean, how else do you account for the rapidly changing events in your relatively young life? You're not doing it all by your little self, are you?"

"People help me," she acknowledged.

"Damn right they help you, because you captivate them into it, that's why they help you. Do you think they'd help you as much if you didn't look the way you do, act the way you do?"

His voice was angry again and Caroline sighed. This was going nowhere and she was getting hungrier. She didn't want to drink with Mike tonight. She didn't drink much, because she hated to lose control over herself, and she didn't want to have to cope with a drunken and maudlin Mike. Especially in bed. She didn't want to have to pretend tonight. Just once she wanted to be allowed to exult. She watched gloomily as Mike ordered another drink.

"I don't want anything," she told the waiter. Mike's eyebrows rose.

"I'm hungry," she said bluntly. "And I think we need a rest from this tonight, Mike. We're—we're chewing on each other, and all we're doing is making each other unhappy."

What she meant was that he was making her unhappy, but she wanted to be tactful about it. Why couldn't he be happy with her?

"You want to go home?"

She noticed he didn't suggest going anywhere to eat, and was grateful.

"Well, why don't you finish your drink? I can get a taxi."

He nodded. "I'm sure you can. You'll always get what you want, when you want it, won't you, Caroline?"

"Mike, please. Try not to be so angry. I mean, I probably won't get the damned job, and all this'll be silly, won't it?"

"If you don't get this one, you'll get the next one. This is your first stepping stone, isn't it? Or was I your first stepping stone? Or was it poor old Franklin?"

Caroline looked around uneasily as his voice rose. His voice was as locally recognizable as Mike was.

"That isn't fair, and it's not true. You know that," she murmured.

"Do I? Do I really, Caroline? He couldn't be as much help to you as I could, could he? And I couldn't be as much help to you as Martha Vogel. Or Mellenkoff. Now there's your target of opportunity, my dear: Mellenkoff. The iceman. There's your real challenge. And I bet you'll make it, Caroline. I just bet you'll make it. Wherever you're going. Because obviously you're not going there with me. Onward and upward through the wreckage."

Most of the bar was now paying fascinated attention.

She picked up her purse.

"Mike, I'm going now. We can talk again. And I'm sorry. I really am. I never thought you'd be this upset. And"—she hesitated—"I'm sorry about Franklin too. Is there anything I'm not to blame for?"

Mike stared into the empty glass and signaled for a refill.

"I hope you get the job," he said quietly and carefully. "I hope you get what you want. Whatever that is. It isn't me. And it wasn't Franklin."

Caroline stood up. "I'll call you later," she said.

He shook his head. "No, don't call me. I'll call you, Caroline. 'Samatter of fact, I'll drive you to the airport. Would you like that?"

"No," said Caroline. "I wouldn't. Good night, Mike."

She left quickly, threading her way past tables of interested onlookers, and found a telephone in a passageway near the restrooms. She called a taxi company, and as she began to walk toward the entrance to wait for the cab, she suddenly turned back to the telephone and dialed the number of the KRT newsroom.

"Is Del Kelly still there?"

He was.

"I was just leaving. As a matter of fact, I was looking around for you. Thought I'd buy you a drink to celebrate. But somebody said you'd left with Mike."

"Yes, well I did. But I—I'm not with him now."

"Something wrong?" She could hear the glee of the born gossip in Del's voice.

"Not really. Obviously, he'd rather I didn't leave, and so would I, in some ways. It's difficult." She had found the best way to defang Kelly was to tell him the approximate truth, which was always duller than what he would fabricate out of reluctance to talk.

"Sure it is." He was sympathetic. He liked Mike Hathaway, but on the other hand, Hathaway had beaten out Kelly with Mitchell, so he was not displeased by the current turn of events. "Hey, you shouldn't be moping around tonight over Mike. I mean, he'll be fine once he thinks about it. How about a drink? Champagne cocktail might be in order."

Caroline giggled. "Not yet, not yet. But God, I'd love to celebrate, Del. I mean, I'm just so thrilled about this. And after all, it was you who told me about the job. I ought to buy you a beer!"

"You're on," said Kelly happily. "Where are you now? You want me to pick you up?"

"No, no, you don't need to do that. Let's meet. . . ." The last thing she needed was for Kelly to pick her up at a bar where Mike was working on getting drunk. She named another KRT hangout. "See you there in ten minutes."

As she stood at the door, waiting for her taxi, Mike appeared behind her. She looked at him nervously. Mike usually carried his liquor well, and even when he didn't, he was a jolly drunk. But tonight he was unpredictable.

"You want a ride home?" His voice was deliberate, but not noticeably slurred. She shook her head.

"No, thank you. I have a cab coming."

"Cancel it. That's silly." He turned toward the phone, and for an instant, she wondered if he had heard her talking to Kelly.

"No," she said, "I'll take the cab."

He paused, and looked at her. "You're not going home, are you?"

Caroline felt as though she were being backed against a wall. Mike had never bullied her. No one had bullied her, except her father. Caroline in the mirror would not have put up with as much. She faced him and her eyes were dark and cold.

"It's none of your business, Mike."

"It's not?"

"No. Especially it's not when you're drunk. Please leave me alone."

"You're sure you don't want me to drive you to the airport? You wouldn't want to miss your plane to Chicago next week."

He put his hand on her shoulder, and Caroline wrenched herself away. Now she felt nothing but fury.

"I don't want you to drive me anywhere. I'm not your property. I never made you think I was. I never pretended. You thought what you wanted to think. Now leave me alone. Leave me *alone.*"

She stepped into the cab, and slammed the door. She rolled up the window before she gave the driver directions, and through the glass, she saw, as in a distorted mirror, the image of Mike's face. He looked suddenly older.

29

THEY CALLED it Josh Henry's show, and it was.
Which was why Barbara Guess, who was almost as ego-
tistic as Josh, had taken herself off to Los Angeles,
where she had decided the competition for the camera
couldn't be any fiercer. Barbara, a tall and frosty frosted-
blonde, had survived remarkably well during three years
of on-air amicability and off-air vituperation with Josh.
She said her problems arose from the fact she had refused to go to bed with him on the grounds that she
didn't want to compete with his ego in bed. He said her
problems arose from the fact that the television audience
liked him better, and the ratings proved it. Those at
JRZ-WNN in Chicago who mopped up after Josh Henry
said there was an element of truth in both versions. Only
Josh and God knew whom he could get along with,
whether he went to bed with them or not. One cynic
suggested the ratings might reach an all-time high if Josh
had sex with his co-anchor on camera in the middle of
"People Are Asking." Josh laughed immoderately when
he heard that; he enjoyed his own publicity, and didn't
take it as seriously as people thought he did. And he
certainly didn't take seriously the women silly enough to
go to bed with him. Josh's wife, Meg, knew that.

Josh and Meg Henry's marriage had lasted for twenty-
six years, and he had never even considered leaving her.
She had once or twice demanded he either cool it with
that person who had taken to calling him at home in the
middle of the night or he could have a divorce. Josh
invariably had cooled it. In his way, Josh was devoted to
Meg. He never told any of his inamoratas that his wife
didn't understand him, because she did, and he happily
admitted it. It had been a source of unending curiosity to

Josh through the years that telling some women "I love
my wife very much, but—" had the immediate effect of
them casting themselves as the one human being who was
the corollary to the "but."

"The trouble with Josh is he's the original man who
can't say no," Meg had observed sardonically to a friend
one night after her husband called and said he had to
take a network executive to dinner and not to wait up.
There were not, said Meg, enough network executives
extant for Josh to spend as much time as he did wining
and dining them. On the other hand, it had worked out
well for everyone, Meg told the man she was in bed with,
because now he didn't have to leave early. At some point,
Meg had decided that although she knew Josh loved her
and would never leave her, his unabashed philandering was
doing little for her self-esteem. In the early years of marriage, she had refused to believe the evidence, even when
it took the form of letters in the mail and notes in his
shirt pocket. Josh was a roving national corespondent for
WNN, after having been a war correspondent for them in
Vietnam, and Meg made allowances for the fact that her
husband was an exceedingly handsome man, with the black
hair and light blue eyes of those known as black Irish,
and a jaunty wit from which his name had sprung when he
was still in junior high school. Meg had been a photographer for a magazine in Washington when she met Josh,
and although she had fallen in love with him, she had
never had any illusions about him.

"You'll run around on me all my life," she told him
when he asked her to marry him.

"But it'll always be you I'll need," he said.

She had gone on taking pictures, and eventually had
wound up taking a lover or two. But she was discreet
about it. She did not particularly care whether Josh found
out about her infidelities, but she took no particular
pride in being unfaithful. It gave her a sense of power
over him that he did not realize that his lovable, depend-
able Meg had her own secrets. He never knew, and his
belief that she was at home, at the theater with friends,
or working in her darkroom while he was indulging in his
favorite recreation always brought him home early enough
to annoy the woman he had been with, full of thanks that
Meg was waiting for him as usual.

Anchoring a talk show where the public was encouraged to ask questions about anything that was on its collective mind had been a change of pace for the peripatetic Josh, but he was almost fifty now, and slowing down just a little. He even spent some nights at home, playing poker with Meg, who was much better at bluffing than he was, and usually won. He had become so domesticated, by comparison with earlier years, that Meg had to trim her own social activities. She was pleased to have him with her, but she had become so accustomed to their unorthodox form of marriage that she occasionally felt a little restricted by the unexpected presence of her husband.

Meg had not been surprised at the enormous success of the show. Josh had precisely the right approach to handling questions, whether rambling, intellectual, original, or obscene. He never lost his temper, never condescended, never mocked. He was patient, quick to grasp, and even quicker with a quip. The televised audience loved him, and viewers loved him. Even Meg, who was used to his drolleries, would click on the show and find herself chuckling. Somehow, he succeeded in rarely antagonizing the questioners, and the station was surprised at how little hate mail he attracted. "Everybody likes an Irish comedian," he told them.

Given his success, Meg wondered why it had been deemed necessary to give him a co-host. She assumed it was because the network bosses decided that adding a woman to the show would be good business to demonstrate their dedication to equality of the sexes. The trouble was that the women chosen—Barbara Guess had been the third—seemed trapped in the role of straight man to Josh. Individual surveys showed them discouragingly far behind him in audience approval. It was because they hadn't found the right woman, Meg suggested to Josh. The first had been fluffy and giggly, the second had been elegant and gravely introspective. And rumors to the contrary, Josh had slept with neither of them. Fluffy-and-Giggly had been receptive to his charms, to the point that the station received calls and letters complaining about her "making eyes at Josh." Gravely Introspective, Meg suspected, was not receptive to the charms of the opposite sex; she had found the format of the show too superficial, said so, and left.

If anyone might have worked out, as far as Meg could tell, it would have been Barbara Guess, who was quick, bright, and funny as well as having a flair for striking clothes. In some respects, Barbara was similar to Josh in her style which made her competitive with him and which, Meg concluded, was why they didn't get along. Josh admitted he didn't like Barbara, and was unusually vehement in his denials of having made any advances to her. "The Barbed Wire Lady," he called her, which was a little unfair, given Josh's capacity to be prickly when assessing competition.

"Why do they bother replacing her? Why not go back to the solo anchor format?" Meg asked Josh, when Barbara's departure was announced. He threw up his hands.

"They feel they must have a woman. Somewhere there must be a woman who will work out. That seems to be the philosophy. God knows I don't care one way or the other. Right now, it's beginning to feel like a railroad station, and the viewers don't like that, either. All this coming and going."

"Well, as long as they have you, they're happy," said his wife soothingly. Josh grinned at her, his eyes warm as he looked at the tall, reed-slender woman with merry gray eyes, to whom he had always been glad to come back. He had sometimes wondered why she put up with him, but anytime he received the impression that she was about to stop putting up with him, Josh had invariably terminated whatever attachment on his part was causing the problem. He could not conceive of life without Meg. She was the ultimate focus around which he revolved, and when he thought about it, he was remorseful about his years of cavorting through fields of recumbent female forms. But he didn't think about it too often.

During what Josh called the "casting anchor period," when a selection of women tried out for the job, he regaled Meg with descriptions of disaster. The show's producer, Gil Tadich, was going bananas, reported Josh, as a result of the past two weeks, during which one of the tryouts had engaged in a furious argument with two female members of the studio audience on the subject of abortion, and another had stalked off the set after accusing Josh of chauvinism.

"That wasn't exactly news to anybody, darling," said

Meg, placidly pouring him the light bourbon and water that was all he permitted himself before dinner now. Josh liked to drink, but he tried not to let his vices jeopardize anything he valued, and he knew the value of ratings.

"You think I'm a male chauvinist?" He looked at her with merry reproach.

"The last and greatest of the breed."

He grinned. "And you should know, my darling."

Meg ruffled the thick, silky black hair.

"Who better? You want to go out to dinner tonight or have you any executives waiting in the wings?"

"You mean you haven't fixed anything?"

"Haven't, don't want to, won't."

"Okay, where?"

They both laughed.

"I wish I'd seen the abortion fight. Where'd they get that one?" asked Meg.

"I think she was a fallen-away Mormon, who got re-born in the middle of the show."

Meg paused in brushing her short ash-blond hair.

"You mean your co-anchor was anti-abortion? I thought it was the other way round."

"Hell, no. That was what made it so chaotic. I thought she was going to lead a pro-life march across the studio at one point. And let me tell you, there was nothing silent about *her* scream."

Meg winced and laughed. "Gil given up yet?"

Josh shook his head.

"New one arriving this week. This one may be interesting, as a matter of fact. She's a Mellenkoff special."

"Well, well. You mean . . . ?"

"I'm not sure. All I know is that Gil said Mellenkoff asked that she have a tryout. Sent her tapes down from New York, but I haven't seen them. Gil said they weren't bad. Said she was gorgeous."

"But?"

"Hard to tell if there's a 'but.' Mellenkoff doesn't have much reputation for playing games with airheads. Come to think of it, I can't remember his ever foisting off somebody on anybody just because he was screwing her."

"He's undoubtedly quite reformed now that he's mar-ried to the lovely Sally."

"It'll take more than that with Mellenkoff. On the

other hand, Eliass is nobody to mess with. Anyway, this Mitchell woman—from Ohio, I think it is—is arriving next week. Very young and not much experience."

"Promising."

"Well, that wouldn't matter so much on this kind of show. It's a question of how she gets along with people. And how people react to her."

"And how she gets along with you," said Meg, as he helped her into a black mink coat.

"By the way," she said, "what's happened with Martha Vogel? I mean how's she doing in the wake of the marriage of the year?"

Josh shrugged. "I hear she's doing better than might be expected, but I don't hear much."

"I liked her that time she was up here, and we had dinner with her."

"Everybody likes Martha," said Josh. "That's probably her trouble. She's so goddamned decent."

"How's that again?"

"I have the feeling Martha thinks everybody in the world is basically as nice as she is. Now that's a dangerous philosophy. What happens when she finds out they're not?"

"Probably a relief."

He shook his head. "It's a relief to find out you're not the worst person you know. That other people are just as bad. But suppose you find out nobody's as good as you thought they were."

"All this is too complicated for me," said Meg. "And I'm hungry. Speaking of food, by the way, don't feel called upon to invite whoever she is to dinner during her tryout. The last two had allergies to seafood and me, in that order."

"And those were the two before the two who nearly gave Gil a nervous breakdown. Very well, I'll take her to dinner myself. I'll sacrifice."

Meg grinned at him. "And you and I both know how much of a sacrifice that will be, darling. How gorgeous did you say she was supposed to be?"

"Very."

30

THE UNCHARITABLE said that Caroline Mitchell's success at JRZ-WNN was because she looked so good by comparison with her predecessors. The venomous said it was because Josh Henry had decided she would make him look good on the show and feel good in bed. The truth, as usual, lay in the gray area in between. Caroline did look better than some of those who had preceded her, although she was not nearly as smooth as the more experienced Barbara Guess had been. On the other hand, she had captured the studio audience and shown remarkable results in snap surveys. Her capacity to listen and to field questions in interviews, which Martha Vogel had been one of the first to recognize, bloomed in the format of "People Are Asking." She was professionally still tentative enough to accept direction from Josh Henry; she had in fact made it clear at their first meeting that she had done research into the background and style of PAA. It was his show, she told Josh. She wanted to succeed and she would do her best, but she hoped he wouldn't mind if she asked for guidance so that they would work well together. Josh, whose basest instincts had been aroused by Caroline's looks, found himself having second thoughts of a more professional nature. She was certainly starting off with the right attitude, and Josh was keenly aware that the string of unsuccessful co-anchors had not been good for the show, from a viewer standpoint. The station's market-research consultant reported grumblings about the "stream" of new faces, and Why was Josh Henry always having trouble getting along with women?

That was the key phrase to Josh, who knew that, whether it was accurate or not, that was the impression left with those who watched, those who were crucial to the success or failure of any show. He had argued for a resumption of the solo format, but the network chiefs pointed out that other dual-anchor talk shows showed better results than solos, and anyway, why *did* he have such a problem with women? The next step, Josh knew, would be a ratings drop, and at that point he would be arguing from a disadvantage. He wanted PAA to stay on the air. He enjoyed the give and take with the studio audience, he had fun doing it, he was exceedingly well paid, and he felt he was too old to go back to roving reporting and batting around the country in a series of red-eye flights in pursuit of breaking news. Consequently, Josh wanted Caroline Mitchell to succeed, especially because her test had been arranged by Mellenkoff himself. It could do Josh no harm to provide vindication of the talent judgment of the great man himself. In addition to all of which, Josh wanted Caroline Mitchell. He had not found a woman so attractive in years, and beyond her warm manner, there was a reserve that intrigued him. He was prepared to provide all the support he could when they did their first show together, and was pleasantly surprised to find that Caroline needed no help when it came to talking to people. He noticed she was inclined to draw out the audience, to let them form their own mini-debates, whereas Josh would banter with them, injecting his own opinions, his own philosophy, as a sounding board.

Caroline would listen to a question or a comment, see a wildly waving hand, and direct her radiant smile at its owner as she asked, "And what do *you* say to that?" She was a combination of a buffer zone and a Band-Aid, displaying dexterity at soothing the snarling, and encouraging the timid. After she had been on the show for two weeks, an early market survey showed highly favorable viewer response. She was, as Mike Hathaway had sensed, a natural.

The chemistry between Caroline and television cameras made her welcome in the living rooms and bedrooms of those who watched, and then there was that smile of hers. They got letters about it. There was the usual scattering of suggestions that she do her hair differently

or wear a different color, but there appeared to be una-
nimity about her smile. It wasn't so much that it was a
lovely smile; it apparently made viewers feel good to
have Caroline Mitchell smile at them. At KRT, Joe Moynihan had occasionally warned Caroline about smiling
too much while doing the weekend news. He pointed out
that a lot of people didn't want somebody grinning at
them while describing an earthquake in Peru. But the
PAA faithful wanted to be cheered up. They liked smiles.
They watched the show to be entertained, and to gratify
the random hope that a couple of the more aggressive
members of the audience would get into a fight on camera. Now they had the wit and wisdom of Josh Henry,
sandwiched between Caroline Mitchell's dimples.

There were a few negative reactions to Caroline.
But for every letter dubbing her the Shirley Temple of
the airways, there were twenty raving about her friend-
liness, her willingness to listen, her smile, and her
"niceness."

"They don't say much about her intelligence," observed Gil Tadich, PAA's producer.

"They say she seems to know what she's talking about,
but she—how does that woman put it?—doesn't shove it
down your throat," Josh pointed out.

"A lot of people on television are perceived by the
public as talking too much, and listening too little," noted
Robert Cohen, the director of market research for JRZ.

"It's damned good for an early reaction," concluded
John Mayer, the station manager.

"In terms of how people see her, especially when you
think about how little experience she's got, it's phenomenal," said Cohen.

"Josh, you're happy with her?" asked Mayer.

Josh nodded. "Hell yes. She couldn't be easier to work
with. No friction at all."

"So far," said the pessimistic Tadich.

Mayer smiled as he glanced over Caroline's file.
"Mellenkoff strikes again."

"He's always had a good eye for talent," said Cohen.
"And speaking of that, have you met the glamorous Mrs.
Mellenkoff yet?"

Josh grinned widely. "Miss California, you mean? She
doesn't even have to be Joel Eliass's niece."

"Anyway"—Mayer was impatient—"are we going to go with Mitchell? And are we dealing with her or does she have an agent?"

"I think," said Tadich, "she said something about maybe she should get an agent. She's a little wide-eyed about the whole thing right now."

"In that case, we should talk with her now," said Mayer quickly.

"Screw her while the going's good," observed Josh.

"Try to restrain yourself," muttered Tadich, as they left Mayer's office, Josh leered exaggeratedly, but Tadich was not far from the truth. Josh had restrained himself during Caroline's tryout, but he saw no need to deprive himself indefinitely. He assumed she was at that delightful stage when she would be ripe for cozy dinners with his advice on her career as the entrée and herself as the dessert. Josh wondered why Mellenkoff had set things up for Caroline Mitchell. It was unlike the network president to reach down from his gray glass eminence and help smooth the path for someone as unknown and untested as Caroline. Might she be Mellenkoff's personal property? That thought gave Josh pause, but he expected he would rapidly find out if that were the case.

In fact, Mellenkoff had been pleased and faintly amused when he heard Caroline Mitchell was doing so well in the test at PAA. He would never have made any call on her behalf had it not been for his need to convince Martha that he was still capable of a generous gesture.

Even his hand outstretched to Caroline had not mollified Martha as much as he had hoped, however. At their brief meeting in Los Angeles, it had taken all of Mellenkoff's knowledge of Martha and all his formidable powers of persuasion to keep her with him for half an hour. She had listened impassively to his account of his disastrous marriage, meditatively stirring her Scotch and soda with its plastic straw, and not drinking much of it, he noticed. After he had finished, she shook her head.

"It's a mess, I grant you that, James. Assuming"—her eyes grew cold—"that you're telling the truth."

"Martha, come on. Why would I lie?"

"You and I both know why you'd lie. You believe in

keeping your options open, and I've resigned as an option."

"We were friends before we were anything else."

She nodded. "That's true. If that weren't true, I wouldn't be here. I said I'd let you cry on my shoulder, and I have. For old times' sake, I suppose."

She looked at her watch.

"You can't have a quick dinner?"

She shook her head. "I'm on the press pool for a reception the President's attending in Beverly Hills."

"When are you going back to D.C.?

"Day after tomorrow."

"I'm going back to New York tomorrow."

He hesitated.

"I'm going to be in Washington next week. Meetings with Sullivan and some others."

She was silent.

"May I call you?"

"What for?"

"Because I'd like to see you, like to talk to you."

Martha rattled the ice cubes in her glass. "I don't know. Everything's different, James. So your forest fire's a fizzle. It doesn't change your status. Nothing will, either, because you'll never split with Eliass's niece."

"I'm practically never going to see her, either. She's made that clear."

Martha looked thoughtful. "Does she have somebody else on the string? Somebody her uncle didn't approve of?"

"God knows. She was very definite about not being interested in sex. Maybe it was just an excuse; I don't know."

"Well"—Martha picked up her purse—"I expect you don't know the whole story yet. She may change her mind, James. Don't despair."

He sat quietly, watching her, until she looked at him and met the intense blue gaze.

"It wouldn't matter if she changed her mind, Martha."

Her smile was small and twisted. "Just don't tell me about that too, if it happens."

"You haven't believed anything I've said, have you? That does make me despair."

She hesitated briefly.

"I do believe you and I even feel a little sorry for you. But the reasons I feel sorry for you aren't the reasons you feel sorry for yourself."

"Explain?"

She shook her head and her laugh sounded for a moment like the old Martha.

"You're playing for time, James, I recognize the ploy. I have to go, really. WNN can't keep the President waiting."

He stood up, left bills on the table, and walked out of the bar to the street with her.

"Next week? Please."

She smiled over her shoulder as she walked away, and he strolled back into the bar to reward himself with another drink after all his hard work. He had never wanted to lose Martha, but he had been reconciled to losing sight of her for a while. Now that was unnecessary. Their relationship could proceed, even flourish, once she adjusted to what could, as far as he could see, become a comfortable arrangement. He knew how much he had hurt Martha, and he was genuinely sorry about that. But he had considered it a situation beyond his control, in that he could not, at this point in his career, flout Joel Eliass. Sally turning out to be a disaster might prove to be a godsend.

Mellenkoff propped his chin on his hand and turned his mind to what really mattered to him, which was how things were going with the ratings at WNN. He was not happy with Roy Chelter, who had been national anchor during the network's worst drop in ratings. A boyish face on a man of forty-three could be a liability, and his camera presence was not solid enough to counterbalance his artless expression. Research marketing reported that focus groups of viewers tended to feel that Chelter didn't sound as if he knew what he was talking about, and, even worse, sounded pompous about what he did know.

"He looks like my teenage son. He sounds like my teenage son," wrote one father, leaving little doubt as to his feelings about his teenage son. The complaints were mounting.

"I don't feel comfortable listening to him. He's nice, but he doesn't act as if he's been around."

"He looks like he spends more time getting all that blond hair cut than doing his homework about what's going on in the world."

"It was bad enough to have a movie star as a President. I don't want to have to listen to somebody else who doesn't know what he's talking about. Somebody else is probably telling him what to say, or that's the way he sounds. I don't want to watch that. And I won't."

The last phrase was the devastating part. How many viewers were switching to another network? It didn't seem to be a landslide yet, but it certainly was a steady flow, according to surveys.

One of the things Mellenkoff wanted to discuss with Sullivan in Washington and other station managers was whether any notable talent was stirring in the pool of possible candidates for coveted network jobs. He knew Martha's name would come up for the anchor job, and he had thought about it. She was good, exceptionally so. But she was also professionally tough. She was the only correspondent he knew who would be prepared to challenge him without worrying about it. That was the price he had paid for their relationship, the price they had both paid, for that matter. Moreover, she would be trouble. He smiled a little grimly to himself as he recalled that she had always been a little trouble and that was one of the things that had drawn him to her. She had always been her own woman, even when she was willing to be his woman. That made her different from anyone else he had known. But he could not afford, would not tolerate, that kind of trouble in a position he wanted to operate by remote control. And he had never been certain of how far he could control Martha. Moreover, there was Eliass, who was complaining about her coverage of the White House.

"She is so tough, so irreverent. The questions she asks the President—no wonder we get complaints. I mean, I believe in standing behind a correspondent, and I know you think highly of her, James, but are you sure this is the right spot for Vogel? I mean, sometimes she doesn't look as if she's even combed her hair."

Mellenkoff was silent.

Eliass cocked his rosy head. "You disagree, James?"

"She is very good," said Mellenkoff.

"Ah? Then you are grooming her for the anchor job?"

"Not necessarily," Mellenkoff said a little too quickly.

Eliass's mouth curled in a smile that was almost a sneer.

"If she is very good, as you say, then what are your reservations about her?"

Mellenkoff raised his head and thought that Eliass's eyes looked like puddles of melting ice.

"There are—problems," he said.

Eliass nodded. "Then you agree with me, James. After all. We usually agree. Do we not?"

"Usually," Mellenkoff acknowledged, and wondered with momentary chill how much the chairman played games with him, and whether he could ever accurately gauge Eliass's thoughts. He also was aware of Eliass's doubts about Mellenkoff's concept of establishing the first female solo national news anchor. Eliass only gambled when he believed he would win. He assumed Mellenkoff was similarly cautious, and in most situations, Mellenkoff was. Even had Mellenkoff been inclined to propose Martha for an already controversial post, however, Eliass's remarks would have warned him of opposition forthcoming at the board level. He wondered about an overseas bureau for her, but that would mean he would not see her, and that would be inconvenient. He needed Martha, but he had to solve the problem of what to do with her professionally. He also had to be prepared to deal with her bewildered resentment at being passsed over for a job she believed, with justification, that she was qualified to do well.

Maybe he could be truthful and tell her what Eliass had said. But that bore the risk of Martha getting mad enough to tackle the chairman the first time she saw him, and Eliass would then blame Mellenkoff. Heaving a sigh, Mellenkoff went back to his drink. He had nowhere to go anyway. He assmed Sally would show up in time to catch the flight back to New York. Meantime, he had been placed in a bizarre position where he could hardly call friends and suggest getting together when he was supposed to be snuggling with Sally at the beach on their honeymoon. Mellenkoff had his pride. It was pride flexible enough to allow him to marry a woman in whom he had no particular interest, because her uncle was his employer, but it would not permit him to risk gossip that he had been abandoned on his honeymoon. Especially as that would eventually get back to Eliass. He didn't know what Sally was up to, and didn't especially care. But he had not expected her simply to disappear as soon as they arrived in California. Idly, he speculated on what she might be doing. He might have been almost as shocked as Joel Eliass, had he been transported to the home of Karen Ward in Emerald Beach, where she and Sally had been spending most of the afternoon in a passionate farewell.

"I can't bear it," said Sally.

"I'll be in New York next month, darling," Karen consoled her.

"But that's two weeks away!"

"So do some shopping. See some shows. Do something useful. Why don't you take a decent course in photography, for that matter?"

Karen sat up, pushing the tangle of her usually smooth dark hair out of her eyes, and pulled the sheet over her breasts against the chilly wind from the ocean.

"That's a very good idea," Karen said briskly.

"What is?" asked Sally sleepily.

"You can't just do nothing but wait for me."

"Why not?"

"Don't be silly. You've got some talent for photography and you ought to develop it. Those people from the *Los Angeles Times* who were over for dinner were quite complimentary about some of your pictures, and that's without training. Anyway, it'd be a useful thing to do. You never know, you might have to contribute to your own support someday, my love."

Sally snuggled against her. "Are you trying to get rid of me?"

"Hardly. But you're going to get awfully bored hanging around the New York social scene, or any social scene, for that matter. You're too bright for that."

Sally yawned. "I'll think about it."

Karen shook her lightly. "You'll do it. I want to hear you've enrolled in some decent courses by the time I get to New York. Okay?"

"Okay."

Karen smiled at the golden face on the pillow. "If you don't, I'll . . ." She put her lips to Sally's ear and whispered.

"Mmmmm," said Sally.

31

MEG HENRY wasn't sure when she first realized that something different was going on with Josh. He'd stayed out all night before, although not often, and usually he'd gone to the trouble of a respectable excuse. But after twenty-six years, she could detect variations on Josh's theme. She assumed he was having a fling with Caroline Mitchell, whom she had seen on "People Are Asking," although she had not met her. Josh had reminded her of her specific request that she not have to cope with his latest co-anchor.

Watching Caroline on the tube, Meg had premonitions of a different kind of disaster. The young woman was beautiful; that she could live with. Josh had succumbed to beauty before, and surfaced after a few days when he discovered that the lady's looks did not mean the lady could talk. Clearly there was something more to Caroline. Meg paid attention to the show, studying Caroline's manner toward Josh, which was an interesting blend of deference and challenge. Meg put two and two together and wondered whether, in this case, it added up to trouble. It seemed unlikely, on the face of it. Her relationship with Josh had not changed. They were as compatible and comfortable as ever, when he was home. When he was home. Meg telephoned her current extramarital interest and suggested a prolonged lunch. She didn't enjoy it as much as usual. Any of it.

Lying in his arms, she found she was breaking her own rule and thinking about Josh. It always seemed to her peculiarly immoral to think about her husband while making love with someone else. She recalled that in one of his rare confessional moments, Josh had told her he shared that self-imposed restriction. Yet, as was her habit,

Meg did not tell Josh she was troubled, and had she done so, he could not have allayed her fears.

Josh himself was breaking the rules with which he had lived happily for more than two decades, and didn't know what to do about it, or why it had happened. For the first time that he could recall, Josh was obsessed by a woman. He loved Meg, but he had never been obsessed by her. She did not invite that kind of reaction. Meg was a woman for all seasons, whereas Caroline might have blown in on a mistral. He could not analyze his fascination with Caroline. The remoteness he had sensed when he met her turned out to linger in bed, where she was affectionately acquiescent rather than passionate. Sometimes that was when her eyes seemed to look beyond him, instead of at him, and Josh found that disconcerting. Caroline rarely closed her eyes when making love, which he wouldn't have minded if he had been able to read adoration in them, but most of the time, he couldn't read anything in them. They were blank; beautiful, but blank. Yet her passivity challenged Josh, a man who had always been in easy control of his checkered love life. In that low, warm voice, she assured him she loved him, and he supposed it wasn't her fault that she sounded as if she had been programmed.

The worst of it was that he could not get enough of her. Whereas he used to reach a point in such relationships when all he wanted to do was get home to Meg and be refreshed by her, with Caroline, he didn't want to go home at all.

He wanted to find out who lived inside that lovely shell. In his more sardonic moments, he wondered if she were a pod, recalling the science fiction movie about body snatchers from another planet. What was strange was that she was at her most communicative when they talked over lunch or dinner, and when she was on the show. Those were the times Caroline came to life. It was in bed that she died. Now I'm a necrophiliac, Josh thought with grisly humor. And he knew that Meg was hurting. That troubled him deeply, but not enough to make him end his affair with Caroline. God knew it wasn't that Caroline made any demands on him. She was sweet and easygoing to the point that he wasn't sure she cared whether he was with her or not.

"Tell me what you're thinking," he urged her as they lay in bed.

She would smile. "Nothing, darling. I'm perfectly happy."

He couldn't exactly chide her for that, even if he knew she were lying. He had even gone so far as to check her file, to see if there was something there that would provide a clue to the Caroline he was sure lived inside the other Caroline. She seemed to have a background of surpassing normalcy, small-town, nothing unusual. He had heard, through diligent digging, that she had been involved with the KRT anchor in Columbus, Mike Hathaway, but that apparently had ended with her departure for Chicago. And apparently she wasn't and had never been involved with Mellenkoff. When he asked her how come Mellenkoff arranged her test, she had been quite open about it.

"Oh, that was Martha, Martha Vogel. She's sort of a friend of mine, and she's been just great. I had some new tapes out, and she asked Mellenkoff to look at them. They're—they're friends."

"Yeah, I know," said Josh. "They were a lot more than friends."

Caroline looked sad. "I had the feeling Martha was upset the time I talked to her. But anyway, that was how it happened. He apparently liked my tapes, and he was nice enough to say I could try out for PAA."

"You ever met Mellenkoff?"

She nodded. "Once, when he first became president of the network. Martha had been showing me around in Washington, and she set up an appointment for me with him in New York. He was—well, I was scared stiff, but he was nice. Very intense."

"He's a monument to his own ambition," observed Josh. "And God knows he's done just about everything he could have, at his age."

He looked at Caroline curiously. "Martha certainly went out of her way to help you, honey, didn't she?"

"God yes," said Caroline. "I really owe Martha. She's been terrific to me. And she's always so friendly and encouraging."

"She's got troubles of her own, too," said Josh.

"Oh?" Caroline frowned.

"Well, you know about that business with Mellenkoff dumping her for the chairman's niece. And I've heard rumors lately that they aren't happy with what she's doing on the White House. You'd think Mellenkoff would protect her, but you never know with him."

"That's terrible," said Caroline, and sounded genuinely distressed. "I wish I could do something to help her."

"Only person who can help Martha is Mellenkoff, at least in this network," said Josh. "And she'd be better off it he didn't."

He did not tell Caroline he had also heard reports that the newly married Mellenkoff already had been seen escorting Martha again. He hoped it wasn't true, because he liked Martha.

"It sounds so depressing. I'll never survive in this jungle," said Caroline disconsolately. Josh laughed and put his arm around her.

"I'd put money on you to survive just about anywhere," he told her affectionately. "You'll always find somebody to take care of you.

Caroline pulled away, to his surprise.

"I don't want people to take care of me," she said coolly. "I want people to help me, so I can do things by myself. The way you have, Josh. I mean, you've taught me a great deal since I've been on PAA."

He grinned, and reached for her again. "And I'd like to teach you a lot more. . . ."

But Caroline gently evaded his grasp and slid out of the bed where they were sitting. She went over to a small wall mirror and looked at herself critically.

"Mayer wants to see me in his office tomorrow. I guess it's about the contract."

"Haven't you signed it yet?"

She shook her head. "Martha said I should have an agent, and she recommended one. So he's been dealing with Mayer. I don't think Mayer was too pleased about it, but Martha said it was very important."

"She was right. What'd you do without Martha?"

Caroline's face was serious. "I don't know. I can't tell you how kind she's been."

"Hey, if you don't have to see Mayer until tomorrow, come back here."

Caroline faced him, a little tentative, but with a stubborn line to her mouth that Mike Hathaway would have recognized.

"Josh, darling, would you mind—I mean I'd sort of like to be by myself for a while. I've got some things to do around here. I don't seem to have had time to get even an apartment this small into shape, and I can't find anything!"

She smiled ravishingly, and Josh felt his resentment melt. He probably ought to go home anyway. He hadn't been home early one night that week, and two of those nights he hadn't been home at all. Meg, he noticed, had said nothing. But then, she was saying less.

He eased himself out of the bed and stretched lazily.

"Okay, I know when I'm not wanted."

"Come on, Josh."

"But I'll be back." He seized her in an exaggerated hug and felt her suddenly stiffen.

"Hey, I'm teasing." He tilted up her face, and this time he could read her eyes. They were full of fear.

"Caroline, what's the matter? Didn't you ever get a bear hug before? What is it, darling?" He petted her, stroked her hair, and slowly the rigidity left her body, and the terror ebbed from her eyes. She shook her head, and essayed a small smile.

"I'm sorry. Must have been some old . . . bad dream or something. Sorry to be so silly."

Suddenly she was her composed self again, but Josh was more intrigued than ever. There *was* another Caroline. He kissed her gently.

"Get some sleep. And don't be frightened of anything, all right?"

She nodded, and now her smile was easy. "Don't pay any attention. I've no idea what that was about."

The hell she didn't, thought Josh. But he kissed her again and left, waiting until he heard her double-lock the door behind him.

Alone in the apartment, Caroline wandered about it aimlessly. She had long ago put it into an orderly state, because she disliked living in disorder. But she was beginning to feel suffocated by Josh, and she was also worried about becoming a focus of JRZ gossip. She was very new and fragile in terms of security at the station, and she didn't want to take chances.

She had to take care of herself, because nobody else would. She would just as soon never sleep with anybody, but it was difficult when people like Mike and Josh put such a premium on it. Caroline sighed and comforted herself by looking around the living room of the apartment, which was a little too expensive, but she had loved its high ceilings and arched doorways. It was part of a mansion that had been divided up and redesigned into flats. It was also furnished, which made it more expensive, but that was what she wanted. She didn't feel secure enough to start buying furniture and curtains, and she didn't care about that kind of thing. She knew what she liked, which was a rather spartan elegance. When she could afford it, she would have a decorator do that for her. In these narrow, lofty-ceilinged rooms, with their shining parquet floors, subtly patterned rugs and sofas, and curtains of delphinium blue, there was a certain starkness, nothing unnecessary, and that was the way Caroline liked it. The bedroom had a four-poster mahogany bed, which she had doubts about at first but had come to enjoy. It made her feel protected. She loved the bathroom, with its huge sunken tub and marble fittings. And in the bedroom was her beloved vanity, lacquered a deep blue so that it no longer reminded her of the peach and ivory room with the crawling trellised wallpaper. Caroline in the mirror looked more comfortable in her new setting. She still talked to Caroline in the mirror, but she didn't need her quite as much as she used to. She had done what Caroline in the mirror told her to do and it seemed to be working. If she could just get this business with Josh tidied up. Curling up in a corner of her blue sofa, Caroline reflected that the only thing about sleeping with men that gave her pleasure was the thought of how it would have tortured her father. She jumped when the telephone rang, and hoped it wasn't Josh.

"Caroline?" said an unfamiliar voice. "This is Tom Roberts."

She gasped in surprise. "Where are you? Is Jill with you?"

"I'm here in Chicago. Jill's in Washington."

"What're you doing here?"

He laughed. "You'll never guess. I wound up taking that advice you gave me about getting into television. I got a job at JRZ, as a reporter. Start next week."

"That's wonderful! Will Jill move here too?"

There was a pause.

"No. At least not now. She's really enthusiastic about the PBS job and she seems to be doing well. They certainly keep her busy enough. Even when I visit, I hardly see her. But she's happy, and that's what counts. I guess."

Caroline's eyebrows had risen slightly.

"Well," she said diplomatically, "she'll probably be coming to Chicago on weekends."

"I suppose so," said Tom sulkily. "I sometimes wonder if she doesn't care about that job more than our marriage. But I shouldn't be grumbling to you, should I?"

"Well, I'm sure it's difficult." She was carefully noncommittal. "Have you found a place to stay?"

"Not yet. I've got a hotel room and the station's paying until I can find something, by which I think they mean next week or something like that. I'm not too elevated in the JRZ scheme of things."

She wondered why he sounded so digruntled, then she remembered how upset Mike had been when she had chosen to think of herself, and shrugged. But on the telephone, her voice was sympathetic.

"This is a nice building where I live, but it's not too cheap. As a matter of fact, it's too expensive for me, but I couldn't resist it."

"Well, if it's expensive for you, it's probably out of the question for me. And I don't know the city at all."

Caroline suppressed a sigh.

"I could help you look for a place, if you like."

"Well, that'd be great. Jill's coming up this weekend and I know she'll want to see you, so maybe we could look around together. Have dinner or something."

"I'd love that," said Caroline, realizing with joy that it would give her a genuine excuse for not seeing Josh Henry.

Tom was suddenly full of enthusiasm. "I hear great things about you on PAA."

"Thank you," said Caroline sincerely. "You don't know how good that makes me feel. I'm still very nervous."

"I saw the show. I thought you were great."

"For that I'll buy you a drink." She hesitated. "Listen, why don't you come by here tomorrow and see if there's anything you might be able to afford. And we could get a bite or something, maybe. I'm dying to see you and Jill. And I'm so glad you like the show. You never know if people like you."

He laughed. "Caroline," he said, "how could anyone not like you?"

32

MARTHA WOKE up with a hangover and with Mellenkoff and was uncertain which was the bigger mistake. He was still asleep, sprawled across three-quarters of the bed, when Martha, clutching her head, padded to the bathroom and grimaced as she looked in the mirror and fumbled in the medicine cabinet for aspirin. She wondered whether a shower would drown her or make her feel minimally better, and decided it didn't matter much either way. Standing beneath the spray of warm water, she reached the conclusion that the events of the previous evening were evidence of a death wish on her part. Certainly the amount of brandy she had drunk was. All she had to be grateful for was that it was Sunday and she didn't have to look at the smug countenance of the White House press secretary delivering his daily dose of assorted platitudes. She could blame no one but herself for the sorry state she was in, physically and psychologically. When she accepted, however reluctantly, Mellenkoff's invitation to dinner, she had known what would happen. She also knew that he knew she knew. The convolution of that thought sent pain needling through her head, and with a small moan, she turned the faucet to cold in the hope of numbing her misery.

The quiet dinner between two old friends, as Mellenkoff had billed it, had promptly deteriorated into bitter recriminations, the illogic of which was cemented by martinis. Mellenkoff had accepted her anger and taken his punishment quietly as she told him several times, in increasing detail, what he had made her suffer. He had looked positively woebegone. She had become afflicted by her usual remorse at being unkind and subsided into picking at an expensive dinner and drinking some unnecessary wine. By the time the coffee arrived, she was remembering all that she had loved about him and he was telling her he had always loved her, would always love her, and she didn't realize how miserable he had made himself. After that they went back to her apartment and drank brandy happily before they went to bed.

Martha stepped blindly out of the shower and groped for a towel. She probably was going to live, although she felt no enthusiasm about the prospect. Wrapped in her own oversized white terry cloth robe, she moved with careful steps toward the kitchen and coffee. She moved carefully because she didn't want her head to fall off and wake Mellenkoff, who was still asleep. When she dropped the lid of the coffeepot, the sound was shattering. She heard a groan from the bedroom, followed a few minutes later by a muffled grumble.

"Where's my robe?"

"In the hall closet."

Mellenkoff marched out of the bedroom wearing nothing but an offended expression, rummaged in the closet, and returned wearing the blue velour robe.

"Just got back before you threw it out the door?" he inquired.

"Barely."

His arms slipped around her. "But I made it."

She kissed him back.

"Let's go back to bed," he said in her ear.

"Only if you promise to let me die quietly there."

"Afterward."

But afterward, she asked him about the rumors that Roy Chelter was going to be out as national anchorman.

"I don't know what's going to happen there," said Mellenkoff, looking around for the cigarettes he rarely smoked.

"If you don't, who does? If you're smoking, you're nervous. Just tell me, for God's sake. I'm a big girl," said Martha, pulling the comforter around her bare shoulders.

"Chelter is in trouble. We know he's negotiating with ABC and we aren't doing a thing to stop him. But if you're raising this for the reason I think you are, you're not going to get the anchor slot."

Mellenkoff inhaled, and the eyes he turned on Martha were a frozen blue.

She nodded, her expression bleak. "That doesn't surprise me too much. What about the White House?"

"What about it?" He kept the surprise out of his voice. To his knowledge, no one had mentioned trouble with White House coverage except Eliass.

"Sullivan seems edgy about the way I'm handling it. Maybe I'm not the best person for that spot. I can't be reverent about a clown like the President."

Mellenkoff breathed an imperceptible sigh of relief. Maybe it wasn't just Eliass and his knee-jerk deference to power. He always underestimated Martha's capacity for cool self-appraisal.

"You're not happy with it yourself?"

Martha stirred restlessly under the comforter.

"I know it's a good assignment, James, and I get a lot of air time. I think I handle it okay. I know what I'm doing and I'm good at it. But Sullivan seems to think I'm too abrasive, and the White House gets back at WNN by giving us last crack at interviews and damned few leaks."

Her voice was tired. Mellenkoff stared at a Van Gogh print on the wall.

"What'd you like to do?"

"I'm not sure. Maybe go abroad? That might be a good idea, James. For both of us."

"That's a possibility."

Eliass was going to be pleased, he thought. Ask Mellenkoff and it shall be done. He wondered if it were only the hangover that was producing a sour taste in his mouth.

"Maybe London? Or Moscow? I've always been curious about Russia, and that would be interesting." Martha's voice became more lively.

He felt her gaze on him, and nodded. "I'll have to check and see what's going to turn over in the foreign bureaus. Then we'll talk about it, all right?"

"Fine." She rolled over suddenly. "You're sure about the anchor slot? I mean, couldn't I try out?"

"I—no, I don't think so, Martha. That wouldn't be entirely up to me, you know."

"Roger Miller would back it."

"Joel Eliass wouldn't."

"Ah. So that's it. Uncle Joel doesn't like me."

He was silent.

"Okay. Let's drop it."

Nothing would have made him happier, but he knew he wouldn't, because she wouldn't.

"When are you going to Chicago?" she asked.

"Tomorrow. Mayer has a couple of problems, and I want to look at some of Jay Erickson's tapes."

"He's another pretty boy, if you're thinking of him for the anchor spot."

"He's got more style than Chelter."

Martha reached for her robe. "I'll fix something to eat."

"Good. I'm starving." He stubbed out the cigarette and felt the knot in his stomach unwind a little. He wished he could do something to make Martha happy. Maybe a foreign assignment might be the answer, if that could be worked out. Except there wasn't anything coming up for a while that he could think of. They had just finished a global reconfiguration of their foreign correspondents. He sighed and got out of bed. Bundled in the blue velour robe, he wandered into the kitchen where Martha was taking eggs from the refrigerator.

"How's my little protégée, Mitchell, doing on PAA?" she asked, critically examining an orange she was about to juice.

"Mayer's very high on her. Of course he gives me all the credit."

"And of course you take it." She grinned at him.

"As a matter of fact, she's evidently turned out a lot better than anybody expected. Josh Henry's crazy about her, I hear, and he's had trouble with just about all his co-anchors."

"I've heard about Josh's trouble with women. I hope Caroline can cope."

"Just so long as they don't screw on camera."

Martha laughed. "You wouldn't care, if the ratings went up."

"True, my dear, true."

They ate, read the papers, watched a political talk show, and slept some more. It was peaceful, yet Martha had a strong sense of something missing. They were not as comfortable together as they once had been. They probably never would be again. And her flickering hope of the national anchor job was gone now. She had also

noticed Mellenkoff's concealed relief at her comments on
her White House assignment. He knew she only wanted
a foreign assignment to get away from him. She was
aware that if she stayed in Washington, or, even worse,
was moved to New York, she would remain tied to him
forever. She knew she should end it; should have ended
it. She certainly shouldn't be spending Sunday in bed
with him.

It would be different if it made her happy, as Roger
Miller had observed recently, but it didn't anymore. It
crumbled her self-esteem and left her with the feeling
that she had abandoned herself. Roger had been urging
her to consider seriously a CBS offer of a weekend anchor slot, plus roving assignment. She had far more chance
over there of receiving an objective assessment of what
she could do, he told her. Martha knew he was right.
That was one reason she had mentioned the White House
situation to Mellenkoff. She had exaggerated it a little,
and his reaction confirmed the warning signals sent out
by Bob Sullivan's uneasy complaint that she seemed left
out of presidential guidance sessions and her interviews
were granted only after other network correspondents
had been taken care of.

"It's not as if you were dealing with a Nixon," Sullivan
had said. "This President is more stupid than sinister.
Sometimes you indulge in overkill about what's beneath
all this, Martha."

It seemed a good bet that the President would lose his
reelection bid, or might not even run. He was a man who
hated to be unpopular, and his income tax hikes had
made him an anathema to what the polls showed as a
large proportion of the voting public. He would be out,
and so would Martha, and probably not too far off. That
would be a natural break, and a good time for a change.
And that would be a good time to tell CBS she would
accept their offer, as Roger wanted her to do. Why the
hell couldn't she be in love with Roger? She moved
restlessly and felt Mellenkoff's arm curl around her.

"Stop brooding," he murmured. "It'll be all right.
You'll see."

Mellenkoff flew to Chicago the next morning and had
lunch with John Mayer and market research director

Robert Cohen. He took a look at Erickson's tapes and
shook his head over them. Erickson had all the flaws of
Roy Chelter and less of his professionalism.

"No?" asked Mayer.

Mellenkoff shrugged. He wasn't about to tell any secrets to the station manager.

"I'm not sure. Doubtful. But nothing's settled yet."

"I'm not surprised," said Mayer.

"How's he doing here?"

"Mixed. Still hanging in there, though."

"And very, very sure of himself."

"God, yes."

Changing the subject, Mayer observed, "That was a
good call of yours on Mitchell, James."

Mellenkoff hid a grin. "Glad to hear it. I just thought
it might be an interesting long shot. You never know how
these things'll work out."

"Well, she has. Once she gets Josh Henry out of her
system, not to mention her pants. I think she's got a
future. Audience reaction's been fantastic. You ought to
take a look at some of the PAA tapes, since you saw the
previous ones," suggested Cohen.

After they ran a tape of the show, Mellenkoff nodded.

"I see what you mean. She's very interesting. Comes
across well."

"Remarkable control," said Cohen. "Our last survey
showed most people are impressed by how much she
seems to know about a lot of things."

"Does she?"

"She really tries to do homework. I see her reading
piles of newspapers, magazines. At times with an addled
expression, but she's in there trying all right."

"What's this about her and Henry?" Mellenkoff asked.

"You know Josh. He can't let anything female pass by
without making a pass at it. Only thing that makes this
different is I think he's fallen for her. Not the other way
around," said Mayer with some amusement.

"So?"

"Well, Mitchell's getting a little jumpy. I think she's
more interested in the job than in Josh and she's trying to
get out and doesn't know how. Especially since she's his
co-anchor."

"Have a word with her about bad publicity. Married

man and all that. Have a word with him, if necessary. I don't want the ratings rocked for this kind of crap, when the show's going the way it is," said Mellenkoff coldly.

"I'll do that," said Mayer.

Mellenkoff was on his way to the elevator when he met Caroline Mitchell on her way into Mayer's office. When she saw him, her face was instantly illuminated by the famous smile.

"Mr. Mellenkoff, I'm glad I ran into you. I wanted to thank you for your help with the test. Giving me the opportunity to try out, I mean."

She assumed he would remember her, and that pleased him. It was the kind of assumption he would have made.

"It's nice to see you again, Caroline, and I'm delighted the test worked out well. I hear good things about your work."

"I'm glad. I'm working hard—as you told me to."

He appraised the simple, well-cut pale wool dress, the delicately patterned gold silk scarf at her throat, the cameo face in its frame of skillfully cut dark hair. The sophistication process was rapid with Caroline Mitchell. He didn't blame Josh Henry for his infatuation with her, although she was not Mellenkoff's type. He considered women like Caroline marketable commodities. She was ambitious and predictable. She would never be a maverick like Martha. Watching her tapes and talking with her, it crossed Mellenkoff's mind that it might be possible to mold Caroline into something special. He believed the raw material was there, was certainly malleable, and needed only the skill of the right sculptor. Like him. An idea was taking shape in his mind. He bestowed one of his warmer smiles on Caroline.

"Keep at it. Perhaps we'll have you up to New York for a chat one of these days."

"I'd be delighted," she said.

Going down in the elevator, he had no doubt she would be delighted. He also had no doubt that he would have her come to New York.

Caroline could hardly wait to tell Tom Roberts what Mellenkoff had said to her. She had spent much of the weekend with Jill and Tom, who had found a tiny studio apartment not far from Caroline's building. She had enjoyed being with them, but she had sensed strain between them.

Tom Roberts seemed to be trying to persuade himself as well as others that it made sense for him to be in Chicago while Jill was in Washington. From one or two bitter-tinged remarks, Caroline had the impression that he felt Jill might have at least offered to consider relocating to Chicago. They had not been married that long, after all, yet Jill had made clear that it was out of the question for her to consider leaving her cherished job in Washington, no matter where Tom was. That apparently rankled with Tom, which Caroline thought was understandable. She was surprised at Jill's attitude; she would not have expected her childhood friend to be so self-centered. Jill seemed to feel that Tom should eventually get himself moved to Washington. Her reaction to his job at JRZ in Chicago reminded Caroline faintly of the attitude of Leslie Hathaway toward Mike. It was as though Jill was doing what she considered real work and Tom was in show business. She had even used that phrase, jokingly, but in a manner that had caused Tom's face to harden. It seemed to Caroline that Jill had changed a little. She was less easygoing and muddled, and more intense and earnest. Her sense of humor seemed to have diminished as her awareness of world tensions had increased. And she had made clear that she expected Tom to come to Washington on weekends. That way, she said, he could meet some interesting people. Some of her friends at PBS might come over. What, asked Jill, could he possibly do on weekends in Chicago, anyway?

33

IT WAS shock as much as anything else. Josh Henry could not, offhand, recall a woman telling him she wanted to put an end to their affair before he did. He had always tried to be gentle about concluding relationships. He didn't just stop calling, or disappear entirely. He took whoever it was out for a last lovely dinner, and toward the end of the meal, he explained in carefully chosen words that it was over. He did it toward the end of the meal, because making such an announcement over cocktails left time for tears, temper, and even tantrums. He usually tried to get most of it over between dessert and coffee, so he could call for the check without being abrupt about things. As far as Caroline Mitchell was concerned, Josh couldn't say he was content with their relationship, but he hadn't reached the stage where he wanted it to end. When it did, he assumed he would be the one to end it. But it was Caroline, elusive and unpredictable as she had been throughout their affair, who chose a dinner at the beginning of what he had hoped would be a lovely weekend, to intimate that she was closing the books on him. It was especially stunning in view of the fact that it followed a suggestion by Meg—the first she had made in many years—that he might be happier living elsewhere for a while. He had not, as he always had before, instantly rejected the idea.

Josh knew that when his wife went that far, she was serious. Anytime it had happened before, he had invariably assured her that if faced with a choice between her and any other woman alive, he would invariably choose her. He had astounded himself by finding it unusually difficult to give that assurance this time around.

What was particularly infuriating about the situation

with Caroline was that she had never made any overtures, never made any demands, and had always been the
one to plead fatigue with work or early-morning plans as
a means of cutting short their time together. She had
remained as remote as ever. He had been angry at himself for always being the one who was reluctant to leave,
and next morning, calling her to arrange another meeting. He felt as though he were pursuing a mirage.

Meg remained noncommittal and pleasant when he
was at home, until the morning he found her packing a
suitcase to spend a few days at their country place in
Wisconsin, as she said. In between folding clothes, she
almost casually suggested he think about moving out.

"Until you feel more settled in your mind, at least,"
she said, calmly choosing between one blouse and another.

He had tried to tell her nothing had changed, and that
was when she leveled that penetrating gray gaze on him
and smiled a little sadly.

"We've never fooled each other, Josh," she said. "Don't
let's start now." She returned to her packing. "We can
talk when I get back, if you're still here."

"Of course I'll still be here—"

"Then we'll talk." Her tone was dismissive. He noticed
she was packing silk dresses and pants, although she
rarely wore anything but jeans and sweaters in the country. She offered no explanation, and there was no reply
when he tried to call her later. It did not occur to Josh
that she might be with anyone else.

What he ought to do, he knew, was spend the weekend
quietly thinking about what Meg had said. He knew that,
even as he picked up the telephone to call Caroline and
announce they could spend the whole weekend together.
She said that was a lovely idea but she couldn't, because
she had plans for Sunday. She couldn't change them? he
asked, crestfallen. She said no, she couldn't. What about
Saturday? There was the faintest hesitation before she
said she was free Saturday evening.

Josh was unaware that Caroline had just been offered
what was described as fatherly advice by John Mayer, the
station manager, who had not failed to mention that he
had the blessing of Mellenkoff for what he was about to
tell her. What he told her was that she was at a critical
point in her career, and the kind of thing that had hap-

pened on the show the previous day could not and would not be repeated. As Caroline sat frozen with fright, Mayer assured her that she had behaved well under trying circumstances, but obviously those circumstances had arisen from her—ah—friendship with Josh Henry.

Both Mayer and Gil Tadich had noticed for some weeks that Josh was performing less smoothly as host, displaying impatience with silly questions with which he had previously been patient, and looking occasionally haggard on camera. Ironically, Caroline's self-confidence on the air had increased, partly because she was determined that Josh's attention would not distract her from her objective of establishing her credentials as a professional and, she hoped, attracting the favorable attention of Mellenkoff.

The incident that had disturbed Mayer had occurred when a member of the studio audience made some suggestive remarks to Caroline. She had remained unperturbed, deflecting the comments with a smile and a shake of her head, but Josh had reacted with a sharpness that bordered on violence, turning a flash of bad taste into an altercation on the air. Finally Tadich had cut off the exchange, but not before Mayer decided things had gone too far. He was surprised at Josh, who should have known better. But he also was aware that if it came to a choice between Caroline Mitchell and Josh Henry, there was no doubt as to whom JRZ would choose. Caroline was still at the expendable stage. He did not put it quite that bluntly when he talked to Caroline, but she was left with no doubt that she had no choice about terminating her relationship with Josh.

"I understand these things are difficult, and I dislike becoming involved in people's personal lives," said Mayer. "But this is a business, and whatever is going on off camera can never be permitted to intrude on camera."

"I know. I understand that and I apologize for having contributed to any problem," said Caroline quietly.

"I might say," Mayer added, "that you handled that well the other day. The problem is not with you but with the—er—situation in which you appear to find yourself."

Tadich had told Mayer that as far as he could tell, Mitchell had been trying to cool the thing for months, and it was Henry who had stayed hot.

"I'll provide her with some ice water to douse him," Mayer had said tersely.

Mayer also told Josh Henry he wanted to talk with him at the beginning of the week, accurately guessing that Caroline would lose no time. He was right. At dinner that Saturday, the entrée had not even been reached before Caroline raised the topic of breaking up. Josh was incredulous. Her words had a bitterly familiar ring.

"I'm very fond of you, Josh," she said, gazing at him with troubled dark eyes. "But I think we shouldn't see each other for a while, outside work that is. I think we both need to sort things out. I mean, I know you must be concerned about Meg, and after all, we—you do have the show to think of, too."

"I've got you to think of." Josh heard himself say it, and was furious with himself.

"Well, that's sort of what I mean. We can't be thinking of each other when we really should be thinking about the show," said Caroline.

"You're talking about that silly business the other day. I'd have put that guy in his place no matter whom he'd insulted on my show," Josh protested.

"I know that," said Caroline soothingly. "But—"

"But what!"

"Josh." She glanced uneasily around as his voice rose, and again he felt as though he were living through a rerun of a past scene.

"I suppose you'd have handled it better yourself. We have come quite a way, haven't we, Caroline?"

"That isn't it. Please. Don't make this more difficult for me than it is. I mean, how do you think I feel? I don't—don't want to stop seeing you."

Her voice was so earnest he would have believed her, had he not used the same tone himself on several occasions in similar circumstances. He drank his bourbon in one gulp. He couldn't believe this was happening to him. The only woman for whom he had ever considered leaving his wife was telling him it was all over. He waved at the waiter and ordered another drink. Caroline looked nervous.

"Shouldn't we order?"

"You go ahead. I'm not hungry." That was another line he had heard while sitting in Caroline's place.

"Josh, this is proving what I'm saying. We're both too involved."

But she was the one who wanted to get uninvolved. Suddenly he missed Meg. His drink arrived, and the waiter looked questioningly at the menus lying beside their plates.

"I don't think I'm very hungry, either," said Caroline.

"Then drink up and let's get out of here. It's hardly an occasion for celebration, is it?"

The waiter reacted with professional impassivity to Josh's abrupt request for a bill before dinner. Doubtless he was regaling the kitchen with the details of Josh Henry's downfall. It had been a mistake to bring Caroline to a restaurant where he was so well known, and where, in fact, he had delivered a coup de grace to earlier affairs.

They drove back to Caroline's apartment in silence. At the front door, Caroline was conscious of relief at the presence of the doorman.

"I assume you don't want me to come up," said Josh.

"I think we're both too upset," said Caroline tactfully. "I'll talk to you over the weekend. If you want to."

She reached over and gave him a feathery kiss on the cheek and he pulled away as if stung. Caroline sighed and let herself out of the car.

She walked swiftly to the elevator and even more swiftly down the corridor to her apartment door. Inside, she kicked off her high-heeled shoes and collapsed on the sofa, burrowing her head into the pillows. It had been as bad as she had thought it would be, and she could only guess at what his demeanor would be on the show. Except that Mayer had some control over that. But Josh could make things difficult for her. And she didn't have the kind of clout he did at the station. Oh God, Caroline thought, why did I ever go to bed with him in the first place? If I hadn't done that . . . On the other hand, if she hadn't, he might have been difficult over that too, and she wasn't sure a sexual harassment suit would have enhanced her budding career either. She groaned into the pillow. Now she was hungry. She'd skipped lunch because she was worried about dinner, and then she hadn't eaten any dinner. All she'd had were about two sips of wine. She wondered if there was anything to eat in her refrigerator, and doubted it.

Caroline sat up, smoothed her skirt, and picked up the phone.

"Tom?" she said after a moment. "Are you busy?"

Tom Roberts, who had been gloomily watching a bad movie on television and wondering what Jill was doing in Washington at that moment, said he wasn't busy at all.

"I'm starving," said Caroline. "Want to get a hamburger?"

She changed into pants and a shirt, pulled on her raincoat, and met him at the corner.

"How come you're not busy?" he asked with a grin.

"I was, but I'm not now. And I need a drink," she said, surprisingly.

"Problems?" he asked, as they slid into a booth in a small bar that served excellent hamburgers.

"Trying to solve them."

"All over?"

"I hope so." She shook her head. "He'll probably crucify me on the show."

"Probably won't. He's got a big ego but he's not mean. You can't fault him for falling for you, Caroline."

She sighed. "What are you going to drink? I've never had a martini.

He laughed. "We can remedy that. But only one, if you've never had one."

Caroline sipped tentatively and gave a small shudder. "Got a real bite, doesn't it?"

"Like a crocodile."

She put her glass down after two experimental swallows.

"What'd you hear from Jill?"

"Not much. She called Tuesday, I think it was. All involved in some big congressional story she's working on. Said she'd be tied up all weekend, so there wasn't much point in my coming down. Not that I'd planned on it. Those trips get expensive."

"Any chance of JRZ moving you to Washington?"

His face grew stubborn. "Why the hell do I have to move? I mean, she could have got a job here, too. I seem to make all the concessions. I'm for equal rights and partnership and all that, but it works both ways. Talk about a double standard—'.

"Hey," said Caroline. "I'm sorry. I didn't mean to—"

"I know." Tom took a bite of his hamburger. "It just

gets to me sometimes that it doesn't seem to bother her.
I mean sometimes I wonder why we . . . oh well. I don't
mean to jump all over you after the kind of day you've
had." He grinned at her. "Listen, it's great to at least
have somebody to talk to. Drink up."

Caroline took another small swallow of her martini,
decided she didn't like it much, and wondered what Josh
Henry was doing.

She would have been vastly relieved had she known
that he had already concluded she was right.

Driving home, Josh realized that as his resentment
ebbed, he was experiencing rising relief. Caroline really
hadn't handled it badly at all, now he thought about it.
She had done what he probably really wanted to, but
couldn't because he'd been hung up on her. He felt
pretty good. So good he decided to stop and have a drink
and call Meg in Wisconsin.

The bar was quiet, the bartender friendly and complimentary about the show, and the drinks were healthy in
size, but Josh's repeated calls to Wisconsin were fruitless.
Where the hell was she, he wondered. Meg rarely went
out at night when she stayed there alone. She liked to
read in front of the fire, and if she had company, she
usually invited them to stay over. It was almost midnight
by the time she answered the telephone, and Josh had
lost count of the bourbons he consumed. He only knew
he felt happier than he had in a long time. He felt
downright fond of Caroline, but he didn't give a damn if
he never saw her again. What he'd like to do was drive to
Wisconsin to Meg. Her voice was cool and composed, as
usual.

"Meg? I'm going home. I mean, I'm really going home,
and I wish to Christ you were there. Why'n't you take a
taxi back tonight or better yet, why'n't I take a taxi to
Wisconsin. Hey, that has a nice ring to it—taxi to
Wisconsin."

Meg laughed. "What're you celebrating? You're obviously in a bar."

"Us. You. You'n me. Meg, I don't know why you put
up—"

"Josh," her voice was clipped. "I don't want to discuss
it now. Why don't you take a taxi home?"

"When're you comin' home?"

"In a few days."

"But I'm home now. I'm back, Meg. For good."

"Yes, Josh. That's fine. We'll talk tomorrow, all right?"

"Meg"—his voice was urgent—"come home tomorrow. Please?"

Meg hesitated.

"Maybe. I'll talk to you in the morning. Now get a taxi, will you? Don't drive."

"Hell," said Josh, "I can drive. I'm in great shape. You wanna ask my friend here if I'm in great shape—"

"Get a taxi," said Meg, and hung up.

Josh was unperturbed. He was going home. Meg was coming home. Everything was going to be fine again. He left a pile of bills on the bar and departed unsteadily into the night, heading for his car. The bartender, finding the money and whistling at the size of the tip, looked worriedly after him, but Josh was gone. And he was very careful as he drove toward the suburb where he lived. He had always said he was more careful when he had been drinking because he was aware of all those problems with reflexes slowing down and blurred vision and all that stuff. He thought about it as he drove, peering at the traffic lights and thinking how well everything had turned out. His foot grew heavier on the accelerator the more he thought about how well everything had turned out, and he sang happily to himself. He was still singing when he drove through a red light and head on into a truck whose driver yelled helpless curses as the dark green Mercedes slammed into him. The truck driver was unhurt, but Josh Henry was flung headfirst through the windshield. He was dead before the police arrived.

34

SOME SAID it showed what Caroline Mitchell could do on her own. Others said it was the least she could do after what she had done to poor Josh. But there was general agreement that the Josh Henry memorial show on "People Are Asking" was a huge success.

"Sensitive and beautifully handled," wrote one television critic.

"Caroline Mitchell showed grace and dignity in a trying situation. Getting people to talk about death and dying without becoming emotional is not easy, and Mitchell accomplished it with understanding and taste," wrote another.

"A tour de force for Mitchell, a newcomer whose work belies her youth and the length of her experience," raved a third.

"Josh would have laughed," said Meg Henry, but nobody quoted her.

Gil Tadich, the show's producer, who had always been cynical about Caroline, suggested Josh had done more for her by dying than he had ever done while he was alive. The memorial show was Caroline's idea, although it had grown from a suggestion by Tom Roberts that she try to talk the station into letting her do the show on her own.

"You need a gimmick to persuade them," Tom had said. Caroline thought about it a lot the weekend Josh died, and when she walked into the office of station manager John Mayer on Monday morning, she knew she had her gimmick.

She had surprised both Mayer and Tadich by arguing that there should be no cancellation of the show that day, as was their inclination.

"Do the show, and let people talk about death. I think a lot of people would like to do that, just talk about it, get their feelings into the open. People who've had friends and relatives die, people who're sick, people who're worried about dying, people who want to talk about keeping patients alive with machines—the whole thing. I think Josh would have thought that was a good idea, too," she told the station executives.

Mayer and Tadich had exchanged glances.

"You're suggesting you host this kind of show on your own?" asked Tadich dubiously.

Caroline nodded. She was paler than usual and her eyes were a little shadowed, but that was because she had stayed up half the night thinking about what she could do for a gimmick that the station would go for and that might be a springboard for her. She wasn't sure she could do it, either, but she had enough confidence in her skill as an interviewer, as the kind of person people liked to confide in, to want to try it.

Mayer, while thoughtful, was less reluctant than Tadich to consider the concept of a memorial to Josh Henry.

"You really think you could deal with it by yourself, Caroline?" he asked. "I mean, people can get hysterical on that kind of subject. You'd have to have control over the show, and you wouldn't have . . . well . . ." He paused awkwardly.

"I wouldn't have Josh to help me." Caroline completed his sentence. "I've thought of that. But Josh did teach me a lot. I worked with him for six months, and that's why I think I can do this. I think it would be a good thing to do. And I think an awful lot of people would watch it."

Those were the magic words. They probably would, Mayer mused. Even if it were a disaster, viewership would be high, especially in light of Henry's death. And if it weren't a disaster, it could be a smash, and thereby a classic in terms of reruns. In any case, it might be well worth the relatively small risk involved, and it wasn't as if Mitchell were a prime property. She might be out on her ear in any case. This would either let her prove herself or let the station fire her if she didn't.

"Let's go for it," he said, and saw Tadich's head come up in surprise.

The Josh Henry memorial show was an unqualified success, and so was Caroline. Dramatic and beautiful in a severe black dress with a soft pink scarf at her throat, she was calm, dignified, understanding, and entirely in control. There was no doubt that the show had touched a vulnerable public nerve. The studio audience had taken an almost audible deep breath as they listened to Caroline tell them this was a very special show.

"We're doing this show in memory of a very special man, of my friend and your friend, Josh Henry," she told them in a low, warm voice that sounded just a note away from breaking, but wasn't.

"So today we want to talk about what all of us think about, at least sometimes, and certainly at some point in our lives, when someone we love is ill or dies. I want you to talk, to me, to each other. Ask the questions that trouble you. Tell us how you feel about that ultimate question. Talk about the one subject no one is entirely sure about, but which haunts us all. Our subject is death," said Caroline.

There was a moment's pause, all the more dramatic in that it was followed by a cascade of voices. They tumbled over each other to talk. She had unleashed a wave of emotional reaction, and Mayer and Tadich uttered a mutual groan as the audience sound rose to a low roar. Then Caroline held up both hands.

"I can't hear you," she said, raising her voice a little.

There was a puzzled hush.

"We can't hear each other," Caroline continued. "It's very important today that we listen to each other, that we speak slowly and clearly, because a lot of people are listening to us, and they want to hear what you all have to say. What you have to say today is very important to many, many people."

She pointed to an elderly man, and the camera caught tears glistening in his eyes.

"My wife . . . ," he said. He stopped, apparently struggling for control, and Caroline nodded.

"Take your time. Don't worry. We'll wait until you're ready," she said gently. And they waited. There was not a sound as the man sat for a moment or two, his face contorted.

"My wife died," he said finally, huskily. "She was in

such pain. I wanted to help her die. And I didn't. And now I feel guilty that I didn't. I begged them to let her die, but they kept her alive." He broke down again.

A young woman was on her feet. Caroline held up a hand to prevent her from speaking until she was sure the man was unable to continue. Then she nodded.

"I know how he feels. My father died that way. And I'm so afraid that I'll do that. I have nightmares about it. What if I'm in an accident, like Josh Henry, and suppose I don't die, and I'm a vegetable? I'd rather be dead. Why couldn't I be dead? That scares me."

"I know what you mean," said Caroline softly. "When I heard about Josh on the weekend, I felt the way you do."

She glanced toward a wildly waving hand.

"He should have helped his wife to die," said a man in a gray turtleneck sweater. "Who'd have blamed him?"

The show took off. Comments, questions, and case histories poured out. Yet the voices were muted, sometimes desperate, but never hysterical. There was no ranting, and when a voice rose too high, Caroline was there at once with a gentle admonition, a reminder of how special this was, how important that it be presented with dignity and responsibility. They listened to her. They obeyed her. And at the end of the hour, several of the members of the audience came up to her and shook hands with her or put their arms around her. There was a magnificent shot of Caroline being embraced by a weeping white-haired woman.

Only Gil Tadich noted that almost everyone in the show, at one point or another, was in tears or on the verge of breaking down, except Caroline.

"Cold-blooded little bitch," he said.

"She couldn't have done this well if she were as cold-blooded as you say," said Mayer.

"Hadn't been for her, he'd still be alive," said Tadich, whose friendship with Josh had gone back a long time. He slammed the door of Mayer's office behind him.

The station manager sighed. He also had been fond of the irrepressible Henry, but he was aware that what Caroline Mitchell had done as a memorial to the late co-host had bestowed on his death a dignity it had previously lacked. She had also established herself as a tele-

vision talent in her own right, and he had to respect that.
On an impulse, Mayer telephoned WNN in New York
and asked to be put through to Mellenkoff.

"I want you to take a look at a tape of today's PAA,"
he said.

"Why? I thought the show was going to be canceled
because of Henry's death?"

Mayer explained. There was a pause, then Mellenkoff
laughed softly.

"I'll be damned," he said. "I didn't realize Mitchell
was capable of something like that."

"Believe me," said Mayer, "neither did anyone else.
But after all, you were the one who liked her tapes when
you first saw them, James. You shouldn't be too surprised."

Mellenkoff grinned at the other end of the line. He
had forgotten his ostensible role in the plucking of Caroline Mitchell from the ranks of the faceless into the thin
line of the favored. He would have to remember to tell
Martha about this, although he expected that Caroline
would be ahead of him. He was amused and pleasantly
surprised that there was more to the beautiful brunette
with a Jackie Onassis smile than what could be seen on
camera.

"It's really that good?" he asked Mayer.

"It's remarkable. She got people to talk about their
feelings about dying without getting maudlin or throwing
a fit about what Uncle Jim's funeral cost. And she held it
together. Very classy."

"I'll be interested to see it."

"I thought you'd like to know," said Mayer, "since
you had some interest in her initial tryout. Maybe we've
got something in her."

"Maybe we do," said Mellenkoff, who was still smiling. "What're you going to do with her now?"

"Well, we haven't decided on what to do about PAA.
It was so much Henry's show. And I don't think she's
ready to run it alone, despite today's performance. We'll
have to see whom we can come up with, play it by ear, I
suppose."

"It might be interesting to try something else with
Mitchell."

"Such as?"

"You don't have a co-anchor on your news at six."

"Mitchell?"

"Maybe. Let's talk about it more. Give her a shot at a weekend anchor. She's done that before. This could be a one-shot deal, this memorial show thing. We don't want to get too optimistic about her."

"Well, there's still a perception of her as a lightweight and a man-eater," Mayer admitted.

"The one I don't care about. The other would be impossible. Anyway, try the weekend thing and let me know your assessment of her."

Mayer hung up with a reflective expression on his face. He was curious about Mellenkoff's interest in Caroline Mitchell. From his knowledge of Mellenkoff, there was nothing personal about that interest, so he wondered what the network president had up his sleeve this time. Mellenkoff was establishing a reputation for gambling with tradition. His criteria for what should be used at greatest length was based less on its importance as news than its potential titillation of the viewer. The news was still there, and if it was dramatic enough, there was ample footage. But he had raised the use of "soft" news to a new high or a record low, depending on which television critic you read. Joel Eliass, who watched the "McNeil-Lehrer Report," had stood by with raised eyebrows watching Mellenkoff radicalize the WNN news broadcast. But the ratings had shot up, proving, as Roger Miller noted to Mellenkoff, the adage of the veteran news editor that what the public really cared about was crime, animals, and sex. Mellenkoff grinned. He was exasperated by an indignant call from Martha asking why he was "gutting" a decent news broadcast.

"It's like a visual version of one of those supermarket tabloids with headlines like 'Uncle Fries Twin Nephews in Oven,' " she sputtered.

"Don't get stuffy with me. Good gray journalism wasn't getting us anywhere, and all I did was pep it up a bit. Put in some new people."

"You mean like Miss Animal Rights?"

Mellenkoff sighed. "Gail Chumley is a life-style reporter. Pets are part of American life-style. And there was a hell of a lot of favorable reaction to that piece on pet cemeteries."

"I don't understand you," said Martha.

"That's the first time you've ever admitted it."

There was a pause.

"Feeling better?" Mellenkoff inquired silkily.

"Okay. I suppose you're going to tell me the ratings are up."

"I am."

"Oh."

"I won't be down this weekend, by the way," he mentioned. "Eliass has the equivalent of a state dinner for the board. Assessment weekend."

"Will you be able to find Sally for the occasion?"

"Only because her uncle will ask if not, why not. She's been conferring with an interior decorator on the new apartment."

"More purple?"

"I trust not. I haven't been asked about her side of the house. Maybe you can advise me on mine."

"Maybe I can. Listen, is there anything coming up abroad? I heard Don Fosdick might be coming back early from Moscow. And I don't want to fall between the cracks of the White House and the Soviet Union, so to speak."

Her voice was casual, but Mellenkoff was frowning. He had mentioned to Eliass the likelihood that Martha would be taken off the White House and reassigned, and the chairman had promptly suggested she do investigative reporting in Washington.

"She's so tough, that woman. She reminds me of some kind of wisecracking detective. I must say, James, I can't quite understand your fondness for her. What does Sally think of her?"

"She thinks she's great on the White House."

"Humph," said Eliass.

"How about sending her abroad—"

Eliass had interrupted him.

"She'd create an international incident. Our correspondents are in the nature of our ambassadors, James, aren't they?"

"I suppose so. But Martha Vogel is an excellent reporter. She's done some good stuff for us."

"It doesn't seem likely to me, James. Not that I ever want to interfere with your staff."

"Of course not," said Mellenkoff.

He was worried about Martha anyway. He had seen as much of her as he could on weekends recently, and she seemed tense, unhappy, and drinking much more. Mellenkoff had nothing against drinking, but it seemed to him that every time he saw Martha, they got drunk. Once he had accused her only half jokingly of having to be smashed before she would go to bed with him. He read in her face that his comment was well taken.

Roger Miller had voiced his concern about the same problem.

"Why the hell don't you leave her alone, James?" he asked with brutal frankness.

Mellenkoff was silent. Some subjects he would not discuss, even with Roger.

But Miller pursued his point. "What're you trying to do to her? She's finished at WNN—you know that. It wouldn't matter what she does, because Eliass doesn't like her, so he'll block any decent assignments. And you won't stand up to Eliass."

Mellenkoff's eyes became blue ice. "My dealings with the chairman—" he began.

"Consist of your saying yessir," finished Miller angrily.

"That's about enough, Roger."

"Maybe it should be." Miller had gone slamming out of the office, leaving Mellenkoff staring at the view from the fortieth floor. It was ironic that what he really wanted to do with Martha was have her somewhere he could talk to her, have her listen to him, have her be there. He sometimes wondered why he hadn't asked her to marry him long ago. But things had been different then for both of them, and Martha had been climbing almost as fast as he. Eliass had offered Mellenkoff the goal of a lifetime. Being president of a network was what he had always wanted, and now he had it. It was true there had been a price, but he had always managed to persuade himself that the price would not involve Martha. Now he seemed inextricably enmeshed in a surrealistic situation in which the favor of Eliass was linked to Mellenkoff's marriage to a woman who was visible less than their housekeeper. Sally, since their return to New York, spent an official thirty minutes a week with Mellenkoff on Mondays, checking which social functions they must attend together, and on which occasions it would be necessary for her to play hostess in their newly acquired house.

Where she was the rest of the time, Mellenkoff had very little idea. They had separate bedrooms, and for all the communication he had with her, could have lived in separate houses. She had mentioned once that she was thinking about studying photography; he assumed that was when she wasn't spending money on clothes. He was grateful when her Aunt Julia was away on one of her many trips, because without her encouragement, Sally was less likely to go shopping for emeralds. Receiving the bill from Cartier for one bracelet, Mellenkoff had suggested she take out an account in her uncle's name. He wasn't even sure that she came home some nights. Yet she played her role admirably in public. On the rare occasions they had dinner in a restaurant together, Sally was all golden charm and wit, especially if her Uncle Joel was present. Occasionally, Mellenkoff thought it was a pity to let all that golden glory go to waste, as it were, but he was still nervous about her rushing to Eliass with tales of woe, and he had enough problems to otherwise occupy his mind. He had also felt a stirring of interest in a woman whom he had met on his social rounds, a wealthy three-time divorcée with a wicked sense of humor, a well-preserved body, and very little enthusiasm for long-term relationships. Mellenkoff had found her refreshingly relaxing after the disinterest of Sally and the intensity of Martha.

But he was intrigued by the latest news on Caroline Mitchell. It strengthened his view of her as a young woman with a future; specifically the prospect of being turned into something that would be of credit to Mellenkoff.

In Chicago, Caroline felt as though she had been consigned to limbo. After the memorial PAA show, her time seemed to be up at JRZ. That was what she told Tom Roberts, who stopped by her office to offer congratulations and a drink.

"Listen, that show has to be the best thing you've ever done," he assured her. "Want a martini to celebrate?"

She shook her head somberly.

"I don't think I'll ever face a martini again without thinking of poor Josh."

Caroline hesitated.

"I just wondered—have you heard how his wife is doing?"

"Pretty well, from everything I hear. But she was always a strong woman. She'd have to be, to deal with somebody like him for twenty years or whatever it was," said Tom.

"Obviously I don't know her, but I felt sorry for her—"

"Again from what I'm told, don't," he said. "She knew what she had on her hands. And it was her he called from that bar before the accident."

Caroline nodded. "That was a mistake," she said.

Roberts frowned. "What was?"

"I was thinking aloud, sorry. And I'm so pleased you liked the show. I didn't get much feedback, but then, practically nobody seems to be speaking to me."

"Mayer really liked it. I heard Tadich say so."

"That must have annoyed Tadich. He didn't want to do it."

"You're really down, aren't you?" said Roberts gently.

"Sort of. I mean, I don't know right now if I'm still working.

"Want to bet?"

Caroline smiled a little. "You're so good for me, Tom. I really appreciate it." She looked at him quizzically. "Any word from Jill?"

He shrugged "The usual weekly call telling what she's doing for twenty minutes and asking what I'm doing for twenty seconds. She's fine, I guess."

"You going to Washington this weekend?"

He shook his head. "She's very busy and I don't feel like being a postscript to her friends. She said maybe she'd get here the end of the month, because Chicago might be part of a story she's doing."

Caroline was silent. There was nothing to say, because the Jill he was describing was not the Jill she knew. The old Jill was worried about people's feelings and whether she was doing the right thing. The new Jill didn't seem to care that her husband was miserable.

"You busy this weekend?" he asked.

She laughed. "Not at all."

"How about taking a drive somewhere, having dinner? I could use getting away from the whole scene, and it sounds like you could too."

She nodded. "I'd love to, Tom. Thanks for suggesting it."

"Caroline." For a moment his hand touched hers. "I can't think of anyone I'd rather be with right now."

Caroline smiled at him. He was sweet and kind and she liked him, but he was the husband of her best friend, and she had the ominous feeling that spending a day with Tom Roberts would wind up in bed. She would be determined that she wouldn't. She remembered how she had dismissed young men when she went to college. But it was as though, since Mike, she had slipped backward into a world where it didn't really matter to her because she didn't feel anything, and it seemed to matter to them. It had surprised her, how easy it was to block out reality in bed, how nobody really seemed to notice she wasn't there. And afterward, they could resume talking, and they were always nice because she had done something that pleased them. Or she supposed she had.

35

"YOU'RE WRONG about her," said Martha, and heard her own voice as at a distance.

"You're drunk," said Mellenkoff.

Martha put down her glass. "And you?"

He sighed, and was grateful that the conversation was being conducted in her living room, and not the restaurant they had just left. It seemed to him that every evening with Martha now ended in anger, with almost desultory lovemaking. He knew she was bitter, and he was aware he was responsible for some of her bitterness. He did not feel responsible for what she had been doing to herself and those closest to her for the past six months. She was no longer covering the White House for WNN, and an assignment to Moscow seemed remote. She was on general assignment, which meant, most of the time, that she covered whatever the news director told her to cover. That could range from a breaking spot story to an out-of-town feature. During the past two weeks she had done pieces about a veteran catalog company in Maine, a school for congressional wives, and a crack in the Lincoln statue. She was floating, professionally and personally. She took long lunches, at which she drank wine, and went out to dinner, at which she drank martinis. For the first time in her life, she was drinking heavily when she was alone. Mellenkoff knew when he arrived from New York and found her asleep on her bed at seven o'clock, that she was not curled up there because of fatigue.

They had eaten quickly, Mellenkoff pleading lack of lunch, hoping they could leave before what Martha was consuming with dinner could form an alliance with what she had drunk at lunch. Back at her apartment, he tried to persuade her to go to bed, tried to caress her into sleep. She poured them both a brandy and said she wanted to talk to him about Caroline Mitchell.

"There's nothing to say," he told her flatly, and left his brandy untouched.

"It's all over the place that she's your baby—that you're going to make her a national anchor. James Pygmalion Mellenkoff," said Martha.

"Listen," said Mellenkoff, "I'm not going to go through this with you. Why don't I go to a hotel and I'll see you in the morning?"

Martha ignored him. "It's true, isn't it? You're leaving me to rot, while you hatch out your latest little chicken. Except this little chicken's going to be a bird of paradise, isn't she?"

Mellenkoff stood up and walked into the bedroom. He began to repack his weekend bag. Martha stood in the doorway, staring at him.

"I ran into your little Mitchell's best friend here the other day. Jill whatsis, with PBS. Caroline's screwing her husband, did you know that?"

"I didn't know and I don't care about gossip." He folded a shirt.

"You don't care about trying to make an anchor out of a pea-headed little tramp, either, do you?"

As Mellenkoff picked up his suitcase and turned to leave, Martha crumpled, sliding slowly down the wall and coming to rest on the pale blue carpeting. The brandy made a pale brown puddle on the rug.

"Oh, Christ," said Mellenkoff.

He picked her up and laid her on the bed, then mopped up the brandy with a sponge from the kitchen. When he came back to the bedroom, she was lying where he had placed her, her breathing shallow, her mouth partly open. Abruptly he felt immense pity for her. He managed to unzip her dress and pull it off, then eased her under the covers, and turned off the lights. In the living room, he undressed, put on the blue velour robe, and lay down on the sofa with his untouched snifter of brandy. He didn't want to leave her alone while she was in that condition, but he was also aware that she had to be somehow forced to face reality. Roger Miller had told him about the CBS offer, and said it was still open, and he had no idea why Martha would not take it. Mellenkoff thought he knew.

Martha was giving up, unless he could persuade her there was some reason not to. He didn't think she was an alcoholic, although she was obviously skirting the edge of a problem. She functioned perfectly well at work, but it was only a matter of time before her drinking ebbed into her working day. He was puzzled as to why she was so vituperative about Caroline Mitchell. It was unlike Martha to be vicious, and in fact, it was she who had helped Caroline take her first steps in television.

Except that those steps had led Caroline to the point where Martha had always wanted to be. Or where she had said she always wanted to be. There was some truth in the gossip sweeping WNN that Caroline, now a co-anchor at JRZ in Chicago, was being groomed by Mellenkoff for bigger things. She was making slow progress at JRZ, working uneasily with her co-anchor, a happily married man who kept ambitious female colleagues at arm's length. Mellenkoff had studied her tapes, talked to her at length, and come away retaining his earlier impression that Caroline could be molded. He had tentatively discussed the idea with Roger Miller, who flatly cautioned him against it.

"She's not ready for that and she'll never be ready," Miller had said.

"The best thing she does is on a talk show. She's good with people. She can get them to talk. We should have cashed in on that Henry memorial show she did, instead of pushing her into news. You've seen her goof on the air, even with Gale to bail her out."

"Everybody does that, even the old-timers," Mellenkoff protested.

"She does it because she panics, because she's got nothing to fall back on. James, she's got the attention span of a houseplant, but she covers it up as well as anybody I've ever seen. She's very high risk as a solo."

"I don't get that feeling," said Mellenkoff stubbornly.

"You don't because you don't want to. It's not Mitchell who's fooling you, it's yourself. You've persuaded yourself you can turn her into a female Cronkite, and you'll commit professional suicide in the attempt, if that's what it takes."

There had been a long silence. Mellenkoff respected Miller's judgment.

"What does Eliass say?" Miller pressed.

"He—he's got some doubts. But says he'll rely on my judgment."

"That's interesting," observed Miller. "He certainly wouldn't rely on it when it came to Martha Vogel, who's a proven professional. But he's willing to let you hang yourself for little Mitchell?"

"He agrees with me about Caroline's potential," said Mellenkoff stiffly. "He just feels she may need more time."

"About fifty years and a brain transplant," said Miller harshly.

"We differ," Mellenkoff told him in a voice of controlled fury, which ended the conversation.

That had been two weeks ago, and Miller had spoken to him only when it was necessary. Mellenkoff didn't know whether Miller was more upset about Martha or about Caroline Mitchell. Yet his opinion of Caroline was unshaken. She had not tried to present herself to him as something she was not. She had expressed her own doubts that she could ever be what he wanted her to be. It was he who insisted that she could do it; that he could do it.

Sometimes he wondered why he was the only one who had faith in Caroline. He had gambled before and won. His revamped news hour had taken WNN to a close second place in the ratings, and there were two situation comedies that he had backed, despite objections, which were doing well with viewers. Caroline, in his view, was not even such a major gamble. Her career record was a spectacular upward spiral, some of which had been luck and being in the right place at the right time, and the rest of it had been Caroline herself. She had worked hard. She did work hard. David Gale, who had been less than thrilled to find that the erstwhile girl friend and co-host of the late Josh Henry was joining him on the six o'clock news, admitted he had been surprised. Caroline was all business, asked no favors, and took advice willingly. She came in early and stayed late, and she was available for anything the station wanted her to do.

Mellenkoff knew all this because he kept tabs on Caroline Mitchell. He was not about to bring her to New York, even as a correspondent, before he thought she might fulfill his dream. Which was also Caroline's dream.

She looked like a child on Christmas morning when he talked about her becoming a national television star. But he had tried to make it clear that nobody was going to leave her anything beneath the network tree. At another time, he would have talked to Martha about Caroline, because he valued Martha's opinions. Of all the people he knew, and the one or two he cared for, it was Martha to whom he listened most. Martha the way she used to be. Martha had let him down, he thought, and glanced resentfully toward the bedroom.

He slept fitfully on the sofa, and fell into a deep sleep shortly before dawn. When he woke, it was to the fragrance of coffee, and Martha, who was sitting in an armchair opposite, watching him. She looked remarkably good in view of the way he assumed she must feel. She was freshly showered, and her dark hair curled in damp tendrils about her face. She was wearing a pair of jeans and a bulky blue sweater. He sat up and stretched, and accepted her proffered cup of coffee.

"How d'you feel?" he asked.

"Better than I should, I expect." She sipped at her coffee. "I don't recall too much of last night, but I suppose I owe you an apology for whatever I did say or didn't do."

"You don't owe me an apology. You're the one who's being chewed up. You're doing it to yourself, for God's sake."

"I know that."

"You know why?"

She was silent for a few moments, staring into the coffee cup.

"I'm unhappy, I guess. I did that to myself too."

"Why don't you take the CBS offer? Roger told me about it."

"You mean before it's too late? The trouble is I don't know if it isn't too late anyway, and I don't mean because I've been getting smashed more often lately. I seem to feel sort of . . . hollow all the time. As if there isn't any future because there isn't any past."

"That doesn't make sense, Martha. You've done very well, and you know it. Your reputation's excellent."

"That isn't what I mean. I think that my good days were . . . well, they were too tied up with you. Most of what I did was for you, or because you encouraged me, you said I could do it. I did it because you thought I could do it, not always because I thought I could do it. I was more scared than you knew a lot of the time. And now I'm beginning to think I didn't really want to do it. What I wanted to do was please you." She grinned ruefully. "How's that for feminism in reverse? I did all the right things for all the wrong reasons. I was good, but I wasn't good so much because I wanted to be good as because you wanted me to be good." Martha put her hands to her head. "Christ, that many goods have to be bad."

"Martha, I'm not sure I understand all this. But you're telling me you're unhappy now because I drove you?"

"I drove myself. I let you drive me. I loved it. But I did it because of you, not because of myself, or what I wanted. What I wanted, James, was you."

He looked at her for a long moment, and put out his hand.

"Come over here."

She moved over to the sofa and sat beside him. He put his arm about her gently.

"You think I don't want you?"

"Not enough. I mean, I know I've been bitter, and I probably always will be. But that was the trouble. You were the center of the world for me. I was no more than a significant part of it for you."

His arm tightened about her. "Martha, I was wrong about a lot of things too. But I never thought I was wrong about you."

"You weren't wrong about me. I was wrong about me. I've just begun to see that. Maybe that's why I've been sloshing it up so much. Realizing you've spent most of your life doing something you didn't *really* want to do is unnerving at my age." She looked up him affectionately. "I'm not saying it's your fault, James. I didn't have to do any of these things. But it was the kind of thing I was supposed to do—the kind of thing women like me are supposed to do, I guess."

She leaned against his shoulder.

"Maybe I'd have been happier if you'd set me up in a fancy apartment and visited me three times a week!—No, no, don't tell me, I know that wouldn't have worked out either. Anyway, I'm trying to tell you what I'm trying to work my way through, because in a strange way, I think I owe it to you."

"What do you think you'll do?"

"I don't know. Maybe the CBS thing'll work out. But I wouldn't be doing them any favors at this point if I took it. They wouldn't be getting what they think they're getting."

"You want to take some time off? Go somewhere? Maybe I could arrange a trip—"

"I have to do it by myself. Whatever I have to do. At least I know that. But I wanted you to know, because I still love you."

She put her arms around his neck and clung to him.

"Martha, for God's sake, you must know I love you. And I want to help. . . ." His voice was muffled by her hair. She stayed curled in his arms for a while, and he rocked her like a child. Slowly, she pulled away, and pushed her hair off her face.

"Something else. I'm sorry if I was bitchy about Caroline Mitchell last night. I'm a little vague on what I said, but I suspect it was nasty."

"It was," he agreed. "I thought you liked Mitchell?"

Martha got up and went to fetch fresh coffee.

"I do," she said reflectively. "Maybe I was reacting because I didn't want to see her become a victim."

"Of me?"

"Well, you have a certain Svengali quality."

"Last night it was Pygmalion."

She grinned. "I think Caroline's done very well, generally speaking. I guess you're getting a lot of flak from Roger about your idea that she can be the first solo female anchor, right?"

"I couldn't have put it better. I seem to be the only defender of little Miss Mitchell."

"You know," said Martha, "she isn't little at all. She's almost as tall as I am. But every man who's ever known Caroline describes her as little. I wonder how and why she conveys a sense of smallness, of fragility. You don't suppose she is, beneath all that charm, made of steel?"

"I've never thought about it. I haven't analyzed Mitchell. I see her as a potentially very valuable property," said Mellenkoff impatiently.

"I'm aware of that," Martha acknowledged. "But maybe you should analyze her, if you're going to put all your eggs in that basket—if you'll pardon the expression."

"All I need to know," Mellenkoff told her curtly, "is that Caroline Mitchell is a talented professional journalist who won't make a fool of the network, and who may propel us into first place in the ratings."

"How do you find that out? You don't know her like you knew me.

"I gauge her performance. I get reports on her. I talk to her. She's under no illusion about what I require of her, and if I don't get it, that'll be the end of the whole concept."

Martha nodded. "I'm sure she's not about to relax, James."

"She can't relax. This is no time for her to relax. She has to do one thousand percent better than she thinks she can do—" He saw her smile, and stopped abruptly.

"Goddamnit, Martha, I'm trying to make this woman a star. I'm not going to baby her. If she needs to be babied, she'll fail long before she gets to the top."

"Just the way I did," said Martha softly. "Just the way I did."

36

THERE WAS a calculated psychology to the decor of Mellenkoff's office. In his home, he had not interfered with the rococo visions of the interior decorator hired by Sally, because his home was not important to him except as a tool to entertain and impress. He slept there briefly and ate there occasionally. He did not care about the French influence in the living room, the Egyptian flavor to the dining room or the Japanese touches in the bedrooms and bathrooms. His office was where he lived, where he exercised power. Black and white, he told the decorator, and specified what should be black, what should be white, and how it should be placed. The oversized desk was topped by black marble. The chairs were upholstered in black leather. The coffee table was ebony inlaid with onyx. The sofa was slipcovered in white linen. The thick wall-to-wall carpeting was black and white. A touch of a dial transformed the lighting from a mellow glow to the glare of a bare bulb, highlighting the blood red poppies of the tapestry on the wall behind the desk. The triple console of television sets at one side of the room was set in ebony, and the curving sweep of the windows was framed in white linen.

"My God, it's Count Dracula's castle!" Roger Miller had exclaimed gleefully the first time he saw the room. Mellenkoff's smile had been wintry. He had wanted the office to startle, even to intimidate, and he was satisfied that it had that effect on most of those who entered it. It was not accidental that the overstuffed black leather armchairs facing his desk were so designed that occupants had to sprawl or sit bolt upright.

Few declined Mellenkoff's waved invitation toward the armchairs. Roger Miller either perched on the edge of

Mellenkoff's desk, or exasperated him by stretching out on the white sofa, which meant his voice floated, disembodied, back across the long room. And Joel Eliass, who permitted himself a smile of amusement when he saw and understood the office, deliberately chose to sit squarely in the middle of the white sofa. That meant Mellenkoff had to sit in one of two white tub chairs across the coffee table. Mellenkoff was too large to be comfortable in a tub chair, but he had not had himself in mind when he ordered them. Caroline Mitchell sat in one of the black armchairs, rigidly upright, and feeling as though she were being X-rayed by the cold blue eyes a few feet away. Mellenkoff was unlike any man she had ever encountered. He had no personal interest in her at all. He discussed her appearance, her personality, her voice, her clothes, her mental capacity—and lack of it—without a shade of expression in his voice. She might have been a robot he was building, nut by bolt by hinge. And that was a fairly accurate description of how Mellenkoff felt about her. He believed he had discovered in Caroline Mitchell star quality like gold glinting in gravel, and he meant to mine it. It had glimmered in those early tapes, and it had shone brightly on the Josh Henry memorial show. Mellenkoff did not care about the housing of the gold. He was grateful for its striking setting, although he would have preferred it be embedded in the rock of intelligence. But he had been looking for someone with the kind of magic that he could transmute into a rainbow with a potful of gold ratings at its end.

He was also aware of the kind of obstacle course he would have to maneuver to place a completed and burnished model of Caroline where he wanted it to be, where it would reflect most credit on his eye for talent. It was paradoxical, he sometimes reflected, that it was Martha who had first brought Caroline to his attention; Martha, who so desperately had wanted what in effect was being thrust upon the younger woman. Martha had her own kind of magic, certainly for him, but not the kind that lit up an audience research chart. Nevertheless, there was an intricate maze of network bureaucracy that Mellenkoff had negotiated successfully himself, notably with his quantum leap from Washington bureau chief to division president to president of the network. And if Caroline were to reach the pinnacle he had in mind for her, her course must be charted with craft and skill, especially while she remained in the learning process. Mellenkoff did nothing without weighing the potential consequences to himself.

Caroline's success at JRZ-WNN in Chicago had permitted him to take the first step of calling Tom Gold, the president of the station, and registering his satisfaction that he had been right in his assessment of the tapes of the beautiful brunette from Ohio. He had not mentioned to Gold that John Mayer, the general manager of JRZ, who was Mellenkoff's old friend, had already called him about Mitchell. When Gold passed on Mellenkoff's comments, Mayer followed through, and set in motion the next stage in Caroline's development. The news director had expressed surprise at the suggestion that Mitchell be so promoted on the basis of what many at the station considered a fluke performance. But he offered no real opposition.

Most of the grumbling came from Gil Tadich, director of programming, whose opinion of Caroline had been set in concrete hostility by her relationship with Josh Henry. Unreasonably, Tadich held her responsible for Henry's death. It was not, he had observed bitterly, a fair exchange to get a Mitchell for a Henry. It was Tadich who remembered that Mellenkoff had suggested testing Mitchell for the co-host spot. It was Tadich who first identified Mellenkoff as Caroline Mitchell's "rabbi" in the network. And while he disagreed with Mellenkoff's judgment and could not comprehend it, he acknowledged that Mitchell's feet seemed to be set on the yellow brick road, although he did not have any idea of her ultimate destination. Tadich assumed that Mellenkoff had taken a fancy to Mitchell, as Josh Henry had, and assumed the infatuation would fade, as it usually did. And because Caroline Mitchell was no longer under his direct jurisdiction, Tadich gave her less thought. She had become the problem of Milt Crosby, the news director, who had a reputation for suffering no fool gladly. Mellenkoff, aware of the intricacies of the chain of command, kept an eye on Caroline from a distance. It could do her as much

harm as good for her co-workers to be aware whose eye
was on her. He also wanted to test her, to make sure his
golden egg was not hatching into a monster. He noticed
that Crosby assigned her to stories on the lighter side,
like a study on unemployed women, or an environmental
controversy, and her performance was creditable. But as
co-anchor with David Gale, she was uneven and unpredictable.

She seemed to be off guard and nervous, which aroused
Mellenkoff's concern and curiosity when he watched the
tapes of the shows. Her co-anchor, Gale, was a news
veteran whose ambition to move upward was well known.
Mellenkoff considered him solid and reliable but without
the flair that captured viewers, which was why Gale
stayed where he was despite his professional designs.
Mellenkoff suspected Gale had not welcomed Caroline's
arrival, concluding that what she presumably had going
for her was not only her looks, but somebody up there
who was watching over her. Mellenkoff knew what a
hostile co-anchor could do, especially to someone still as
vulnerable as Caroline. That was something else he wanted
her to learn: the capacity to be knocked flat and fight
back.

Caroline had been in her new job for eight months
when Mellenkoff received a call from John Mayer. He
had a complaint from Crosby about Mitchell, he said,
and it seemed solidly based. The show that Crosby was
most upset about had Caroline blithely reading a story
about a mass murderer accused of slaughtering ten people, while on the videotape there was the earnest face of
a United States senator campaigning locally for reelection. That was bad enough, but what was worse, as
Mellenkoff knew, was that Caroline had not instantly
noticed, corrected her error, and apologized to the viewers. The senator had gotten his apology, but the viewers,
as Mayer put it, probably were either snickering or wondering what they had voted for. Crosby, he said, had
provided a list of grievances about Mitchell. This had
been the worst.

Mellenkoff watched the tape grimly. He assumed that
Crosby had already chewed her out. The other complaints were of carelessness, inattentiveness to changes in

copy, problems with ad-libbing in that she talked too long about too little, slow reaction to instructions on changes relayed to her during a show by the producer, via her earpiece. Yet what Mellenkoff found just as interesting were the viewer research studies showing audience reaction to Mitchell as phenomenally favorable. Research reported that, like Ronald Reagan, Caroline's fluffs seemed to be forgiven because viewers liked her so much. The worst that was said about her was that sometimes she didn't seem too sure of herself, but that was considered refreshing by comparison with the talky omniscience of some of her colleagues. She was so warm, so pleasant to listen to, according to surveys of focus groups chosen to comment on their television watching. And although she was so pretty, she didn't look plastic. That was a real smile, they said, and she seemed to be trying to make things clear instead of just reading at you. Mellenkoff went on checking charts, and noted that the ratings for JRZ's early news show had risen by two points since Caroline joined the team. True, the improvement was not necessarily linked to her arrival, but it was an interesting coincidence. He thought for a while, then called Mayer back, and told him he wanted to see Mitchell in New York. He had been disturbed by the tape and the complaints, he mentioned. It was somewhat disappointing after her earlier showing. Mayer nodded to himself, as Mellenkoff knew he would. The word would be passed that Mitchell was in trouble.

Two days later, Caroline found herself sitting in one of the famous black leather chairs, impaled by the icy blue eyes. Mellenkoff wasted no time on small talk.

"I'm disappointed in you and you should be disappointed in yourself," he began.

Caroline tensed, and Mellenkoff was reminded of a black and pink butterfly poised for flight. He hoped the analogy was superficial.

"I have placed some faith in you, given you a chance. At this time, you aren't justifying it. This is your opportunity to tell me why. It may be your only opportunity."

Had she cringed, he would have lost interest in her there and then.

"I don't have any excuses," said Caroline in a voice

that bordered on defiance. "I know I've screwed up a few times on the air, but I've tried not to make the same mistake twice. I'm learning, but it's on-the-job training, Mr. Mellenkoff, because that's what you wanted me to do. You said it was the fastest, hardest way to learn, and you told me I was high risk. Well, maybe I still am. But I am learning."

Mellenkoff concealed a faint smile of approval. She was justifying his belief that there was stuff behind the Teflon charm. It was only a matter of time. And he didn't know too many WNN correspondents, especially at her stage of development, who would have stood up to him. Most would have groveled or defended themselves by blaming somebody else.

"Inexperience can be overcome," he said. "Is there any problem other than your own carelessness?"

Caroline's eyes didn't flicker.

"My co-anchor doesn't like me. And he gets along better with the producer than I do. I know somebody has to stop me when I ad-lib too long, but when the producer's screaming 'Shut up! shut up!' through my earpiece and David is sneering two feet away, it doesn't do much for my dignity on camera. The other side of that coin is I've decided maybe it's good for me because it means I don't have anybody really to rely on but myself, and when I get something right, I get a real high out of it because I've done it in spite of all of them."

Mellenkoff listened impassively. What she said came as no surprise. And he was pleased by her reaction to what he considered survival training, a crash course to speed up the learning process. He knew her troubles were the result of her inexperience, but his response to that was that she must work harder. With the kind of unprecedented opportunity dangling before her, she would be willing to devote twenty-four hours a day, seven days a week, to eliminate her weaknesses.

"You apparently haven't learned to watch the monitor while you're reading your script. Or to at once apologize and make a correction."

Again there was that unexpected flicker of defiance.

"I would have, if I'd known I'd done it. You're right I wasn't careful about watching the monitor. But I have been since."

"The producer didn't tell you."

"No."

Mellenkoff looked at her with appraising eyes. She had changed considerably since he first met her, when she had looked like an exquisite kitten. She was maturing into a spectacular cat, with a sleekness and self-confidence softened by that dazzling camera combination of wide-set, luminous eyes and the irresistible smile. With Mitchell, he was relying—he admitted it to himself—on his visceral reaction to her as a potential television star of Cronkite caliber. And James Mellenkoff would have discovered her, molded her, trained her, defended her against early doubters, turned her into the first female anchor who could inspire the kind of confidence that had been reposed by the public in the legendary, avuncular Cronkite. That was why market research was crucial to tracking her progress. She could be force-fed techniques and journalistic expertise, but nobody could teach her how to enchant a nation. She needed time and polishing, but he liked her philosophy about learning from mistakes and doing well in spite of those who disliked her. He wasn't about to do anything about David Gale, although the co-anchor should have known better than to show signs of enmity on the air, for the simple reason that viewers sensed such currents and usually took the side of the underdog, who was obviously Caroline, the new girl on the team. But Mellenkoff would make sure something was done about a producer who allowed his own prejudice to prevent his telling her to make an on-the-air correction of a major mistake. That reflected on the station as well as on the anchor.

The caustic remarks made to him by Martha while she was in her cups had put Mellenkoff on notice that network gossip about Mitchell was intensifying, and presumably, so was the level of resentment. The kind of thing he was doing with Caroline Mitchell, or the kind of thing he hoped to do with her, could be expected to generate jealousy, objections, and anger, at all levels of the bureaucracy, and particularly among those striving to attain what was ostensibly being handed to an unqualified young woman who had acquired a powerful ally. Mellenkoff didn't care about the gossip and he was prepared to take on any opposition, with the exception of Joel Eliass, who had to persuaded. But he also had to be sure that Caroline Mitchell was worth the risk, and no one knew better than he how costly failure could be.

He leaned forward. "I told you you would have to work very hard, Caroline. Now I'm telling you to work a lot harder. You have to remember what's riding on you as an anchor. It's far more than learning to do a credible job of reading and looking as though you understand it. You have to learn to think ahead, read ahead, see mistakes before they become inevitable. Be alert for errors in what you read, in what you're told. Learn to hedge. Don't be afraid to tell the viewers you don't know, but you're going to find out. That's reassuring to them. What isn't reassuring is seeing you sitting there with your face hanging out while you're earning a ridiculous amount of money. Remember they can see every flicker on your face, catch every word you screw up.

"They'll forgive your mistakes," he continued, "most of the time, but only if you admit them and correct them. You can only blame a co-anchor or a producer so long. In the end it'll be your responsibility if you fuck up. And it could very well be the end of your career too. Keep that firmly in your mind anytime you feel like goofing off."

Caroline's eyes were fixed on his face. "I will try," she promised.

"Don't tell me you'll try. Tell me you'll do it. I'm only interested in a winner," he said flatly.

She hesitated.

"May I ask you a question?"

He nodded.

"Why me? I mean, I'm flattered and honored and all that when you take an interest in how I'm doing. But why me? Maybe I shouldn't say this, but there are a lot of people in this business with more experience than I have—I mean, they wouldn't give you so much trouble. . . ." Her voice trailed away and her eyes were apprehensive.

Mellenkoff laughed. "That's a legitimate question. It was my judgment that you were different, that you could do what people with more experience couldn't and can't. Because you have something they don't have. You can gather experience, as you're doing now, but you can't manufacture or simulate the kind of thing you project on camera. You never had to learn that. You had it. It won't take you all the way, but it'll sure as hell help. If I wanted a responsible, competent journalist, I wouldn't pick you, to be blunt. But in our time a television star is a cult figure. People watch television the way they used to read the Bible. So they have to have faith in the face on the screen. And whatever the quality is that inspires such faith, you can't distill it. It's the old business: some people have it, some don't. But even if you have it, Caroline, you've got to know how to use it. Do I make myself clear?"

Her eyes were wider than usual, and Mellenkoff could not know that she was wondering if it was Caroline in the mirror who was being groomed as the next guru of the airways, or the Caroline who had spent so much time trying to armor herself against fear of what crept in the dark. Perhaps now there was only Caroline in the mirror, sublimely sure and self-confident.

She looked at Mellenkoff. "It's very clear."

"Good. Then I can expect to get good reports from JRZ. And after a while, we'll talk about what's next."

She stood up, assuming dismissal, but Mellenkoff looked at his watch.

"You're spending the night in New York?"

She nodded.

"Good. I'll take you to dinner. I'd like to spend a little time talking with you. Find out what you know. I'll pick you up at your hotel at eight."

"Thank you," said Caroline, speculating for a brief instant what his reaction would be if she declined the invitation. Not that she wanted to, although she dreaded spending an evening with Mellenkoff. She could only pray she would prove to know a fraction of what he probably expected of her.

In her hotel room, she lay gratefully in a tub of warm water, trying to relax tense muscles. She didn't think she had moved at all during the time she had sat in that impossible chair. Why did he have people he was talking to sit in chairs in which they couldn't relax? she thought, and realized she had answered her own question. She

savored what he had said, though. He had put her wild-
est dreams into words, and suddenly she found she was
smiling from pure excitement. When the telephone rang,
she answered it with a joyful lilt that evoked a surprised
reaction from Tom Roberts, who was calling her from
Chicago.

"I gather he didn't cut your head off after all?"

"No. He didn't." Caroline had learned the value of
discretion.

"Just a lecture?"

"Pretty much."

"You mean Mellenkoff called you to New York to give
you a lecture? What is he, Caroline, your godfather?"

He's my "rabbi," she thought, having newly learned
the network version of a protector, but she knew better
than to say so.

"Well, I guess he felt I'd let him down because he was
the one who got me the tryout because he liked my
tapes."

"He must have plans for you." Tom's voice had a sour
edge, and Caroline realized abruptly how isolated she
had become and must remain.

"Not so far as I know. He thought I ought to work
harder and do better, or I won't be in the job. He really
came down on me about that mass murderer mess."

Roberts laughed, the sharpness fading from his voice,
and Caroline relaxed a little. She could not afford to
have Mellenkoff think she repeated anything he said to
her, but it had to be obvious to him that the JRZ staff
would be curious about her visit to New York, and a
warning about her recent disaster on live camera was a
logical consequence.

"What's doing with you?" she asked, mildly curious
why he was calling her. Caroline had been seeking to
reinstate a platonic friendship between Tom Roberts and
herself. In the wake of her uncertainty and fright over
her professional prospects after Josh Henry's death, she
had spent a weekend with Tom, and had been grateful
for the comfort of his presence and his arms around her
in the night. But she had regretted that weekend almost
as soon as it was over. She had needed him, but only for
a weekend. And Tom had persuaded himself that he had

married the wrong woman. His resentment at what he felt as Jill's indifference to their marriage had erupted into revenge, which had made his apparent conquest of Caroline all the sweeter. Caroline had spent the next few months trying to persuade him that she had been wrong, they had been wrong, and they must be no more than friends. She did not especially care about Tom's feelings, as she did not care about the feelings of any man she had known, with the exception—and even that was qualified—of Mike Hathaway. In a strange way he might have been the father she never had. She did not want to make an enemy of Tom Roberts; she seemed to have enough enemies already.

Nor did she want to lose Jill's friendship, one of the only pleasant memories of her childhood. So her behavior with Tom had become guarded, and she had watched with weariness his rising reproach. Now, his response was confused, and Caroline felt an anticipatory chill.

"Well, I guess I'm okay. Jill and I had a bust-up."

"Oh? I'm sorry. Maybe you should get together and try to talk things out."

"Caroline." His voice was harsh. "I don't want to get together with her and talk things out. There isn't anything to talk out. I mean I told her it was over. I told her . . ." He hesitated.

"What did you tell her?"

"Well, I told her about us."

Anger swept Caroline. "There was nothing to tell. Why did you do that? To get back at her?"

He blustered uncertainly. Caroline's sharp words were accurate and it was difficult for him to entirely deny them. He had wanted to hurt Jill, as she had hurt him. And Caroline was her best friend.

"What d'you mean there was nothing to tell?"

"Tom." Caroline's voice was toneless. "We spent a weekend together when we were both unhappy, and that was it. How could you tell Jill any more than that? How could you tell her that?"

He was silent, because he had no defense and his fierce little flurry of vengeance had dissolved into dismay at himself.

"I guess I'll . . . well, maybe I'll call her back—"

Caroline dismissed him. "I don't care what you do,

Tom. You had no right to do this to me or to Jill. You've destroyed—" Her voice hardened instead of breaking. "You had no right at all. I'm very disappointed in you."

As she hung up without waiting for his response, she thought with a wry flicker of a smile that she was echoing Mellenkoff's words to her earlier that day. Caroline sighed and began to brush her hair, because that still soothed her. And as she looked at Caroline in the mirror, her distress about Jill faded before the vision of a future that Mellenkoff had painted for her. By the time she dressed in a simple black suit, with gold at her throat and wrists, Tom Roberts and Jill had both receded into the vast recesses of Caroline's memory.

And she was pleasantly surprised by her evening with Mellenkoff, who took her to a restaurant as quiet and discreet as it was exorbitantly priced, ordered her food and wine for her, and chattered in an entertaining, apparently casual manner about books, plays, politics, history, and a recent murder.

Yet he drew her out, weighing and assessing her responses, and as Caroline relaxed, she did what came most naturally to her, and began to question him on his opinions and observations. By the time they reached dessert, Mellenkoff realized with amusement that she was interviewing him. She did not evade questions; she turned them around and asked why he thought that.

He understood why she had done so well on a talk show. She had a personality like warm velvet when it came to asking even difficult questions. Caroline, he thought, could ask if you had enjoyed murdering your mother, without being offensive about it. Calling for the bill, he bestowed on her a glance of qualified approval.

"Do more homework on politics, especially national politics. Make sure you're up to date on recent history as well as current events. Read all the newspapers and magazines you can find time for, and try to keep some files of your own. It helps keep stuff fresh in your mind."

"I will. And thank you," she said.

He took her to her hotel in his limousine and formally shook hands with her as they parted.

"Good luck," he said.

From all she had heard, she would need it, Caroline thought. Mellenkoff watched her mount the steps and saw the admiring glances of men whom she passed on her way into the hotel. He found Caroline Mitchell beautiful in an abstract way, but she did not interest him as a person, perhaps because he had not completed his sculpting of the person he wished her to be. He smiled faintly, reflecting that had he been inclined to sleep with Caroline, which he was not, it would have seemed, in the circumstances, almost incestuous.

37

SALLY ELIASS Mellenkoff wandered the elaborate, empty rooms of the house on East Seventy-eighth Street where she co-existed with her husband, and thought she might as well live in a hotel. Their dinner parties were catered, the housekeeping was done by a couple who came in four times a week, and during the months of their marriage, Sally had never made so much as a cup of coffee for Mellenkoff. He was usually going out to work in the morning when she came home; they said good morning in passing. She took no interest in where he was, and as far as she knew, he was equally uninterested in her whereabouts. She kept her clothes in the large dressing room off her bedroom, located at the other end of the upstairs hall from Mellenkoff's bedroom, only because Karen had complained she had no more closet space in her apartment into which to cram Sally's lavish wardrobe. Sally was much more familiar with Karen Ward's apartment, with its decor reflecting the subtle blues and greens of Karen's beloved ocean, than she was with the house she and Mellenkoff had bought. Or she used to be more familiar with Karen's apartment, she thought bitterly. She followed the trail of her thoughts to the nearest telephone in the living room, which reflected the interior decorator's penchant for pink and gold, and dialed Karen's number. She sat there on the pink sofa, listening to it ringing, listening to Karen not answering. She didn't believe Karen was out; she was sure she was refusing to pick up the receiver out of spite.

Sally slammed the receiver back in its cradle and resumed her restless prowling over inlaid floors and heavy-piled carpeting. She could not understand why Karen had become so difficult over such a trivial matter. Sally had been delighted that things had worked out so well after she married Mellenkoff. Uncle Joel had been downright jovial when they had dinner with him and Aunt Julia, and Mellenkoff barely spoke to her, which was exactly the way she liked it. They had talked a lot during the brief weeks of the courtship sponsored by Joel Eliass, but Sally had learned very little about Mellenkoff himself and had not tried to elicit more information than he was willing to give. She had been preoccupied with thoughts of Karen during her evenings with Mellenkoff, and their conversation had been of a lighthearted nature, punctuation of parties with other people or attendance at the ballet or theater. Mellenkoff had been charming, having little choice but to be on his best behavior with the niece of the chairman of the board, and Sally had been charming because she was, as long as she got her own way. She had learned more about Mellenkoff from correspondents who worked for WNN, who were closer to Sally's age, whom she had met at network parties. They were delighted to be invited to lunch with Joel Eliass's niece, especially since she turned out to love gossip. And they gossiped. Sally heard about most of the scandals in the business— who was sleeping with whom and why, who was on the way up or down and why. It was all speculation, she knew, but since she was looking and listening, as one watching a film unroll, she came to consider it her personal soap opera. It also provided useful insight into Mellenkoff and how people who worked for him saw him.

When it came to references to Mellenkoff, the conversation became more discreet, which Sally expected and understood. But there were enough unspoken clues for her to begin to piece together a portrait of the man to whom she was legally married, and she came to dislike him without caring very much about it. Mellenkoff had little reality for her, so she had no emotional reactions about him, but she did react to what he apparently was capable of doing to other people. There were those who had no illusions about him and might have hesitated to turn their backs on him, but who liked him for his rapacious charm and a certain buccaneering quality. Like Roger Miller, whom Sally liked, who laughed and called Mellenkoff "Captain Kidd" to his face. But Roger's world was not dependent on Mellenkoff's whim. Miller was far more his own man than Mellenkoff was, Sally had concluded, and consequently more interesting, because he was less predictable. And Sally felt sympathy for Martha Vogel, whom she had met at an official WNN reception and liked immensely. She could not understand the enduring loyalty of such a woman for such a man, but as Karen had pointed out, Martha probably would have been equally perplexed by Sally's feelings for Karen.

"But he's such a bastard to her," Sally protested.

"She'd think we're strange," said Karen.

"Maybe not."

"Don't try to find out," Karen advised with a grin.

Sally had also discovered that her Uncle Joel was inclined to use her as a conduit to Mellenkoff, making observations to her that she was obviously supposed to pass on. Eliass was unaware of how little the Mellenkoffs saw of each other or that what he saw as a convenient system of keeping Mellenkoff aware of reaction at the highest level could not operate when there was no communication. Eliass was quite capable of calling Mellenkoff in and telling him what he wanted, but occasionally he chose to indulge in heavyfooted tact, and that was how he saw transmitting an attitude, opinion, or warning through Sally. For example, the rumors still floating about Mellenkoff and Vogel: Eliass had little concern for their accuracy, but he felt Mellenkoff should exercise more discretion, if the speculation was true. He was aware that Mellenkoff had been involved romantically with Vogel, and Eliass had left him in no doubt that it was inappropriate for the president of the network to be sleeping with a woman whose career was dependent on his decisions. It was around the time that Eliass had decided to make sure that no favoritism was extended toward Vogel, who was no favorite of his. He disliked a woman with a mocking look in her eye and what he thought of as an excessively forthright manner. Eliass did not permit himself to be mocked, especially by women. He was perplexed by the suggestion that the relationship with Vogel had continued after Mellenkoff's marriage to Sally. What could he want with a woman with as little style as Vogel when he had at his disposal a creature as exquisite as Sally, Eliass wondered. When Mellenkoff assured him it was no more than leftover chitchat, Eliass was inclined to accept that.

It was almost relief that Mellenkoff had offered so little opposition to Eliass's condemnation of Vogel that made the chairman lean toward tolerance of the network president's latest favorite, this Mitchell person. Mellenkoff had been emphatic about the professional nature of his interest in Caroline Mitchell, persuading Eliass to see some of her tapes, including one of her acting as host of a Chicago talk show about death. Eliass was not certain that a show about death was in the best of taste, but he had to concede she had handled it well. There was no question about her beauty. Caroline Mitchell reminded Eliass a little of Julia when she was younger. She had an undeniable charm, none of the harshness he so disliked in Vogel. On the one occasion they had met, Eliass had found Caroline attractive to look at and appropriately respectful. As a matter of fact, he had talked to her longer than he had realized, because she was such an excellent listener, and was so clearly fascinated by what he had to tell her about his beginnings as an entrepreneur in California. She obviously had made an effort to do her homework about him, and he approved of that. She had asked intelligent questions and listened intently to his answers, and hadn't tried to flirt with him. Eliass was embarrassed by women who flirted with him or tried to tease him. He thought it was inappropriate behavior, and made sure Mellenkoff knew what he thought of those who resorted to such dalliance to advance their career prospects. Mitchell was a beautiful and charming young woman, but Eliass was far from being persuaded that she should be considered as a national news anchor, which he had reason to believe was Mellenkoff's goal for her.

"She doesn't have the experience, my dear James," he had said. Very reasonably, he thought. Mellenkoff had launched a monologue about Mitchell's magic on camera, her incredible effect on viewers, the unprecedented market research reports on reaction to her. Eliass disliked monologues unless he conducted them, and became irritable when Mellenkoff displayed singlemindedness about projects and people. The chairman had listened patiently, agreed they would have to wait and see, and promised he would not close his mind on the subject.

But he took the first opportunity to comment to Sally that James seemed unhealthily obsessed by this Mitchell woman, and Did James realize the damage he could do to his own career by indulging in obsession? Sally, who had heard more than her uncle knew about the rumors that Mellenkoff was Mitchell's "rabbi," said she was sure James didn't want to do anything that would imperil his future. Eliass said approvingly that was just what he hoped she would make clear to James. Not, he added, that he wanted Sally to worry. No matter what happened to James, she would be perfectly all right. After all, Sally was his niece, a member of the Eliass family, and she seemed to have settled down quite nicely after getting married, which was what Eliass had expected she would do. Nevertheless, the fact that she was married to a Mellenkoff did not make her any the less an Eliass. And Julia had been such a good influence on her, guiding her away from those awful hippie clothes, if that's what they were. He certainly hoped James could afford those diamonds she was wearing.

Sally had not conveyed her uncle's warning to Mellenkoff immediately. She probably would never have told him at all, had she not become distraught over her estrangement from Karen Ward. Karen was annoyed because of Sally's procrastination about taking photography classes. Karen had asked about it every other week, and Sally had always said she was going to enroll the very next day, and then there had been a party or a matinee, or she just hadn't gotten up in time. She had been stunned when Karen picked a fight about it, which was how Sally saw it. Karen thought she'd been patient and reasonable about the whole thing, despite the fact that Sally's flitting had been getting on her nerves for weeks.

"You've got to come to terms with what you're going to do with yourself, darling. You can't play this silly dilettante business forever. At least not with me, you can't."

Sally's shining blue eyes had instantly been clouded by hurt tears.

"But you told me to marry him. You said it would work out for us, if I did," she hiccuped. Karen looked at the tousled blond head compassionately and resisted an impulse to stroke it.

"I also said you had to figure out what you wanted to do with your life. You were working more at your photography on the coast than you are now, when you've got nothing at all to do that matters. A lot of people have told you that you have talent, but you haven't even enrolled in school, and it's been too long. You don't take it seriously. You don't seem to take anything seriously."

"I take you seriously," said Sally reproachfully, and Karen sighed. She'd walked into that one. "I mean," said Sally pathetically, "I only go to those dumb parties and things because you aren't here all the time, and last time you went to California, you wouldn't let me come along. What was I supposed to do?"

"Go to photography class. Or any other class, for that matter."

"Why? Why does that matter so much?"

Karen lit a cigarette, reflecting that the only time she smoked much anymore was when she was trying to reason with Sally.

"Because you've got nothing to occupy your life and I'm not your playmate. If you'd just give it a try— photography, I mean—I think you'd really get involved in it and you'd feel you're doing something satisfying. You might even make some money eventually."

"I don't need money."

"If you left Mellenkoff you'd need money, unless Uncle Joel has changed his tune."

Sally looked at her through reddened eyes. "I don't need to leave Mellenkoff. I practically never see him."

"Well, you only married him to mollify your uncle and because, as we both know, you're not exactly accustomed to a spartan lifestyle. But you could make something of yourself by yourself. I'm not suggesting you go live in a photographic darkroom, for God's sake. You love doing it, you just don't try. You float. And I don't."

Sally scratched disconsolately at a stain on the knee of her black silk pants.

"I don't understand why you're making such a big deal out of this. I thought we were happy," she said petulantly.

Karen's eyes narrowed. "Sally," she said, "if I'd wanted a child, I'd have adopted one. If you're going to stay a child, we're not going to last."

She braced herself for a tidal wave of tears, but Sally only looked incredulous.

"You can't mean we're through because I'm not taking photography classes?"

"All I'm suggesting," said Karen patiently, "is that you do something useful occasionally so you don't spend your time partying in between waiting for me. All you've got to talk about nowadays is Manhattan social gossip. I don't think you've read a newspaper in six months. If you watch television, it's probably a soap opera. You go to what's fashionable at the theater and you go to parties to find out who's screwing who and talk about it. When we met, you had a lot going for you. You were fresh and fun and lively. Now you're addicted to trash, and God knows what else."

"What's that supposed to mean?" Sally asked sullenly.

"Kay Keller's little soirees are not my scene. I am not into scatology," said Karen quietly.

Sally looked defensive. "I only went the once, and I told you I left early. I didn't like it."

"But you went after I warned you. And you went the next time she asked you. Are you going to become one of Kay's little whores?"

"That's not fair. I was just curious. And you were gone—and I'd nothing to do."

Karen shrugged. "Where you go and what you do is your business. It's only my business in that it affects how I think of you and what I feel about you. It depends how much that matters to you, if it matters at all."

Sally flung herself into Karen's arms. "You know how much it matters! How can you say these awful things? You know nobody matters to me except you."

Karen gently disengaged herself. "Then show it. And I think we probably shouldn't see each other for a little while. Give us both a chance to think."

Sally stared at her wildly. "I can't come here again?"

"Darling, I didn't say that. Of course I want you to come back here. I'm just saying we need a breathing space."

"Are you going to the coast?"

"Not until next month."

"Can I call you?"

Karen shook her head. "It'd be better not." She

cocked her head to one side and smiled. "You can write me a note telling me how you're doing in class."

Sally's tears gave way to temper. "All I want is to be with you, and all you care about is whether I go to a damned photography school. Why do you have to tell me what to do? It's my life."

"I know that," said Karen. She walked past Sally toward the door of the apartment and opened it. "It's your life. Go ahead," she said.

Sally stormed out, cried all the way home in a taxi, and as soon as she got there, called Karen to apologize, to promise she'd do anything Karen wanted. There was no reply. Next time she called, the line was busy, and when she had the operator check after an hour, she was told that telephone was out of order. Sally knew it was off the hook. She went back to the apartment the next day, and the security guard, who had always been remote, said Mrs. Ward was out of town. Karen had never given her a key to her apartment, something else that had rankled Sally. She wavered between desperation and defiance. She made herself promises she would never speak to Karen Ward again, and plunged into a round of social activity. She went to two parties a night, shopped frantically with her Aunt Julia, slept until noon, and in a final gesture of rebellion, accepted an invitation to another of Kay Keller's parties. Kay, a wealthy art dealer, had an unfortunate resemblance to a giant wasp, accentuated by bulbous black eyes and a fondness for acid yellow and black. Karen had once accused her of giving depravity a bad name.

Keller parties were notorious, with guests whose ages ranged from twelve to fifty, taking part in activities that would have gotten Kay arrested for contributing to the delinquency of minors, had one of the participants not been a member of the New York City Vice Squad. Sally disliked Kay, but Kay had assiduously cultivated Sally, especially after hearing about Karen's comment. And Kay had heard at one point that Karen was being seen around town with a group from which Sally was suddenly absent. She called Sally three times; it was going to be such a devastating do, she said. Everybody in really, really original costumes. Why didn't Sally come as something really, really fun? Sally went as a werewolf, knowing it wasn't the kind of thing Kay had in mind. Peering through a furry, fanged mask, with taloned gloves on her hands, and fake fur sprouting from a wet suit, she arrived at the Keller penthouse to find it festooned in toilet tissue, with clotheslines of silk underwear stretched from wall to wall. Kay was wearing yellow and black see-through chiffon pajamas and a yellow and black silk miniature toilet seat around her neck. Most of the guests appeared to be naked except for the toilet seats around their necks, and Sally could hear squeals and shrieks from the direction of the black marble-walled bathroom, where some of the fixtures were hardly traditional.

"My gorgeous little wolfie," hissed Kay, and stroked the fur on Sally's suit. Sally left, muttering about having left her purse in the taxi.

When she let herself into the house on East Seventy-eighth Street, Mellenkoff was strolling into the living room, carrying a drink, which he almost dropped when he saw her.

"Your night to howl?" he inquired, with a glance at her costume.

Sally took off her wolf's head. "Do me a favor and fix me a drink," she said.

Mellenkoff raised his eyebrows. It was the first time since their wedding that Sally had suggested they have a drink together. He couldn't remember what she drank, so he hazarded a guess and put together a Scotch and water. When she came downstairs, wearing blue jeans and a loose red shirt, she nodded approval.

"Fine," she said.

She sat down on the sofa and curled her legs under her. Mellenkoff, who had planned to study some ratings charts, looked at her curiously. She looked drawn and tense, which was unusual.

"My God, this is positively domestic. Unheard of," he observed amiably.

Sally grinned. "Yeah, I guess we haven't seen each other since last week when we went to that godawful reception at Winkie's."

"That was grim," he agreed, and bent to his charts, having no reason to assume she desired conversation with him.

Sally sipped her Scotch, and was grateful to be somewhere quiet, warm, and peaceful, even if it was pink and gold. She wondered why she'd let the decorator get away with that, but she hadn't cared enough to argue. She'd been in California while most of the damage was done, aesthetically speaking, and Mellenkoff hadn't seemed to care. Their guests usually appeared rendered speechless by the decorator's efforts to recreate a Louis XIV salon, and Sally didn't care what they said after they left. At least it was a conversation piece, once they found their tongues, and only the boldest asked her why. She usually told the truth, that she'd been gone and it had been too expensive to have the whole thing ripped out. She'd especially liked a woman who had suggested that, if their insurance was up to it, a good fire might be the solution. Sally had dissolved into helpless laughter.

Contemplating Mellenkoff, Sally tried to remember the last thing Uncle Joel had said to her that she was obviously supposed to pass along, and hadn't. Something about the anchor. Mitchell. Vogel? No, he'd apparently subsided on that. Mitchell. Anchor. Now she remembered.

"I hear WNN's thinking about a new news anchor."

That got his attention, she noted. Mellenkoff's head came up. "Where'd you hear that?"

"I have my sources. As you know," she said mischievously.

He nodded. "Uncle Joel, no doubt."

Sally went on sipping her drink.

"What's Uncle Joel saying these days?" Mellenkoff inquired with studied carelessness.

"He doesn't understand why you're risking so much on this Caroline Mitchell," said Sally, choosing her words for effect. She had nothing against Caroline, whom she had never met, and given Mellenkoff's instinct for self-preservation, he could be expected to lose interest in anyone who threatened his cherished power. She glanced at him and was surprised to see his expression remain unruffled.

"Well, he's a bit premature in his concern," said Mellenkoff, also choosing his words.

"He seemed to think you were obsessed about her," said Sally, watching the restless blue eyes for reaction. Mellenkoff smiled frostily.

"I can't afford obsessions, as your uncle knows better than anyone."

"Probably true," agreed Sally, and yawned. She was becoming bored by the conversation. Her encounter with the twilit world of Kay Keller had depressed her more than she expected. And she missed Karen more than she had imagined possible. She looked at Mellenkoff with distaste; he was so venal. That was Karen's favorite description of him and she was right. She was usually right.

"Uncle Joel have anything else to say?" asked Mellenkoff. So he was more perturbed than he looked, Sally thought. She shrugged.

"Not that I remember. I guess I recalled about Mitchell because I'd heard her name mentioned at WNN parties."

"She's high on the gossip circuit, I expect," said Mellenkoff.

"Oh, he did make one other remark. That he didn't know why you weren't going after a Dan Rather or a Peter Jennings and cash in on known success."

That sounded like Eliass, Mellenkoff thought, acknowledging that in other circumstances, the chairman's instincts would have been similar to his own. But he would never have achieved the kind of control over two strongly established anchors that he could exert over a Caroline Mitchell. She would be a reflection of his glory.

"I may do just that. That's very much a possibility," he told Sally, assuming that at some point, all this would trickle back to Eliass and be fed into the chairman's convoluted reasoning processes. He also did not want Eliass's hostility to be aroused toward Caroline Mitchell as it had been toward Martha. Apparently Caroline had taken care of the social side of things on her own, when she had succeeded in making a favorable impression on the chairman. That was all to the good, but it would have little bearing on Eliass's judgment of her as a potential anchorwoman. Mellenkoff did not delude himself that he could sway an Eliass whose computerized mind had reached a final negative decision. Eliass's approval was crucial to any future for Caroline of the kind that Mellenkoff envisaged, but that he rarely put into words. He saw Sally's mouth stretch in a yawn and realized she had lost interest.

"I assume you'll pass this along the Eliass family grapevine," he said, again striving to sound casual.

Sally nodded. "Oh, sure."

As she wandered toward the stairs, Mellenkoff noticed that she was thinner, and that she looked wan and tired.

"You're looking a bit pale. Coming down with flu?" This time his casualness was genuine.

Sally did not turn her head. Over her shoulder, she said, "I'm bored. I've decided I'm going to school."

Mellenkoff was mildly surprised. "School? Here?"

"Photography school," said Sally.

38

SITTING ACROSS a lunch table from Jill Starling Roberts, Martha Vogel saw a reflection of herself. Or a reflection of the way she had visualized herself, the way she should have been. Sipping a glass of wine, only half hearing Jill's animated descripton of a story she had been working on for PBS, Martha remembered when she had been imbued with the same kind of enthusiasm. And she had been good. She was still good, as soundings from other networks assured her. But she seemed to be slipping gradually into darkness and she was unable to stop that ominous slide. She could do what Roger Miller wanted her to do—leave WNN and take another job, start over, which wasn't quite the same when you were starting so close to the top. She could still become an anchor, yet now she wondered whether her desire for the job had been inexorably linked to her desire that Mellenkoff give her that position, thereby bestowing on her the final seal of his professional approval. So much of her life since she met Mellenkoff had been preoccupied by her struggle to possess him, and now she was uncertain that goal would have fulfilled her illusions about it. She had known the truth about their relationship when, with his characteristic capacity for rationalizing cruelty by investing it with the virtue of candor, Mellenkoff had admitted to her that he had not recommended her to Joel Eliass as a potential national anchor. It had not come as a surprise to her; she was sharply aware of Mellenkoff's tenacity at fighting for what he wanted. Her rejection as a candidate for the anchor job had suggested indifference on the part of Mellenkoff more than real opposition by Eliass. The chairman was inclined to take Mellenkoff's advice on matters pertaining to personnel, which of course left the president in a situation where he was being given enough rope to hang himself, but it also left correspondents dependent on Mellenkoff.

What had upset Martha was the discovery that at the point at which Mellenkoff demolished her chances for anchor, he had been simultaneously assuring her it was a live possibility. When she pointed that out, he had observed irritably that it would have been discouraging to her professionally to have been aware of such facts at a time when he wanted her to be engrossed in White House coverage. She had always complained about that job, yet most correspondents were delighted to be offered it, he reminded her. She said she had never wanted it, especially with a chairman like Eliass who thought the President was synonymous with God.

"It was that attitude that finally got you out of the White House," Mellenkoff had said coldly. "And into a hole," she'd rejoined.

He was silent, she supposed rather than tell her The way to get out of a hole you had got yourself into was to climb up and start again. Which got her back to where she was today, foundering in a hole at least partially of her own digging.

She became aware that Jill was eyeing her worriedly across the table.

"I'm sorry. I was daydreaming. Senility. Nothing that another glass of wine won't help." She smiled brightly at Jill, and signaled a waiter. "I gather things are going well for you?"

Jill, who had been on the verge of asking Martha what in God's name was happening to her, found herself neatly sidestepped, as usual, and was so absorbed by her own happiness that she was not as ready to probe the older woman's reserve. Martha had never been one to reveal what she didn't want to, and Jill was preoccupied by events in her own life. She still woke up in the morning with a feeling of pleased surprise that the world was suddenly so full of promise. She had been promoted to correspondent at PBS, she had received a substantial salary increase, and she was in love.

She had to admit to herself that her personal life was more complicated, but the lightness of her spirits seemed to invigorate her. Not even a grim discussion with Tom about their pending divorce could shadow her day. She didn't quite see why such talks had to be grim.

Their marriage had disintegrated almost before it had begun, and its frail structure had collapsed entirely when Tom had made his pious confession about sleeping with Caroline Mitchell. It hadn't mattered to either of them, he assured Jill, whose reaction was primarily exasperation. "Why is that supposed to make me feel better?" she'd snapped. "If I'm expected to forgive and forget, wouldn't it be easier if you had become involved in something that mattered? In any case," she added vindictively, "only a fool would believe you could matter to Caroline. What could you do for her?"

"You're spiteful and vicious," said Tom.

"Perceptive and accurate," said Jill. "I've known Caroline a lot longer than you have."

"And you've always been jealous of her," said Tom.

With a small laugh, Jill conceded that in some respects that was true. Caroline was beautiful, and so far she'd gotten everything she wanted, as well as a few things she didn't want, which probably included him. As a matter of passing interest, did Caroline still want him, and did Caroline know he'd been busy confessing his sins? He certainly planned to tell her, said Tom, and Jill had laughed. She'd bet he wouldn't be so anxious to tell her the reaction, because she'd be willing to predict that Caroline would be furious. That was nonsense, said Tom, but his voice was uncertain. And Jill knew she was right. Caroline's pragmatism would be outraged at the idea of a perfectly good friendship being wrecked because a man she didn't care about was stupid enough to talk. If there was one thing Jill did know about her former roommate, it was Caroline's indifference to the opposite sex, except as a means of getting her where she wanted to go. Without that incentive, Jill strongly suspected Caroline would never have had anything to do with men beyond letting them buy her dinner.

Tom had never mentioned Caroline again, which Jill interpreted correctly as vindication of her theory. His conversations with Jill were becoming rarer and terser. There wasn't that much to settle anyway. They had never really set up housekeeping together, and he seemed to be building himself a life as a WNN correspondent in Chicago, which was far enough away that Jill didn't have to worry about encountering his reproachful face.

She wondered if he knew about Mike, and whether that was the reason for the often unreasonable incivility of his remarks. She didn't care if he knew about Mike, and she rather hoped that Caroline knew. That would give her a little gleeful satisfaction, Jill reflected. She couldn't believe what had happened to her with Mike Hathaway, couldn't yet believe that they had left that terrible party, had two drinks, no dinner, and gone back to her apartment and climbed into bed together. When she was alone, she would remember, savoring each step, how they had stood for a moment in the dark apartment. She had switched on a light, murmuring about a drink and thinking at the same time that an after-dinner drink wasn't entirely appropriate when they'd had no dinner. Mike had pointed that out, and they had begun to laugh again. Jill could not remember an evening when she had laughed so much and so happily, when she had known so clearly what she wanted to do.

Mike had switched off the light and begun to kiss her, and they had undressed each other as they moved slowly, unhurriedly, toward the bedroom. The bed wasn't made, as usual, about which Tom had always complained. Mike didn't seem to notice. His hands and mouth roved her body, tracing and seeking and caressing, yet with patience.

"I want to know everything about you. I want this to last forever," he had murmured into her mouth as his body entered hers. They made love and slept and waked to make love again. Once, the telephone rang, and Mike stirred and asked drowsily, "Who's that at this hour? Whatever hour this is?"

Jill giggled. "Probably my husband calling to tell me he's been getting advice from Caroline."

They had shaken the bed with their mirth.

Since that night, they had seen each other as much as possible. Mike was negotiating for a job with another network in Washington or New York, and when he could not get to Washington, Jill flew to Columbus, spending weekends in the apartment he had taken when he left his wife for Caroline. They were relaxed in occasional reference to Jill's husband or Caroline, as they were in their whole relationship. Jill had never felt so comfortable with anyone, except her father. She felt complete with Mike, as though he complemented her in personality and need. So much of their relationship was ribboned with laughter that they rarely argued. It was as though they were grateful to have found each other, she thought, reveling in a mutual warmth of discovery. Sometimes she thought of Tom with surprising compassion. It hadn't been all his fault; she had blamed him because it was the obvious and easy reaction. What he had done had been in part the result of his hurt that his wife didn't need him at all on any level. She had married Tom because he was there, and there didn't seem any good reason not to. She had liked him, but not enough to live with him, to grow with him.

But she didn't think about that often. She was so glad to have found Mike that she didn't think about anyone else. She even caught herself thinking about him while she was at work, and for Jill, that was unusual. Sometimes they looked at each other and smiled, and there was unspoken understanding.

Mike felt as though he had been reborn. When he first made love to her, he was almost overwhelmed by the difference between Jill and other women he had known. Leslie had been as condescending in bed as she had been at the dinner table, and Caroline had been an exquisite doll with predictably mechanical reactions. Even when Caroline had done the right thing in bed, he had occasionally wondered whether there was anything spontaneous about her affection. It was as though she had practiced to please, perhaps as she had practiced in her mirror to perfect her performance before the camera. Only when Caroline hugged him had she seemed spontaneous, and that had been the embrace of an impulsive child. She had never sensed his moods, never, he suspected, had enough interest to try to do so. The Carolinian radar was limited to gauging people in interviews. That was why she had been so unperturbed about switching her affections to him from Frank. That thought still hurt; that was the only aspect of his relationship with Caroline that had left Mike bitter. For the rest, he looked at Jill lying in his arms, and sighed with relief. She was everything Caroline and Leslie had not been. She even laughed gleefully when he told her he thought she was the most aggressive woman he had ever met when Frank brought her home to dinner.

"I thought I was pretty demure that night you seduced me," she said with a grin.

"That was psychic rape," said Mike, "except it was the first time we had both laughed in a while. Or that's how I remember it."

Jill touched his cheek tenderly. "I don't care what it was, I just want to remember it," she told him.

When Jill assured Martha that yes, things were going wonderfully well, Martha toasted her and said she was glad, and meant it. She particularly envied Jill her capacity to deal with a problem and get over it. Jill could shut out personal difficulties, compartmentalizing them in her mind so that they did not interfere with her work. Martha thought with regret that she had never perfected that art. She could perform creditably, but the problem was always there, a sadness at the back of her mind. As soon as she stopped working, it pounced on her, engulfing her.

"Caroline's called me once or twice to chat," she told Jill. "Sometimes I think she's lonely."

Jill chewed meditatively on shrimp salad.

"Caroline's very much alone," she said slowly. "I don't know that she's lonely. She sort of lives in her own world a lot. I remember when we were kids, I'd go over to her house and she had this absolutely gorgeous room—her father worshipped her—and she'd sit in front of the mirror for hours. She talked to herself in the mirror."

Jill laughed. "Maybe that's why she's doing so well on camera now. She's been preparing herself since she was seven."

Martha was intrigued. "What'd she talk about when she talked to herself in the mirror?"

"Well, sometimes—at least, when we were rooming together at school—she'd read newspaper stories to herself. As if she were reading the news. Before that, when she was small, it was kind of strange, the way she'd sit staring into the mirror, as if she were trying to see through herself, it was that intense." Jill shook her head. "What was really strange was that when we went to school, that was the only thing she took from her room. The vanity with the mirror."

"You mean she's still got it?"

"I know she took it with her to Chicago."

"My God," said Martha, "mirror, mirror on the wall?"

Jill laughed. "I told you Caroline was in a world of her own. But she's always known where she was going. That's why Tom was being so idiotic to think he mattered."

"From what I hear," observed Martha, "she may get where she wants to go."

"It wouldn't surprise me," said Jill. She ate the last of her salad, took a sip of wine, and looked sharply at Martha, who had barely touched her food.

"We haven't said a word about you. How are things?"

Martha retreated almost visibly. She hated being asked that now, because it meant she had to lie. She preferred impersonal topics, or casual analyses of people she knew, because it allowed her to be dispassionate, as she could not be about herself. She had not seen Mellenkoff for several weeks, and when he called, she felt no familiar rush of excitement, no warm surge of affection. Most of the time, she felt nothing. She carried out her assignments competently and mechanically. She was on the air only occasionally and had reconciled herself to accept she would not be sent abroad. Her only comfort was in the patient devotion of Roger Miller, who shuttled between New York and Washington.

She listened to Roger. Sometimes she watched him with a desperate wistfulness, wondering why she could not accept the caring he displayed and demonstrated. Sometimes he stayed with her, but they rarely made love. Martha had come to remember the first time she had made love with Roger as something to cherish in her mind, a small flicker of comfort when she woke at dawn and looked about the empty room. Now she only wanted him to hold her, so that she could feel the warmth of his body, yet not have to deal with its demands. And he never questioned her about that. He was always there when she needed him, and the irony was that increasingly she needed nothing and nobody. She had taken to sitting for hours at night, looking out at the Washington Monument in the distance and watching the black lace of tree branches against a moonlit sky. Her drinking had dropped, not because of her concern about developing dependence on it, but because she had lost interest in getting drunk.

She was depressed when sober and more depressed when drunk. She also didn't eat much. She couldn't remember the last time she had gone grocery shopping, except for coffee. She had lost so much weight, the news director had suggested she take some vacation and get some sun. She expected she looked like a death's head on camera. She didn't want to go on vacation. She'd been everywhere she wanted to go and done almost everything she'd thought she wanted to do. Now she felt as though she had been driving for a long time along a winding road fringed by flowering hedgerows, where every corner held promise, and at the end of the beautiful road, there was a wasteland where nothing grew, and there was nowhere else to go.

Even Mellenkoff had become a remote figure in her mind, a memory of other times and places. When he did come to Washington, she only got drunk to avoid remembered pain. She had come to despise herself for the extent to which she had allowed herself to become psychologically dependent on Mellenkoff. He had never encouraged that, merely accepted it and made use of it. And he had never pretended with her. He had tried to warn her what and whom she was dealing with, and clearly considered that the extent of his responsibility toward her. It was she who had pretended. She belonged to the breed of women who felt called upon to win the approbation of others, usually that of men, who remained the power figures, in order to feel secure in success. Jill was the new generation, candid in self-appraisal, secure in self-worth, and practical about what she wanted professionally without being obsessed by it. Caroline Mitchell, Martha thought, was closer to the stereotype of the climbing woman dependent on what she looked like and her impact on those she met, rather than the kind of independent intelligence that characterized Jill.

Sitting in the dark, Martha flagellated herself and withdrew into hollow despair. Her mother's letters piled up unanswered and sometimes unread. Everyone seemed distant in her mind, and only Roger Miller pounded at the wall rising around her.

So she drank her wine and smiled at Jill without seeing her and assured her she was fine, just a bit anemic, she lied, hoping to deflect the steady, skeptical gaze.

"I'm sorry," said Jill. "I don't mean to pry."

Martha smiled more naturally.

"I know," she said gently. "And I appreciate your asking. But I'm all right. You know—we all have bad patches. It'll pass."

She insisted on paying for lunch, and on an impulse, took a taxi home after leaving the restaurant. She was suddenly tired. She called in to say she was coming down with something, and Sullivan was unusually sympathetic.

"Take all the time you need. Let us know if you need anything."

Martha hung up and reflected that judging from her recent assignments, they wouldn't miss her if she didn't show up for a year. She sighed and looked around the long room with the rosewood bookcases, fluffy white rugs, and oversized red sofa. She had always loved this room because it cheered her up to look at it. Especially the sofa. She'd had a lot of fun on that sofa, when she thought about it, and her mouth turned up a little at the corners in recollection. She went into the bedroom and opened the closet to find pants and a sweater. Hanging at the back, she saw Mellenkoff's blue velour robe. She touched it and smiled. She'd had a lot of fun with that too. She pulled on a pair of jeans and a sweater and wandered barefoot back into the living room. Curling into a corner of the red sofa, she read a magazine until she realized the words had no meaning because her mind was not focusing. She looked at her watch, and picked up the telephone. Mellenkoff answered his private line on the third ring.

"I've been thinking about you," he said.

"That's nice."

"I was thinking of coming down this weekend."

Martha hesitated.

"James, I don't think so," she said slowly. There was a surprised silence at the other end of the line.

"You have other plans?"

She smiled. It was characteristic of Mellenkoff to assume there could be no reason for rejection except competition.

"No, I don't have other plans. I'm feeling sickie. I'm home as a matter of fact. Feel as if I've got flu."

"Oh. Well, I'm sorry." He had always been uncomfortable with sickness. She could not remember his ever being ill, and he seemed to view it as a weakness that afflicted those who didn't know how to deal with it. She knew she would receive an immense floral arrangement in the morning, sent by his secretary, but there would be no solicitous calls from him until he could talk to her without having to ask how she felt.

"It's nothing serious," she assured him. "What's new with you?"

"Not much really." He mentioned a few comings and goings by people she knew in New York. They did not speak of Martha's job. There no longer was anything to say about it. Idly, she mentioned her lunch with Jill Roberts and asked, "What's happening with your protégée, Mitchell?"

There was a pause.

"I'm transferring her to New York," he said.

Martha was silent.

"She'll be a correspondent. Do some cut-ins on the morning show, some weekend anchor stuff."

"She's going to be busy."

"She's been busy. She's been working her tail off in Chicago."

Martha smiled. "I hear she's done well there."

His voice lifted suddenly. "Well, that's what I think. Hell of an improvement. Even Gale has stopped bitching, and Mayer says she's improved out of all recognition. Very professional."

"I'm glad for her," said Martha.

"You should be glad for me too," said Mellenkoff. "I've got a lot riding on her."

Martha said, "But she's doing what you want her to do, isn't she?"

"Martha, don't start analyzing the situation. Mitchell's one hell of an ambitious woman. She wants this very badly."

Not as badly as you do, she thought, but did not say it.

"I wasn't analyzing, James," she said quietly. "I was warning you."

He was incredulous. "Warning me?"

"Be very sure she can do what you've told her she can do. You aren't going to be the one sitting there on camera."

"How's that a warning?"

"You're going to make her news anchor, aren't you?"

"Well, I didn't say that—"

She interrupted him. "That's what you've always had in mind, practically since the first time you saw her. But how much do you know about what's inside her head?"

He was irritable now. "I don't need to know what's in her head, for Christ's sake. All I need to be sure of is that there is something in her head. And let me tell you, she can outperform people you'd never believe."

"In terms of personality, that's probably true. She's got incredible charisma on the air. But what you want her to do isn't soft stuff. If she were going to be an anchor bunny burbling through interviews on the morning show, I'd say you were on a real winner. I mean, she isn't the type to ask a hijacker to hug a hostage. But she still doesn't have much to fall back on in the way of solid experience."

The pause that followed was thoughtful.

"She's been pushed along, I grant you," he acknowledged. "But she's come along faster and farther than I ever thought she would. I tell you, Martha, she's going to be all right. And she is absolute magic in market research. They say audience reaction to her is phenomenal. Viewers love her."

"I can never remember—" said Martha, "is it good or bad if the audience's palms get sweaty over an anchor? I remember the time you told me I was getting the reverse of favorable reaction along those esoteric lines."

"That isn't used anymore," said Mellenkoff impatiently. "And anyway, Mitchell goes beyond that kind of stuff. Gale told Mayer she was really pulling her weight now. We've been using her as a co-anchor on the six and eleven shows the past few weeks. Reports were excellent, and the reviewers have been very favorable."

"You mean they aren't saying 'She's gorgeous but . . .'?"

"They're saying she's competent and gorgeous. I know what you're saying. The priorities with her are in the right order.

"Listen," he went on, "I'll bet you a dinner that ratings will be up within three months of her taking over."

"I assume you have agreement with Eliass on all this?" Martha inquired.

"Not exactly. He's said he'll leave it up to my judgment."

"And God help both of you if she fails."

"She isn't going to fail. You don't have any confidence in me anymore, do you?" He sounded almost plaintive.

"I have a great deal of confidence in you, James, obviously. I mean, you made me what I am today."

She could hear her words falling, plummeting into the silence that followed.

"At least you can derive comfort from holding me responsible," he said in a clipped, cool voice.

Martha sighed. "Sorry. Age and sickness must be sharpening my tongue. Listen, you know I don't want her to fail. Or you. You do know that, James?"

"I suppose so. And you don't need to remind me I'm taking a risk. I've always taken risks."

"I know you have." She was tired and her voice was soft and slow.

"And I wish you luck with this one."

"You obviously think I'll need it." His voice was harsh.

Martha looked out at the darkening sky. "Yes," she said. "I think you may."

39

THEY GAVE a party for Caroline when she left JRZ in Chicago to go to New York, partly because they were glad she was leaving and partly because they had come to like her. She was still the center of a rumor mill that thrived on speculation about her relationship with Mellenkoff, her relationship with Eliass (somebody had seen her shake hands with him at a reception), her chances of becoming a national anchor, how many people she was sleeping with and why, the mistakes she had made on air in the past, and the likelihood of how she would screw up in the future. Listening to the latest Mitchell gossip one day, John Mayer, the general manager, observed cynically, "If there hadn't been a Caroline, we'd have had to invent her."

"We did invent her," said Milt Crosby, the news director, whose reaction to evidence of Mellenkoff's cloak around Caroline's shoulders, had been to assign her to stories where it was unlikely she would find herself in trouble. Crosby was a highly competent pragmatist who took the position that if he had to deal with what he considered a professional aberration on the part of the president of television news at WNN, then he would do it at the smallest possible cost to himself. He had no intention of allowing Caroline the opportunity to embarrass the station and himself because she was not qualified for the kind of assignment that would have been appropriate for someone on her way to the top. Given the independence to move Caroline as he would have liked, Crosby would have left her on a talk show, or emphasized her interviewing skill, for which he had considerable respect. Beyond those areas, he believed she was often out of her depth, although he gave her credit for an enormous effort at self-improvement.

Crosby, who had been around a long time and had seen relationships such as that of Mitchell and Mellenkoff bud, bloom, and fade at a dizzying pace, suspected that she lived in terror of the disapproval of her mentor, and probably led a much duller existence than any of her colleagues thought. He was right, in that Caroline had taken to heart Mellenkoff's lecture and had devoted herself to what he had made plain was his blueprint for her future. Her personal life was almost nonexistent, which was fortunate, because she often worked seven days a week, and not even Gil Tadich, who was still wary of her, could say she had ever complained about being called in. She contributed the brief reports called cut-ins to the morning shows, did reporting on stories about female unemployment, missing children, the homeless, and local politics, and was news anchor on weekends. In between, she took Mellenkoff's advice and read. She subscribed to the Chicago newspapers, the *New York Times,* the *Washington Post,* the *Wall Street Journal,* and the news magazines. She found another role for Caroline in the mirror. She had always read to herself in the mirror to see how she looked reading. Now she read aloud to herself in the mirror so that she might be more likely to remember what she was reading. She kept a boxful of clippings of major stories and reread them in the hope that she would retain their content. And she was getting better at keeping things straight, although strange pronunciations and stories about crises in the Middle East still made her stomach churn. Some of the best or worst Mitchell stories from her early days on JRZ were of those occasions when she muddled nations, regions, and names.

"At least she doesn't burst into tears," Crosby observed once when he could think of nothing better to say about her. Caroline had heard him, and the wry thought crossed her mind that she had her father to thank for that. She rarely heard from Mellenkoff, and when she did, she dreaded it, because it was usually in response to complaints about her. The last time he called, however, she had been puzzled, because even Crosby had given her his terse nod of approval once or twice, and the postshow critiques were no longer devoted to her failings. She was as much astonished as pleased when Mellenkoff said he had called to tell her he thought her work was improving. It was about time, he added, lest the unaccustomed praise permit her any illusions, and she still had a long way to go. But she seemed to be making progress. She had thanked him and he had hung up. She had nothing else to say to him. He had always done the talking, always given the orders. She permitted herself a smile when she heard the rumors that she was sleeping with Mellenkoff. Caroline wasn't sleeping with anybody. The old barriers had gone up after her unfortunate and brief affair with Tom Roberts, who now treated her with the deference due a colleague who may have the ear of the man at the top. Sometimes she missed Mike Hathaway, because he had cuddled her and let her chatter. But she never invited anyone into her apartment.

Nearly all of her time was devoted to becoming what Mellenkoff wanted. In addition to her homework, she had discussions with the station's experts on hair and clothes, and she read letters from readers who wanted to know everything from why she didn't smile more to why she didn't smile less, why she didn't wear her hair shorter, and why she didn't wear more blue. Why had she looked so supercilious when she was talking about the new ruling on abortion, how could she possibly have mispronounced Himalayas, and why was she in a man's job? She even read letters from her parents, who wrote once or twice a month to say they had seen her on television, and why was she so thin? She rarely replied to those letters, although she had endeared herself to Glory Swimmers by sending her a letter full of nostalgic references to Glayville, enclosing a signed color photograph. Glory ran the picture on the front page, along with most of the letter, and told several of her dearest friends that Caroline was still the same sweet girl she had always been, and she sometimes wondered just what was behind her being estranged from her parents. It might not, implied Glory, be all Caroline's fault. She gave the impression she was in Caroline's confidence, and the *Gazette* sold out that week.

When Caroline was told she was being transferred to WNN in New York to work as a correspondent and weekend anchor, she was pleased, but she was not transported with joy as she once would have been. She occasionally had dreams in which she was always running and never reached her destination. Like a mouse on a wheel, she thought. She had said that once to Martha Vogel, whom she still called occasionally because Martha had always been kind.

Martha had laughed a little, but she had been sympathetic.

"Don't let them eat you alive," she told Caroline.

"I just have such a lot to learn. And I'm not as good at it as you," said Caroline in a tone of total sincerity.

"You seem to be doing very well at a tremendous speed," observed Martha, and thought she heard Caroline sigh.

Caroline could hardly complain that she had been plucked out of obscurity and set on the path to stardom, but she increasingly felt that her days spun by, out of her control. The people she worked with were friendly, sometimes effusive, especially the executive producer, who was desperate to get to New York and thought Mitchell might be the bandwagon to jump on. But she had no friends, especially because she could hardly call Jill anymore. All she had was Caroline in the mirror, more glamorous than ever, and full of confidence, especially when she became Caroline on camera. Somewhere, another Caroline cowered in the grip of an old terror, but as long as Caroline in the mirror was there, she was safe.

It was a very nice farewell party, with champagne and hors d'oeuvres and compliments, and Caroline did not hear Crosby and Mayer agreeing they'd been lucky to get off so lightly with her.

"It could have been a lot worse," said Mayer, who knew Mellenkoff well enough to have sympathy for anyone caught up in the fierce embrace of his ambition.

"It would have been a lot worse if we hadn't been careful," said Crosby, who was on his third glass of champagne.

"I put a lot of work into her. I hope she appreciated it," he added.

"You protected your own ass with her," said Mayer tartly, and Crosby grinned.

"You really think Mellenkoff's going to go all the way with her?" he asked.

Mayer shook his head.

"God knows. He's got the worst case of tunnel vision I know sometimes. Always had. But I hear there've been blowups in New York already over the idea. Heard Eliass wanted them to go after Jennings."

"Was he interested?"

"Hard to tell. Mellenkoff's playing the hardest ball anybody's seen him play, from what floats out here. And I'm damned if I know why."

Crosby nodded. "He's not screwing her, apparently."

"Hell no. That's not his style. He thinks he's objective about his work, but he gets blinded by his own visions of himself. She's just a little pawn. She's scared stiff of him."

"Well. They can dig their own way out of their hole," said Crosby callously. "This business can do without the goddamned star system."

They looked across the room to where Caroline, radiant in red velvet, was holding an untouched glass of champagne and smiling on her retinue of admirers, most of whom wanted to do what she was doing, as soon as she proved to be the disaster everybody said she·would be.

"I feel sort of sorry for her," said Mayer.

Crosby accepted another glass of champagne from a passing waiter and shrugged.

"I suppose so. But she doesn't have to do it, does she? I mean, she's got to know her own strengths and weaknesses. She's no fool."

"Yeah, but she's still pretty young, and looking like that can be a handicap in this business. I mean, people assume you're an airhead, which she isn't. But she's no brain, either. Best thing she'll probably ever do was that memorial show for Josh. She's got a feel for that kind of thing. Funny thing is the market research doesn't show audiences question her credibility, and that's where she seems weakest to me."

"Tell me about it," said Crosby.

"Going to be interesting to see how much blood's on the floor in New York," said Mayer.

There was considerable blood on the thickly carpeted floors of the WNN offices in New York a few weeks later, when James Mellenkoff defended his proposal that Caroline Mitchell be considered as a national anchor. He already had fought his battle with Joel Eliass, and felt he had won it. Eliass conceded that Mitchell's progress had been spectacular, that market research on her had remained remarkable even during periods when she was clearly having difficulties, and that she might indeed have the potential to light up the screens of viewers.

"I still think she is lacking in experience, James," he said in his ice cube voice.

"What she has, she can't be taught. The rest of it, she's learned. You've seen the tapes—a whole range of them over the past few years. Believe me, she's the real thing. We're sitting up top of the biggest star since Cronkite," Mellenkoff told him fervently.

Eliass contemplated him gravely. "You realize that this young woman is your responsibility, professionally speaking, James," he said.

Mellenkoff looked the chairman in the eye, and nodded.

Eliass raised his pale eyebrows slightly. "Why are you so sure about her?" he inquired.

"I just know. I've watched her. I mean, I've had worries about her, but she's come through. She's done it herself. And you can't deny the audience surveys—fantastic."

"It is true that market research shows her to be, ah— quite outstanding," admitted Eliass. "I still say you are taking a risk with her. I may be wrong, James, and I shall be the first to congratulate you if I am. But I see a risk."

"I'll take it," said Mellenkoff, "if I have you behind me."

Eliass smiled. Without him, Mellenkoff could take no risks, and Mellenkoff knew it.

"I shall not stand in your way in this matter," said the chairman, "but I still have reservations. And as I understand it, I am not alone in that."

That was an understatement. Rumblings had risen from the ranks about the prospect that Caroline Mitchell might become the first woman news anchor in the business. The general feeling seemed to be that she should become co-anchor of the morning show, following in a lengthening line of those who excelled in what was referred to as "fluff talk."

Roger Miller was one of the few who dared challenge Mellenkoff, reiterating Eliass's warnings, and hinting that some resignations might even be forthcoming in the wake of such a gigantic promotion for Mitchell.

"Why are you doing this?" Miller asked wearily. Mellenkoff looked resentfully at the Texan's large feet planted on the end of his white linen sofa and said he couldn't understand what all the uproar was about.

"It is not the first time in this business," he observed, "that talent has been recognized in the place of experience. Why is everyone so reluctant to accept my judgment? I've been proved right before."

Miller groaned. "It wouldn't be the first time in this business either that somebody like you became stuck in cement about something, James. Can't you see people are concerned about WNN? It's not just a question of Mitchell. Granted she's damn near unbeatable when it comes to using a camera to build a relationship with the viewers. But you're putting her out there on her own, with no backup."

"Because I think she can do it," said Mellenkoff patiently. "I tried her out in Chicago, built her up. She learned. Hell, she made all the mistakes in the book. But they'll tell you there, Mayer and Crosby—Crosby complained like hell for the first few months—they'll tell you how she learned. She's a natural."

"Because you say so."

"Because I say so," said Mellenkoff.

Miller took his feet off the white sofa, leaving gray smudges, and loped to the door.

"I'm surprised you aren't telling me not to say you didn't warn me," said Mellenkoff.

Miller shook his head. "You're missing the point, James."

As the door closed behind him, Mellenkoff leaned his head back on his black leather chair and closed his eyes. He was sure. He had to be sure. It was a gamble. He had reached where he was by gambling, taking risks. And he had proved himself loyal to Eliass. The chairman owed him some allegiance. Hell, he had even married the man's niece as a favor. He sighed at the prospect of going home to a house now awash in photographic equipment, with the downstairs bathroom turned into a darkroom.

He hoped the photographic craze Sally seemed to be going through would be cheaper than her shopping expeditions with her Aunt Julia. At least she was more cheerful, although she seemed to have stopped going to the hairdresser, and her wardrobe consisted of blue jeans and shirts. Maybe she was taking pictures of her Aunt Julia. Eliass would like that.

Mellenkoff felt tired. He wished he could go home and talk to Martha. She might not be entirely sympathetic, but she would understand, and in the end, she would comfort him. She hadn't sounded too good these past months; of course, she'd had flu or something the last time they had talked, when she'd been a bit waspish. He missed Martha. She was the only woman he had ever cared about enough to call back when he couldn't reach her. She was the only woman he had ever cared about. And she seemed to be vegetating, professionally speaking. But Martha would snap back. Martha was a professional. Martha was a survivor.

40

THERE WAS only darkness around her now, as she sat at the arched window in the living room. She could see rain on the glass, and her eyes followed the trickling droplets, but beyond was a moonless blackness. The trees, which made the view green and graceful by day, were merged into the somber mass. She looked into it as through a tunnel, and even when she closed her eyes there was before her the garish rerun of tragedy translated into personal disaster. Again and again she relived her misery. She had been seated at the horseshoe-shaped desk in the studio, framed by the familiar blue backdrop, in the midst of a routine news broadcast, when it had begun. It had been a quiet news day, and the voice of her executive producer, attached to her like an aural umbilical cord via her tiny earpiece, had barely interrupted her with changes in the scheduling or content of the stories neatly stacked before her. She had been relaxed, almost happy. She had been in the anchor spot for almost three months, and that morning, Mellenkoff had told her there was a perceptive upward movement in the ratings. She knew how worried he had been, knew how worried she had been. Everybody had been worried, except those who had licked their chops and waited for her to fall on her face.

"Disappoint them," Mellenkoff had challenged her.

And she had. The television reviewers, who had been part of the doomsday chorus united in pessimism over her "shallow background . . . lack of credibility . . . lack of experience behind the pretty face" had gradually given her grudgingly fair grades. She was better than they had expected, they conceded. Market research, that vital gauge of the decline and fall of dreams and fantasies, had stayed on her side, as it had from the beginning.

People out there, from Boston to Kansas to California, liked her. There was a percentage that would have preferred her to be a man. Some complained they didn't like the news read by somebody who might have been their daughter. But the majority handed down the verdict that she handled herself well, seemed to understand what she was talking about, even if they suspected she didn't write it herself. She didn't "act condescending," and didn't ask dumb questions. She saw the reaction as a public acknowledgment of her private effort. Her homework was more intensive than ever. Her readings to Caroline in the mirror had become lectures, at the end of which, she questioned herself. Every morning, she snatched up the bundle of newspapers delivered to the door of her apartment and read them with a concentration that would have astounded her childhood teachers. She marked in red ink, took notes, studied names and places, familiarizing herself so that she could confront the still dubious faces at the morning meeting and be able to comment knowledgeably on what was going on at home and abroad. She had even begun to offer an occasional opinion, her eyes scanning the faces for reactions of approval or scorn. She saw Mellenkoff only occasionally, unless he called her to his office, and she had to admit he had been supportive, even considerate. Her opponents had been left in no doubt that this was his choice and they could live with it or leave. Once he had told her that Joel Eliass had commented favorably on her performance, and she had seen her own relief mirrored in the blue ice of his eyes.

She knew they were being careful with her. She went over stories written for her to read, and then the senior producer went over them again, she supposed to make sure she hadn't changed them. She was heavily briefed by correspondents for the White House, the State Department, the Pentagon, and any other government agencies involved in the day's news. Now and again, she sensed a growing protectiveness, as though even those who had opposed her were increasingly willing to see she got a fair chance, even to prevent her from failing. Like Roger

Miller, who had been as curtly courtly as only a South-
erner could be when he first met her. She had felt his
eyes on her, felt him assessing her during those tense first
weeks, and one day, he invited her to have a cup of
coffee. She had been unreasonably pleased, as she sat
with him in the executive dining room, knowing that
somehow, she had done something right. She liked Miller,
who had a reputation for toughness and decency, a rare
combination in the business he had chosen.

When she asked for milk instead of coffee, he had
grinned.

"You don't look like you need anything to make you
more tense, Caroline," he observed.

"I drink warm milk at night," she confided. "With a
splash of Scotch."

"I'd need more than a splash," said Miller. "I'd drink
Scotch with a splash of milk if I were you."

"I don't imagine you'd want to be me," Caroline said
with a faint edge of bitterness.

Miller's look was not unkindly. "Frankly, no, I wouldn't,
honey, and I'm not calling you honey to be condescending. Always seemed a friendly kind of word to me, if it's
used in the proper sense, that is."

She laughed. "Doesn't bother me a bit. I can use all
the friendly words I can get."

He nodded. "Expect you can, at that. But you're beginning to settle in, aren't you? Feeling a little less like a
chicken in a fox coop?"

Caroline began to relax a little. She wished Mellenkoff
were like Miller, but if he had been, she wouldn't have
been sitting where she was, she was sure of that.

"People have been very helpful," she said carefully.
Miller laughed heartily.

"Hell they have," he said. "But you're bearing up
pretty well. Hang in there. That's not an easy job. Ask
Rather or Jennings."

"I don't really know them well enough."

"They might be more helpful than you'd expect. They
know what you're dealing with. Now whether you're up
to dealing with it, that's up to you. But they're in the
same boat in that respect."

She smiled at him tentatively. "It was nice of you to
ask me for coffee."

"We'll do it again."

And they had. She had even begun to ask his advice occasionally, and he gave it without making her feel a fool for asking. Sometimes she had the feeling he was sorry for her. She didn't care, as long as he would help her if she needed it. She tried not to make any enemies, recalling her problems in Chicago. She walked the finest line she could, working as hard as she could, paying grim attention to what she was told, listening to all advice, even if she had reached a point of self-confidence when she didn't always take it. When she was off, she collapsed into an exhausted sleep, and when she got up, she went back to her reading, in case she'd missed something she would be expected to know. She accepted few social engagements, preferring to go to dinner parties where the guest list included high government officials or diplomats who might be of use to her. She was pleased when Martha Vogel sent her flowers and a warm little note. But she was delighted when she received a letter from Jill Starling Roberts, congratulating her, and observing, "I never thought you could do it, to be candid." Caroline called her to thank her, urged her to visit her in New York. Jill thought later that she sounded almost pathetically grateful, which was certainly unlike the Caroline she used to know. Yet Caroline was too busy to be lonely, too remote to realize her isolation. All she desired was to be successful in the job she had always wanted.

And it had been going fairly well. Even Mellenkoff said so. Until sixteen minutes after seven on the rainy evening of November tenth, when the voice in her earpiece abruptly warned her to be prepared to break into the broadcast with a bulletin bearing the first report that the President had been shot. Her mouth had gone dry and her stomach had clenched, but she'd told herself it was normal to be nervous. She just had to stay in control. And she'd always prided herself on being in control. She had done the bulletin, tried to look attentive and composed and reliable as the senior producer, Jay Klinger, told her she would have to wing it, ad lib, until more solid material came in from the remotes, the correspondents and crews in the field. She'd been glad it was Martha who would be doing live shots from the hotel where it had happened. She had more faith in Martha than she had in herself. She'd tried not to think about Mellenkoff at all, but as she sat down at her desk, feeling uncomfortably naked without her prepared script, she could almost feel his eyes on her. For the first few minutes, she'd repeated what she didn't know, read improvised accounts of what the President had been doing that day, what he'd been doing in the hotel. She'd been tense, but she had looked tranquil. It was when the pace began to pick up that her mind had begun to spin. She'd never been able to keep facts in order unless they were tidily arrayed before her in print. Wire-service copy appeared before her, carefully highlighted to guide her on what to read, what to leave out. She'd managed that. But she had been grateful when the voice in her ear said, "Throw to Vogel live."

"We go now to Martha Vogel, who is at the scene in Washington, at the hotel in Washington where the President was attending a private reception when he was shot. Martha," she said.

Martha was magnificent, which didn't surprise Caroline. She delivered a vivid, smoothly phrased account of what she had seen: the blank-faced young man who had come out of shadows and rain to kill the President, the dark wet street, the President's blood trickling into the gutter, the agents suddenly bristling with guns, the tears on the face of the White House press secretary as he bent over the dying Chief Executive, the smile of the President, frozen by bullets, the sense of despair among those who watched, the feeling of hopelessness. It was all there, and Caroline watched Martha on the monitor with admiration. Even when Martha finished speaking, Caroline was still watching her, until she was jarred back to the reality of her situation by the voice in her ear.

"Read your copy," it hissed. The sheets of paper in front of her were piling up. She fumbled through them, fighting back confusion. The voice went on buzzing insistently in her ear.

"AP has a report that an agent may have been injured."

"UPI says the killer was chanting when they took him away. Rumor he was a member of a West Coast cult."

"We've got Tom Potter standing by at the hospital. He's got a live interview with one of the doctors."

"Graham will be doing a piece on the First Lady."

"Colter's got the Vice-President's press secretary. Stand by to throw to Jameson."

"Fill, Caroline, fill. Stay cool. You'll be okay."

She couldn't remember when she lost control. But she could hear her voice rising and see her hands begin to shake as she shuffled the frighteningly meaningless papers in front of her, and she knew her eyes had to be like saucers.

A producer who had materialized at the horseshoe-shaped desk, out of camera range but close enough to talk to her when she was not on camera, was looking at her with horrified eyes.

"Talk," said the voice in her ear with desperate patience. "Please, Caroline, talk. You're all right. Just keep cool. Read what's in front of you. Listen to what I tell you. Just listen. And TALK!"

She talked, or rather, she babbled.

"The assassin of the President has been taken to—"

The voice rose to a yelp. "*Alleged* assassin! Alleged!" Alleged!"

"The alleged assassin of the President . . ." she began again; hopelessly she stared at the words in front of her for help—"has been identified as Joseph Warton, a former member of the American Nazi party, who has a record of criminal convictions. He belonged to a survivalist cult in California—"

The voice came to life again. "Qualify, for God's sake. 'Was *reported* to be a member, *reported* to have convictions, *reported* to belong to.' You're convicting him. Qualify."

She knew that. That was one of the things that had been hammered into her head. Convict somebody on camera and you've got a million-dollar libel suit. Hedge. Qualify. Back off. She peppered her sentences with "alleged" and "waiting to confirms" but she wasn't sure she was making sense, and the expression of the producer a few feet away suggested her fears were well grounded.

When she confused the Vice-President with Carl Olson, the White House press secretary, and talked through a comment from the First Lady, the voice became wild.

When she was told to throw to Vogel again, Caroline suspected it was a desperate effort to let her regain composure. Martha had more eyewitness reports from the assassination scene, as well as an interview with the real Carl Olson, and Caroline contemplated the monitor with speechless gratitude. She wished Martha were beside her.

"Talk to her!" howled the voice as Martha waited patiently for Caroline to respond to a question.

"Caroline? I think we're having trouble with our connection," she said in that warm, reassuring voice.

"I—ah—I wondered if—did Carl Olson see—know the—the killer?"

Even Martha looked briefly startled, and there was a moaning sound on Caroline's earpiece. Martha at once proceeded with an interview with a White House assistant who had been behind the President when the fatal shots were fired. He told how he had felt a bullet fly by his head, heard the President's gasped exclamation, seen him crumple, knelt by him. He had heard no last words.

"Thank you, Martha," said Caroline unsteadily, and looked down blindly at the papers in front of her.

"Throw live to Potter at the hospital," said the voice.

"Now we go to the hospital where the President's body was taken—where, I—where the President was pronounced dead. The President's doctor is standing by—"

"It's one of the hospital staff," snarled the voice.

Caroline gulped. "I—I mean we're now going live to Tom Potter at the hospital. Tom?"

She hoped the connection would not break, that the monitor would not be obscured by communications "snow," which would mean she was left alone with her nightmare. She felt sick. She watched Potter speaking quietly, almost casually, gazing confidently at the camera, and grasped the papers in front of her so hard that she felt them tear in her hand. The senior producer took the opportunity when she was off camera to grasp her wrist.

"Caroline, get a grip on yourself. Take a sip of water. Just listen and read. Take a deep breath. You know what to do. You've done all this before."

His voice and the warmth of his hand on her wrist were meant to be reassuring, but nothing could stem the tide of terror now flooding through her. She looked at his anxious face and wondered if an anchor had ever thrown up on camera. The words on the script in front of her were blurring, and she knew several million viewers— half the world—were watching her hands shake. She realized Potter had disappeared from the monitor, and the relentless voice in her ear was adjuring her to talk, to read. She focused, with a desperate effort, on a script with sentences carefully highlighted for her attention.

"We have a report that the mother of the young man who killed the President—"

"*Allegedly* killed! *Allegedly* killed! Jeeeezus!" wailed the voice on a level of one pushed past endurance.

"—who allegedly killed the President has tried to commit suicide."

She saw the senior producer holding up a piece of paper on which he had printed QUALIFY.

"We are checking out this report and will get back to you as soon as we have more information."

There was a steady stream of reports from the White House correspondent, the State Department correspondent, and more from Martha Vogel, who appeared as indefatigable as she was unruffled. Caroline put her hand to her forehead and found her skin wet with perspiration. And still the voice brayed in her ear.

"Read! Talk! Listen! Read! Talk! Listen!"

Her voice was shaking so badly she could hardly talk now. Another correspondent, the weekend anchor, appeared beside her abruptly. He looked at her with disbelief, and to her horror, she felt her eyes fill with tears. She never cried. She hadn't cried since she was five years old. She couldn't cry now. But she felt tears spill down her cheeks, and she said abruptly, "I—I'm sorry."

Two minutes later, there was a station break and the senior producer took her by the arm.

"Caroline, let's get you a cup of coffee."

She stared at him, half resisting, but his grasp was firm. She was led, supported by his arm, to her office, planted in a chair, and left there.

She didn't know how long she sat there, her head on her desk, sobbing quietly. No one came near her. She could hear people rushing about, worried, excited voices, but she was not part of it any longer. Perhaps she never had been part of it. Perhaps she had seen it all in a mirror. Cocooned in misery, she waited until the traffic past her door seemed to have slackened. She looked at her watch, and it was three in the morning. She must have slept, fainted—she didn't know, didn't care. She crept out of the office, peering nervously up and down the corridor, pulling up the collar of her coat, finding a scarf in the pocket and wrapping it around her head, and somehow she reached the elevator and the rear entrance.

"I need a taxi," she told the security guard in a muffled voice, and after a curious glance, he called one for her. She stood leaning against a wall until it arrived, her eyes half closed. If she could only reach her apartment, and be somewhere dark and quiet, where there were no voices at all. The taxi driver wanted to talk about the assassination, but he didn't care if his audience responded, although he did glance around once and ask if she knew the President had been shot.

"Yes," she said.

At the apartment, she did not go to bed. She took off her clothes, the damp, bedraggled silk blouse, the creased skirt. She bathed and changed, and drank four cups of coffee. She knew she had to go back to the studio at least once more. She had to face Mellenkoff, had to have confirmed what she already knew. She telephoned him, left messages, knowing he wouldn't return her calls. She felt as though she were dead. She sat beside the silent telephone until she looked out of the window and saw a pale gray morning. Even the trees looked gray. She put on her raincoat and tried to brush her hair without looking in the mirror. She was afraid there would be no one there. The doorman hailed her a taxi and she went back to the studio, staring sightlessly in front of her. She did not know why she had to see Mellenkoff. She only knew she must. She had to play out the farce, she thought suddenly. And she saw him, brushing past Betsy Cooley. And once she had confronted him, reading in Mellenkoff's eyes that she no longer existed, she walked out of the studio, oblivious to the murmurs and glances through which she walked. Roger Miller was the only person who tried to talk to her. He touched her arm, and she looked at him as if she'd never seen him before.

"Caroline? Are you—do you need anything?"

She shook her head. "I'm going home."

"Can I—get you a car?"

"No, thank you."

She turned and walked away, and he stood staring after her, disturbed by the vacant look in her eyes, the flat, toneless voice. She looked like a different person, he thought, maybe he ought to . . . but he was too busy to think about Caroline Mitchell then. He'd call her later. He was damned sure Mellenkoff wouldn't call her. But somebody should make sure she was at least alive. Suddenly he shivered.

Back in her apartment, Caroline sat down by the window, unsure she would ever get up again. She couldn't remember feeling so tired, so overwhelmed by numbness. But there was silence, and she was grateful for that. She sat there all day, gazing out of the window, watching the gray day dissolve into the ashes of a bleak evening. The telephone did not ring. It might never ring again, and she didn't care. Her mind wandered, roamed, and suddenly she thought of Glory Swimmers. Poor Glory; what would she put in the *Glayville Gazette* now that Caroline had failed her? Caroline's pale lips twisted. Perhaps she should call and explain she was ill. Nobody would believe it anywhere but in Glayville. She supposed she should write to her mother, tell her the same fragile lie. Or call her. That might be easier. She couldn't talk to anyone who would know what had happened. It had to be someone she could pretend to, because she couldn't talk about what had happened yet. She might never be able to talk about it, no matter where she went, and she didn't know where she would go. She'd think about that later. She picked up the telephone and dialed her parents' number. Her father answered the telephone on the sixth ring, and his voice had a familiar, aching tension.

"Daddy? This is Caroline."

There was a pause. She supposed he was surprised. She almost never called, except at Christmas.

"Yes?" he said with an odd harshness.

"I . . . thought you might be worried. You and Mother. I mean, I guess I . . . got sick on the air last night. Sort of a mess. I just wanted you to know—"

"You'd better tell your mother." He cut into her faltering words. "You seem to have talked a lot to your mother."

Caroline frowned. She heard him shouting her mother's name, over and over again. There was a long silence, then she heard his voice again.

"She doesn't want to talk to you. She doesn't want to talk to either of us, I gather. She's doing all the talking now, Caroline. Since last night, when you screwed up on television, she's never stopped talking. All my fault, she says. All because I screwed the little bitch. That's what she said, Caroline. She's going to turn me in now. For raping you, she says. You hear that? But you told her, didn't you? You told her. You betrayed me. And now she's going to send me to jail. Me and all the other perverts, she says. You hear what I'm saying, Caroline? You hear me?"

He was drunk and he was frightened. She could hear the fear seeping through his voice. She didn't care about that. What she did care about was that her mother must have known. Known the secret all along. Known what Carlton was doing to Caroline. Known what was happening in the lovely peach and ivory room. Known Caroline was being tortured. Known and done nothing at all. Stayed in the kitchen and eaten her way through the refrigerator.

Caroline looked dully at the babbling telephone. Halfway to replacing the receiver, she stopped herself, and put it to her mouth again.

"You listen to me," she said in a voice so cold and lifeless that her father whined into silence. "Tell her she's worse than you. Tell her I'll never have anything to do with either of you again as long as I live. Tell her I hate her more than I hated you. You don't have a daughter anymore. You never had a daughter."

She hung up, quietly. She sat there until she could control the shaking in her legs enough to stand up, then she walked slowly into the bedroom. She looked around the room until her eye fell on the brass lantern clock which sat beside her bed. It had been a farewell gift from the staff at KRT in Columbus, and she treasured it. She picked it up, and moved to the vanity, now a burnished tortoiseshell, with the mirror shining above it. She did not look into the mirror because she was afraid of what she would see there. She took a step back and with all her strength, hurled the clock at the mirror. It did not make as much noise as she had expected. The glass cracked and splintered, and when she finally looked at the broken mirror, she could see only fragments of herself.

41

FLOWERS WERE the first thing she saw, dark red roses, pale pink azaleas, a scarlet poinsettia in a green pot, brilliant yellow chrysanthemums. They came into bright but blurred focus, their colors in sharp contrast to the pale yellow wash of the walls. She blinked, and felt a movement close to her.

"It's about time," said Roger Miller,

Martha looked at the tired, leathery face, which still wore its customary sardonic grin.

"Checking up on me again," she said, and was surprised when her voice emerged as a muffled croak.

"We needed a good second-day story," he said, and abruptly took her hand and held it so tightly that her fingers hurt. He looked behind him, and Martha saw a white-coated stranger.

"Hello there," said the stranger, "I'm Doctor Louis. Glad you decided to wake up. Lot of people been worried about you. Especially Mr. Miller here."

He moved over to the side of the bed and Roger stepped back while Louis checked Martha's pulse, temperature, and heartbeat and peered into her eyes.

"You seem to be in pretty good shape, considering," he observed. "How d'you feel?"

"Not bad, probably better than I've any right to expect." She sat up a little. "I'm thirsty."

"She's fine," said Roger's voice from the corner. The doctor smiled faintly.

"We'll get you some orange juice."

"Can I go home? I'm afraid I've caused a lot of trouble," said Martha apologetically.

"We'll see." Louis smiled briefly at her and ambled out. He nodded to Roger on the way, but Miller didn't notice him leave. Sitting awkwardly on the straight chair beside the bed, Roger took her hand again, and this time her fingers curled around his.

"How do you feel?" he asked.

"Surprisingly cheerful," said Martha. She raised her other hand and touched his cheek. "A lot better than when I last wrote to you."

His eyes darkened. "That was about the worst moment you've ever given me, Vogel. I was mad enough to wring your neck."

She grinned, and she looked like the old Martha, but he wasn't sure, and he knew they were both hiding behind their usual badinage.

Martha lay and looked at him for a little while, then she smiled.

"At least it had a nice ending, didn't it?" she asked softly.

"What had? The letter—or things in general?" His voice was cautious.

"I meant the letter to have a nice ending. But I'm beginning to be sort of glad about how everything turned out."

"Are you?"

She heard the tension in his voice and held her arms out to him.

"Dear Roger," she said against his cheek. "You were the only reason I didn't want to die, or that was the way I saw it. Now I don't see it the same."

"How do you see it now? Or would you rather not talk about it for a while?"

"It's okay. I'd just had it with myself, I guess. I didn't find life at the bottom of the well much fun."

"I'd have sent down a bucket, if I'd known."

"You did know. And you tried. You were all that kept me going, most of the time."

"And now?"

"Now I'm back. All right, so I'm not exactly fine. But I'm not sorry I'm alive, if that's what's worrying you. And it was wonderful to wake up and find you here, grumbling away as usual."

"Get used to it."

Martha's eyebrows rose, but her eyes were bright. "How do we work that out?"

"I haven't figured out the details, but we will. Okay?"

She nodded, and her arms tightened around his neck for a moment.

A nurse arrived with a tray on which sat a glass of orange juice and another vase of flowers.

"The doctor said you wanted something to drink," she said cheerfully.

Martha drank the juice eagerly, and peered around the small, flower-filled room.

"The place looks like a greenhouse," she observed.

"You have a lot of messages too," the nurse told her. "I'll bring them in."

As she left, Martha looked warily at Roger.

"What's officially wrong with me?"

"Collapse. Exhaustion. Terminal bad temper? Labor pains? Take your pick."

"Fooling nobody, no doubt."

"Fooling nobody you'd care about. Your mother's here, by the way.

Martha lay back and closed her eyes. "Oh God. She's come to take care of her little girl. Now what'll I do? She'll move in with me and bake cookies."

"Tell her your doctor said you needed total quiet and a lot of sun. I'll make reservations for the Bahamas."

"She'll go with me."

"I shall make clear to her, in as courteous a manner as possible, that three remains a crowd, ma'am."

The dimple deepened in Martha's chin. "You mean you'd prefer the two of us."

He bowed. "If that's agreeable to you."

"That's agreeable to me. When do we leave?"

"We could charter an air ambulance, but short of that, let's get you out of here as soon as they'll let you, and we'll try to get out of town at the end of the week. That give you time to pack?"

"What about the office?"

"I doubt that'll be a problem. Incidentally, what went out on the air and on the wires was that you had collapsed, were undergoing medical tests. And it doesn't seem to have dampened anybody's emthusiasm for your work, especially after your performance the other night. Bob Kingsley at CBS, who, as you know, is my old-time buddy, was making interested sounds only yesterday. Raving about your assassination stuff."

He watched her face and saw the faint clouding of her eyes.

"But we don't have to think about anything like that for a while. Certainly not until you wash your hair."

Martha groaned. "That bad, eh?"

He shuddered, and she laughed and began to poke at the cards attached to the flowers. Roger detached the card from a giant arrangement of dark red roses, and handed it to her without comment.

"James," it read, in the familiar sprawling script.

Martha looked at it for a while, and Roger was silent.

"He always sent enormous quantities of flowers," she said.

"I expect there are messages too."

She shook her head. "He dislikes people who are sick. He waits for them to get better before he feels comfortable with them again."

Roger said nothing.

"I'll send him a note thanking him," she said.

He waited.

"From the Bahamas, I think."

Roger's slow smile deepened the lines on his face. "That simple?" he inquired.

"Not really. But I didn't write him a farewell note, did I?"

"No, you didn't."

Martha replaced the card in its envelope and put it on the bedside table.

"What happened the other night, Roger? I mean to Caroline? My God, she came unglued. I was so damned sorry for her."

"You were one of the few," he said dryly. "Most of the people at WNN wanted to strangle her."

She shook her head. "Poor little thing. What a disaster for her." She frowned. "They pulled her off, didn't they?"

"It was either that or they were going to hang her on camera."

"And now everybody's saying 'I told you so,' I suppose."

"Well, it goes beyond that, I'm afraid. I mean, it was a disaster for WNN. You were the only good thing about our coverage, because she couldn't hold anything to-

gether, and although Steiner did his best, once they put
him on, it was still a mess."

He saw her eyes harden a little.

"They could have called me in. I mean, I'm not being
bitter, but they could have. It would have made sense."

"That's what I told him. That's what a lot of people
told him."

"Him." Now her smile was bitter. "James never did
admit he was wrong, did he? And that would have been a
real turnaround after all the years of saying I was wrong
for the job."

"He's admitted he was wrong now."

"But not about me," Martha said quickly. "I'll bet that
what he's admitting he was wrong about is poor goddamned Caroline, his victim."

Roger patted her hand. "Don't get worked up about it,
sweetie."

"I'm not, don't worry. But I'm sorry for Caroline. She
didn't have anything to do with it, practically."

Roger snorted. "Come on now, Martha. She had all
the damned ambition in the world. She was dying to be
an anchor."

"That's not the point," said Martha. "A lot of women
in this business—and a lot of men—are dying to be
anchor. But if it hadn't been for Mellenkoff, nobody
would have even thought of Caroline for the job. She'd
probably have done very well on a talk show, somewhere
she could have used that talent she has for interviewing.
She wasn't up to the anchor spot, that's true. God knows,
people warned him about that. Maybe nobody could
have predicted she'd come apart the way she did, and
maybe if there'd never been an assassination, she'd have
rocked along for a while. But she had no basic underpin-
nings. And I'll tell you something else: I don't think she
had any real faith in herself. What she was," said Martha
thoughtfully, "was a little machine that James built. And
under pressure, it self-destructed."

Roger sighed. "Last I saw her, I almost didn't recognize her," he said.

"When was that?"

"She more or less forced her way into Mellenkoff's
office the morning after the assassination. You can imagine what he did to her."

"She die of frostbite?"

"She looked like it. She didn't—I swear to God, she was barely recognizable. She looked like a death's head."

"Where is she now?"

Roger shrugged. "I've no idea. She said she was going home. I asked if I could do anything and she said no. I just saw her in passing; she was heading out the door."

"Jesus," said Martha feelingly. "Does she have any friends?"

Roger shrugged again.

"People like Caroline have groupies, but they don't usually have many friends. She called me once or twice, and I remember telling Jill Roberts I thought she was lonely," Martha commented.

"Hell, she used you," said Roger. "She used everybody."

"Everybody except Mellenkoff. He used her."

"Maybe they deserve each other."

Martha shook her head. "I guess she's not friends with Jill anymore. She was having a thing with Jill's husband at one time—"

"That would put a chill on friendship," he observed. "Why are you being so goddamned tenderhearted about her? Maybe she wasn't as bad as she's been painted, but she was Mellenkoff's anchor bunny and she blew it—that's what it amounts to. She'll find her feet. The Carolines of this world always do."

"There's such a thing as kicking somebody when they're down," said Martha severely.

Roger sighed. "Are you leading up to something, my dear one?"

Martha grinned. "Sort of."

"What is it you want me to do? Send her flowers?"

"Are you going back to New York tonight?"

He nodded. "I have to. There's a meeting in the morning which I fear may prove to be a lynching. Eliass is out for blood, and I'm sure he'll get it."

"And I know whose."

"Probably. Although his survival instincts are formidable."

"He's never taken on an Eliass before." She grimaced. "Anyway. Roger, when you get home, why don't you call her?"

He groaned. "What do I say? Hi, how are you tonight, Mrs. Lincoln?"

"It's not much to do. Just make sure she's all right. I mean, Christ, Roger, she isn't a monster."

"As a matter of fact, she is. She was Mellenkoff's little monster. But all right, all right. To prevent you from doing it yourself, I shall call as soon as I get home. And I'll let you know how she is. That make you feel better?"

She nodded, and pulled his head down to hers. "Get some sleep," she said.

"You'll still love me in the morning?"

"I'll still love you in the morning."

When he looked back at her from the door, she was smiling. She looked a lot like the old Martha, and even if she hadn't, her determination to be kind to Caroline Mitchell would have convinced him. Miller slept through the fifty-minute flight to New York; the drink he had ordered sat untouched on his lap tray. He looked at his watch and decided to call Caroline from LaGuardia. He wanted to get it over with, because he didn't really want to do it. He was tired of the Mellenkoff-Mitchell axis, and whatever happened at tomorrow's meeting, he didn't think things could get much worse. He had been disturbed for months about the direction in which WNN seemed to be heading, and he didn't know that he wanted to go on working for a network dedicated to the glorification of the ego of James Mellenkoff. He had not mentioned it to Martha yet, but he had also been approached by CBS, which was one reason he was so aware of their interest in hiring her. He had wanted her to leave WNN for a long time, in the hope that she would simultaneously leave Mellenkoff. Now it seemed that she didn't have to leave the network for that reason, which delighted him. But he still wanted her out of there, cut loose from the memories. Both of them cut loose from the memories, for that matter.

Miller looked in his list of home numbers for people at the office, and found Caroline. He dialed, and listened to the telephone ring for a long time. He was about to hang up, with a sense of vast relief, when the receiver was picked up. The voice was a whisper.

"Hello."

"Caroline? Caroline, this is Roger Miller. I—I just wondered how you were doing?"

There was a pause so long that he thought they had been disconnected.

"Caroline? Are you there? Are you all right?"

There was an odd, choking sound at the other end. Jesus Christ, Roger thought. His voice rose.

"Caroline? Caroline? Caroline!"

It sounded as if she were crying.

"Caroline," he said urgently, "I'll be there in a few minutes. All right? You're going to be all right. Tell the doorman to let me in, you hear me?"

The gulping sound went on.

"Caroline," he said harshly, "tell the doorman to let me in or I'll call the police."

There was a pause, and a muttered affirmative whispered over the line. Roger put the phone down and ran for a taxi. He felt as if his head were lined in gravel, he was so tired, and he also knew he had to find out what was happening. Martha's compassion was contagious, he thought wearily. At the front door to Caroline's small, exclusive, and expensive apartment house, he told the uniformed guardian of the door to tell the uniformed guardian of the elevator that Miss Mitchell was ill and he was there to see her. The two men conferred briefly, and one picked up a telephone. He waited for a long time.

"She isn't answering, sir."

"Let it ring," said Roger firmly. "Because if she doesn't answer, we'll have to get the manager."

The doorman lived in New York a long time, and much of his work had been spent around celebrities. He nodded impassively, and continued to let the phone ring. Suddenly, he nodded.

"Miss Mitchell. Mr. Miller is here."

He signaled to Roger to go in, and rolled his eyes at the elevator operator.

"You want me to wait, Mr. Miller?" inquired the elevator operator.

"I'm not sure," said Miller.

"If there's any problem . . . we can call a doctor around the corner. He's a friend of the manager . . . I mean, if it's necesary . . ."

Miller was grateful for the man's quick grasp of the

situation. Presumably, among the millions who had witnessed Caroline's collapse on the air had been some of
the employees at the building where she lived. He walked
out of the elevator to a door to the left, and found it
slightly open. He turned his head and saw the elevator
operator behind him.

"I'll let you know if any help is needed," he said.
"And thanks."

"Certainly, sir," said the operator, and nodded his
thanks for the twenty-dollar bill Miller handed him.

The apartment was dark, and he could see nothing as
he pushed open the door.

"Caroline?" he called gently. "It's Roger Miller. Where
are you?"

There was no reply. Miller sighed and wished he were
at home in the peace and solitude of his own bedroom,
catching up on what was beginning to feel like a year's
lost sleep. His eyes becoming accustomed to the gloom,
he groped his way through the living room toward a door
that turned out to lead to the kitchen, and made his way
back across the room to a short passageway. He found a
light switch and clicked it on.

"Please don't turn on the lights," said a wavering voice
from the darkness ahead of him.

"Okay, I won't. I just don't want to fall on my face,"
he said and turned it off. He was too tired and irritable to
want to play any role in the latest chapter of the Mitchell
drama. He'd made sure she was alive, because he'd promised Martha he would, and now all he wanted was to get
out of there. In the doorway of what he assumed was the
bedroom, he finally managed to discern a figure sitting
on the floor.

"Caroline?"

The figure moved slightly. "Be careful of your feet," it
said. "There's some broken glass."

Roger thought, Oh God.

"I'm sorry, I'm going to get some lights on," he told
her. He fumbled until he found a lamp on a table to his
right and switched it on.

With relief, he saw no signs of blood. Caroline was
sitting on the floor, leaning against a chair. Most of her
face was hidden by the tangled mass of her hair, but what
he could see was ashen. She was wearing a dark robe that

seemed to be too big for her. The pale blue rug was littered with pieces of broken glass, which apparently had come from a mirror set in an elaborate tortoiseshell vanity table. Roger leaned against the wall. Caroline did not look up.

"We—I—wanted to be sure you were all right," he said.

She nodded. "That was kind of you. I'm all right."

"Well—you're sure?" He couldn't very well turn around and walk out, although that was what he wanted to do.

Suddenly, she scrambled to her feet and faced him. She didn't look as bad as he had expected. She was colorless, and her eyes were smudged with shadow, but there was a certain composure in her expression that surprised him.

He gestured toward the shards of glass near her bare feet.

"Be careful."

She looked down, and when she looked up, she was smiling. It wasn't the dazzling smile with which she used to woo the camera; it was a small, mischievous sort of smile. Like the smile of a child caught out and unrepentant.

"Would you like a drink?" she asked politely.

Roger peered at her. Now what? But his curiosity was roused.

"As a matter of fact," he said, "I would like a drink, and if I may, I'd like to sit down while I drink it, because otherwise I may fall down. But I really don't want to impose."

Caroline padded past him to the living room, and switched on another lamp.

"Sit down," she said. He sat down and hoped he would not fall asleep before she got back with the drink. He heard ice cubes clink, and realized she had not asked him what he wanted to drink. As he opened his mouth to tell her, she appeared with a glass of amber liquid.

"Scotch all right?"

"Fine." He took the glass and sipped gratefully. "Aren't you having one?" What a goddamned ridiculous situation, he thought.

"No." She sat down on the sofa opposite him and curled her feet under her. She looked more and more like a child with a rather dirty, tired face.

"It was very nice of you to come here," she said.

"Not at all," said Roger, with a sense of the surreal.

"I broke my mirror," said Caroline. For a wild moment, he thought of asking her if she'd been trying to get through the looking glass, then remembered that kind of humor had to be reserved for someone he knew would understand it, like Martha. He had never had any reason to think that Caroline Mitchell had much of a sense of humor.

"Why did you break it? Was it an accident?" He phrased the questions carefully. She shook her head.

"I threw my clock at it."

"Oh." He took another sip, and felt his head throb. "Any particular reason?"

"I wanted to get rid of Caroline in the mirror. She got me into a lot of trouble."

She's snapped, he thought. Now what do I do? He studied her. She didn't look particularly upset. Her face was placid.

"Who was Caroline in the mirror? If I may ask."

She uttered a croaky little laugh. "I invented her when I was seven. She was sort of an invisible playmate. She helped me get away from my father."

"I see," said Roger untruthfully. "Why did you want to get away from your father?"

"He raped me when I was five, and he went on screwing me until I was fourteen."

The hideous words came out calmly. She might have been discussing the weather. He stared at her, his fingers tight on the glass.

"Caroline, for God's sake, I—"

She waved a hand. "I'm sorry. This is an awful thing to do to you. But I'm just glad I can talk about it. Tell somebody. I'm sorry it had to be you."

He looked at her helplessly. She took his glass and refilled it, and he let her.

"In a way," she said, "what happened the other night, well maybe it was the best thing that could have happened to me. Because it made me cry. I hadn't cried since I was five. I wouldn't let my father make me cry. Anyway, I really was screwed up. And I still am. But now I know why I'm screwed up. And after I talked to them—"

"Them?" asked Roger faintly.

"My parents," said Caroline. "I called them. I was going to pretend some more. Say I'd got sick on the air. Then I found my mother had known all along. And she never tried to help me. My mother. My bitch of a mother."

"That was when you broke the mirror?" Roger asked.

"I didn't need it anymore," she explained with a certain astounding cheerfulness.

"That's good," said Roger.

"I'm sorry," said Caroline. "I know I sound crazy. But I'm not. I think I'm better than I ever was. I'm not afraid anymore; I don't need the damned mirror to find out who I am."

"Who did you think you were before?" Roger asked.

"I was the girl in the mirror. Except she didn't exist either." She laughed again, and this time, it was a harsher sound.

"It's sort of funny," she said. "Poor old Mellenkoff didn't realize he was dealing with a cripple. I mean, his shining star was—well just a façade. And he risked it all for that."

"Caroline," said Roger, putting down his glass, "are you saying that you couldn't have succeeded in that job, no matter what?"

"Of course," she said. "I couldn't have succeeded in any job where I had to . . . well, you know, dig into myself and come up with any inner strength. There wasn't any inner anything, if you understand what I mean?"

"You've been sitting on the floor in the middle of broken glass figuring all this out?" he asked.

"Well, sort of. I haven't really figured it all out yet, and I'm not all put together either. I mean, no miracle's happened. But it was as if a lot of things became clear all at once, so I just sat and remembered things and thought, and put things together."

"How d'you feel now?"

"Sort of empty. But that's nothing new for me, so I don't feel as bad as people probably think I do. I mean, what happened the night before last wasn't nearly as bad as what happened to me a lot of nights when I was a kid. And it's like a jigsaw. The pieces are fitting. It's sort of exciting for me."

It was, Roger thought with disbelief, one of the more

bizarre conversations he had ever participated in, and what made it especially strange was that it was the first time he could recall seeing Caroline Mitchell relaxed. Her formal politeness, her anxiety to please, her self-consciousness—all were gone. She was still beautiful, but the lacquer had disappeared.

"What now?" he asked.

Caroline looked thoughtful. "I'm not sure. Obviously I'm through at WNN." She smiled maliciously. "Who'd have thought I'd bring down the mighty Mellenkoff."

"Quite a few people predicted it, if you want to know," said Miller, finishing his Scotch.

"Well, they were right, weren't they," said Caroline. She sounded indifferent. "What will I do? Well, I've had some pretty good training, haven't I? Maybe I can find a job working for someboy who doesn't like Mellenkoff." She smiled again. "That shouldn't be too hard to find, should it?"

Miller looked at her with a mixture of awe and distaste. Poor little Caroline, indeed. He couldn't wait to tell Martha. Caroline stretched with the grace of a weary cat.

"I guess I'd better get this place cleaned up. Throw out the rest of that damned mirror. And I'm hungry."

Suddenly, she was in the kitchen, rattling cupboard doors.

"Soup!" she cried.

She reappeared triumphantly waving a can of vegetable soup. "You want some?"

Miller shook his head. "Thanks, no. I've got to get home and get some sleep."

Caroline put the can down and came over to him. "Listen, I am truly grateful, Roger. You came by when nobody else cared whether I was still alive. Although I suppose from the network's viewpoint, I'm dead anyway. But I didn't mean to scare you on the phone. I was sort of surfacing when you called, that's why I sounded so odd."

"Yeah, you did," said Roger, who had been nursing a vague resentment that he had been lured up there on false pretenses.

"I guess I sound pretty matter of fact about it all—I mean, I'm supposed to be a wreck, aren't I?"

"Well, it would be a more traditional reaction," he acknowledged. "But nobody ever said there was anything too traditional about you, Caroline."

She smiled and he had a brief vision of a cat grooming its fur.

"I'll be all right, Roger."

"My dear," he said, "I am quite certain you will."

He was beginning to think Mellenkoff was the one he should be sorry for, although he wasn't.

He stood up and moved to the door. Caroline opened it for him and offered her hand, which was warm and firm in its clasp.

"Good-bye, Roger," she said.

As he went to the elevator, he turned his head and saw her standing in the doorway, her face wreathed in that feline smile.

"Give my regards to Mellenkoff," she said.

42

WHEN MELLENKOFF went back to his black and white office, it was no longer his. Staring out of the window at the rain that had lashed New York for a week, he thought the most humiliating moment of the day had come when Eliass, in a dreadful parody of a considerate gesture, had assured him he could continue to use an office at the WNN building, and even someone from the typing pool, while he looked for another job.

"Not your office, of course, James," said the chairman.

"Of course not," said Mellenkoff through stiff lips.

He had known for forty-eight hours that he was out as president of WNN television, but the knowledge had not lessened the pain of the official confirmation of his downfall. The meeting of the board had been mechanical. He had offered his resignation and it had been accepted, as had been his suggestion that his presence at the meeting was no longer needed. What had been worst had been the private meeting with Eliass that had preceded it. It was then Mellenkoff realized just how much he had lost. On Eliass's desk, a heavy, mahogany desk, less dramatic than Mellenkoff's, was a pile of clippings. Mellenkoff had read them already, bleakly. They were, in a way, his epitaph.

"Mitchell bombed, but Mellenkoff blew it," wrote the *New York Daily News* television critic.

"Melenkoff, WNN mogul, ignored warnings that Caroline Mitchell was an anchor bunny. He made a star without making sure that she could handle the job, and her failure should be laid on his doorstep. WNN's assassination coverage made Mitchell, Mellenkoff, and the network look ridiculous. Not even the brilliant reporting of

Martha Vogel, who was the obvious choice for the anchor job, could save them."

"Caroline Mitchell's pathetic performance as anchor during coverage of the presidential assassination provided the ultimate example of television's capacity for miscasting. Ms. Mitchell's woeful lack of experience became immediately and glaringly apparent, as did her total lack of qualification for a job in which she was entirely out of her depth. Why James Mellenkoff, the shrewd president of WNN, should have selected Ms. Mitchell for one of the most responsible positions in a network is a total mystery, especially when there was available to him the experience and competence of a correspondent such as Martha Vogel, whose live reporting from the scene was outstanding." That was the *New York Times*.

Eliass had gestured grimly toward the clippings. "We certainly ah . . . attracted attention, James."

His eyes resembled two shiny pebbles protruding from beneath his eyebrows. Mellenkoff nodded silently. There was nothing he could say that would not fuel the chairman's fury. He could not even think of an excuse to make to himself.

"You cannot say you were not warned," said the chairman. "Repeatedly." He savored the word.

"Yes," said Mellenkoff. Eliass looked at the clippings, then at Mellenkoff. He was obviously waiting.

"I shall offer my resignation at the board meeting," said Mellenkoff quietly.

Eliass nodded. "I think that would be best, James. That would be best."

It was the only time in Mellenkoff's life he had felt as though he were wriggling. He had not sat down, nor been invited to, and he found himself moving nervously from foot to foot.

"I do . . . regret what happened, very much. I was wrong," he said. He owed the bastard that much. Eliass's tightly closed mouth did not soften.

"Yes," said Eliass relentlessly. "You were, James. You were. Which was unfortunate for all of us. Including your, ah, protégée."

Mellenkoff stood rigidly, awaiting an opportunity to escape.

"By the way," said Eliass. "How is Vogel?"

Mellenkoff realized he didn't know. He knew that Roger Miller had been practically commuting to Wahington, but Miller appeared to be avoiding him, and he assumed that Martha was recovering. He had thought about her, wished she were there to talk to. Martha had always been there when he needed her. He had sent flowers, left a message at the hospital, tried to reach her, when he heard she had regained consciousness, but had been told she was resting and taking no calls.

"I understand she—she's improving," he said lamely, and his gaze dropped under the piercing Eliass stare.

"She did an excellent job the other night," said the chairman.

Mellenkoff nodded. "Yes. Yes, she did."

"Perhaps you were wrong about her too."

"Perhaps I was," said Mellenkoff, and thought, You bastard; you had nothing good to say about her until today.

"Perhaps," said Eliass, "she might make a good anchor after all, James."

"Perhaps she might," said Mellenkoff dully.

The chairman said, "You know how sorry I am, James, about, ah, you."

"Thank you," said Mellenkoff. The chairman wasn't sorry at all, and Mellenkoff knew it. Eliass's anger over the Caroline Mitchell disaster was exacerbated by his awareness that he had allowed himself to rely on a man whose ego had overwhelmed his judgment. Although Mellenkoff had shown signs of being on a power trip, Eliass had assumed the man realized that ultimate authority did not lie in his hands. He had reposed such faith in Mellenkoff, based on his record of consistent compentence and unflinching ruthlessness, that he had allowed him to take a giant leap upward in the network hierarchy, admitted him into Eliass family circles, and permitted him to make a dangerously risky choice for a crucial job. Mitchell had failed Mellenkoff, but Mellenkoff had failed Eliass, and the chairman was not a forgiving man. As he had used his influence and power to advance Mellenkoff, he was equally prepared to demolish him.

The chairman's offer of a place—a cubicle, he thought—from which Mellenkoff could seek a new job, was in keeping with his disdain for his former favorite. Mellenkoff would learn how foolish he had been in his arrogance. Not that it would require any great effort or expenditure of time on the part of the chairman. A word here and there in an appropriate ear at high levels would suffice. Sally Eliass Mellenkoff would present no problem. Eliass would have made sure that Mellenkoff's disgrace would not affect his niece, who had, after all, married the man at his bidding.

But Sally had come to her uncle's house the previous evening and talked with him. She seemed to have become more mature than he recalled. Eliass had paid little attention to his niece since she ceased to be a problem. She had wanted to know what his reaction would be if she left Mellenkoff, and he admitted to himself that his reaction might have been quite different, had it not been for the Mitchell matter. What, he asked, did she plan to do if she left her husband? Sally explained that she had been taking photography classes and planned to go to work as a photographer. Eliass did not view such plans with disapproval. In fact, he was pleased that his niece appeared to have developed a constructive approach to dealing with her life. She had shown him some of her photographs, which, he had been relieved to see, involved nothing he would have considered improper, such as nudity. She seemed to be taking photographs of various celebrities, and doing a good job of it, although he was no expert on camera angles. But she appeared to have put her contacts on both coasts to good use, and to be embarking on a career of her own, which he wouldn't have believed possible at an earlier time. He assumed her dreadful leanings toward perversion were now part of a misspent past, so the marriage to Mellenkoff might have been of some use after all. And he told his niece what she wanted to know; that he would not offer any objections to her ending her marriage, and that his financial aid to her mother and herself would continue. Sally had pleased him further by emphasizing that she hoped to do well enough from her photography that she would not have to impose on him for such assistance. Perhaps, he thought, she was an Eliass after all.

Because Mellenkoff had not raised the subject, Eliass assumed, correctly, that James was unaware of Sally's impending departure. Doubtless, he would become aware

of it when he went home that night. The thought brought
a facsimile of a smile to the chairman's fuchsia tinted
face, as he watched Mellenkoff leave. His walk had lost
much of its swinging confidence. And in the office that
used to be a symbol of his success, Mellenkoff felt strangely
lost. He looked at the desk and the clutter of papers that
no longer meant anything, no longer required his sprawling signature to give them authority. He pulled open one
or two of the desk drawers and closed them. He would
have the contents packed up and sent to his home. He
had no stomach for clearing out his desk that day. And
he certainly had no intention of returning to WNN to
make free phone calls from an unoccupied cubicle. It was
enough that Eliass had savored the satisfaction of the
offer. He wondered if Eliass had meant what he said
about offering Martha the anchor job, or whether that
was another calculated gibe.

Martha. Mellenkoff picked up the telephone and called
the hospital in Washington. Miss Vogel had left the hospital that morning, he was told. His spirits lifted. That
meant she was fine. He dialed her number in Washington. She answered on the fifth ring, and her voice sounded
like the Martha he used to know. Maybe he would go
down there on the weekend; hell, maybe he'd go spend
some time there. He could use some comfort, God knows,
and there was nobody who could comfort him better.

"How are you?" he asked. There was a pause, a rather
lengthy pause.

"Fine," she said.

"You sure? You worried the hell out of me."

She was silent. Maybe she was peeved because he hadn't
gone to Washington, but she knew he couldn't leave New
York at a time like that. Especially in the situation he
was in. Martha, of all people, knew that.

"I wanted to come down," he said anxiously, "but,
well . . . you can imagine what it's been like."

"Yes," she said, "I can."

The terse responses puzzled him. He assumed she was
aware of what was happening at the network. She must
know how much trouble he was in. He was sure Roger
Miller had kept her informed.

"I'm out," he said, and waited for the warm flow of
sympathy, reassurance, affection.

"I know," said Martha.

Mellenkoff felt a sinking in his stomach. She couldn't be that mad at him, not at a time like this. Didn't she realize what he was going through?

"It's been pretty bad up here," he said.

"I expect it has."

"What's wrong?"

"Nothing."

"Well, I mean, I thought you'd be . . . sympathetic, honey."

"Why?"

"Why!" He was flustered, and sounded it.

"Why should I be sympathetic, James? Give me one good reason."

"Christ, Martha, I didn't expect you, of all people, to be petty. I mean, I really need you."

At the other end of the line there was a sound that might have been a laugh, except he knew she wouldn't do such a thing to him.

"James," said Martha quietly, "I know you're having a bad time. But you'll bounce back. You always do. And you certainly don't need me. You never did."

"That's not true," he began, but she interrupted him, which also was unusual.

"I don't really want to talk right now," Martha went on. "And I'm going to take some time off, try to put myself back together, come back to the real world, I suppose. I'm sorry I can't be there to hold your hand, James. For one thing, I don't really want to."

He was bereft of words. Not Martha.

"Please," he said. "Everything's changed. Believe me. You're all I want—"

Again she interrupted him. "Please, James. I'm not up to this. All that's changed is that you've had a career setback. But a lot of things have changed for me. And I can't afford you anymore. I wish I could, in a way, but I can't. The price is a little too high."

"I don't understand," he said. "I know you've been depressed—"

"It's not just that," said Martha. "You've never understood at all. You never took the time to try."

She took a deep breath, and suddenly her voice sounded tired.

"Don't call me back. Don't call for a while. Maybe some day we can have lunch together, but not now. Not for a long time."

"Listen." His voice was urgent. "You're just exhausted, worn out. You need me to take care of you for a while. We'll go to Europe, look around. See what the job market's like there. I've still got a lot of contacts—"

"James," said Martha, "for God's sake, will you listen to what I'm saying? I'm not going anywhere with you. I don't want you to come here. You're right, you've still got a lot of contacts, so sit down and use them. You're good at that. But I want no part in any of it. I want no part of you, James. Not anymore."

"Is this because I didn't come down to Washington after you—tried to kill yourself?" His voice was almost petulant.

"No, it's not. It's got nothing to do with that, but it's typical that you would think it did. James, let's have lunch next year. Or the year after that."

He heard the soft click at the other end with disbelief. He'd never heard Martha talk to him like that before. She had to be really upset with him. He had to admit she'd sounded as if she meant what she was saying. Except she couldn't have meant it. Martha had always been there, would always be there, had to be there. He did need her, and maybe he'd been less attentive than he might have been in recent months. Mellenkoff sighed. Come to think of it, maybe she was right about his taking off on his own. He had a lot of friends in London; maybe he'd go over there, relax a little, look around, have a little fun. God knows he hadn't had much fun lately.

He didn't suppose Sally would give a damn where he was. Suddenly, Mellenkoff grinned wolfishly. He wondered whether Uncle Joel was prepared to go on supporting his dear niece in the style she preferred, which was damned expensive. Mellenkoff would pick up a nice chunk of severance pay, a couple of years, according to his contract, but he didn't plan to spend it on catering to the taste in emeralds of his alleged wife. Now that he wasn't dependent on her uncle for every breath he took, maybe he could be a little more insistent about the lovely Sally's marital obligations. He shrugged. He didn't need her in bed. He'd never had any trouble finding partners for sex.

But he'd enjoy watching her face when he told her he'd resigned. Unless Eliass had already told her, but he doubted that. The chairman had more things on his mind today than his niece's welfare.

He walked across to the built-in ebony bar and poured himself a stiff Scotch. It was probably the last drink he'd have at Eliass's expense, and he'd earned it. He'd been wrong about Mitchell, but he'd been right about a lot of other things—not that Eliass would remember any of them now. Mellenkoff drank deeply, and felt a little better. He'd go home, wipe the smile off Sally's blank little face with his news, and start making some plans. He had to move fast. Nobody knew better than he how fast bad news sped around the business. But his track record was damned good. He shouldn't have too much trouble relocating, and at least he wouldn't have to deal with that tomato-faced bastard anymore. He finished his drink and poured another. It occurred to him that his telephone hadn't rung all the time he was in the office. He couldn't recall a time when it had not been constantly buzzing. But that was when *everybody* wanted to reach him.

He picked up the phone and pressed the button for Betsy Cooley's desk. It rang for several minutes, which was most unusual. It wasn't even five yet, and Betsy was most conscientious. When the receiver was picked up, it wasn't her voice.

"Where's Betsy?" he asked.

There was a pause.

"She—she had to go out," said an unfamiliar voice.

Christ, the world must be coming to an end if Betsy had left her post.

"When's she coming back?"

"I—don't know." The voice sounded unhappy.

Mellenkoff frowned. "Who is this?" he asked sharply.

"Oh—wait a minute," said the voice in obvious relief. "Betsy's here."

He sat back. But Betsy didn't sound like herself either.

"I'm sorry, Mr. Mellenkoff," she said.

"No problem, Betsy," he said easily. "I just wanted to let you know I'm going to be leaving shortly. Will you call for the car?"

She hesitated.

"Betsy? What's going on?"

"Mr. Mellenkoff, I—I was going to come in. I didn't
know you were leaving now. I—wanted to say good-bye."

So that was it.

"Well, I may be in and out getting things cleared up."

"What I mean, is that I've been—transferred."

"Oh?"

"I'm temporarily in Mr. Eliass's suite. Until—ahh—"

"Until my successor is named." He completed the
awkward sentence.

"I'm sorry, Mr. Mellenkoff."

He noticed she hadn't said she was sorry he was leaving. Maybe she wasn't.

"Never mind, Betsy. Just make sure the limousine's
downstairs."

He cut off another confused sentence by hanging up,
and went back to the bar for another drink. Nobody had
come to say good-bye. The word had been passed. Not
even Miller, his old friend. Rats and the sinking ship. He
finished the drink, picked up his overcoat, and walked
out. Betsy Cooley was not at her desk in the outer room.
Neither was anyone else. And in the elevator, he imagined that the operator looked uncomfortable as he greeted
him.

He went to the side entrance where network limousines waited for WNN executives. The guard was there,
but there was no chauffeur and no car. He peered around.
Nothing was working anymore. The whole place was
falling apart. He turned to the guard.

"Mrs. Cooley called for a car for me, George. Was
there a problem?"

George looked as if he wished he were anywhere else
in the world except sitting there under Mellenkoff's eye.

"Mr. Mellenkoff, I guess Mrs. Cooley didn't tell you.
You're—you're off the list. For limo service, I mean."

George studied his feet. Mellenkoff stared at him for a
moment. He was off the list. Eliass had lost no time. Use
a cubicle to look for a job and take a taxi home. He
couldn't bring himself to ask George to call a taxi for
him. Mellenkoff turned on his heel and walked out into
the street, where everybody in New York seemed to be
hailing taxis in rush hour traffic.

He thought of going to a bar and waiting until the rush
was over. He hated crowds, hated traffic, and had had to

deal with neither for some time. As he stood, uncertain, one of the sleek and shining WNN cars purred past him, came to a halt. He sprinted toward it; he'd been sure it was a mistake. But inside the car, Roger Miller was peering at him. Mellenkoff stopped, his hand on the door handle. Miller beckoned him in, winding down a window.

"You want a ride, James?"

Mellenkoff almost hit him. Miller was offering *him* a ride? But the door was open, and he needed to get home. He was beginning to feel as if he were unraveling. He climbed into the long black car. When had Miller rated a limo to get home? Executive vice-presidents weren't on that level. Miller answered the unspoken question.

"I borrowed this from the vice-chairman of the board. Have to get to the airport," he explained.

"I'm not taking you out of your way, I hope." Mellenkoff was studiedly polite.

"Hell no. You're going home, I assume? George said—" He stopped, and Mellenkoff suddenly knew just what George had said. Felt so bad about that poor Mr. Mellenkoff. He felt rage rise within him.

"George was correct," he said icily. "I'd appreciate a ride home."

Miller was silent as they navigated a slow course through the wet, crowded streets.

"You said the airport. You've a flight-time problem?" Mellenkoff's anger was subsiding. It wasn't Miller's fault. He'd always liked Roger. He and Roger and Martha had been a threesome a long time ago.

"No. I'm catching the shuttle. No problem."

Mellenkoff nodded. He'd always wondered why Miller had to spend so much time at the Washington bureau of WNN, but he supposed there were reasons. He didn't care anymore. It was none of his business. The thought was like probing a nerve. As the car neared Mellenkoff's house, Miller stirred and spoke again, sounding slightly uneasy.

"You'll be back around the office?"

"I doubt it."

Miller held out his hand. "I'm sorry, James. You'll be all right?"

Mellenkoff shook hands with him, and nodded curtly.

"Yes. I'll be fine. Got a couple of good prospects, as a matter of fact. No point in wasting my time."

Miller said, "Of course not. Good luck, James."

Mellenkoff got out of the car without looking back. He felt for his house key. The windows were dark. Sally was probably out as usual. He unlocked the front door, let himself in. The foyer light was on. He dropped his coat on a chair, went into the living room, where the pink and gold struck him as more hideous than usual. He thought of having a drink, walked about the room restlessly, then went upstairs. Glancing down the passageway as he went toward his room, he noticed that Sally's door was open. One of the reasons they had bought the house was that it had two master suites. He couldn't remember her leaving her door open before.

Impulsively, he turned and walked down the heavily carpeted corridor, pausing before the open door. A lamp was on in the bedroom, but he could hear no sound. He went in, and stopped, puzzled. The room had an empty look to it. The bed was neatly made up, but there was an unnatural tidiness. There were no toiletries on the vanity table, no hairbrushes, no perfume bottles. The tops of the bedside stands were bare. He walked over to the closets, pulled a door open. The clothes were gone. He pulled open a dresser drawer. It was empty. Maybe she'd gone on a trip. But she wouldn't have taken everything with her, would she? He spun around as he heard a sound downstairs, hurried to the top of the stairs. Sally apparently had been in the library, perhaps had gone in there when she heard the car. She was loading suitcases into a taxi, with the aid of the driver. He called to her, and she looked up, and waved casually.

"Hi."

"Where're you going?"

"California."

"For how long this time?"

"For good."

He stared at her.

"I left you a note. It's in your room. I'll send for some other stuff, but you can have most of it."

"Wait a minute." He ran down the stairs. Sally paused, looking uncertainly between him and the taxi driver.

"I'll wait," said the driver hurriedly, and removed himself from a domestic scene.

"What's all this about, for Christ's sake?" Mellenkoff asked.

"Nothing really. I decided I wanted a divorce, that's all."

"A divorce?"

"Why not? Hell, we could get an annulment." Sally smiled, and for an instant, Mellenkoff wanted to strike her.

"What are you going to do?"

"Be a photographer."

"Support yourself, I hope," he said.

"More or less."

"I forgot." His smile was sneering. "There's always Uncle Joel."

"Not anymore, or not much longer. I talked to him."

"He knew about this?"

She nodded.

"And he approves?"

She shrugged. "He doesn't care one way or the other. He never cared whom I married. He just wanted me to be married."

"Why?"

"Oh, he just didn't approve of me, I guess." Her voice was lighthearted. Mellenkoff thought she had never looked prettier.

"Who's the guy?" he asked with sudden bitterness.

Sally laughed. "No guy."

"All by your little self, I suppose."

"No, not all by myself." Her smile was pure happiness.

Mellenkoff was tired of this conversation, and his head ached, which he supposed was partly the result of three Scotches and no food.

"Well, I assume you won't want alimony, at least."

"Hardly. Listen, James, I have to go."

Automatically, he opened the front door for her, and as she hurried through the rain, he saw the white blur of a face at the taxi window. The door opened, Sally scrambled in, and he heard laughter and the voice of another woman. Slowly, he closed the door on the darkness and went back into the pink and gold living room. He sat down heavily on the pink sofa and closed his eyes. Maybe another drink would be a good idea after all. He got up and poured himself a Scotch from a crystal decanter on a side table. The house was silent around him, enfolding him in the quietness he had longed for throughout the endless day. He wondered where Sally was going, and who the woman in the taxi was. A thought flickered in his mind, and he dismissed it, refusing to contemplate its possibility. His head throbbed and he wished Martha were there. He'd feel so much better if she were with him. He thought about calling her. Perhaps she wasn't angry with him anymore. Martha never stayed angry with him very long. He'd always been able to rely on that; it was one of the great things about their relationship. He reached out for the telephone and dialed her number. It rang for a long time before she answered it. She sounded breathless, happy.

"Hey there," he said. It was their old familiar greeting code, and he waited, smiling. The telephone clicked softly in his ear. He looked at the receiver. Could they have been disconnected? But he knew they hadn't. Holding his drink, he went over to the window and stood there in the echoing silence of the hollow house, looking into the dark emptiness of the street.

DORIS MORTMAN

FIRST BORN

Franyu Rostov is dead. As her children mourn, they each vow to name their first-born daughters Frances Rebecca. These four girls grow up known as Cissie, Frankie, Jinx and Becca:

Cissie is a fashion entrepreneur, with an international reputation.

Frankie, a stunning model, New York's hottest property.

Jinx, a super-rich businesswoman, married to a devastating multi-millionaire.

Becca, an ambitious golfer, whose real talent is for manipulating human beings.

They are four women inextricably linked by blood, love and destiny. Their story moves from Paris to New York, from politics to international high finance, to a dramatic climax in which one, or more, must inevitably suffer . . .

ANNE TOLSTOI WALLACH

PRIVATE SCORES

Cornelia Fuller is a determined woman – independent and successful. And she has managed, alone, to give her daughter the most precious gift for the future that money can buy: a place at the Boston School.

But Livvie is failing. Behind the genteel façade, the school is not what it seems. Old traditions are despised, pupils like Livvie – neither rich nor brilliant – are shunned, and fear lurks beneath the surface.

Then undercurrents turn to real danger and Livvie disappears into the snowy New York night. Cornelia reaches out for help at last ... and discovers her daughter's heartbreaking secret.

'This cogent, penetrating tale juxtaposes innocence and tyranny with uncommon subtley'

Publishers Weekly

HODDER AND STOUGHTON PAPERBACKS